Extraordinary praise for The Strain Trilogy and Guillermo del Toro and Chuck Hogan

"*The Strain* was the most credible and frightening of all the vampire books of the past decade, relentless in the pace of its narrative, utterly convincing in its details, and forthright in the depiction of characters we can care about. . . . Those of you interested in utterly engrossing, high-level entertainment who haven't read *The Strain* have some catching up to do. . . . Most readers will find themselves turning pages with the momentum of an engaged movie viewer, with their own normal reality imperiled. . . . Del Toro and Hogan have managed—for this reader certainly, someone always on the watch for a novel that will give him the chance to leave mainstream literature and life behind for a few days—to turn this on it head. I thirst! I thirst! Bring on volume three!"

—*San Francisco Chronicle*

"A cross between *The Hot Zone* and *'Salem's Lot*."   —*Entertainment Weekly*

"Potent cinematic imagery welded onto crime fiction pacing. . . . Reads like an extra grisly screenplay for a prime-time police procedural; a horror-infused *CSI*. . . . This is a monstrous vision, one where all the romantic ideas of Bela Lugosi and George Hamilton are stripped bare and what is revealed is a new vampire biology—but with links to the past. . . . [The authors] create a vivid scene of a New York where something has gone terribly wrong."

—*Chicago Sun Times*

"A fast-paced mix of gruesome horror and straightforward investigative crime fiction."   —*Philadelphia Inquirer*

"Guillermo del Toro and Chuck Hogan have crafted a deliciously creepy story that will literally make the hairs on your neck stand up. *The Strain* is Bram Stoker meets Stephen King meets Michael Crichton. It just doesn't get much better than this."   —Nelson DeMille

"An imaginative and genuinely frightening mashup of *Dracula* and *Outbreak*. . . . Takes the vampire genre into bold new territory while still staying grounded in the classical motifs. . . . Intriguing [and] frightening. An engrossing war between humanity and an enveloping darkness. . . . A gripping page-turner that's bound to be one of the hottest novels of the year. A captivating thrill ride that injects new life into the vampire genre. More important, it's a horror novel that's actually frightening. Its monsters are so fully rendered, its scenes so well-crafted, that the story takes over your imagination. It will give you nightmares and make you think you see something moving out of the corner of your eye when you're walking to your car at night. . . . An incredible fiction debut for Del Toro, who shows that his eye for detail and dark imagination are not limited to film. In terms of sheer horror and atmosphere, *The Strain* can stand beside the best of Stephen King or Peter Straub. It combines the elemental fears of antiquity with the unique fear and anxiety of an age of terrorist threats and biological weapons. It's the quintessential horror story of this decade."   —*Buffalo News*

"Guillermo del Toro and Chuck Hogan are not interested in chaste adolescent vampires or sexy rock-star vampires or vampires who drink artificial blood. The vampires in *The Strain* are just plain evil."   —*New York Times*

"Chuck Hogan is known for his taut thrillers, Guillermo del Toro for his surreal horror films (including *Pan's Labyrinth*), and their new book, *The Strain*, brings out the best of each. . . . Riveting from the start. Scenes are so vividly drawn that you can almost smell the moldering soil that clings to the undead, feel their unnatural heat. Page-turning suspense."   —*Minneapolis Star Tribune*

"A high-tech vampire epic. . . . Terrifying. The biological rationale behind the metamorphosis of the undead is cleverly and vividly explicated, and the authors concoct a number of riveting action sequences. . . . With echoes of Richard Matheson's *I Am Legend* and Stephen King's *'Salem's Lot*, *The Strain* is a solid opener for a twenty-first-century vampire saga."   —*San Francisco Chronicle*

"Creepy fun."   —*Detroit Free Press*

"Del Toro and thriller writer Hogan treat a vampire outbreak as a massive public-health crisis, with chilling results. The book boasts a plethora of arresting images and many terrific macabre touches. Del Toro and Hogan also succeed in constructing a driving plot and delivering a gripping conclusion. Great characters . . . and a flair for striking scenes get this trilogy off to a first-rate start."

—*Kirkus Reviews*

"Though elements of the story are familiar, the sharp, propulsive language helps invest them with new power. . . . Uniquely compelling. . . . It's not hard to think that were the partners' novels to be combined into one lengthy narrative, the result would be something akin . . . to the best of Stephen King's early, expansive sagas: a sprawling, detailed examination of a world gone mad . . . and a sparse group of heroes must do whatever they can to prevent the Earth from being consumed by perpetual night. . . . You have to hand it to Del Toro and Hogan. At a time when brooding, sexy vampires are so ubiquitous . . . the authors finally have given the creatures back some of their nasty, vicious, delicious bite."

—*Los Angeles Times*

"Have your heart medicine close: *The Strain* may sneak up on you—and it's scary enough to kill. I loved it."

—Gregory Maguire, bestselling author of
A Lion Among Men and *Wicked*

"Eerie [and] truly terrifying. . . . [It] will have the hairs on your neck standing for quite a while. . . . Full of the blood and sinew of terrific horror fiction and nightmarish passages that will haunt you for days. These big bad bloodsuckers will convince you they are real and that they will be marching into your town— soon. This combination of classic folk tale and modern biological nightmare will have you shivering in the night and double-checking the deadbolts."

—*Louisville Courier Journal*

"Apocalyptic action. . . . Part *The Andromeda Strain*, part *Night of the Living Dead*."

—Salon.com

"A fresh approach to vampires. . . . Both gritty and real. . . . Engaging [and] compelling."

—*Deseret News*

"Doesn't necessarily reinvent the vampire script but it certainly reinvigorates. . . . A truly creepy, intense thriller whose characters . . . will consume readers from the first page to the last. . . . What makes it special is plain old-fashioned storytelling. For those jaded by a genre that's become a tad anemic and oversaturated, *The Strain* will inspire as it terrifies."

—*Anniston Star*

"The first in a trilogy that soars with spellbinding intrigue. Truly, an unforgettable tale you can't put down once you read the first page. I can't wait until the next one."

—Clive Cussler

"Blood and apocalypse mix in a terrifying story that feels like it was ripped from today's headlines. Vividly wrought and relentlessly paced, *The Strain* haunts as much as it terrifies. I cannot wait to see where Del Toro and Hogan take us next."
—James Rollins, author of *Altar of Eden*

"Every few decades the vampire genre grows a tad anemic, as it were, and the lore of the undead threatens to die on us. But then along comes a Richard Matheson or Stephen King and . . . license renewed. This time around, the reanimators are Guillermo del Toro and Chuck Hogan with their terrifying new novel, *The Strain*, an unholy spawn of *I Am Legend* out of *'Salem's Lot*."
—Dan Simmons, author of *Drood* and *The Terror*

"*The Strain* might be the purest example of entertainment for entertainment's sake I've read in quite some time."
—Sarah Weinman, *Confessions of an Idiosyncratic Mind*

"Fans of the director will not want to miss this fresh take on the undead that will demand a little elbow room at local bookstores. . . . Fans of horror will lap this up and be watching their calendar for the next release. . . . *The Strain* demands attention and it demands that, yet again, we put away our old ideas and make room for a fresh take on the primordial monster."
—theonering.net

"What makes *The Strain* special, what in fact makes the trilogy it begins to seem a likely candidate to join the gallery of classic vampire portrayals, is its absolute technical conviction. . . . [This] is what *Dracula* would have been like if written today by a writer of heavily-researched, nuts-and-bolts techno-thrillers. Combined with strong characterization, it's a mix that winds up being commendably scary, the most viscerally exciting vampire novel since *'Salem's Lot*."
—*Blastr*

"Maybe you're tired of all the good-looking vampires wooing pretty girls. . . . Maybe you just like the kind of horror that makes you feel cold while you're sitting in the sunshine. . . . [*The Strain*] brings old-time folklore together with high-tech New York, whose citizens are in denial over creeping, ugly death. . . . One of those just-one-more-chapter books for readers."
—*Toronto Star*

GUILLERMO DEL TORO
and
CHUCK HOGAN

HARPER

NEW YORK • LONDON • TORONTO • SYDNEY

THE
STRAIN

Book I
OF
The Strain Trilogy

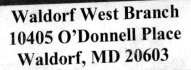

HARPER

A hardcover edition of this book was published in 2009 by William Morrow, an imprint of HarperCollins Publishers.

HarperCollins books may be purchased for educational, business, or sales promotional use. For information please write: Special Markets Department, HarperCollins Publishers, 10 East 53rd Street, New York, NY 10022.

FIRST HARPER PAPERBACK PUBLISHED 2011.

Designed by Shubhani Sarkar

The Library of Congress has catalogued the hardcover edition as follows:

Toro, Guillermo del, 1964–
   The Strain / Guillermo Del Toro and Chuck Hogan — 1st ed.
     p. cm. — (The Strain trilogy; bk. 1)
   ISBN: 978-0-06-155823-8
   1. Vampires—Fiction. I. Hogan, Chuck. II. Title.
   PS3620.O5875S77 2009
   813'.6—dc22
                                   2008043520

ISBN 978-0-06-206825-5 (pbk.)

11 12 13 14 15 OV/RRD 10 9 8 7 6 5 4 3 2 1

To Lorenza, Mariana, and Marisa . . .

and

to all the monsters in my nursery:

May you never leave me alone

—GDT

For Lila

—CH

THE STRAIN

The Legend of Jusef Sardu

O nce upon a time," said Abraham Setrakian's grandmother, "there was a giant."

Young Abraham's eyes brightened, and immediately the cabbage borscht in the wooden bowl got tastier, or at least less garlicky. He was a pale boy, underweight and sickly. His grandmother, intent on fattening him, sat across from him while he ate his soup, entertaining him by spinning a yarn.

A *bubbeh meiseh*, a "grandmother's story." A fairy tale. A legend.

"He was the son of a Polish nobleman. And his name was Jusef Sardu. Master Sardu stood taller than any other man. Taller than any roof in the village. He had to bow deeply to enter any door. But his great height, it was a burden. A disease of birth, not a blessing. The young man suffered. His muscles lacked the strength to support his long, heavy bones. At times it was a struggle for him just to walk. He used a cane, a tall stick—taller than you—with a silver handle carved into the shape of a wolf's head, which was the family crest."

"Yes, Bubbeh?" said Abraham, between spoonfuls.

"This was his lot in life, and it taught him humility, which is a rare thing indeed for a nobleman to possess. He had so much compassion—for the poor, for the hardworking, for the sick. He was especially dear to the children of the village, and his great, deep pockets—the size of turnip sacks—bulged with trinkets and sweets. He had not much of a childhood himself, matching his father's height at the age of eight, and surpassing him by a head at age nine. His frailty and his great size were a secret source of shame to his father. But Master Sardu truly was a gentle giant, and much beloved by his people. It was said of him that Master Sardu looked down on everyone, yet looked down on no one."

She nodded at him, reminding him to take another spoonful. He chewed a boiled red beet, known as a "baby heart" because of its color, its shape, its capillary-like strings. "Yes, Bubbeh?"

"He was also a lover of nature, and had no interest in the brutality of the hunt—but, as a nobleman and a man of rank, at the age of fifteen his father and his uncles prevailed upon him to accompany them on a six-week expedition to Romania."

"To here, Bubbeh?" said Abraham. "The giant, he came here?"

"To the north country, *kaddishel*. The dark forests. The Sardu men, they did not come to hunt wild pig or bear or elk. They came to hunt wolf, the family symbol, the arms of the house of Sardu. They were hunting a hunting animal. Sardu family lore said that eating wolf meat gave Sardu men courage and strength, and the young master's father believed that this might cure his son's weak muscles."

"Yes, Bubbeh?"

"Their trek was long and arduous, as well as violently opposed by the weather, and Jusef struggled mightily. He had never before traveled anywhere outside his family's village, and the looks he received from strangers along the journey shamed him. When they arrived in the dark forest, the woodlands felt alive around him. Packs of animals roamed the woods at night, almost like refugees displaced from their shelters, their dens, nests, and lairs. So many animals that the hunters were unable to sleep at night in their camp. Some wanted to leave, but the elder Sardu's obsession came before all else. They could hear the wolves, crying in the night, and he wanted one badly for his son, his only son, whose gigantism was a pox upon the Sardu line. He wanted to cleanse the house of Sardu of this curse, to marry off his son, and produce many healthy heirs.

"And so it was that his father, off tracking a wolf, was the first to become separated from the others, just before nightfall on the second evening. The rest waited for him all night, and spread out to search for him after sunrise. And so it was that one of Jusef's cousins failed to return that evening. And so on, you see."

"Yes, Bubbeh?"

"Until the only one left was Jusef, the boy giant. That next day he set out, and in an area previously searched, discovered the body of his father, and of all his cousins and uncles, laid out at the entrance to an underground cave. Their skulls had been crushed with great force, but their bodies remained uneaten—killed by a beast of tremendous strength, yet not out of hunger or fear. For what reason, he could not guess—though he did feel himself being watched, perhaps even studied, by some being lurking within that dark cave.

"Master Sardu carried each body away from the cave and buried them deep. Of course, this exertion severely weakened him, taking most of his strength. He was spent, he was *farmutshet*. And yet, alone and scared and exhausted, he returned to the cave that night, to face what evil revealed itself after dark, to avenge his forebears or die trying. This is known from a diary he kept, discovered in the woods many years later. This was his last entry."

Abraham's mouth hung empty and open. "But what happened, Bubbeh?"

"No one truly knows. Back at home, when six weeks stretched to eight, and ten, with no word, the entire hunting party was feared lost. A search party was formed and found nothing. Then, in the eleventh week, one night a carriage with curtained windows arrived at the Sardu estate. It was the young master. He secluded himself inside the castle, inside a wing of empty bedrooms, and was rarely, if ever, seen again. At that time, only rumors followed him back, about what had happened in the Romanian forest. A few who did claim to see Sardu—if indeed any of these accounts could be believed—insisted that he had been cured of his infirmities. Some even whispered that he had returned possessed of great strength, matching his superhuman size. Yet so deep was Sardu's mourning for his father and his uncles and cousins, that he was never again seen about during work hours, and discharged most of his servants. There was movement about the castle at night— hearth fires could be seen glowing in windows—but over time, the Sardu estate fell into disrepair.

"But at night . . . some claimed to hear the giant walking about the village. Children, especially, passed the tale of hearing the *pick-pick-pick* of his walking stick, which Sardu no longer relied upon but used to call them out of their night beds for trinkets and treats. Disbelievers were directed to holes in the soil, some outside bedroom windows, little poke marks as from his wolf-handled stick."

His *bubbeh*'s eyes darkened. She glanced at his bowl, seeing that most of the soup was gone.

"Then, Abraham, some peasant children began to disappear. Stories went around of children vanishing from surrounding villages as well. Even from my own village. Yes, Abraham, as a girl your *bubbeh* grew up just a half-day's walk from Sardu's castle. I remember two sisters. Their bodies were found in a clearing of the woods, as white as the snow surrounding them, their open eyes glazed with frost. I myself, one night, heard not too distantly the *pick-pick-pick*—such a powerful, rhythmic noise—and pulled my blanket fast over my head to block it out, and didn't sleep again for many days."

Abraham gulped down the end of the story with the remains of his soup.

"Much of Sardu's village was eventually abandoned and became an accursed place. The Gypsies, when their carriage train passed through our town, told of strange happenings, of hauntings and apparitions near the castle. Of a giant who prowled the moonlit land like a god of the night. It was they who warned us, 'Eat and grow strong—or else Sardu will get you.' Why it is important, Abraham. *Ess gezunterhait!* Eat and be strong. Scrape that bowl now. Or else—he will come." She had come back from those few moments of darkness, of remembering. Her eyes came back to their lively selves. "Sardu will come. *Pick-pick-pick.*"

And finish he did, every last remaining beet string. The bowl was empty and the story was over, but his belly and his mind were full. His eating pleased his *bubbeh*, and her face was, for him, as clear an expression of love that existed. In these private moments at the rickety family table, they communed, the two of them, sharing food of the heart and the soul.

A decade later, the Setrakian family would be driven from their woodwork shop and their village, though not by Sardu. A German officer was billeted in their home, and the man, softened by his hosts' utter humanity, having broken bread with them over that same wobbly table, one evening warned them not to follow the next day's order to assemble at the train station, but to leave their home and their village that very night.

Which they did, the entire extended family together—all eight of them—journeying into the countryside with as much as they could carry. Bubbeh slowed them down. Worse—she *knew* that she was slowing them down, *knew* that her presence placed the entire family at risk, and cursed herself and her old, tired legs. The rest of the family eventually went on ahead, all except for Abraham—now a strong young man and full of promise, a master carver at such a young age, a scholar of the Talmud, with a special interest in the Zohar, the secrets of Jewish mysticism—who stayed behind, at her side. When word reached them that the others had been arrested at the next town, and had to board a train for Poland, his *bubbeh*, wracked with guilt, insisted that, for Abraham's sake, she be allowed to turn herself in.

"Run, Abraham. Run from the Nazi. As from Sardu. *Escape.*"

But he would not have it. He would not be separated from her.

In the morning he found her on the floor of the room they had shared—in the house of a sympathetic farmer—having fallen off in the night, her lips charcoal black and peeling and her throat black through her neck, dead from the animal poison she had ingested. With his host family's gracious permission, Abraham Setrakian buried her beneath a flowering silver birch. Patiently, he carved her a beautiful wooden marker, full of flowers and birds and all the things that had made her happiest. And he cried and cried for her—and then run he did.

He ran hard from the Nazis, hearing a *pick-pick-pick* all the time at his back . . .

And evil followed closely behind.

THE
BEGINNING

Excerpts, NTSB transcription, Flight 753, Berlin (TXL) to New York (JFK), 9/24/10:

2049:31 [Public-address microphone is switched ON.]

CAPT. PETER J. MOLDES: "Ah, folks, this is Captain Moldes up in the flight deck. We should be touching down on the ground in a few minutes for an on-time arrival. Just wanted to take a moment and let you know we certainly 'preciate you choosing Regis Airlines, and that, on behalf of First Officer Nash and myself and your cabin crew, hope you come back and travel with us again real soon . . ."

2049:44 [Public-address microphone is switched OFF.]

CAPT. PETER J. MOLDES: ". . . so we can all keep our jobs." [cockpit laughter]

2050:01 Air-traffic control New York (JFK): "Regis 7-5-3 heavy, approaching left, heading 1-0-0. Clear to land on 13R."

CAPT. PETER J. MOLDES: "Regis 7-5-3 heavy, approaching left, 1-0-0, landing on runway 13R, we have it."

2050:15 [Public-address microphone is switched ON.]

CAPT. PETER J. MOLDES: "Flight attendants, prepare for landing."

2050:18 [Public-address microphone is switched OFF.]

FIRST OFFICER RONALD W. NASH IV: "Landing gear clear."
CAPT. PETER J. MOLDES: "Always nice coming home . . ."
2050:41 [Banging noise. Static. High-pitched noise.]

END OF TRANSMISSION

THE
LANDING

The dish, they called it. Glowing green monochrome (JFK had been waiting for new color screens for more than two years now), like a bowl of pea soup supplemented with clusters of alphabet letters tagged to coded blips. Each blip represented hundreds of human lives, or, in the old nautical parlance that endured in air travel to this day, *souls*.

Hundreds of souls.

Perhaps that was why all the other air-traffic controllers called Jimmy Mendes "Jimmy the Bishop." The Bishop was the only ATC who spent his entire eight-hour shift standing rather than sitting, wielding a number 2 pencil in his hand and pacing back and forth, talking commercial jets into New York from the busy tower cab 321 feet above John F. Kennedy International Airport like a shepherd tending his flock. He used the pink pencil eraser to visualize the aircraft under his command, their positions relative to one another, rather than relying exclusively upon his two-dimensional radar screen.

Where hundreds of souls beeped every second.

"United 6-4-2, turn right heading 1-0-0, climb to five thousand."

But you couldn't think like that when you were on the dish. You couldn't dwell on all those souls whose fates rested under your command: human beings packed inside winged missiles rocketing miles above the earth. You couldn't big-picture it: all the planes on your dish, and then all the other controllers muttering coded headset conversations around you, and then all of the planes on *their* dishes, and then the ATC tower over at neighboring LaGuardia . . . and then all the ATC towers of every airport in every city in the United States . . . and then all across the world . . .

Calvin Buss, the air-traffic-control area manager and Jimmy the Bishop's immediate supervisor, appeared at his shoulder. He was back early from a break, in fact, still chewing his food. "Where are you with Regis 7-5-3?"

"Regis 7-5-3 is home." Jimmy the Bishop took a quick, hot look at his dish to confirm. "Proceeding to gate." He scrolled back his gate-assignment roster, looking for 7-5-3. "Why?"

"Ground radar says we have an aircraft stalled on Foxtrot."

"The taxiway?" Jimmy checked his dish again, making sure all his bugs were good, then reopened his channel to DL753. "Regis 7-5-3, this is JFK tower, over."

Nothing. He tried again.

"Regis 7-5-3, this is JFK tower, come in, over."

He waited. Nothing, not even a radio click.

"Regis 7-5-3, this is JFK tower, are you reading me, over."

A traffic assistant materialized behind Calvin Buss's shoulder. "Comm problem?" he suggested.

Calvin Buss said, "Gross mechanical failure, more likely. Somebody said the plane's gone dark."

"Dark?" said Jimmy the Bishop, marveling at what a near miss that would be, the aircraft's gross mechanicals shitting the bed just minutes after landing. He made a mental note to stop off on the way home and play 753 for tomorrow's numbers.

Calvin plugged his own earphone into Jimmy's b-comm audio jack. "Regis 7-5-3, this is JFK tower, please respond. Regis 7-5-3, this is the tower, over."

Waiting, listening.

Nothing.

Jimmy the Bishop eyed his pending blips on the dish—no conflict alerts, all his aircraft okay. "Better advise on a reroute around Foxtrot," he said.

Calvin unplugged and stepped back. He got a middle-distance

look in his eyes, staring past Jimmy's console to the windows of the tower cab, out in the general direction of the taxiway. His look showed as much confusion as concern. "We need to get Foxtrot cleared." He turned to the traffic assistant. "Dispatch somebody for a visual."

Jimmy the Bishop clutched his belly, wishing he could reach inside and somehow massage the sickness roiling at its pit. His profession, essentially, was midwifery. He assisted pilots in delivering planes full of souls safely out of the womb of the void and unto the earth. What he felt now were pangs of fear, like those of a young doctor having delivered his very first stillborn.

Terminal 3 Tarmac

LORENZA RUIZ was on her way out to the gate, driving a baggage conveyor, basically a hydraulic ramp on wheels. When 753 didn't show around the corner as expected, Lo rolled out farther for a little peek, as she was due her break soon. She wore protective headphones, a Mets hoodie underneath her reflective vest, goggles—that runway grit was a bitch—with her orange marshaling batons lying next to her hip, on the seat.

What in the hell?

She pulled off her goggles as though needing to see it with her bare eyes. There it was, a Regis 777, a big boy, one of the new ones on the fleet, sitting out on Foxtrot in darkness. *Total* darkness, even the nav lights on the wings. All she saw was the smooth, tubular surface of the fuselage and wings glowing faintly under the landing lights of approaching planes. One of them, Lufthansa 1567, missing a collision with its landing gear by a mere foot.

"Jesus Santisimo!"

She called it in.

"We're already on our way," said her supervisor. "Crow's nest wants you to roll out and take a look."

"Me?" Lo said.

She frowned. That's what you get for curiosity. So she went, following the service lane out from the passenger terminal, crossing the taxiway lines painted onto the apron. She was a little nervous, and very watchful, having never driven out this far before. The FAA had strict rules about how far out the conveyors and baggage trailers were supposed to go.

She turned past the blue guide lamps edging the taxiway. The plane appeared to have been shut down completely, stem to stern. No beacon light, no anticollision light, no lights in the cabin windows. Usually, even from the ground, thirty feet below, through the tiny windshield like eyes slanting over the characteristic Boeing nose, you could see up and inside the cockpit, the overhead switch panel and the instrument lights glowing darkroom red. But there were no lights at all.

Lo idled ten yards back from the tip of the long left wing. You work the tarmac long enough—Lo had eight years in now, longer than both of her marriages put together—you pick up a few things. The trailing edge flaps and the ailerons—the spoiler panels on the back sides of the wings—were all straight up like Paula Abdul, which is how pilots set them after runway touchdown. The turbojets were quiet and still, and they usually took a while to stop chewing air even after switch off, sucking in grit and bugs like great ravenous vacuums. So this big baby had come in clean and set down all nice and easy and gotten this far before—*lights out.*

Even more alarmingly, if it had been cleared for landing, whatever had gone wrong happened in the space of two, maybe three minutes. *What can go wrong that fast?*

Lo pulled a little bit closer, rolling in behind the wing. If those turbofans were to start up all of a sudden, she didn't want to get sucked in and shredded like some Canadian goose. She drove near the freight hold, the area of the plane she was best acquainted with, down toward the tail, stopping beneath the rear exit door. She set the locking brake and worked the stick that raised her ramp, which at its height topped out at about a thirty-degree incline. Not enough, but still. She got out, reached back in for her batons, and walked up the ramp toward the dead airplane.

Dead? Why did she think that? The thing had never been alive—

But for a moment, Lorenza thought of the image of a large, rotting corpse, a beached whale. That was what the plane looked like to her: a festering carcass; a dying leviathan.

The wind stopped as she neared the top, and you have to understand one thing about the climate out on the apron at JFK: the wind never stops. As in *never ever*. It is *always* windy out on the tarmac, with the planes coming in and the salt marsh and the friggin' Atlantic Ocean just on the other side of Rockaway. But all of a sudden it got real silent—so silent that Lo pulled down her big-muff headphones, just to be certain. She thought she heard pounding coming from inside the plane, but realized it was just the beating of her own heart. She turned on her flashlight and trained it on the right flank of the plane.

Following the circular splash of her beam, she could see that the fuselage was still slick and pearly from its descent, smelling like spring rain. She shined her light on the long row of windows. Every interior shade was pulled down.

That was strange. She was spooked now. Majorly spooked. Dwarfed by a massive, $250-million, 383-ton flying machine, she had a fleeting yet palpable and cold sensation of standing in the presence of a dragon-like beast. A sleeping demon only *pretending* to be asleep, yet capable, at any moment, of opening its eyes and its terrible mouth. An electrically psychic moment, a chill running through her with the force of a reverse orgasm, everything tightening, knotting up.

Then she noticed that one of the shades was up now. The fine hairs went so prickly on the back of her neck, she put her hand there to console them, like soothing a jumpy pet. She had missed seeing that shade before. It had always been up—always.

Maybe . . .

Inside the plane, the darkness stirred. And Lo felt as if something were observing her from within it.

She whimpered, just like a child, but couldn't help it. She was paralyzed. A throbbing rush of blood, rising as though commanded, tightened her throat . . .

And she understood it then, unequivocally: *something in there was going to eat her . . .*

The gusting wind started up again, as though it had never paused, and Lo didn't need any more prompting. She backed down the ramp and jumped inside her conveyor, putting it in reverse with the alert beeping and her ramp still up. The crunching noise was one of the blue taxiway lights beneath her treads as she sped away, half on and half off the grass, toward the approaching lights of half a dozen emergency vehicles.

JFK International Control Tower

CALVIN BUSS had switched to a different headset, and was giving orders as set forth in the FAA national playbook for taxiway incursions. All arrivals and departures were halted in a five-mile airspace around JFK. This meant that volume was stacking up fast. Calvin canceled breaks and ordered every on-shift controller to try to raise Flight 753 on every available frequency. It was as close to chaos in the JFK tower as Jimmy the Bishop had ever seen.

Port Authority officials—guys in suits muttering into Nextels—gathered at his back. Never a good sign. Funny how people naturally assemble when faced with the unexplained.

Jimmy the Bishop tried his call again, to no avail.

One suit asked him, "Hijack signal?"

"No," said Jimmy the Bishop. "Nothing."

"No fire alarm?"

"Of course not."

"No cockpit door alarm?" said another.

Jimmy the Bishop saw that they had entered the "stupid questions" phase of the investigation. He summoned the patience and good judgment that made him a successful air-traffic controller. "She came in smooth and set down soft. Regis 7-5-3 confirmed the gate assignment and turned off the runway. I terminated radar and transitioned it over to ASDE."

Calvin said, one hand over his earphone mic, "Maybe the pilot had to shut down?"

"Maybe," said Jimmy the Bishop. "Or maybe it shut down on him."

A suit said, "Then why haven't they opened a door?"

Jimmy the Bishop's mind was already spinning on that. Passengers, as a rule, won't sit still for a minute longer than they had to. The previous week, a jetBlue arriving from Florida had very nearly undergone a mutiny, and that was over *stale bagels*. Here, these people had been sitting tight for, what—maybe fifteen minutes. Completely in the dark.

Jimmy the Bishop said, "It's got to be starting to get hot in there. If the electrical is shut down, there's no air circulating inside. No ventilation."

"So what the hell are they waiting for?" said another suit.

Jimmy the Bishop felt everyone's anxiety going up. That hole in your gut when you realize that something is about to happen, something really, really wrong.

"What if they can't move?" he muttered before he could stop himself from speaking.

"A hostage situation? Is that what you mean?" asked the suit.

The Bishop nodded quietly . . . but he wasn't thinking that. For whatever reason, all he could think was . . . *souls*.

Taxiway Foxtrot

THE PORT AUTHORITY'S aircraft rescue firefighters went out on a standard airliner distress deployment, six vehicles including the fuel spill foamer, pumper, and aerial ladder truck. They pulled up at the stuck baggage conveyor before the blue lamps edging Foxtrot. Captain Sean Navarro hopped off the back step of the ladder truck, standing there in his helmet and fire suit before the dead plane. The rescue vehicles' lights flashing against the fuselage imbued the aircraft with a fake red pulse. It looked like an empty plane set out for a nighttime training drill.

Captain Navarro went up to the front of the truck and climbed in with the driver, Benny Chufer. "Call in to maintenance and get those staging lights out here. Then pull up behind the wing."

Benny said, "Our orders are to hang back."

Captain Navarro said, "That's a plane full of people there. We're not paid to be glorified road flares. We're paid to save lives."

Benny shrugged and did as the cap told him. Captain Navarro climbed back out of the rig and up onto the roof, and Benny raised the boom just enough to get him up on the wing. Captain Navarro switched on his flashlight and stepped over the trailing edge between the two raised flaps, his boot landing right where it said, in bold black lettering, DON'T STEP HERE.

He walked along the broadening wing, twenty feet above the tarmac. He went to the over-wing exit, the only door on the aircraft installed with an exterior emergency release. There was a small, unshaded window set in the door, and he tried to peer through, past the beads of condensation inside the double-thick glass, seeing nothing inside except more darkness. It had to be as stifling as an iron lung in there.

Why weren't they calling out for help? Why wasn't he hearing any movement inside? If still pressurized, then the plane was airtight. Those passengers were running out of oxygen.

With his fire gloves on, he pushed in the twin red flaps and pulled the door handle out from its recess. He rotated it in the direction of the arrows, nearly 180 degrees, and tugged. The door should have popped outward then, but it would not open. He pulled again, but knew immediately that his effort was useless—no give whatsoever. There was no way it could have been stuck from the inside. The handle must have jammed. Or else something was holding it from the inside.

He went back down wing to the ladder top. He saw an orange utility light spinning, an airport cart on its way out from the international terminal. Closer, he saw it was driven by blue-jacketed agents of the Transportation Security Administration.

"Here we go," muttered Captain Navarro, starting down the ladder.

There were five of them, each one introducing himself in turn, but Captain Navarro didn't waste any effort trying to remember names. He had come to the plane with fire engines and foaming equipment; they came with laptops and mobile handhelds. For a while he just stood and listened while they talked into their devices and over each other:

"We need to think long and hard before we push the Homeland Security button here. Nobody wants a shit storm for nothing."

"We don't even know what we have. You ring that bell and scramble fighters up here from Otis Air Force Base, you're talking about panicking the entire eastern seaboard."

"If it *is* a bomb, they waited until the last possible moment."

"Explode it on U.S. soil, maybe."

"Maybe they're playing dead for a while. Staying radio dark. Luring us closer. Waiting for the media."

One guy was reading from his phone. "I have the flight originating from Tegel, in Berlin."

Another spoke into his. "I want someone on the ground in Germany who sprechen ze English. We need to know if they've seen any suspicious activity there, any breaches. Also, we need a primer on their baggage-handling procedures."

Another ordered: "Check the flight plan and reclear the passenger manifest. Yes—every name, run them again. This time accounting for spelling variations."

"Okay," said another, reading from his handheld. "Full specs. Plane reg is N323RG. Boeing 777–200LR. Most recent transit check was four days ago, at Atlanta Hartsfield. Replaced a worn duct slider on the left engine's thrust reverser, and a worn mount bushing on the right. Deferred repair of a dent in the left-aft inboard flap assembly due to flight schedule. Bottom line—she got a clean bill of health."

"Triple sevens are new orders, aren't they? A year or two out?"

"Three hundred and one max capacity. This flight boarded two ten. A hundred and ninety-nine passengers, two pilots, nine cabin crew."

"Any unticketed?" That meant infants.

"I'm showing no."

"Classic tactic," said the one focused on terror. "Create a disturbance, draw first responders, gain an audience—then detonate for max impact."

"If so, then we're already dead."

They looked at each other uncomfortably.

"We need to pull these rescue vehicles back. Who was that fool up there stomping on the wing?"

Captain Navarro edged forward, surprising them with a response. "That was me."

"Ah. Well." The guy coughed once into his fist. "That's maintenance personnel only up there, Captain. FAA regs."

"I know it."

"Well? What'd you see? Anything?"

Navarro said, "Nothing. Saw nothing, heard nothing. All the window shades are drawn down."

"Drawn down, you say? All of them?"

"All of them."

"Did you try the over-wing exit?"

"I did indeed."

"And?"

"It was stuck."

"Stuck? That's impossible."

"It's stuck," said Captain Navarro, showing more patience with these five than he did with his own kids.

The senior man stepped away to make a call. Captain Navarro looked at the others. "So what are we going to do here, then?"

"That's what we're waiting to find out."

"Waiting to find out? You have how many passengers on this plane? How many 911 calls have they made?"

One man shook his head. "No mobile 911 calls from the plane yet."

"Yet?" said Captain Navarro.

The guy next to him said, "Zero for one-ninety-nine. Not good."

"Not good at all."

Captain Navarro looked at them in amazement. "We have to do something, and now. I don't need permission to grab a fire ax and start smashing in windows when people are dead or dying in there. There is no air inside that plane."

The senior man came back from his phone call. "They're bringing out the torch now. We're cutting her open."

Dark Harbor, Virginia

CHESAPEAKE BAY, black and churning at that late hour.

Inside the glassed-in patio of the main house, on a scenic bluff overlooking the bay, a man reclined in a specially made medical chair. The lights were dimmed for his comfort as well as for modesty. The industrial thermostats, of which there were three for this room alone, maintained a temperature of sixty-two degrees Fahrenheit. Stravinsky played quietly, *The Rite of Spring*, piped in through discreet speakers to obscure the relentless *shush*ing pump of the dialysis machine.

A faint plume of breath emerged from his mouth. An onlooker might have believed the man near death. Might have thought they were witnessing the last days or weeks of what was, judging by the sprawling seventeen-acre estate, a dramatically successful life. Might even have remarked on the irony of a man of such obvious wealth and position meeting the same end as a pauper.

Only, Eldritch Palmer was not at the end. He was in his seventy-sixth year, and he had no intention of giving up on anything. Nothing at all.

The esteemed investor, businessman, theologian, and high-powered confidant had been undergoing the same procedure for three to four hours every evening for the past seven years of his life. His health was frail and yet manageable, overseen by round-the-clock physicians and aided by hospital-grade medical equipment purchased for his private, in-home use.

Wealthy people can afford excellent health care, and they can also afford to be eccentric. Eldritch Palmer kept his peculiarities hidden from public view, even from his inner circle. The man had never married. He had never sired an heir. And so a major topic of speculation about Palmer was what plans he might have for his vast fortune after his death. He had no second-in-command at his primary investment entity, the Stoneheart Group. He had no public affiliation with any foundations or charities, unlike the two men jockeying for number one with him on the annual *Forbes* list of the world's richest Americans, Microsoft founder Bill Gates and Berkshire Hathaway investor Warren Buffett. (If certain gold reserves in South America and other holdings by shadow corporations in Africa were factored into Forbes's accounting, Palmer alone would hold the top spot on the list.) Palmer had never even drafted a will, an estate-planning lapse unthinkable for a man with even one one-thousandth of his wealth and treasure.

But Eldritch Palmer was, quite simply, not planning to die.

Hemodialysis is a procedure in which blood is removed from the body through a system of tubing, ultrafiltered through a dialyzer, or artificial kidney, and then returned to the body cleansed of waste products and impurities. Ingoing and outgoing needles are inserted into a synthetic arteriovenous graft semipermanently installed in the forearm. The machine for this procedure was a state-of-the-art Fresenius model, continuously monitoring Palmer's critical parameters and alerting Mr. Fitzwilliam, never more than two rooms away, of any readings outside the normal range.

Loyal investors were accustomed to Palmer's perpetually gaunt appearance. It had essentially become his trademark, an ironic symbol of his monetary strength, that such a delicate, ashen-looking man should wield such power and influence in both international finance and politics. His legion of faithful investors numbered thirty thousand strong, a financially elite bloc of people: the buy-in was two million dollars, and many who had invested with Palmer for decades were worth mid-nine figures. The buying power of his Stoneheart Group gave him enormous economic leverage, which he put to effective and occasionally ruthless use.

The west doors opened from the wide hallway, and Mr. Fitzwilliam, who doubled as the head of Palmer's personal security detail, entered with a portable, secure telephone on a sterling-silver serving tray. Mr. Fitzwilliam was a former U.S. Marine with forty-two confirmed combat kills and a quick mind, whose postmilitary medical schooling Palmer had financed. "The undersecretary for Homeland Security, sir," he said, with a plume of breath steaming in the cold room.

Normally Palmer allowed no intrusions during his nightly replenishment, preferring instead to use the time contemplatively. But this was a call he had been expecting. He accepted the telephone from Mr. Fitzwilliam, and waited for him to dutifully withdraw.

Palmer answered, and was informed about the dormant airplane. He learned that there was considerable uncertainty as to how to proceed by officials at JFK. The caller spoke anxiously, with self-conscious formality, like a proud child reporting a good deed. "This is a highly unusual event, and I thought you'd want to be apprised immediately, sir."

"Yes," Palmer told the man. "I do appreciate such courtesy."

"Ha-have a good night, sir."

Palmer hung up and set the phone down in his small lap. A good night *indeed*. He felt a pang of anticipation. He had been expecting this. And now that the plane had landed, he knew it had begun—and in what spectacular fashion.

Excitedly, he turned to the large-screen television on the side wall and used the remote control on the arm of his chair to activate the sound. Nothing about the airplane yet. But soon . . .

He pressed the button on an intercom. Mr. Fitzwilliam's voice said, "Yes, sir?"

"Have them ready the helicopter, Mr. Fitzwilliam. I have some business to attend to in Manhattan."

Eldritch Palmer rang off, then looked through the wall of windows out over the great Chesapeake Bay, roiling and black, just south of where the steely Potomac emptied into her dark depths.

Taxiway Foxtrot

THE MAINTENANCE CREW wheeled oxygen tanks underneath the fuselage. Cutting in was an emergency procedure of last resort. All commercial aircraft were constructed with specified "chop-out" areas. The triple seven's chop out was in the rear fuselage, beneath the tail, between the aft cargo doors on the right side. The LR in Boeing 777–200LR stood for long range, and as a C-market model with a top range exceeding 9,000 nautical miles (nearly 11,000 U.S.) and a fuel capacity of up to 200,000 liters (more than 50,000 gallons), the aircraft had, in addition to the traditional fuel tanks inside the wing bodies, three auxiliary tanks in the rear cargo hold—thus the need for a safe chop-out area.

The maintenance crew was using an Arcair slice pack, an exothermic torch favored for disaster work not only because it was highly portable, but because it was also oxygen powered, using no hazardous secondary gases such as acetylene. The work of cutting through the thick fuselage shell would take about one hour.

No one on the tarmac at this point was anticipating a happy outcome. There had been no 911 calls from passengers inside the aircraft. No light, noise, or signal of any kind emanating from inside Regis 753. The situation was mystifying.

A Port Authority emergency services unit mobile-command vehicle was cleared through to the terminal apron, set up behind powerful construction lights trained on the jet. Their SWAT team was trained for evacuations, hostage rescue, and antiterrorism assaults on the bridges, tunnels, bus terminals, airports, PATH rail lines, and seaports of New York and New Jersey. Tactical officers were outfitted with light body armor and Heckler-Koch submachine guns. A pair of German shepherds were out sniffing around the main landing gear—two sets of six enormous tires—trotting around with their noses in the air as if they could smell the trouble here too.

Captain Navarro wondered for a moment if anyone was actually still on board. Hadn't there been a *Twilight Zone* where a plane landed empty?

The maintenance crew sparked up the torches and was just starting in on the underside of the hull when one of the canines started howling. The dog was baying, actually, and spinning around and around on his leash in tight circles.

Captain Navarro saw his ladder man, Benny Chufer, pointing up at the midsection of the aircraft. A thin, black shadow appeared before his eyes. A vertical slash of darkest black, disrupting the perfectly smooth breast of the fuselage.

The exit door over the wing. The one Captain Navarro hadn't been able to budge.

It was open now.

It made no sense to him, but Navarro kept quiet, struck dumb by the sight. Maybe a latch failure, a malfunction in the handle . . . maybe he had not tried hard enough . . . or maybe—just maybe—someone had finally opened the door.

JFK International Control Tower

THE PORT AUTHORITY had pulled Jimmy the Bishop's audio. He was standing, as always, waiting to review it with the suits, when their phones started ringing like crazy.

"It's open," one guy reported. "Somebody opened up 3L."

Everybody was standing now, trying to see. Jimmy the Bishop looked out from the tower cab at the lit-up plane. The door did not look open from up here.

Calvin Buss said, "From the inside? Who's coming out?"

The guy shook his head, still on his phone. "No one. Not yet."

Jimmy the Bishop grabbed a small pair of birders off the ledge and checked out Regis 753 for himself.

There it was. A sliver of black over the wing. A seam of shadow, like a tear in the hull of the aircraft.

Jimmy's mouth went dry at the sight. Those doors pull out slightly when first unlocked, then swivel back and fold against the interior wall. So, technically, all that had happened was that the airlock had been disengaged. The door wasn't quite open yet.

He set the field glasses back on the ledge and backed away. For some reason, his mind was telling him that this would be a good time to run.

Taxiway Foxtrot

THE GAS AND RADIATION SENSORS lifted to the door crack both read clear. An emergency service unit officer lying on the wing managed to pull out the door a few extra inches with a long, hooked pole, two other armed tactical officers covering him from the tarmac below. A parabolic microphone was inserted, returning all manner of chirps, beeps, and ring tones: the passengers' mobile phones going unanswered. Eerie and plaintive sounding, like tiny little personal distress alarms.

They then inserted a mirror attached at the end of a pole, a large-size version of the sort of dental instrument used to examine back teeth. All they could see were the two jump seats inside the between-classes area, both unoccupied.

Bullhorn commands got them nowhere. No response from inside the aircraft: no lights, no movement, no nothing.

Two ESU officers in light body armor stood back from the taxiway lights for a briefing. They viewed a cross-section schematic, showing passengers seated ten abreast inside the coach cabin they would be entering: three each on the row sides and four across the middle. Airplane interior was tight, and they traded their H-K submachine guns for more manageable Glock 17s, preparing for close combat.

They strapped on radio-enabled gas masks fitted with flip-down night-vision specs, and snapped mace, zip cuffs, and extra magazine pouches to their belts. Q-tip–size cameras, also with passive infrared lenses, were mounted onto the tops of their ESU helmets.

They went up the fire rescue ladder onto the wing, and advanced to the door. They pulled up flat against the fuselage on either side of it, one man folding the door back against the interior wall with his boot, then curling inside, low and straight ahead to a near partition, staying down on his haunches. His partner followed him aboard.

The bullhorn spoke for them:

"*Occupants of Regis 753. This is the New York–New Jersey Port*

Authority. We are entering the aircraft. For your own safety, please remain seated and lace your fingers on top of your heads."

The lead man waited with his back to the partition, listening. His mask dulled sound into a jarlike roar, but he could discern no movement inside. He flipped down his NVD and the interior of the plane went pea-soup green. He nodded to his partner, readied his Glock, and on a three count swept into the wide cabin.

NOW
BOARDING

Worth Street, Chinatown

Ephraim Goodweather couldn't tell if the siren he heard was blaring out in the street—which is to say, *real*—or part of the sound track of the video game he was playing with his son, Zack.

"Why do you keep killing me?" asked Eph.

The sandy-haired boy shrugged, as though offended by the question. "That's the whole point, Dad."

The television stood next to the broad west-facing window, far and away the best feature of this tiny, second-story walk-up on the southern edge of Chinatown. The coffee table before them was cluttered with open cartons of Chinese food, a bag of comics from Forbidden Planet, Eph's mobile phone, Zack's mobile phone, and Zack's smelly feet. The game system was new, another toy purchased with Zack in mind. Just as his grandmother used to juice the inside of an orange half, so did Eph try to squeeze every last bit of fun and goodness out of their limited time together. His only son was his life, was his air and water and food, and he had to load up on him when he could, because sometimes a week could pass with only a phone call or two, and it was like going a week without seeing the sun.

"What the . . ." Eph thumbed his controller, this foreign-feeling wireless gadget in his hand, still hitting all the wrong buttons. His soldier was punching the ground. "At least let me get up."

"Too late. Dead again."

For a lot of other guys Eph knew, men in a situation similar to his own, their divorce seemed to have been as much from their children as from their wives. Sure, they would talk the talk, how they missed their kids, and how their ex-wives kept subverting their relationship, blah, blah, but the effort never really seemed to be there. A weekend with their kids became a weekend *out* of their new life of freedom. For Eph, these weekends with Zack *were* his life. Eph had never wanted the divorce. Still didn't. He acknowledged that his married life with Kelly was over—she had made her position perfectly clear to him—but he refused to relinquish his claim on Zack. The boy's custody was the only unresolved issue, the sole reason they still remained wed in the eyes of the state.

This was the last of Eph's trial weekends, as stipulated by their court-appointed family counselor. Zack would be interviewed sometime next week, and soon afterward a final determination would be made. Eph didn't care that it was a long shot, his getting custody; this was the fight of his life. *Do the right thing for Zack* formed the crux of Kelly's guilt trip, pushing Eph to settle for generous visitation rights. But the right thing for Eph was to hang on to Zack. Eph had twisted the arm of the U.S. government, his employer, in order to set up his team here in New York instead of Atlanta, where the CDC was located, just so that Zack's life would not be disrupted any more than it had been already.

He could have fought harder. Dirtier. As his lawyer had advised him to, many times. That man knew the tricks of the divorce trade. One reason Eph could not bring himself to do so was his lingering melancholy over the failure of the marriage. The other was that Eph had too much mercy in him—that what indeed made him a terrific doctor was the very same thing that made him a pitiful divorce-case client. He had conceded to Kelly almost every demand and financial claim her lawyer requested. All he wanted was time alone with his only son.

Who right now was lobbing grenades at him.

Eph said, "How can I shoot back when you've blown off my arms?"

"I don't know. Maybe try kicking?"

"Now I know why your mother doesn't let you own a game system."

"Because it makes me hyper and antisocial and . . . OH, FRAGGED YOU!"

Eph's life-capacity bar diminished to zero.

That was when his mobile phone started vibrating, skittering up against the take-out cartons like a hungry silver beetle. Probably Kelly, reminding him to make sure Zack used his asthma inhaler. Or just checking up on him, making sure he hadn't whisked Zack away to Morocco or something.

Eph caught it, checked the screen. A 718 number, local. Caller ID read JFK QUARANTINE.

The Centers for Disease Control and Prevention maintained a quarantine station inside the international terminal at JFK. Not a detainment or even a treatment facility, just a few small offices and an examining room: a way station, a firebreak to identify and perhaps stall an outbreak from threatening the general population of the United States. Most of their work involved isolating and evaluating passengers taken ill in flight, occasionally turning up a diagnosis of meningococcal meningitis or severe acute respiratory syndrome (SARS).

The office was closed evenings, and Eph was not to be on call tonight, or anywhere on the depth chart through Monday morning. He had cleared his work schedule weeks ago, in advance of his weekend with Zack.

He clicked off the vibrate button and set the mobile back down next to the carton of scallion pancakes. Somebody else's problem. "It's the kid who sold me this thing," he told Zack. "Calling to heckle me."

Zack was eating another steamed dumpling. "I cannot *believe* you got Yankees–Red Sox tickets for tomorrow."

"I know. Good seats too. Third-base side. Tapped into your college fund to get them, but hey, don't worry—with your skills, you'll go far on just a high school degree."

"Dad."

"Anyway, you know how it pains me to put even one green dollar in Steinbrenner's pocket. This is essentially treason."

Zack said, "Boo, Red Sox. Go, Yanks."

"First you kill me, then you taunt me?"

"I figured, as a Red Sox fan, you'd be used to it."

"That's it—!" Eph wrapped up his son, working his hands in along his ticklish rib cage, the boy bucking as he convulsed with laughter. Zack was getting stronger, his squirming possessed of real force: this boy who he used to fly around the room on one shoulder. Zachary had his mother's hair, both in its sandy color (her original color, the way it was when he first met her in college) and fine texture. And yet, to Eph's amazement and joy, he recognized his own eleven-year-old hands dangling uncannily from the boy's wrists. The very same broad-knuckled hands that used to want to do nothing more than rub up baseball cowhide, hands that hated piano lessons, that could not wait to get a grip on this world of adults. Uncanny, seeing those young hands again. It was true: our children do come to replace us. Zachary was like a perfect human package, his DNA written with everything Eph and Kelly once were to each other—their hopes, dreams, potential. This was probably why each of them worked so hard, in his and her own contradictory ways, to bring out his very best. So much so that the thought of Zack being brought up under the influence of Kelly's live-in boyfriend, Matt—a "nice" guy, a "good" guy, but so middle of the road as to be practically invisible—kept Eph up at night. He wanted challenge for his son, he wanted inspiration, greatness! The battle for the custody of Zack's person was settled, but not the battle for the custody of Zack's spirit—for his very soul.

Eph's mobile started vibrating again, crabbing across the tabletop like the chattering gag teeth his uncles used to give him for Christmas. The awakened device interrupted their roughhousing, Eph releasing Zack, fighting the impulse to check the display. Something was happening. The calls wouldn't have come through to him otherwise. An outbreak. An infected traveler.

Eph made himself *not* pick up the phone. Someone else had to handle it. This was his weekend with Zack. Who was looking at him now.

"Don't worry," said Eph, putting the mobile back down on the table, the call going to his voice mail. "Everything's taken care of. No work this weekend."

Zack nodded, perking up, finding his controller. "Want some more?"

"I don't know. When do we get to the part where the little Mario guy starts rolling barrels down at the monkey?"

"Dad."

"I'm just more comfortable with little Italian stereotypes running around gobbling up mushrooms for points."

"Right. And how many miles of snow was it you had to trudge through to get to school each day?"

"*That's it—!*"

Eph fell on him again, the boy ready for him this time, clamping his elbows tight, foiling his rib attack. So Eph changed strategy, going instead for the ultrasensitive Achilles tendon, wrestling with Zack's heels while trying hard not to get kicked in the face. The boy was begging for mercy when Eph realized his mobile was vibrating *yet again.*

Eph jumped up this time, angry, knowing now that his job, his vocation, was going to pull him away from his son tonight. He glanced at the caller ID, and this time the number bore an Atlanta prefix. Very bad news. Eph closed his eyes and pressed the humming phone to his forehead, clearing his mind. "Sorry, Z," he told Zack. "Just let me see what's up."

He took the phone into the adjoining kitchen, where he answered it. "Ephraim? It's Everett Barnes."

Dr. Everett Barnes. The director of the CDC.

Eph's back was to Zack. He knew Zack was watching and couldn't bear to look at him. "Yes, Everett, what is it?"

"I just got the call from Washington. Your team is en route to the airport now?"

"Ah, sir, actually—"

"You saw it on TV?"

"TV?"

He went back to the sofa, showing Zack his open hand, a plea for patience. Eph found the remote and searched it for the correct button or combination of buttons, tried a few, and the screen went blank. Zack took the remote from his hand and sullenly switched to cable.

The news channel showed an airplane parked on the tarmac. Support vehicles formed a wide, perhaps fearful, perimeter. JFK International Airport. "I think I see it, Everett."

"Jim Kent just reached me, he's pulling the equipment your Canary team needs. You are the front line on this, Ephraim. They're not to make another move until you get there."

"They who, sir?"

"The Port Authority of New York, the Transportation Security Administration. The National Transportation Safety Board and Homeland Security are winging there now."

The Canary project was a rapid-response team of field epidemiologists organized to detect and identify incipient biological threats. Its purview included both naturally occurring threats, such as viral and rickettsial diseases found in nature, and man-made outbreaks—although most of their funding came thanks to Canary's obvious bioterrorism applications. New York City was the nerve center, with smaller, university-hospital-based satellite Canaries up and running in Miami, Los Angeles, Denver, and Chicago.

The program drew its name from the old coal miner's trick of bringing a caged canary underground as a crude yet efficient biological early warning system. The bright yellow bird's highly sensitive metabolism detected methane and carbon monoxide gas traces before they reached toxic or even explosive levels, causing the normally chirpy creature to fall silent and sway on its perch.

In this modern age, every human being had the potential to be that sentinel canary. Eph's team's job was to isolate them once they stopped singing, treat the infected, and contain the spread.

Eph said, "What is it, Everett? Did somebody die on the plane?"

The director said, "They're all dead, Ephraim. Every last one."

Kelton Street, Woodside, Queens

KELLY GOODWEATHER sat at the small table across from Matt Sayles, her live-in partner ("boyfriend" sounded too young; "significant other" sounded too old). They were sharing a homemade pizza made with pesto sauce, sun-dried tomatoes, and goat cheese, with a few curls of prosciutto thrown in for flair, as well as an eleven-dollar bottle of year-old merlot. The kitchen television was tuned to NY1 because Matt wanted the news. As far as Kelly was concerned, twenty-four-hour news channels were her enemy.

"I am sorry," she told him again.

Matt smiled, making a lazy circle in the air with his wineglass.

"It's not my fault, of course. But I know we had this weekend set up all to ourselves . . ."

Matt wiped his lips on the napkin tucked into his shirt collar. "He usually finds a way to get in between the two of us. And I am not referring to Zack."

Kelly looked over at the empty third chair. Matt had no doubt been looking forward to her son's weekend away. Pending resolution of their drawn-out, court-mediated custody battle, Zack was spending a few weekends with Eph at his flat in Lower Manhattan. That meant, for her, an intimate dinner at home, with the usual sexual expectations on Matt's part—which Kelly had no qualms about fulfilling, and was inevitably worth the extra glass of wine she would allow herself.

But now, not tonight. As sorry as she was for Matt, for herself she was actually quite pleased.

"I'll make it up to you," she told him, with a wink.

Matt smiled in defeat. "Deal."

This was why Matt was such a comfort. After Eph's moodiness, his outbursts, his hard-driving personality, the mercury that ran through his veins, she needed a slower boat like Matt. She had married Eph much too young, and deferred too much of herself—her own needs, ambitions, desires—helping him advance his medical career. If she could impart one bit of life advice to the fourth-grade girls in her class at PS 69 in Jackson Heights, it would be: never marry a genius. Especially a good-looking one. With Matt, Kelly felt at ease, and, in fact, enjoyed the upper hand in the relationship. It was her turn to be tended to.

On the small white kitchen television, they were hyping the next day's eclipse. The reporter was trying on various glasses, rating them for eye safety, while reporting from a T-shirt stand in Central Park. KISS ME ON THE ECLIPSE! was the big seller. The anchors promoted their "Live Team Coverage" coming tomorrow afternoon.

"It's gonna be a big show," said Matt, his comment letting her know he wasn't going to let disappointment ruin the evening.

"It's a major celestial event," said Kelly, "and they're treating it like just another winter snowstorm."

The "Breaking News" screen came on. This was usually Kelly's cue to change the channel, but the strangeness of the story drew her in. The TV showed a distant shot of an airplane sitting on the tarmac at JFK, encircled by work lights. The plane was lit so dramatically, and surrounded by so many vehicles and small men, you would have thought a UFO had touched down in Queens.

"Terrorists," said Matt.

JFK Airport was only ten miles away. The reporter said that the airplane in question had completely shut down after an otherwise unremarkable landing, and that there had as yet been no contact either from the flight crew or the passengers still aboard. All landings at JFK had been suspended as a precaution, and air traffic was being diverted to Newark and LaGuardia.

She knew then that this airplane was the reason Eph was bringing Zack back home. All she wanted now was to get Zack back under her roof. Kelly was one of the great worriers, and home meant safety. It was the one place in this world that she could control.

Kelly rose and went to the window over her kitchen sink, dimming the light, looking out at the sky beyond the roof of their backyard neighbor. She saw airplane lights circling LaGuardia, swirling like bits of glittering debris pulled into a storm funnel. She had never been out in the middle part of the country, where you can see tornadoes coming at you from miles away. But this felt like that. Like there was something coming her way that she could do nothing about.

Eph pulled up his CDC-issued Ford Explorer at the curb. Kelly owned a small house on a tidy square of land surrounded by neat, low hedges in a sloping block of two-story houses. She met him outside on the concrete walk, as though wary of admitting him into her domicile, generally treating him like a decade-long flu she had finally fought off.

Blonder and slender and still very pretty, though she was a different person to him now. So much had changed. Somewhere, in a dusty shoe box probably, buried in the back of a closet, there were wedding photos of an untroubled young woman with her veil thrown back, smiling winningly at her tuxedoed groom, two young people very happily in love.

"I had the entire weekend cleared," he said, exiting the car ahead of Zack, pushing through the low iron gate in order to get in the first word. "It's an emergency."

Matt Sayles stepped out through the lighted doorway behind her, stopping on the front stoop. His napkin was tucked into his shirt, obscuring the Sears logo over the pocket from the store he managed at the mall in Rego Park.

Eph didn't acknowledge his presence, keeping his focus on Kelly and Zack as the boy entered the yard. Kelly had a smile for him, and Eph couldn't help but wonder if she preferred this—Eph striking out with Zack—to a weekend alone with Matt. Kelly took him protectively under her arm. "You okay, Z?"

Zack nodded.

"Disappointed, I bet."

He nodded again.

She saw the box and wires in his hand. "What is this?"

Eph said, "Zack's new game system. He's borrowing it for the weekend." Eph looked at Zack, the boy's head against his mother's chest, staring into the middle distance. "Bud, if there's any way I can get free, maybe tomorrow—hopefully tomorrow . . . but if there's *any* way at all, I'll be back for you, and we'll salvage what we can out of this weekend. Okay? I'll make it up to you, you know that, right?"

Zack nodded, his eyes still distant.

Matt called down from the top step. "Come on in, Zack. Let's see if we can get that thing hooked up."

Dependable, reliable Matt. Kelly sure had him trained well. Eph watched his son go inside under Matt's arm, Zack glancing back one last time at Eph.

Alone now, he and Kelly stood facing each other on the little patch of grass. Behind her, over the roof of her house, the lights of the waiting airplanes circled. An entire network of transportation, never mind various government and law enforcement agencies, was waiting for this man facing a woman who said she didn't love him anymore.

"It's that airplane, isn't it."

Eph nodded. "They're all dead. Everybody on board."

"All dead?" Kelly's eyes flared with concern. "How? What could it be?"

"That's what I have to go find out."

Eph felt the urgency of his job settling over him now. He had blown it with Zack—but that was done, and now he had to go. He reached into his pocket and handed her an envelope with the pin-striped logo. "For tomorrow afternoon," he said. "In case I don't make it back before then."

Kelly peeked at the tickets, her eyebrows lifting at the price, then tucked them back inside the envelope. She looked at him with an expression approaching sympathy. "Just be sure not to forget our meeting with Dr. Kempner."

The family therapist—the one who would decide Zack's final custody. "Kempner, right," he said. "I'll be there."

"And—be careful," she said.

Eph nodded and started away.

JFK International Airport

A CROWD HAD GATHERED outside the airport, people drawn to the unexplained, the weird, the potentially tragic, the *event*. The radio, on Eph's drive over, treated the dormant airplane as a potential hijacking, speculating about a link to the conflicts overseas.

Inside the terminal, two airport carts passed Eph, one carrying a teary mother holding the hands of two frightened-looking children, another with an older black gentleman riding with a bouquet of red roses across his lap. He realized that somebody else's Zack was out there on that plane. Somebody else's Kelly. He focused on that.

Eph's team was waiting for him outside a locked door just below gate 6. Jim Kent was working the phone, as usual, speaking into the wire microphone dangling from his ear. Jim handled the bureaucratic and political side of disease control for Eph. He closed his hand around the mic part of his phone wire and said, by way of greeting, "No other reports of planes down anywhere else in the country."

Eph climbed in next to Nora Martinez in the back of the airline cart. Nora, a biochemist by training, was his number two in New York. Her hands were already gloved, the nylon barrier as pale and smooth and mournful as lilies. She shifted over a little for him as he sat down. He regretted the awkwardness between them.

They started to move, Eph smelling marsh salt in the wind. "How long was the plane on the ground before it went dark?"

Nora said, "Six minutes."

"No radio contact? Pilot's out too?"

Jim turned and said, "Presumed, but unconfirmed. Port Authority cops went into the passenger compartment, found it full of corpses, and got right out again."

"They were masked and gloved, I hope."

"Affirmative."

The cart turned a corner, revealing the airplane waiting in the distance. A massive aircraft, work lights trained on it from multiple angles, shining as bright as day. Mist off the nearby bay created a glowing aura around the fuselage.

"Christ," said Eph.

Jim said, "A 'triple seven,' they call it. The 777, the world's largest twin jet. Recent design, new aircraft. Why they're flipped out about the equipment going down. They think it's something more like sabotage."

The landing-gear tires alone were enormous. Eph looked up at the black hole that was the open door over the broad left wing.

Jim said, "They already tested for gas. They tested for everything man-made. They don't know what else to do but start from scratch."

Eph said, "Us being the scratch."

This dormant aircraft mysteriously full of dead people was the HAZMAT equivalent of waking up one day and finding a lump on your back. Eph's team was the biopsy lab charged with telling the Federal Aviation Administration whether or not it had cancer.

Blue-blazer-wearing TSA officials pounced on Eph as soon as the cart stopped, trying to give him the same briefing Jim had just had. Asking him questions and talking over each other like reporters.

"This has gone on too long," said Eph. "Next time something unexplained like this happens, you call us second. HAZMAT first, us second. Got it?"

"Yes, sir, Dr. Goodweather."

"Is HAZMAT ready?"

"Standing by."

Eph slowed before the CDC van. "I will say that this doesn't read like a spontaneous contagious event. Six minutes on the ground? The time element is too short."

"It has to be a deliberate act," said one of the TSA officials.

"Perhaps," said Eph. "As it stands now, in terms of whatever might be awaiting us in there—we have containment." He opened the rear door of the van for Nora. "We'll suit up and see what we've got."

A voice stopped him. "We have one of our own on this plane."

Eph turned back. "One of whose?"

"A federal air marshal. Standard on international flights involving U.S. carriers."

"Armed?" Eph said.

"That's the general idea."

"No phone call, no warning from him?"

"No nothing."

"It must have overpowered them immediately." Eph nodded, looking into these men's worried faces. "Get me his seat assignment. We'll start there."

Eph and Nora ducked inside the CDC van, closing the rear double doors, shutting out the anxiety of the tarmac behind them.

They pulled Level A HAZMAT gear down off the rack. Eph stripped down to his T-shirt and shorts, Nora to a black sports bra and lavender panties, each accommodating the other's elbows and knees inside the cramped Chevy van. Nora's hair was thick and dark and defiantly long for a field epidemiologist, and she swept it up into a tight elastic, arms working purposefully and fast. Her body was gracefully curved, her flesh the warm tone of lightly browned toast.

After Eph's separation from Kelly became permanent and she initiated divorce proceedings, Eph and Nora had a brief fling. It was just one night, followed by a very awkward and uncomfortable morning after, which dragged on for months and months . . . right up until their second fling, just a few weeks ago—which, while even more passionate than the first, and full of intention to avoid the pitfalls that had overwhelmed them the first time, had led again to another protracted and awkward détente.

In a way, he and Nora worked too closely: if they had anything resembling normal jobs, a traditional workplace, the result might have been different, might have been easier, more casual, but this was "love in the trenches," and with each of them giving so much to Canary, they had little left for each other, or the rest of the world. A partnership so voracious that nobody asked, "How was your day?" in the downtime—mainly because there was no downtime at all.

Such as here. Getting practically naked in front of each other in the least sexual way possible. Because donning a biosuit is the antithesis of sensuality. It is the converse of allure, it is a withdrawal into prophylaxis, into sterility.

The first layer was a white Nomex jumpsuit, emblazoned on the back with the initials CDC. It zipped from knee to chin, the collar and cuffs sealing it in snug Velcro, black jump boots lacing up to the shins.

The second layer was a disposable white suit made of papery Tyvek. Then booties pulled on over boots, and Silver Shield chemical protective gloves over nylon barriers, taped at the wrists and ankles. Then lifted on self-contained breathing apparatus gear: a SCBA harness, lightweight titanium pressure-demand tank, full-face respirator mask, and personal alert safety system (PASS) device with a firefighter's distress alarm.

Each hesitated before pulling the mask over his or her face. Nora formed a half smile and cupped Eph's cheek in her hand. She kissed him. "You okay?"

"Yup."

"You sure don't look it. How was Zack?"

"Sulky. Pissed. As he should be."

"Not your fault."

"So what? Bottom line is, this weekend with my son is gone, and I'll never get it back." He readied his mask. "You know, there came a point in my life where things came down to either my family or my job. I thought I chose family. Apparently, not enough."

There are moments like these, which usually come at the most inconvenient of times, such as a crisis, when you look at someone and realize that it will hurt you to be without them. Eph saw how unfair he had been to Nora by clinging to Kelly—not even to Kelly, but to the past, to his dead marriage, to what once was, all for Zack's sake. Nora liked Zack. And Zack liked her, that was obvious.

But now, right now, was not the time to get into this. Eph pulled on his respirator, checking his breathing tank. The outer layer consisted of a yellow—canary yellow—full encapsulation "space" suit, featuring a sealed hood, a 210-degree viewport, and attached gloves. This was the actual level A containment suit, the "contact suit," twelve layers of fabric which, once sealed, absolutely insulated the wearer from the outside atmosphere.

Nora checked his seal, and he did hers. Biohazard investigators operate on a buddy system much the same as that of scuba divers. Their suits puffed a bit from the circulated air. Sealing out pathogens meant trapping sweat and body heat, and the temperature inside their suits could rise up to thirty degrees higher than room temperature.

"Looks tight," said Eph, over the voice-actuated microphones inside his mask.

Nora nodded, catching his eye through their respective masks. The glance went on a moment too long, as if she was going to say something else, then changed her mind. "You ready?" she said.

Eph nodded. "Let's do this."

Outside on the tarmac, Jim switched on his wheeled command console and picked up both their mask-mounted cameras, on separate monitor feeds. He attached small, switched-on flashlights on lanyards from their pull-away shoulder straps: the thickness of the multilayered suit gloves limited the wearer's fine-motor skills.

The TSA guys came up and tried to talk to them some more, but Eph feigned deafness, shaking his head and touching his hood.

As they approached the airplane, Jim showed Eph and Nora a laminated printout containing an overhead view of the interior seat assignments, numbers corresponding to passenger and crew manifests listed on the back. He pointed to a red dot at 18A.

"The federal air marshal," Jim said into his microphone. "Last name Charpentier. Exit row, window seat."

"Got it," Eph said.

A second red dot. "TSA pointed out this other passenger of interest. A German diplomat on the flight, Rolph Hubermann, business class, second row, seat F. In town for UN Council talks on the Korean situation. Might have been carrying one of those diplomatic pouches that get a free pass at customs. Could be nothing, but there is a contingent of Germans on their way here right now, from the UN, just to retrieve it."

"Okay."

Jim left them at the edge of the lights, turning back to his monitors. Inside the perimeter, it was brighter than day. They moved nearly without shadow. Eph led the way up the fire engine ladder onto the wing, then along its broadening surface to the opened door.

Eph entered first. The stillness was palpable. Nora followed, standing with him shoulder to shoulder at the head of the middle cabin.

Seated corpses faced them, in row after row. Eph's and Nora's flashlight beams registered dully in the dead jewels of their open eyes.

No nosebleeds. No bulging eyes or bloated, mottled skin. No foaming or bloody discharge about the mouth. Everyone in his or her seat, no sign of panic or struggle. Arms hanging loose into the aisle or else sagged in laps. No evident trauma.

Mobile phones—in laps, pockets, and muffled inside carry-on bags—emitted waiting message beeps or else rang anew, the peppy tones overlapping. These were the only sounds.

They located the air marshal in the window seat just inside the open door. A man in his forties with black, receding hair, dressed in a baseball-style button-up shirt with blue and orange piping, New York Mets colors, the baseball-headed mascot Mr. Met depicted on the front, and blue jeans. His chin rested on his chest, as though he were napping with his eyes open.

Eph dropped to one knee, the wider exit row giving him room to maneuver. He touched the air marshal's forehead, pushing back the man's head, which moved freely on his neck. Nora, next to him, teased her flashlight beam in and out of his eyes, Charpentier's pupils showing no response. Eph pulled down on his chin, opening his jaw and illuminating the inside of his mouth, his tongue and the top of his throat looking pink and unpoisoned.

Eph needed more light. He reached over and slid open the window shade, and construction light blasted inside like a bright white scream.

No vomit, as from gas inhalation. Victims of carbon monoxide poisoning evinced distinct skin blistering and discoloration, leaving them with a bloated, leathered appearance. No discomfort in his posture, no sign of agonal struggle. Next to him sat a middle-aged woman in resort-style travel wear, half-glasses perched on her nose before her unseeing eyes. They were seated as any normal passengers would be, chairs in the full and upright position, still waiting for the FASTEN SEAT BELTS sign to be turned off at the airport gate.

Front-exit-row passengers stow their personal belongings in mesh containers bolted to the facing cabin wall. Eph pulled a soft Virgin

Atlantic bag out of the pocket before Charpentier, running the zipper back along the top. He pulled out a Notre Dame sweatshirt, a handful of well-thumbed puzzle books, an audio-book thriller, then a nylon pouch that was kidney shaped and heavy. He unzipped it just far enough to see the all-black, rubber-coated handgun inside.

"You seeing this?" said Eph.

"We see it," said Jim over the radio. Jim, TSA, and anyone else with enough rank to get near the monitors were watching this whole thing on Eph's shoulder-mounted camera.

Eph said, "Whatever it was, it took everyone completely unaware. Including the air cop."

Eph zipped the bag closed and left it on the floor, straightening, then proceeding down the aisle. Eph reached across the dead passengers in order to raise every second or third window shade, the harsh light casting weird shadows and throwing their faces into sharp relief, like travelers who had perished by flying too close to the sun.

The phones kept singing, the dissonance becoming shrill, like dozens of personal distress alarms overlapping. Eph tried not to think about the concerned callers on the other end.

Nora moved close to a body. "No trauma at all," she noted.

"I know," said Eph. "Goddamn spooky." He faced the gallery of corpses, thinking. "Jim," he said, "get an alert out to WHO Europe. Bring in Germany's Federal Ministry of Health on this, contacting hospitals. On the off chance this thing is transmissible, they should be seeing it there too."

"I'm on it," said Jim.

In the forward galley between business and first, four flight attendants—three female, one male—sat buckled into their jump seats, bodies pitched forward against their shoulder belts. Moving past them, Eph had the sensation of floating through a shipwreck underwater.

Nora's voice came through. "I'm at the rear of the plane, Eph. No surprises. Coming back now."

"Okay," said Eph as he walked back through the window-lit cabin, opening the segregating curtain to the wider-aisle seats of business class. There, Eph located the German diplomat, Hubermann, sitting on the aisle, near the front. His chubby hands were still folded in his lap, his head slumped, a forelock of sandy silver hair drooped over his open eyes.

The diplomatic pouch Jim mentioned was in the briefcase beneath his seat. It was blue and vinyl with a zipper along the top.

Nora approached him. "Eph, you're not authorized to open that—"

Eph unzipped it, removing a half-eaten Toblerone bar and a clear plastic bottle full of blue pills.

"What is it?" Nora asked.

"My guess is Viagra," said Eph, returning the contents to the pouch and the pouch to the briefcase.

He paused next to a mother and young daughter traveling together. The young girl's hand was still nestled inside her mother's. Both appeared relaxed.

Eph said, "No panic, no nothing."

Nora said, "Doesn't make sense."

Viruses require transmission, and transmission takes time. Passengers becoming sick or falling unconscious would have caused an uproar, no matter what the FASTEN SEAT BELTS sign said. If this was a virus, it was unlike any pathogen Eph had ever encountered in his years as an epidemiologist with the CDC. All signs instead pointed to a lethal poisoning agent introduced into the sealed environment of the airplane cabin.

Eph said, "Jim, I want to retest for gas."

Jim's voice said, "They took air samples, measured in parts per million. There was nothing."

"I know but . . . it's as if these people were overcome by something without any warning whatsoever. Maybe the substance dissipated once that door opened. I want to test the carpeting and any other porous surfaces. We'll test lung tissue once we get these people in post."

"Okay, Eph—you got it."

Eph moved quickly past the widely spaced, leather-appointed seats of first class to the closed cockpit door. The door was grated and framed in steel along each edge, with an overhead camera in the ceiling. He reached for the handle.

Jim's voice in his suit hood said, "Eph, they're telling me it works on a keypad lock, you won't be able to get—"

The door pushed open under his gloved hand.

Eph stood very still at the open doorway. The lights from the taxiway shone through the tinted cockpit windshield, illuminating the flight deck. The system displays were all dark.

Jim said, "Eph, they're saying to be very careful."

"Tell them thanks for the expert technical advice," said Eph before moving inside.

The system displays around the switches and throttles were all dark. One man wearing a pilot's uniform sat slumped in a jump seat to Eph's immediate right as he entered. Two more, the captain and his first officer, were seated in the twin chairs before the controls. The first officer's hands lay curled and empty in his lap, his head drooped to the left with his hat still on. The captain's left hand remained on a control lever, his right arm hanging off the armrest, knuckles brushing the carpeted floor. His head was forward, his hat resting in his lap.

Eph leaned over the control console between the two seats in order to push up the captain's head. He checked the captain's open eyes with his flashlight, the pupils fixed and dilated. He eased the man's head back down gently onto his chest, and then stiffened.

He felt something. He sensed something. A presence.

He stepped back from the console and scanned the flight deck, turning in one complete circle.

Jim said, "What is it, Eph?"

Eph had spent enough time around corpses not to be jumpy. But there was something here . . . somewhere. Here or nearby.

The strange sensation passed, like a dizzy spell, leaving him blinking. He shook it off. "Nothing. Claustrophobia, probably."

Eph turned to the third man inside the cockpit. His head hung low, his right shoulder propped up against the side wall. His jump seat harness straps hung down.

Eph said aloud, "Why isn't he belted in?"

Nora said, "Eph, are you in the cockpit? I'm coming to you."

Eph looked at the dead man's silver tie pin with the Regis Air logo. The nameplate over his pocket read REDFERN. Eph dropped to one knee before him, pressing his thickly gloved fingers against the man's temples to raise his face. His eyes were open and down turned. Eph checked his pupils, and thought he saw something. A glimmer. He looked again, and suddenly Captain Redfern shuddered and emitted a groan.

Eph jerked backward, falling between the two captains' chairs and against the control console with a clatter. The first officer slumped against him, and Eph pushed back at him, trapped for a moment by the man's limp, dead weight.

Jim's voice called to him sharply, "Eph?"

Nora's voice held a note of panic. "Eph, what is it?"

With a surge of energy, Eph propelled the first officer's body back into its chair and got to his feet.

Nora said, "Eph, are you all right?"

Eph looked at Captain Redfern, spilled onto the floor now, eyes open and staring. His throat, though, was working, bucking, his open mouth seeming to gag on the air.

Eph said, wide-eyed, "We have a survivor here."

Nora said, "What?"

"We have a man alive here. Jim, we need a Kurt isolation pod for this man. Brought directly to the wing. Nora?" Eph was talking fast, looking at the pilot twitching on the floor. "We have to go through this entire airplane, passenger by passenger."

ABRAHAM SETRAKIAN

THE OLD MAN STOOD ALONE ON THE CRAMPED SALES floor of his pawnshop on East 118th Street, in Spanish Harlem. An hour after closing and his stomach was rumbling, yet he was reluctant to go upstairs. The gates were all pulled down over the doors and windows, like steel eyelids, the night people having claimed the streets outside. At night, you don't go out.

He went to the bank of dimmers behind the loan desk, and darkened the store lamp by lamp. He was in an elegiac mood. He looked at his shop, the display cases of chrome and streaked glass. The wristwatches showcased on felt instead of velvet, the polished silver he couldn't get rid of, the bits of diamond and gold. The full tea sets under glass. The leather coats and now-controversial furs. The new music players that went fast, and the radios and televisions he didn't bother taking in anymore. And there were, here and there, treasures: a pair of beautiful antique safes (lined with asbestos, but just don't eat it); a suitcase-size wood-and-steel Quasar VCR from the 1970s; an antique 16mm film projector.

But, on balance, lots of low-turnover junk. A pawnshop is part bazaar, part museum, part neighborhood reliquary. The pawnbroker provides a service no one else can. He is the poor man's banker, someone people can come to and borrow twenty-five dollars with no concern as to credit history, employment, references. And, in the grip of an economic recession, twenty-five dollars is real money to many people. Twenty-five dollars can mean the difference between shelter or homelessness. Twenty-five dollars can put life-prolonging medicine within reach. So long as a man or woman has collateral, something of value to borrow against, he or she can walk out of his door with cash in hand. Beautiful.

He trudged on upstairs, turning out more lights as he went. He was fortunate to own his building, bought in the early 1970s for seven dollars and change. Okay, maybe not for so little, but not for so much either. They were burning down buildings for heat back then. Knickerbocker Loans and Curios (the name came with the shop) was never a means to wealth for Setrakian, but rather a conduit, a point of entry into the pre-Internet underground marketplace of the crossroads city of the world, for a man interested in Old World tools, artifacts, curios, and other arcana.

Thirty-five years of haggling over cheap jewelry by day, while amassing tools and armaments by night. Thirty-five years of biding his time, of preparation and waiting. Now his time was running out.

At the door, he touched the mezuzah and kissed his crooked, wrinkled fingertips before entering. The ancient mirror in the hallway was so scratched and faded that he had to crane his neck in order to find a reflective patch in which to view himself. His alabaster white hair, starting high up on his creased forehead and sweeping back below his ears and neck, was long overdue for a trim. His face continued to fall, his chin and earlobes and eyes succumbing to that bully named gravity. His hands, so broken and badly mended so many decades before, had curved into arthritic talons that he kept permanently hidden behind wool gloves with cut-off fingertips. Yet, beneath and within this crumbling facade of a man: strength. Fire. Grit.

The secret of his interior wellspring of youth? One simple element. Revenge.

Many years before, in Warsaw and later in Budapest, there was a man named Abraham Setrakian who had been an esteemed professor of Eastern European literature and folklore. A Holocaust survivor who survived the scandal of marrying a student, and whose field of study took him to some of the darkest corners of the world.

Now, an aged pawnbroker in America, still haunted by unfinished business.

He had good soup left over, delicious chicken soup with kreplach and egg noodles, that a regular had brought him all the way from Liebman's, in the Bronx. He put the bowl in the microwave and worked at his loose necktie knot with his gnarled fingers. After the beeping, he carried the hot bowl over to the table, pulling a linen napkin—never paper!—from the holder and tucking it snugly into his collar.

Blowing on soup. A ritual of comfort, of reassurance. He remembered his grandmother, his *bubbeh*—but this was more than mere memory; it was *sense*, a *feeling*—blowing on it for him when he was a boy, sitting next to him at the rickety wooden table in the cold kitchen of their house in Romania. Before the troubles. Her old breath stirring the rising steam into his young face, the quiet magic of that simple act. Like blowing life into the child. And now, as he blew, an old man himself, he watched his breath given shape by the steam, and wondered just how many of these respirations he had left.

He took the spoon, one of a drawer full of fancy, mismatched implements, into the crooked fingers of his left hand. Blowing onto the spoon now, rippling the tiny pool of broth there, before taking it into his mouth. Taste came and went, the buds on his tongue dying like old soldiers: the victims of many decades of pipe smoking, a professor's vice.

He found the thin remote for the outdated Sony TV—a kitchen model finished in white—and the thirteen-inch screen warmed up, further illuminating the room. He rose and walked to the pantry, leaning his hands on the stacks of books squeezing the hallway into a narrow tread of worn rug—books were everywhere, piled high against the walls, many of them read, all of them impossible to part with—and lifting the cover off the cake tin to retrieve the last of the good rye bread he had been saving. He carried the paper-wrapped loaf back to his cushioned kitchen chair, settling heavily, and went about picking off the little bits of mold as he enjoyed another tender sip of the delicious broth.

Slowly, the image on the screen claimed his attention: a jumbo jet parked on a tarmac somewhere, lit up like an ivory piece upon jeweler's black felt. He pulled on the black-rimmed glasses that hung at his chest, squinting in order to make out the bottom graphic. Today's crisis was taking place across the river, at JFK Airport.

The old professor watched and listened, focused on the pristine-looking airplane. One minute became two, then three, the room fading around him. He was transfixed—nearly transported—by the news report, the soup spoon still in his no-longer-tremulous hand.

The television image of the dormant airplane played across the lenses of his eyeglasses like a future foretold. The broth in the bowl cooled, its steam fading, dying, the picked-apart slice of rye bread remaining uneaten.

He *knew*.

Pick-pick-pick.

The old man *knew*—

Pick-pick-pick.

His malformed hands began to ache. What he saw before him was not an omen—it was an incursion. It was the act itself. The thing he had been waiting for. That he had been preparing for. All his life until now.

Any relief he had felt initially—at not having been outlived by this horror; at getting one last-minute chance at vengeance—was replaced immediately by sharp, painlike fear. The words left his mouth on a gust of steam.

He is here . . . He is here. . .

Regis Air Maintenance Hangar

Because JFK needed the taxiway cleared, the entire aircraft was towed as is into the Regis Air long-span maintenance hangar in the hour before dawn. No one spoke as the lame 777 full of dead passengers rolled past like an enormous white casket.

Once the wheel chocks were put down and the airplane was secured, black tarpaulins were laid out to cover the stained cement floor. Borrowed hospital screens were erected to curtain off a wide containment zone between the left wing and the nose. The plane was isolated in the hangar, like a corpse inside a massive morgue.

At Eph's request, the Office of the Chief Medical Examiner of New York dispatched several senior medicolegal investigators from Manhattan and Queens, bringing with them several cartons of rubber crash bags. The OCME, the world's largest medical examiner's office, was experienced in multiple-casualty disaster management, and helped devise an orderly process of cadaver retrieval.

Port Authority HAZMAT officers in full contact suits brought out the air marshal first—solemnly, officers saluting the bagged corpse as it appeared at the wing door—and then, laboriously, everyone else in the first row of coach. They then removed those emptied seats, using the added space to bag the corpses before evacuating them. Each body, one at a time, was strapped to a stretcher and lowered from the wing to the tarp-covered floor.

The process was deliberate and, at times, gruesome. At one point, about thirty bodies in, one of the Port Authority officers suddenly stumbled away from the retrieval line moaning and gripping his hood. Two fellow HAZMAT officers converged on him, and he lashed out, shoving them into the hospital screens, in effect breaching the containment border. Panic erupted, people clearing the way for this possibly poisoned or infected officer clawing at his containment suit on his way out of the cavernous hangar. Eph caught up with him out on the apron, where, in the light of the morning sun, the officer succeeded in throwing off his hood and peeling off his suit, like a constricting skin. Eph grabbed the man, who then sank down onto the tarmac, sitting there with sweaty tears in his eyes.

"This city," sobbed the officer. "This damn city."

Later, word went around that this Port Authority officer had worked those hellish first few weeks on the pile at Ground Zero, first as part of the rescue mission, and then the recovery effort. The specter of 9/11 still hung over many of these Port Authority officers, and the current bewildering mass-casualty situation had brought it crashing down again.

A "go team" of analysts and investigators from the National Transportation Safety Board in Washington, D.C., arrived aboard an FAA Gulfstream. They were there to interview all involved with the "incident" aboard Regis Air Flight 753, to document the aircraft's final moments of navigability, and to retrieve the flight-data recorder and the cockpit voice recorder. Investigators from the New York City Department of Health, having been leapfrogged by the CDC in the crisis response, were briefed on the matter, though Eph rejected their jurisdiction claim. He knew he had to keep control of the containment response if he wanted it done right.

Boeing representatives en route from Washington State had already disclaimed the 777's complete shutdown as "mechanically impossible." A Regis Air vice president, roused from his bed in Scarsdale, was insisting that a team of Regis's own mechanics be the first to board the aircraft for inspection, once the medical quarantine was lifted. (Corruption of the air-circulation system was the current prevailing cause-of-death theory.) The German ambassador to the United States and his staff were still awaiting their diplomat's pouch, Eph leaving them cooling their heels in Lufthansa's Senator Lounge inside terminal 1. The mayor's press secretary made plans for an afternoon news conference, and the police commissioner arrived with the head of his counterterrorism bureau inside the rolling headquarters of the NYPD's critical response vehicle.

By midmorning, all but eighty corpses had been unloaded. The identification process was proceeding speedily, thanks to passport scans and the detailed passenger manifest.

During a suit break, Eph and Nora conferred with Jim outside the containment zone, the bulk of the aircraft fuselage visible over the curtain screens. Airplanes were taking off and landing again outside; they could hear the thrusters gaining and decelerating overhead, and feel the stir in the atmosphere, the agitation of air.

Eph asked Jim, between gulps of bottled water, "How many bodies can the M.E. in Manhattan handle?"

Jim said, "Queens has jurisdiction here, but you're right, the Manhattan headquarters is the best equipped. Logistically, we're going to be spreading the victims out among those two and Brooklyn and the Bronx. So, about fifty each."

"How are we going to transport them?"

"Refrigerated trucks. Medical examiner said that's how they did the World Trade Center remains. Fulton Fish Market in Lower Manhattan, they've been contacted."

Eph often thought of disease control as a wartime resistance effort, he and his team fighting the good fight while the rest of the world tried to get on with their daily lives under the cloud of occupation, the viruses and bacteria that plagued them. In this scenario, Jim was the underground radio broadcaster, conversant in three languages, who could procure anything from butter to arms to safe passage out of Marseilles.

Eph said, "Nothing from Germany?"

"Not yet. They shut down the airport for two hours, a full security check. No employees sick at the airport, no sudden illnesses being reported to hospitals."

Nora was anxious to speak. "Nothing here adds up."

Eph nodded in agreement. "Go ahead."

"We have a plane full of corpses. Were this caused by a gas, or some aerosol in the ventilation system—accidental or not—they would not have all gone so . . . I have to say, so *peacefully*. There would have been choking, flailing. Vomiting. Turning blue. People with different body types going down at different times. And attendant panic. Now—if instead this was an infectious event, then we have some kind of crazy-sudden, totally new emerging pathogen, something none of us have ever seen. Indicating something man-made, created in a lab. And at the same time, remember, it's not just the passengers who died—the plane itself died too. Almost as though some *thing*, some incapacitating *thing*, hit the airplane itself, and wiped out everything inside it, including the passengers. But that's not exactly accurate, is it? Because, and I think this is the most important question of all right now, who opened the door?" She looked back and forth between Eph and Jim. "I mean—it *could* have been the pressure change. Maybe the door had already been unlocked, and the aircraft's decompression forced it open. We can come up with cute explanations for just about anything, because we're medical scientists, that's what we do."

"And those window shades," said Jim. "People always look out the windows during landing. Who closed them all?"

Eph nodded. He had been so focused on the details all morning, it was good to step back and see strange events from a distance. "This is why the four survivors are going to be key. If they witnessed anything."

Nora said, "Or were otherwise involved."

Jim said, "All four are in critical but stable condition in the isolation wing at Jamaica Hospital Medical Center. Captain Redfern, the third pilot, male, thirty-two. A lawyer from Westchester County, female, forty-one. A computer programmer from Brooklyn, male, forty-four. And a musician, a celebrity from Manhattan and Miami Beach, male, thirty-six. His name is Dwight Moorshein."

Eph shrugged. "Never heard of him."

"He performs under the name Gabriel Bolivar."

Eph said, "Oh."

Nora said, "Ew."

Jim said, "He was traveling incognito in first class. No fright makeup, no crazy contact lenses. So there will be even more media heat."

Eph said, "Any connection between the survivors?"

"None we see yet. Maybe their med workup will find something. They were scattered throughout the plane, the programmer was flying coach, the lawyer in business, the singer first class. And Captain Redfern, of course, up in the flight deck."

"Baffling," said Eph. "But it's something anyway. If they regain consciousness, that is. Long enough for us to get some answers out of them."

One of the Port Authority officers came around for Eph. "Dr. Goodweather, you better get back in there," he said. "The cargo hold. They found something."

Through the side cargo hatch, inside the underbelly of the 777, they had already begun off-loading the rolling steel luggage cabinets, to be opened and inspected by the Port Authority HAZMAT team. Eph and Nora sidestepped the remaining train-linked containers, wheels locked into floor tracks.

At the far end of the hold lay a long, rectangular box, black, wooden, and heavy looking, like a grand cabinet laid out on its back. Unvarnished ebony, eight or so feet long by four feet wide by three high. Taller than a refrigerator. The top side was edged all around with intricate carving, labyrinthine flourishes accompanied by lettering in an ancient or perhaps made-to-look-ancient language. Many of the swirls resembled figures, flowing human figures—and perhaps, with a little imagination, faces screaming.

"No one's opened it yet?" asked Eph.

The HAZMAT officers all shook their heads. "We haven't touched the thing," one said.

Eph checked the back of it. Three orange restraining straps, their steel hooks still in the floor eyelets, lay on the floor next to the cabinet. "These straps?"

"Undone when we came in," said another.

Eph looked around the hold. "That's impossible," he said. "If this thing was left unrestrained during transit, it would have done major damage to the luggage containers, if not the interior walls of the cargo hold itself." He looked it over again. "Where's its tag? What does the cargo manifest say?"

One of the officers had a sheaf of laminated pages in his gloved hand, bound by a single ring clasp. "It's not here."

Eph went over to see for himself. "That can't be."

"The only irregular cargo listed here, other than three sets of golf clubs, is a kayak." The guy pointed to the side wall where, bound by the same type of orange ratchet straps, a plastic-wrapped kayak lay plastered with airline luggage stickers.

"Call Berlin," said Eph. "They must have a record. Somebody there remembers this thing. It must weigh four hundred pounds, easy."

"We did that already. No record. They're going to call in the baggage crew and question them one by one."

Eph turned back to the black cabinet. He ignored the grotesque carvings, bending to examine the sides, locating three hinges along either top edge. The lid was a door, split down the middle the long way, two half doors that opened out. Eph touched the carved lid with his gloved hand, then he reached under the lid, trying to open the heavy doors. "Anybody want to give me a hand?"

One officer stepped forward, wrapping his gloved fingers underneath the lip of the lid opposite Eph. Eph counted to three, and they opened both heavy doors at once.

The doors stood open on sturdy, broad-winged hinges. The odor that wafted out of the box was corpselike, as though the cabinet had been sealed for a hundred years. It looked empty, until one of the officers switched on a flashlight and played the beam inside.

Eph reached in, his fingers sinking into a rich, black loam. The soil was as welcoming and soft as cake mix and filled up the bottom two-thirds of the box.

Nora took a step back from the open cabinet. "It looks like a coffin," said Nora.

Eph withdrew his fingers, shaking off the excess, and turned to her, waiting for a smile that never came. "A little big for that, isn't it?"

"Why would someone ship a box of dirt?" she asked.

"They wouldn't," Eph said. "There had to be something inside."

"But how?" said Nora. "This plane is under total quarantine."

Eph shrugged. "How do we explain anything here? All I know for sure is, we have an unlocked, unstrapped container here without a bill of lading." He turned to the others. "We need to sample the soil. Dirt retains trace evidence well. Radiation, for example."

One of the officers said, "You think whatever agent was used to overcome the passengers . . . ?"

"Was shipped over in here? That's the best theory I've heard all day."

Jim's voice called from below them, outside the plane. "Eph? Nora?"

Eph called back, "What is it, Jim?"

"I just got a call from the isolation ward at Jamaica Hospital. You're going to want to get over there right away."

Jamaica Hospital Medical Center

THE HOSPITAL FACILITY was just ten minutes north of JFK, along the Van Wyck Expressway. Jamaica was one of the four designated Centers for Bioterrorism Preparedness Planning in New York City. It was a full participant in the Syndromic Surveillance System, and Eph had run a Canary workshop there just a few months before. So he knew his way to the airborne infection isolation ward on the fifth floor.

The metal double doors featured a prominent blaze-orange, tripetaled biohazard symbol, indicating a real or potential threat to cellular materials or living organisms. Printed warnings read:

ISOLATION AREA:
CONTACT PRECAUTION MANDATORY,
AUTHORIZED PERSONNEL ONLY.

Eph displayed his CDC credentials at the desk, and the administrator recognized him from previous biocontainment drills. She walked him inside. "What is it?" he asked.

"I really don't mean to be melodramatic," she said, waving her hospital ID over the reader, opening the doors to the ward, "but you need to see it for yourself."

The interior walkway was narrow, this being the outer ring of the isolation ward, occupied mainly by the nurses' station. Eph followed the administrator behind blue curtains into a wide vestibule containing trays of contact supplies—gowns, goggles, gloves, booties, and respirators—and a large, rolling garbage barrel lined with a red biohazard trash bag. The respirator was an N95 half mask, efficiency rated to filter out 95 percent of particles 0.3 microns in size or larger. That meant it offered protection from most airborne viral and bacteriological pathogens, but not against chemical or gas contaminants.

After his full contact suiting at the airport, Eph felt positively exposed in a hospital mask, surgical cap, barrier goggles, gown, and shoe covers. The similarly attired administrator then pressed a plunger button, opening an interior set of doors, and Eph felt the vacuumlike pull upon entering, the result of the negative-pressure system, air flowing into the isolation area so that no particles could blow out.

Inside, a hallway ran left to right off the central supply station. The station consisted of a crash cart packed with drugs and ER supplies, a plastic-sheathed laptop and intercom system for communicating with the outside, and extra barrier supplies.

The patient area was a suite of eight small rooms. Eight total isolation rooms for a borough with a population of more than two and a quarter million. "Surge capacity" is the disaster preparedness term for a health care system's ability to rapidly expand beyond normal operating services, to satisfy public health demands in the event of a large-scale public health emergency. The number of hospital beds in New York State was about 60,000 and falling. The population of New York City alone was 8.1 million and rising. Canary was funded in the hopes of mending this statistical shortfall, as a sort of disaster preparedness stopgap. The CDC termed that political expedience "optimistic." Eph preferred the term "magical thinking."

He followed the administrator into the first room. This was not a full biological isolation tank; there were no air locks or steel doors. This was routine hospital care in a segregated setting. The room was tile floored and fluorescently lit. The first thing Eph saw was the discarded Kurt pod against the side wall. A Kurt pod is a disposable, plastic-boxed stretcher, like a transparent box coffin, with a pair of round glove ports on each long side, and fitted with removable exterior oxygen tanks. A jacket, shirt, and pants were piled next to it, cut away from the patient with surgical scissors, the Regis Air winged-crown logo visible on the overturned pilot's hat.

The hospital bed in the center of the room was tented with transparent plastic curtains, outside which stood monitoring equipment and an electronic IV drip tree laden with bags. The railed bed bore green sheets and large white pillows, and was set in the upright position.

Captain Doyle Redfern sat in the middle of the bed, his hands in his lap. He was bare-legged, clad only in a hospital johnny, and appeared alert. But for the IV pick in his hand and arm, and the drawn expression on his face—he looked as though he had dropped ten pounds since Eph had found him inside the cockpit—he looked for all the world like a patient awaiting a checkup.

He looked up hopefully as Eph approached. "Are you from the airline?" he asked.

Eph shook his head, dumbfounded. Last night, this man had gasped and tumbled to the floor inside the cockpit of Flight 753, eyes rolling back into his skull, seemingly near death.

The thin mattress creaked as the pilot shifted his weight. He winced as though from stiffness, and then asked, "What happened on the plane?"

Eph couldn't hide his disappointment. "That's what I came here hoping to ask you."

Eph stood facing the rock star Gabriel Bolivar, who sat perched on the edge of the bed like a black-haired gargoyle draped in a hospital johnny. Without the fright makeup, he was surprisingly handsome, in a stringy-haired, hard-living way.

"The mother of all hangovers," Bolivar said.

"Any other discomfort?" asked Eph.

"Plenty. *Man.*" He ran his hand through his long, black hair. "Never fly commercial. That's the moral of this story."

"Mr. Bolivar, can you tell me, what is the last thing you remember about the landing?"

"What landing? I'm serious. I was hitting the vodka tonics pretty hard most of the flight—I'm sure I slept right through it." He looked up, squinting into the light. "How about some Demerol, huh? Maybe when the refreshment cart swings by?"

Eph saw the scars crisscrossing Bolivar's bare arms, and remembered that one of his signature concert moves was cutting himself on-stage. "We're trying to match passengers with their possessions."

"That's easy. I had nothing. No luggage, just my phone. Charter plane broke down, I boarded this flight with about one minute to spare. Didn't my manager tell you?"

"I haven't spoken to him yet. I'm asking specifically about a large cabinet."

Bolivar stared at him. "This some kind of mental test?"

"In the cargo area. An old box, partially filled with soil."

"No idea what you're talking about."

"You weren't transporting it back from Germany? It seems like the kind of thing someone like you might collect."

Bolivar frowned. "It's an act, dude. A fucking show, a spectacle. Goth greasepaint and hard-core lyrics. Google me up—my father was a Methodist preacher and the only thing I collect is pussy. Speaking of which, when the hell am I getting out of here?"

Eph said, "We have a few more tests to run. We want to give you a clean bill of health before we let you go."

"When do I get my phone back?"

"Soon," said Eph, making his way out.

The administrator was having trouble with three men outside the entrance to the isolation ward. Two of the men towered over Eph, and had to be Bolivar's bodyguards. The third was smaller and carried a briefcase, and smelled distinctly of lawyer.

Eph said, "Gentlemen, this is a restricted area."

The lawyer said, "I'm here to discharge my client Gabriel Bolivar."

"Mr. Bolivar is undergoing tests and will be released at the earliest possible convenience."

"And when will that be?"

Eph shrugged. "Two, maybe three days, if all goes well."

"Mr. Bolivar has petitioned for his release into the care of his personal physician. I have not only power of attorney, but I can function as his health care proxy if he is in any way disabled."

"No one gets in to see him but me," said Eph. To the administrator, he said, "Let's post a guard here immediately."

The attorney stepped up. "Listen, Doctor. I don't know much about quarantine law, but I'm pretty sure it takes an executive order from the president to hold someone in medical isolation. May I, in fact, see said order?"

Eph smiled. "Mr. Bolivar is now a patient of mine, as well as the survivor of a mass casualty. If you leave your number at the nurses' desk, I will do my best to keep you abreast of his recovery—with Mr. Bolivar's consent, of course."

"Look, Doc." The attorney put his hand on Eph's shoulder in a manner Eph did not like. "I can get quicker results than a court injunction simply by mobilizing my client's rabid fan base." He included the administrator in this threat. "You want a mob of Goth chicks and assorted freaks protesting outside this hospital, running wild through these halls, trying to get in to see him?"

Eph looked at the attorney's hand until the attorney removed it from his shoulder. He had two more survivors to see. "Look, I really don't have time for this. So let me just ask you some questions straight out. Does your client have any sexually transmitted diseases I should know about? Does he have any history of narcotics use? I'm only asking because, if I have to go look up his entire medical record, well, those things have a way of getting into the wrong hands. You wouldn't want his full medical history leaked out to the press—right?"

The attorney stared at him. "That is privileged information. Releasing it would be a felony violation."

"And a real potential embarrassment," said Eph, holding the attorney's eye another second for maximum impact. "I mean, imagine if somebody put *your* complete medical history out there on the Internet for everyone to see."

The attorney was speechless as Eph started away past the two bodyguards.

Joan Luss, law-firm partner, mother of two, Swarthmore grad, Bronxville resident, Junior League member, was sitting on a foam mattress in her isolation-ward hospital bed, still tied up in that ridiculous johnny, scribbling notes on the back of a mattress-pad wrapper. Scribbling and waiting and wiggling her bare toes. They wouldn't give her back her phone; she'd had to cajole and threaten just to get a lead pencil.

She was about to buzz again when finally her nurse walked in the door. Joan turned on her get-me-results smile. "Hi, yes, there you are. I was wondering. What was the doctor's name who was in here?"

"He's not a doctor from the hospital."

"I realize that. I was asking his name."

"His name is Dr. Goodweather."

"Goodweather." She scribbled that down. "First name?"

"Doctor." Her flat smile. "They all have the same first name to me—Doctor."

Joan squinted as if she wasn't sure she'd heard that right, and shifted a bit on the stiff sheets. "And he was dispatched here from the Centers for Disease Control?"

"I guess so, yes. He left orders for a number of tests—"

"How many others survived the crash?"

"Well, there was no crash."

Joan smiled. Sometimes you had to pretend that English was their second language in order to make yourself understood. "What I am asking you is, how many others did not perish on Flight 753 from Berlin to New York?"

"There are three others in this wing with you. Now, Dr. Goodweather wants to take blood and . . ."

Joan tuned her out right there. The only reason she was still sitting in this sickroom was because she knew she could find out more by playing along. But that ploy was nearing its end. Joan Luss was a tort attorney, "tort" being a legal term meaning "a civil wrong," recognized as grounds for a lawsuit. A plane full of passengers all die, except for four survivors—one of whom is a tort attorney.

Poor Regis Air. As far as they would be concerned, the wrong passenger had lived.

Joan said, talking right over the nurse's instructions, "I would like a copy of my medical report to date, along with a complete list of lab tests already performed, and their results . . ."

"Mrs. Luss? Are you certain you feel all right?"

Joan had swooned for a moment, but it was just a remnant of whatever had overcome them at the end of that horrible flight. She smiled and shook her head fiercely, asserting herself anew. This anger she was feeling would power her through the next one thousand or so billable hours spent sorting through this catastrophe and bringing this dangerously negligent airline to trial.

She said, "Soon I will feel very well indeed."

Regis Air Maintenance Hangar

"NO FLIES," SAID EPH.

Nora said, "What?"

They were standing before rows of crash bags laid out before the airplane. The four refrigerated trucks had pulled inside the hangar, sides respectfully canvassed in black to obscure the fish market signage. Each body had already been identified and assigned a bar-coded toe tag by the Office of the Chief Medical Examiner of New York. This tragedy was a "closed universe" mass disaster, in their parlance, with a fixed and knowable number of casualties—the opposite of the collapse of the Twin Towers. Thanks to passport scans, passenger manifests, and the intact condition of the remains, identification of the decedents was a simple, straightforward task. Determining the cause of their deaths was to be the real challenge.

The tarp crinkled under the HAZMAT team's boots as the blue vinyl bags were hoisted by straps at either end and loaded aboard their appointed truck with all solemnity.

Eph said, "There should be flies." The work lights set up around the hangar showed that the air above the corpses was clear but for a lazy moth or two. "Why aren't there any flies?"

After death, the bacteria along the digestive tract that, in life, co-habited symbiotically with the healthy human host, begins to fend for itself. It starts feeding on the intestines, eventually eating its way through the abdominal cavity and consuming the organs. Flies can detect the putrid off-gassing from a decomposing carcass as far as one mile away.

Two hundred and six meals were set out here. The hangar should have been buzzing with pests.

Eph started across the tarp toward where a pair of HAZMAT officers was sealing another crash bag. "Hold on," he said to them. They straightened and stepped back as Eph knelt and unzipped the seam, exposing the corpse inside.

It was the young girl who had died holding her mother's hand. Eph had memorized her body's location on the floor without realizing it. You always remember the children.

Her blond hair lay flat, a smiling sun pendant hanging from a black cord rested against the pit of her throat. Her white dress made her look almost bridelike.

The officers moved on to seal and take the next bag. Nora came up behind Eph, watching him. With his gloved hands, he grasped the girl gently by the sides of her head, rotating it on her neck.

Rigor mortis fully sets in about twelve hours after death, holding for twelve to twenty-four more hours—they were in that middle range now—until the fixed calcium bonds inside the muscles break down again and the body returns to flexibility.

"Still flexible," said Eph. "No rigor."

He grasped her shoulder and hip and rolled the girl over onto her front. He unbuttoned the back of her dress, revealing the flesh of her lower back, the small bulbous nodes of her spine. Her skin was pallid and lightly freckled.

After the heart stops, blood pools inside the circulatory system. The capillary walls, being just one cell thick, soon succumb to the pressure, bursting and spilling blood into the surrounding tissues. This blood settles in the lowest, "dependent" side of the body, and coagulates quickly. Lividity is said to become fixed after about sixteen hours.

They were beyond that time limit now.

From expiring in a seated position, and then being laid out flat, the pooled, thickened blood should have rendered the skin along her lower back a deep, dark purple.

Eph looked out over the rows of bags. "Why aren't these bodies decomposing as they should?"

Eph eased the girl back flat again, then thumbed open her right eye with a practiced hand. Her cornea was clouded, as it should have been, and the sclera, the opaque white protective layer, was suitably dry. He examined the fingertips of her right hand—the one that had been tucked into her mother's—and found them slightly wrinkled, due to evaporation, as they should have been.

He sat back, annoyed by the mixed signals he was receiving, then inserted his two gloved thumbs between her dry lips. The gasplike noise that escaped from her parted jaw was the simple venting of gas. The immediate interior of the mouth was unremarkable, but he wriggled one gloved finger inside to depress her tongue, checking for more dryness.

The soft palate and tongue were completely white, as though carved in ivory. Like anatomical netsuke. The tongue was rigid and oddly erect. Eph manipulated it to the side and revealed the rest of the mouth, equally drained.

Drained? What's next? he thought. "*The bodies have been drained—there's not a drop of blood left.*" If not that line, then one from a Dan Curtis 1970s TV horror show: "*Lieutenant—the corpses—they're . . . drained of blood!*" Cue organ music.

Fatigue was starting to set in. Eph held the firm tongue between his thumb and index finger, using a small flashlight to peer down her white throat. It looked vaguely gynecological to him. Porn netsuke?

Then the tongue moved. He jerked back, pulling out his finger. "Jesus Christ!" The girl's face remained a placid mask of death, lips still slightly parted.

Nora, next to him, stared. "What was it?"

Eph was wiping his gloved finger on his trousers. "Simple reflex action," he said, standing. He looked down at the girl's face until he couldn't look anymore, then drew the zipper up along the bag, sealing her inside.

Nora said, "What could it be? Something that slows tissue decay somehow? These people are dead . . ."

"In every way except decomposition." Eph shook his head uneasily. "We can't hold up the transport. Bottom line is, we need these bodies at the morgue. Cut them open. Figure out this thing from the inside."

Nora, he noticed, was gazing off in the direction of the ornate cabinet, laid out on the hangar floor away from the rest of the unloaded luggage. "Nothing's right about this," she said.

Eph was looking the other way, at the great aircraft overhead. He wanted to get back aboard. They must have missed something. The answer had to be in there.

But before he could do this, he saw Jim Kent escorting the director of the CDC inside the hangar. Dr. Everett Barnes was sixty-one years old, and still very much the southern country doctor he had started out as. The Public Health Service that the CDC was a part of had been born of the navy, and though the PHS had long since branched off on its own, many top CDC officials still favored military-style uniforms, including Director Barnes. So you had the contradiction of a folksy, down-home, white-goateed gentleman dressing like a retired admiral in a trim khaki field uniform complete with chest candy. Looking very much like a combat-decorated Colonel Sanders.

After the preliminaries, and a cursory examination of one of the airplane dead, Director Barnes asked about the survivors.

Eph told him, "None of them has any memory of what happened. They are no help at all."

"Symptoms?"

"Headaches, some severe. Muscle pain, ringing in the ears. Disorientation. Dry mouth. Problems with balance."

Director Barnes said, "Generally, not much worse than anyone else getting off a transatlantic flight."

"It's uncanny, Everett," said Eph. "Nora and I were the first ones on the plane. These passengers—all of them—were flat-lined. Not breathing. Four minutes without oxygen is the threshold for permanent brain damage. These people, they might have been out for more than an hour."

"Evidently not," said the director. "And they couldn't tell you *anything*?"

"They had more questions for me than I had for them."

"Any commonality among the four?"

"I'm pursuing that now. I was going to ask for your help in confining them until our work is done."

"Help?"

"We need these four patients to cooperate."

"We have their cooperation."

"For now. I just . . . we can't take any chances."

The director smoothed down his trim white beard as he spoke. "I'm sure that, with a little tactical use of bedside manner, we can leverage their appreciation for having been spared this tragic fate, and keep them compliant." His smile revealed an upper row of heavily enameled dentures.

"What about enforcing the Health Powers Act—"

"Ephraim, you know there is a world of difference between isolating a few passengers for voluntary preventive treatment, and confining them in quarantine. There are larger issues—media issues, to be frank—to consider."

"Everett, I'm going to have to respectfully disagree—"

The director's small hand came down gently on Eph's shoulder. He exaggerated his drawl a bit, maybe in order to soften the blow. "Let me save us both some time here, Ephraim. Looking at this objectively now, this tragic incident is, thankfully—one might say, blessedly—contained. We've had no other deaths or illnesses on any other airplanes or in any other airports around the globe, in what is approaching eighteen hours since that plane landed. These are positives, and we must stress them. Send a message to the public at large, reinforcing their confidence in our system of air travel. I am certain, Ephraim, that engaging these fortunate survivors, appealing to their sense of honor and duty, will be enough to compel them to cooperate." The director removed his hand, smiling at Eph like a military man humoring his pacifist son. "Besides," continued Barnes, "this has all the hallmarks of a goddamn gas leak, doesn't it? So many victims so suddenly incapacitated? The closed environment? And the survivors rallying after being removed from the plane?"

Nora said, "Except that the air circulation quit when the electrical did, right after landing."

Director Barnes nodded, folding his hands in consideration of this. "Well, it's a lot to process, no question. But, look here—this was a very good drill for your team. You've handled it well. And now that things appear to be settling down, let's see you get right to the bottom of it. Just as soon as this damn press briefing is done with."

Eph said, "Hang on. What?"

"The mayor and the governor are holding a press conference, along with airline representatives, Port Authority officials, and so on. You and I will represent the federal health response."

"Oh—no. Sir, I don't have the time. Jim can do that—"

"Jim *can* do it, but today it will be you, Ephraim. As I said, it is time for you to be the point man on this. You are the head of the Canary project, and I want someone up there who has been dealing with victims firsthand. We need to put a face on our efforts."

That was why all this bluster about no detention or quarantine. Barnes was laying down the party line. "But I really don't know anything yet," said Eph. "Why so soon?"

Director Barnes smiled, showing his enamel again. "The doctor's code is, 'First—do no harm.' The politician's code is, 'First—go on television.' Plus, I understand that there is a time element involved. Something about wanting to get the broadcast out before this damn solar event. Sunspots affecting radio waves, or something."

"Solar . . ." Eph had forgotten all about it. The rare total solar eclipse that was to occur around three thirty that very afternoon. The first such solar event in the New York City region in more than four hundred years, since the advent of America. "Christ, I forgot."

"Our message to the people of this country will be simple. A profound loss of life has occurred here, and is being investigated fully by the CDC. It is a human catastrophe, but the incident has been contained, and is apparently unique, and there is absolutely no further cause for alarm."

Eph hid his scowl from the director. He was being made to stand up in front of cameras and say that everything was just dandy. He walked out of the containment area and through the narrow space between the great doors of the hangar, into the doomed light of the day. He was still trying to figure a way out of this when the mobile inside his pants pocket buzzed against the top of his thigh. He pulled it out, an envelope icon slowly revolving on the LCD screen. A text message from Matt's mobile. Eph opened it:

Yanks 4 Sux 2. gr8t seats, wish u wre here, Z.

Eph stood staring at this electronic dispatch from his son until his eyes lost focus. He was left staring at his own shadow on the airport tarmac, which, unless he was imagining things, had already begun to vanish.

OCCULTATION

Approaching Totality

A nticipation grew on the ground as the slender nick in the western side of the sun—the lunar "first contact"—became a creeping blackness, a rounded bite gradually consuming the afternoon sun. At first there was no obvious difference in the quality or quantity of light on the ground. Only the black gouge high in the sky, making a crescent of the normally reliable sun, marked this day as being different from any other.

The term "solar eclipse" is in fact a misnomer. An eclipse occurs when one object passes into a shadow cast by another. In a solar eclipse, the moon does not pass *into* the sun's shadow, but instead passes *between* the sun and the earth, obscuring the sun—*causing* the shadow. The proper term is "occultation." The moon *occults* the sun, casting a small shadow onto the surface of the earth. It is not a solar eclipse, but in fact an eclipse of the earth.

The earth's distance from the sun is approximately four hundred times the moon's distance from the earth. In a remarkable coincidence, the diameter of the sun happens to be approximately four hundred times the diameter of the moon. This is why the area of the moon and the sun's photosphere—its bright disk—appear roughly the same size from the perspective of earth.

A total occultation is possible only when the moon is in its new phase, and near its perigee, its closest distance to the earth. The duration of totality depends upon the orbit of the moon, never to exceed seven minutes and forty seconds. This occultation was due to last exactly four minutes and fifty-seven seconds: just under five minutes of uncanny nighttime in the middle of a beautiful early fall afternoon.

Half-covered now by the new (and otherwise invisible) moon, the still bright sky began to take on a dusky cast: like a sunset, only without any warming of the light. At ground level, the sunlight appeared pale, as though filtered or diffused. Shadows lost their certainty. The world, it seemed, had been put on a dimmer.

As the crescent continued to thin, being consumed by the lunar disk, its smothering brightness blazed as though in a panic. The occultation appeared to gain momentum and a kind of desperate speed as the ground landscape went gray, colors bleeding off the normal spectrum. The western sky darkened faster than the east as the shadow of the moon approached.

The eclipse was to be partial in much of the United States and Canada, achieving totality along only a lengthy, narrow trail measuring ten thousand miles long by one hundred miles wide, describing the moon's dark umbral shadow upon the earth. The west-to-east course, known as the "path of totality," began at the horn of Africa and curved up the Atlantic Ocean, ending just west of Lake Michigan, moving at more than one thousand miles per hour.

As the crescent sun continued to narrow, the complexion of the sky became a strangled violet. The darkness in the west gathered strength like a silent, windless storm system, spreading throughout the sky and closing in around the weakened sun, like a great organism succumbing to a corrupting force spreading from within.

The sun grew perilously thin, the view—through safety glasses—like that of a manhole lid being slid shut high above, squeezing out the daylight. The crescent blazed white, then turned to silver in its agonal last moments.

Strange, roving bands of shadow began moving over the ground. Oscillations formed by the refraction of light in the earth's atmosphere—similar to the effect of light moving on the floor of a swimming pool—writhed like shadowy snakes at the corner of one's vision. These ghostly tricks of light made the hair stand on the back of every viewer's neck.

The end came quickly. The last throes were chilling, intense, the crescent shrinking to a curved line, a slicing scar in the sky, then fragmenting into individual pearls of fiery white, representing the last of the sun's rays seeping through the deepest valleys along the lunar surface. These beads winked and vanished in rapid succession, snuffed out like a dying candle flame drowned in its own black wax. The crimson-colored band that was the chromosphere, the thin upper atmosphere of the sun, flared for a precious, final few seconds—and then the sun was gone.

Totality.

Kelton Street, Woodside, Queens

KELLY GOODWEATHER could not believe how quickly the day went dark. She stood out on the sidewalk, as did the rest of her Kelton Street neighbors—on what was normally, at that time of day, the sunny side of the street—staring up at the darkened sky through the cardboard-framed glasses that had come free with two two-liter bottles of Diet Eclipse soda. Kelly was an educated woman. She understood on an intellectual level what was occurring. And still she felt an almost giddy surge of panic. An impulse to run, to hide. This lining up of celestial bodies, the passing into the shadow of the moon: it reached something deep inside her. Touched the night-frightened animal within.

Others surely felt it. The street had grown quiet at the moment of total eclipse. This weird light they were all standing in. And those wormy shadows that had wriggled on the lawn, just out of their vision, against the sides of the house, like swirling spirits. It was as though a cold wind had blown down the street and not ruffled any hair but had only chilled their insides.

That thing people say to you, after you shiver: *Someone just walked over your grave.* That was what this whole "occultation" seemed like. Someone or something walking over everyone's grave at once. The dead moon crossing over the living earth.

And then, looking up: the solar corona. An anti-sun, black and faceless, shining madly around the nothingness of the moon, staring down at the earth with glowing, gossamer white hair. A death's head.

Her neighbors, Bonnie and Donna, the couple renting next door, stood together with their arms around each other, Bonnie with her hand in the back pocket of Donna's saggy jeans. "Isn't it amazing?" Bonnie called, smilingly, over her shoulder.

Kelly could not respond. Didn't they get it? To her, this was no mere curiosity, no afternoon entertainment. How could anyone not see this as some kind of omen? Astronomical explanations and intellectual reasoning be damned: how could this not mean something? So maybe it had no *inherent* meaning, per se. It was a simple convergence of orbits. But how could any sentient being not imbue it with *some* significance, positive or negative, religious or psychic or otherwise? Just because we understand how something works doesn't necessarily mean we *understand* it . . .

They called back to Kelly, alone in front of her house, telling her it was safe now to remove her glasses. "You don't want to miss this!"

Kelly was not going to remove her glasses. No matter what the television said about it being safe to do during the "totality." The television also told her she wouldn't age if she bought expensive creams and pills.

Oohhs and aahhs all up and down the street, a real communal event as people got comfortable with the singularity, embracing the moment. Except for Kelly. *What is wrong with me?* she wondered.

Part of it was just having seen Eph on TV. He didn't say much at the press conference, but Kelly could tell by his eyes and the way that he spoke that something was wrong. Really wrong. Something beyond the governor's and the mayor's rote assurances. Something beyond the sudden and unexplained deaths of 206 transatlantic passengers.

A virus? A terror attack? A mass suicide?

And now this.

She wanted Zack and Matt home. She wanted them here with her right now. She wanted this solar occultation thing to be over with, and to know that she would never have to experience this feeling again. She looked up through the filtered lenses at the murdering moon in all its dark triumph, worried that she might never see the sun again.

Yankee Stadium, the Bronx

ZACK STOOD ON HIS SEAT next to Matt, who stared at the eclipse with his nose scrunched up and his mouth hanging open like a driver squinting into oncoming traffic. Fifty-thousand-plus Yankees fans wearing special collector's pin-striped eclipse glasses, on their feet now, faces upturned, looking at the moon that darkened the sky on a perfect afternoon for baseball. All except Zack Goodweather. The eclipse was cool and all, but now he had seen it, and so Zack turned his attention to the dugout. He was trying to see Yankees players. There was Jeter, wearing the same exact specs as Zack, perched on the top step on one knee as though waiting to be announced to hit. Pitchers and catchers were all outside the bullpen, gathered on the right-field grass like anyone else, taking it all in.

"Ladies and gentlemen," said Bob Sheppard, the public address announcer, "boys and girls, you may now remove your safety glasses."

And so they did. Fifty thousand people, nearly in unison. An appreciative gasp went up, then some ballpark applause, then full-out cheering, as though the crowd were trying to lure the unfailingly modest Matsui out of the dugout for a cap tip after slugging one into Monument Park.

In school, Zack had learned that the sun was a 6,000-degree Kelvin thermonuclear furnace, but that its corona, the outer edge, consisting of superheated hydrogen gas—visible from earth only during totality—was unexplainably hotter, its temperature reaching as high as *2,000,000* degrees Kelvin.

What he saw when he removed his glasses was a perfect black disk edged by a thin blaze of crimson, surrounded by an aura of wispy white light. Like an eye: the moon a wide, black pupil; the corona the white of the eye; and the vivid reds bursting from the rim of the pupil—loops of superheated gas erupting from the edge of the sun—the bloodshot veins. Kind of like the eye of a zombie.

Cool.

Zombie Sky. No: *Zombies of the Eclipse. Zombies of the Occultation. Occult Zombies from the Planet Moon!* Wait—the moon isn't a planet. *Zombie Moon.* This could be the concept for the movie he and his friends were going to make this winter. Moon rays during a total earth eclipse transform members of the New York Yankees into brain-slurping zombies—yes! And his buddy Ron looked almost just like a young Jorge Posada. "Hey, Jorge Posada, can I have your autograph . . . wait, what are you . . . hey, that's my . . . what's wrong with . . . your eyes . . . gah . . . no . . . NOOO!!!"

The organ was playing now, and a few of the drunks turned into conductors, waving their arms and exhorting their section to sing along with some corny "I'm Being Followed by a Moon Shadow" song. Base-ball crowds rarely need an excuse to make noise. These people would have cheered even if this occultation were an asteroid hurtling toward them.

Wow. Zack realized, with a start, that this was exactly the sort of thing his dad would have said if he were here.

Matt, now admiring his free specs next to him, nudged Zack. "Pretty sweet keepsake, huh? I bet eBay'll be flooded with these suck-ers by this time tomorrow."

Then a drunk guy jostled Matt's shoulder, sloshing beer onto his shoes. Matt froze a moment, then rolled his eyes at Zack, kind of a *What-are-you-going-to-do?* face. But he didn't say or do anything. He didn't even turn around to look. It occurred to Zack now that he'd never seen Matt drink a beer before, only white or red wine on nights at home with Mom. Zack got the sense then that Matt, for all his enthu-siasm about the game, was essentially afraid of the fans sitting around them.

Now Zack really wished his dad were there. He dug Matt's phone out of his jeans pocket and checked again for a text reply.

Searching for signal, it read. Still no service. Solar flares and radia-tion distortion messing with radio waves and orbiting satellites; they said that would happen. Zack put the phone away and craned his head toward the field, looking for Jeter again.

International Space Station

TWO HUNDRED AND TWENTY MILES above earth, astronaut Thalia Charles—the American flight engineer on Expedition 18, along with a Russian commander and a French engineer—floated in zero gravity through the vestibule joining the *Unity* module to the aft hatch of lab mod *Destiny.* The ISS research facility orbited earth sixteen times each day, or about once every hour and a half, at a speed of seventeen thousand miles per hour. Occultations were no great feat in low earth orbit: blocking the sun with any round object in a window revealed the spectacular corona. Thalia's interest therefore was not in the alignment of the moon and the sun—from her fast-moving perspective, there was indeed no occultation—but rather the result of this phenomenon upon the slow-rotating earth.

Destiny, the primary research lab on the ISS, measures twenty-eight by fourteen feet—although the interior working space of this cylindrical module, due to the amount of equipment tied down to the squared-off sides, is tighter than that, measuring roughly five humans long by one human across. Every duct, pipe, and wire connection was directly accessible and therefore visible, such that each of *Destiny*'s four walls looked like the back of a panel-size motherboard. At times Thalia felt like little more than a tiny microprocessor dutifully carrying out computations inside a great space computer.

Thalia walked her hands along the nadir, the "floor" of *Destiny*—in space there is no up or down—to a broad, lenslike ring studded with bolts. The portal shutter was designed to protect the integrity of the module from micrometeoroids or collisions with orbital debris. She maneuvered her sock-covered feet against a wall grip and manually opened it, revealing the two-foot-diameter optical-quality window.

The blue-white ball of earth came into view.

Thalia's duty assignment was to point and shoot some earth photos with a hard-mounted Hasselblad camera via remote trigger. But when she first looked out on the planet from her unusual vantage point, what she saw made her shudder. The great black blot that was the shadow of the moon looked like a dead spot on the earth. A dark and threatening flaw in the otherwise healthy blue orb that was home. Most unnerving was that she could see nothing at all within the umbra, the central, darkest part of the moon's shadow, that entire region disappearing into a black void. It was something like viewing a postdisaster satellite map showing devastation caused by a mighty fire that had consumed New York City, and was now spreading out over a broad patch of the eastern seaboard.

Manhattan

NEW YORKERS CONGREGATED in Central Park, the fifty-five-acre Great Lawn filling up as though for a summertime concert. Those who had set out blankets and lawn chairs earlier in the morning now stood on their feet with the rest, children perched on their fathers' shoulders, babies cradled in their mother's arms. Belvedere Castle loomed purple-gray over the park, an eerie touch of the gothic in this pastoral open space dwarfed by the East and West Side high-rises.

The great island metropolis ground to a halt, the stillness of the city at that hour felt by all. It was a blackout vibe, anxious yet communal. The occultation imposed a sort of equality upon the city and its denizens, a five-minute suspension of social stratification. Everyone the same under the sun—or the lack thereof.

Radios played up and down the lawn, people singing along with Z100's spinning of the seven-minute Bonnie Tyler karaoke favorite "Total Eclipse of the Heart."

Along the East Side bridges connecting Manhattan to the rest of the world, people stood next to their stopped vehicles, or sat on the hoods, a few photographers with specially filtered cameras clicking from the walkways.

Many rooftops hosted early cocktail hours, a New Year's Eve–type celebration dampened, for the moment, by the fearsome spectacle in the sky.

The giant Panasonic Astrovision screen, in night-dim Times Square, simulcast the occultation to the terrestrial masses, the sun's ghostly corona shimmering over "the crossroads of the world" like a warning from a distant sector of the galaxy, the broadcast interrupted by flickers of distortion.

Emergency 911 and nonemergency 311 systems took a torrent of calls, including a handful from preterm pregnant women reporting early "eclipse-induced" labor. EMTs were dutifully dispatched, even though traffic all over the island was at a virtual standstill.

The twin psychiatric centers on Randall's Island in the northern East River confined violent patients to their rooms and ordered all blinds drawn. Nonviolent patients were invited to assemble in the blacked-out cafeterias, where they were being shown movies—broad comedies—although, during minutes of the totality, a noticeable few grew restless, anxious to leave the room but unable to articulate why. At Bellevue, the psych ward had already seen an uptick in admittances that morning, in advance of the occultation.

Between Bellevue and the New York University Medical Center, two of the largest hospitals in the world, stood perhaps the ugliest building in all of Manhattan. The headquarters of the chief medical examiner of New York was a misshapen rectangle of sickly turquoise. As the fish truck off-loaded bagged corpses, wheeled on stretchers into the autopsy rooms and walk-in refrigerators in the basement, Gossett Bennett, one of the office's fourteen medical examiners, stepped outside for a quick break. He could not see the moon-sun from the small park behind the hospital—the building itself was in his way—so he instead watched the watchers. All along FDR Drive, which the park overlooked, people stood between parked cars on the never-idle throughway. The East River beyond was dark, a river of tar reflecting the dead sky. Across the river, a gloom overhung all of Queens, broken only by the glow of the sun's corona reflected in a few of the highest, west-facing windows, like the white-hot flame of some spectacular chemical-plant blaze.

This is what the beginning of the end of the world will look like, he thought to himself before returning to the M.E.'s office to assist in the cataloging of the dead.

JFK International Airport

THE FAMILIES OF the deceased passengers and crew of Regis Air Flight 753 were encouraged to take a break from paperwork and Red Cross coffee (decaf only for the aggrieved), and walk outside onto the tarmac in the restricted area behind terminal 3. There, with nothing in common but their grief, the hollow-eyed mourners huddled together and faced the eclipse arm in arm—some leaning on others in solidarity, others in need of actual physical support—their faces turned to the dark western sky. They did not know yet that they would be split up soon into four groups and shuttled in school buses to their respective medical examiner's offices where, one family at a time, they would be invited into a viewing room and shown a postmortem photograph and asked to formally identify their loved one. Only families who demanded to view the actual physical remains would be allowed to do so. They then would be issued hotel room vouchers to the airport Sheraton, where a complimentary dinner buffet would be offered and grief counselors placed at their disposal all night and into the next day.

For now, they stared up at the black disk glowing like a spotlight in reverse, sucking light away from this world and back up to the heavens. This obliterating phenomenon was to them a perfect symbol of their loss at that very moment. To them, the eclipse was the opposite of remarkable. It seemed merely appropriate that the sky and their God would see fit to mark their despair.

Outside the Regis Air maintenance hangar, Nora stood apart from the other investigators, waiting for Eph and Jim to return from the press conference. Her eyes were turned toward the ominous black hole in the sky, but her vision was unfocused. She felt caught up in something she did not understand. As though a strange new foe had arisen. The dead moon eclipsing the living sun. Night occulting day.

A shadow flowed past her then. She detected it as a shimmer from out of the corner of her eye, something like the slithering worm shadows that had undulated over the tarmac just before totality. Something just outside her field of vision, at the very edge of perception. Fleeing the maintenance hangar like a dark spirit. A shadow she *felt*.

In the split second it took her pupil to move to it, the shadow was gone.

Lorenza Ruiz, the airport baggage-conveyer operator who had been the first to drive out to the dead airplane, found herself haunted by the experience. Standing in the aircraft's shadow that previous night, Lo couldn't get it out of her mind. She hadn't slept at all, tossing and turning, finally rising to pace. A late-night glass of white wine failed to do the trick. It weighed on her like something she could not let go of. When sunrise finally came, she found herself eyeing the clock—in anticipation, she realized, of returning to work. She found she couldn't wait to get back to JFK. Not out of morbid curiosity. It was the image of that dormant plane, impressed upon her mind like a bright light flashed into her eye. All she knew was that she had to get back to see it again.

Now this eclipse, and for the second time in twenty-four hours, the airport was shut down. This stoppage had been in the planning for months—the FAA had cleared a fifteen-minute window of downtime for airports within the range of the occultation, out of concern for the vision of the pilots, who couldn't very well wear filtered glasses during takeoff or landing—but still, the math struck her as pretty damning and pretty simple:

Dead Airplane + Solar Eclipse = Not Good.

When the moon snuffed out the sun, like a hand covering up a scream, Lo felt the same electric panic as when she had stood on top of the luggage ramp beneath the belly of the darkened 777. The very same impulse to run, this time coupled with the knowledge that there was absolutely no place to go.

Now she was hearing it again. Same noise she'd been hearing since arriving for her shift, only steadier now, louder. A humming. A droning sound, and the weird thing was, she heard it at the same volume whether she wore her protective headphones or not. Headachelike, in that way. Interior. And yet, like a homing beacon, it strengthened in her mind once she returned to work.

With the fifteen minutes of downtime during the eclipse, she decided to set off on foot in search of the source of the tone, following it. Without any sense of surprise, she now found herself looking at the cordoned-off Regis Air maintenance hangar where the dead 777 was being stored.

The noise sounded like no machine she had ever heard. A churning, almost, a rushing sound, like coursing fluid. Or like the murmur of a dozen voices, a hundred different voices, trying to make sense. Maybe she was picking up radar vibrations in her teeth fillings. There was a group of people out in front, officials gazing up at the blocked sun— but no one else like her, lurking there, bothered by or even cognizant of a hum. So she kept it to herself. And yet, for some weird reason, it felt momentous, being right here, this very moment, hearing the noise and wishing—to salve her curiosity, or was it more than that?—that she could get inside the hangar for another look at the plane. As though seeing the plane would somehow resolve the thrumming in her head.

Then suddenly she felt a charge in the atmosphere, like a breeze changing course, and now—yes—it seemed to her that the source of the noise had moved somewhere off to her right. This sudden change startled her, and she followed it under the negative light of the glowing moon, carrying her headphones and protective glasses in her hand. Dumpsters and storage trailers lay ahead, before a few large box containers, and then some scrub brush and hardy, gray, wind-whipped pine trees, their branches full of snagged trash. Then the hurricane fence, beyond which lay hundreds of acres of scrub wilderness.

Voices. It was more like voices to her now. Trying to rise to one single voice, a word . . . something.

As Lo neared the trailers, an abrupt rustling in the trees, a *lifting*, made her leap back. Gray-bellied seagulls, apparently spooked by the eclipse, exploded out of the branches and Dumpsters, like winged shards of glass from a smashed window, scattering in all directions.

The droning voices were sharper now, grown almost painful. Calling on her. Like a chorus of the damned, the cacophony rising from a whisper to a roar and back again, struggling to articulate one word, sounding like, as best she could make out:

" . . . . . . *hhrrhhrrhhrrhhrrhhrrHERE."*

She set down her headphones on the edge of the tarmac, hanging on to her filtered glasses for when the eclipse ended. She veered away from the Dumpsters and their rank garbage smell, instead going toward the large storage trailers. The sound seemed to be emanating not from inside the trailers, but maybe from behind them.

She walked between two six-foot-tall containers and around an old decaying airplane tire, coming upon another row of older, pale green containers. Now she felt it. Not just heard the thrum but *felt* it, a nest of voices vibrating in her head and in her chest. Beckoning to her. She placed her hand on the containers but felt no pulsation there, then continued forward, slowing at the corner, leaning out.

Set on top of the blown trash and uncut, sun-bleached grass was a large, ancient-looking, ornately carved black wooden box. She ventured into the small clearing, wondering why someone would throw such an obviously well-maintained antique all the way back here. Theft—organized and otherwise—was a fact of life at the airport; maybe someone had stashed it here, planning to swing by later to pick it up.

Then she noticed the cats. The outer airport was crawling with wild cats. Some of them were pets who had escaped their transport cages. Many had simply been released onto airport property by locals looking to get rid of unwanted pets. Worst of all were the travelers who abandoned their cats at the airport rather than pay high kennel fees. Domestic cats who did not know how to fend for themselves in the wild, and who, if they avoided becoming prey to larger animals and survived, joined the colony of feral cats roaming the hundreds of acres of undeveloped airport property.

The skinny cats all sat on their hindquarters, facing the cabinet. A few dozen of these mangy, dirty felines—until Lo looked at the trash-strewn tree and along the hurricane fence, and saw that there were in fact close to a hundred of these feral cats, sitting and facing the wooden box, paying her no attention.

The box wasn't vibrating, wasn't emitting the noise she had been attuned to. She was mystified, after coming all this way, to discover something this strange here on the outskirts of the airport—and that was not, in fact, the source she was seeking. The thrumming chorus went on. Were the cats tuned in to it as well? No. Their focus was on the closed cabinet.

She was starting to back away when the cats stiffened. The fur along their backs prickled—each of them, all at once. Their scabby heads all turned her way, one hundred pairs of wild cat eyes staring at her in the gloaming night-day. Lo froze, fearing an attack—and then a darkness fell over her, like a second eclipse.

The cats turned and ran. They fled the clearing, claws grabbing willy-nilly at the high fence or scrambling through predug holes beneath it.

Lo could not turn. She felt a rush of heat from behind her, as from an oven door when you open it. A presence. As she tried to move, the sounds in her head coalesced into one single horrible voice.

"HERE."

And then she was lifted off the ground.

When the legion of cats returned, they discovered her body with its head crushed, cast deep into their side of the hurricane fence like so much litter. The gulls had found her first—but the cats quickly scared them off and got right to work, hungrily shredding her clothes to get to the feast within.

Knickerbocker Loans and Curios, East 118th Street, Spanish Harlem

THE OLD MAN SAT BEFORE the three adjacent windows at the western end of his dimmed apartment, gazing up at the occluded sun.

Five minutes of night in the middle of the day. The greatest naturally occurring celestial event in four centuries.

The timing could not be ignored.

But to what purpose?

Urgency seized him like a fevered hand. He had not opened the shop that day, instead spending the hours since daybreak hauling things up from his basement workshop. Items and curiosities he had acquired over the years . . .

Tools of forgotten function. Rare implements of obscure origin. Weapons of lost provenance.

Why he sat here tired now, his gnarled hands aching. No one else but he could foresee what was coming. What was—by every indication—already here.

No one else who would believe him.

Goodfellow. Or *Goodwilling.* Whatever was the last name of that man who had spoken at the otherwise ridiculous news conference on the television, standing next to the doctor in the navy uniform. How cautiously optimistic all the others had seemed. Exulting over the four survivors, while claiming not to know the final tally of all the dead. *We want to assure the public that this threat is contained.* Only an elected official would dare to declare a thing safe and finished when he or she didn't even know yet what it was.

This man was the only one behind the microphones who seemed to think there might be more to this than a malfunctioning aircraft full of dead passengers.

Goodwater?

From the disease control center, the one in Atlanta. Setrakian didn't know, but he thought his best chance might be with this man. Maybe his only chance.

Four survivors. If they only knew . . .

He looked out again at the glowing black disk in the sky. Like staring at an eye blinded by a cataract.

Like staring into the future.

Stoneheart Group, Manhattan

THE HELICOPTER touched down on the helipad of the Stoneheart Group's Manhattan headquarters, a building of black steel and glass in the heart of Wall Street. Its top three floors were occupied by Eldritch Palmer's private New York residence, a regal penthouse constructed with onyx floors, its tables laden with Brancusis, its walls papered with Bacons.

Palmer sat alone in the media room with the shades all drawn, the glowing black eyeball rimmed in fierce crimson and ringed with flaming white staring out at him from a seventy-two-inch viewing screen. This room, like his home in Dark Harbor and the cabin of his medical helicopter, was kept regulated at exactly sixty-two degrees.

He could have gone outside. It was, after all, cold enough for him; he could have been taken up to the roof to witness the occultation. But technology brought him closer to the event itself—not the resulting shadow, but the image of the sun subordinated to the moon—that was the prelude to the devastation. His Manhattan sojourn would be brief. New York City would not be a very pleasant place to visit, not for much longer.

He placed a few phone calls, a few discreet consultations over his secure line. His cargo had indeed arrived as expected.

Smiling, he rose from his chair, walking slowly but straight at the giant viewing screen, as though it were not a screen at all but a portal he was about to step through. He reached out and touched the LCD screen over the image of the angry black disk, liquid pixels squirming bacteria-like beneath the wrinkled pads of his fingers. As though he were reaching through it to touch the eye of death itself.

This occultation was a celestial perversion, a violation of the natural order. A cold, dead stone deposing a burning, living star. For Eldritch Palmer, it was proof that anything—*anything*, even the grossest betrayal of natural law—was indeed possible.

Of all the human beings watching the occultation that day, in person or via broadcast around the globe, he was perhaps the only one rooting for the moon.

JFK International Control Tower

THOSE IN THE VIEWING CAB of the air-traffic-control tower 321 feet above the ground glimpsed the eerie sunsetlike twilight way off to the west, out beyond the reach of the great moon shadow, past the edge of the umbra. The brighter penumbra, illuminated by the sun's blazing photosphere, had turned the distant sky yellow and orange, not unlike the healing edge of a wound.

This wall of light was advancing on New York City, which had now been dark for exactly four minutes and thirty seconds.

"Glasses on!" came the order, and Jim Kent put his on, anxious for sunlight's return. He glanced around, looking for Eph—everyone from the press conference, including the governor and the mayor, had been invited up into the tower cab for the viewing—and, not seeing him, assumed that Eph had slipped back to the maintenance hangar.

In fact, Eph had used this enforced time-out in the best way he knew: by grabbing a chair as soon as the sun had disappeared and going through a packet of construction diagrams showing cutaway views and schematics of the Boeing 777, ignoring the occultation altogether.

The End of Totality

THE END WAS MARKED BY an extraordinary phenomenon. Dazzling prominences of light appeared along the western edge of the moon, combining to form a single bead of dazzling sunlight, like a rip in the darkness, giving the effect of a blindingly radiant diamond set upon the moon's silver ring. But the price for such beauty, despite a vigorous public service campaign dedicated to eye safety during the occultation, was that more than 270 people across the city, 93 of them children, suffered permanent blindness by watching the sun's dramatic reappearance without wearing proper eye protection. There are no pain sensors in the retina, and the afflicted did not realize they were damaging their eyes until it was too late.

The diamond ring expanded slowly, becoming a band of jewels known as "Baily's beads," which merged into the reborn crescent of the sun, essentially pushing the interloping moon away.

On earth, the shadow bands returned, shimmering over the ground like inaugural spirits heralding the passing from one form of existence to another.

As natural light began filling back in, the human relief on the ground was epic. Cheers and hugs and spontaneous applause. Automobile horns sounded all across the city, and Kate Smith's recorded voice sang over the loudspeakers at Yankee Stadium.

Ninety minutes later, the moon had completely departed from the path of the sun, and the occultation was over. In one very real sense, nothing at all had happened: nothing in the sky had been altered or otherwise affected, nothing had changed on earth except for the few minutes of late-afternoon shade across the northeastern United States. Even in New York itself, people packed up afterward as though the fireworks show was over, and those who had traveled away from home transferred the focus of their dread from the occluded afternoon sun to the traffic awaiting them. A compelling astronomic phenomenon had cast a shadow of awe and anxiety across all five boroughs. But this was New York, and when it was over—it was over.

AWAKEN-ING

E ph returned to the hangar by electric cart, leaving Jim behind with Director Barnes, giving Eph and Nora some breathing room.

The hospital screens had all been wheeled away from beneath the 777's wing, the tarp pulled up. Ladders were now hung from the fore and aft exit doors, and a gang of NTSB officials was working near the aft cargo hatch. The aircraft was being regarded as a crime scene now. Eph found Nora wearing a Tyvek jumper and latex gloves, her hair pulled up under a paper cap. She was dressed not for biological containment but for simple evidence preservation.

"That was pretty amazing, huh?" she said, greeting him.

"Yeah," said Eph, his sheaf of airplane schematics under his arm. "Once in a lifetime."

There was coffee set out on a table, but Eph instead plucked a chilling milk carton from its bowl of ice, tore it open, and emptied it down his throat. Ever since giving up liquor, Eph, like a calcium-hungry toddler, craved whole milk.

Nora said, "Still nothing here. The NTSB is pulling out the cockpit voice recorder and the flight data recorder. I'm not sure why they think the black boxes will work when everything else on the airplane failed catastrophically, but I guess I admire their optimism. So far, technology has gotten us exactly nowhere. We're twenty hours in now, and this thing is still wide open."

Nora was perhaps the only person he had ever known who worked better and smarter through emotion rather than the other way around. "Anyone been through the inside of the plane since the bodies came out?"

"I don't think so. Not yet."

Eph carried his schematics up the wheeled stairs and into the aircraft. The seats were all empty now, and the lighting inside was normal. The only other difference from Eph's and Nora's perspective was that they were no longer sealed inside contact suits. All five senses were available to them now.

Eph said, "You smell that?"

Nora did. "What is it?"

"Ammonia. That's part of it."

"And . . . phosphorous?" The odor made her wince. "Is this what knocked them out?"

"No. The plane is clean for gas. But . . ." He was looking around— looking around for something they could not see. "Nora, go get the Luma wands, would you?"

While she went back out for them, Eph went throughout the cabin closing the window shades, as they had been the night before, darkening the cabin.

Nora returned with two Luma light wands that emitted a black light, similar to the one used on amusement park rides, that made laundered white cotton glow spectrally. Eph remembered Zack's ninth birthday party at a "cosmic" bowling alley, and how every time Zack smiled, the boy's teeth shone bright white.

They switched on the lights, and immediately the dark cabin was transformed into a crazy swirl of colors, a massive staining all throughout the floor and over the seats, leaving dark outlines of where the passengers had been.

Nora said, "Oh my God . . ."

Some of the glowing substance even coated the ceiling in a splashed-out pattern.

"It's not blood," said Eph, overwhelmed by the sight. Looking through to the aft cabin was like staring into a Jackson Pollock painting. "It's some sort of biological matter."

"Whatever it is, it's sprayed all over the place. Like something exploded. But from where?"

"From here. From right where we are standing." He knelt down, examining the carpet, the smell more pungent there. "We need to sample this and test it."

"You think?" said Nora.

He stood again, still amazed. "Look at this." He showed her a page of the airplane schematics. It diagrammed emergency rescue access for the Boeing 777 series. "See this shaded module at the front of the plane?"

She did. "It looks like a flight of stairs."

"Right in back of the cockpit."

"What's 'OFCRA' stand for?"

Eph walked down to the galley before the cockpit door. Those very initials were printed on a wall panel there.

"Overhead flight crew rest area," said Eph. "Standard on these long-distance big birds."

Nora looked at him. "Did anybody check up here?"

Eph said, "I know we didn't."

He reached down and turned a handle recessed in the wall, pulling open the panel. A trifolding door revealed narrow, curving steps leading up into the dark.

"Oh, shit," said Nora.

Eph played his Luma lamp up the stairs. "I take it that means you want me to go first."

"Wait. Let's get somebody else."

"No. They won't know what to look for."

"Do we?"

Eph ignored that, and climbed the tight, curling stairs.

The upper compartment was tight, low-ceilinged. There were no windows. The Luma lights were better suited for forensic examination than indoor illumination.

Inside the first module, they made out two side-by-side business-class-size seats folded down. Behind these were two inclined bunks, also side by side, not much larger than a crawl space. The dark light showed both modules to be empty.

It also, however, showed more of the same multicolored mess they had discovered below. On the floor and tracked over the seats and one of the bunks. But here it was smudged, almost as though tracked in while still wet.

Nora said, "What the hell?"

The ammonia smell was here as well—and something else. A pungent odor.

Nora noticed it too, bringing the back of her hand beneath her nostrils. "What is it?"

Eph stood almost doubled over under the low ceiling between the two chairs. He was trying to put a word to it. "Like earthworms," he said. "Used to dig them up as kids. Cut them in half in order to watch each section wriggle away. Their smell was earth, the cold soil they crawled through."

Eph ran his black light over the walls and floors, scouring the chamber. He was about to give up when he noticed something behind Nora's paper booties.

"Nora, don't move," said Eph.

He leaned to one side for a better angle on the carpeted floor behind her, Nora frozen as though she were about to trip a land mine.

A small clump of soil lay on the patterned carpet. No more than a few grams of dirt, a trace amount, richly black.

Nora said, "Is that what I think it is?"

Eph said, "The cabinet."

They climbed back down the outside stairs to the area of the hangar reserved for cargo, where food-service carts were now being opened and inspected. Eph and Nora scanned the piles of luggage, the golf bags, the kayak.

The black wooden cabinet was gone. The space it had previously occupied, on the edge of the tarpaulin, was bare.

"Someone must have moved it," said Eph, still looking. He walked away a few steps, scanning the rest of the hangar. "Couldn't have gotten far."

Nora's eyes were blazing. "They are just starting to go through all this stuff. Nothing's been taken out yet."

Eph said, "This one thing was."

"This is a secure site, Eph. That thing was what, about eight by four by three? It weighed a few hundred pounds. Would have taken four men to carry it."

"Exactly. So somebody knows where it is."

They went to the duty officer manning the hangar door, the keeper of the site log. The young man consulted his master list, a time log of everyone's and everything's entrances and exits. "Nothing here," he said.

Eph sensed Nora's objection rising and spoke before she could. "How long have you been here—standing right here?"

"Since about twelve, sir."

"No break?" said Eph. "What about during the eclipse?"

"I stood right out here." He pointed to a spot a few yards away from the door. "No one went by me."

Eph looked back at Nora.

Nora said, "What in the hell is going on?" She looked at the duty officer. "Who else might have seen a great big coffin?"

Eph frowned at the word "coffin." He looked back into the hangar, and then up at the security cameras in the rafters.

He pointed. "They did."

Eph, Nora, and the Port Authority site log duty officer walked up the long, steel staircase to the control office overlooking the maintenance hangar. Below, mechanics were removing the aircraft's nose for a look at the internals.

Four drone cameras ran constantly inside the hangar: one at the door leading to the office stairs; one trained on the hangar doors; one up in the rafters—the one Eph had pointed to—and one in the room they were standing in now. All displayed on a four-square screen.

Eph asked the maintenance foreman, "Why the camera in this room?"

The foreman shrugged. "Prolly 'cause this is where the petty cash is."

He took his seat, a battered office chair whose armrests were striped with duct tape, and worked the keyboard beneath the monitor, expanding the rafter view to full screen. He scanned back through the security recording. The unit was digital, but a few years old, and too distorted to make out anything clearly during the rewind.

He stopped it. On the screen, the cabinet lay exactly where it had, on the edge of the off-loaded cargo.

"There it is," said Eph.

The duty officer nodded. "Okay. So let's see where it went."

The foreman punched it forward. It ran more slowly than the rewind, but was still pretty fast. The light in the hangar darkened with the occultation, and when it brightened again, the cabinet was gone.

"Stop, stop," said Eph. "Back it up."

The foreman backed up a little, pressed play again. The time code on the bottom showed the image playing more slowly than before.

The hangar dimmed and at once the cabinet was again gone.

"What the—?" said the foreman, hitting pause.

Eph said, "Go back just a bit."

The foreman did, then let it play through in real time.

The hangar dimmed, still lit by the interior work lights. The cabinet was there. And then it vanished.

"Wow," said the duty officer.

The foreman paused the video. He was confounded too.

Eph said, "There is a gap. A cut."

The foreman said, "No cut. You saw the time code."

"Go back a bit then. A bit more . . . right there . . . now again."

The foreman played it again.

And again the cabinet disappeared.

"Houdini," grumbled the foreman.

Eph looked at Nora.

"It didn't just *disappear*," said the duty officer. He pointed out the other luggage nearby. "Everything else stays the same. Not a flicker."

Eph said, "Back it up again. Please."

The foreman ran it yet again. The cabinet disappeared yet again.

"Wait," said Eph. He'd seen something. "Step it back—*slowly*."

The foreman did, and ran it again.

"There," said Eph.

"Christ," exclaimed the foreman, almost jumping out of his creaky seat. "I saw it."

"Saw what?" said Nora, together with the duty officer.

The foreman was into it now, rewinding the image just a few steps.

"Coming . . . ," said Eph, readying him. "Coming . . ." The foreman held his hand over the keyboard like a game show contestant waiting to press a buzzer. ". . . *there*."

The cabinet was gone again. Nora leaned close. "What?"

Eph pointed to the side of the monitor. "Right there."

Just evident on the wide right edge of the image was a black blur.

Eph said, "Something bursting past the camera."

"Up in the rafters?" said Nora. "What, a bird?"

"Too damn big," Eph said.

The duty officer, leaning close, said, "It's a glitch. A shadow."

"Okay," Eph said, standing back. "A shadow of what?"

The duty officer straightened. "Can you go frame by frame?"

The foreman tried. The cabinet disappeared from the floor . . . almost *simultaneously* with the appearance of the blur in the rafters. "Best I can do on this machine."

The duty officer studied the screen again. "Coincidence," he declared. "How could anything move at that speed?"

Eph asked, "Can you zoom in?"

The foreman rolled his eyes. "This here ain't CSI—it's Radio-fucking-Shack."

"So, it's gone," Nora said, turning to Eph, the other men unable to help. "But why—and how?"

Eph cupped his hand over the back of his neck. "The soil from the cabinet . . . it must be the same as the soil we just found. Which means . . ."

Nora said, "Are we formulating a theory that someone got up into the overhead flight crew rest area from the cargo hold?"

Eph recalled the feeling he had gotten, standing in the cockpit with the dead pilots—just before discovering that Redfern was still alive. That of a presence. Something nearby.

He moved Nora away from the other two. "And tracked some of that . . . whatever swirl of biological matter in the passenger cabin."

Nora looked back to the image of the black blur in the rafters.

Eph said, "I think someone was hiding up in that compartment when we first entered the plane."

"Okay . . . ," she said, grappling with that. "But then—where is it now?"

Eph said, "Wherever that cabinet is."

Gus

GUS SAUNTERED DOWN the lane of cars in the low-ceilinged, long-term parking garage at JFK. The echoing screech of balding tires turning down the exit ramps made the place sound like a madhouse. He pulled out the folded index card from his shirt pocket and double-checked the section number, written in someone else's hand. Then he double-checked that there was no one else near.

He found the van, a dinged-up, road-dirtied, white Econoline with no back windows, at the very end of the lane, parked astride a coned-off corner work area of fluttering tarp and crumbled stone where part of the overhead support had cracked.

He pulled out a hand rag and used it to try the driver's door, which was unlocked, as advertised. He backed off from the van and looked around the isolated corner of the garage, quiet but for those monkey squeals in the distance, thinking *trap*. They could have a camera in any one of these other cars, watching him. Like on *Cops*, he'd seen that one: PD'd hooked up little cameras inside trucks and pulled them over on a city street, Cleveland or somewhere, and watched as kids and other yo-yos jumped in and took off on a joyride or a trip down to the local chop shop. Being caught was bad, but being tricked like that, getting hosed on prime-time TV, was much worse. Gus would rather be shot dead in his underwear than be branded a fool.

But he had taken the $50 the dude offered him to do this. Easy money, which Gus still had on him, tucked inside the band of his pinch-front hat, holding on to it for evidence in case things went south.

Dude was in the market when Gus went in for a Sprite. Behind him in line when he paid. Outside, a half block away, Gus heard someone coming up on him and turned fast. It was the dude—hands out, showing them empty. Wanting to know if Gus wanted to make some quick money.

White guy, neat suit, way out of place. He didn't look cop but he didn't look queer neither. Looked like some sort of missionary.

"A van in the airport parking garage. You pick it up, drive it into Manhattan, park it, and walk away."

"A van," said Gus.

"A van."

"What's in it?"

Dude just shook his head. Handed over an index card folded over five new tens. "Just a taste."

Gus pulled out the bills, like lifting the meat out of a sandwich. "If you PD, this entrapment."

"The pickup time is written on there. Don't be early, and don't be late."

Gus thumbed the folded tens in his hand like sampling a fine fabric. Dude saw this. Dude also saw, Gus realized, the three small circles tattooed onto the webbing of Gus's hand. Mex gang symbol for thief, but how would this dude know that? Was that why he made him back in the store? Why the dude had picked him?

"Keys and further instructions will be in the glove compartment."

The dude started walking away.

"Yo," said Gus after him. "I didn't say yes yet."

Gus pulled open the door—waited; no alarm—and climbed inside. Didn't see no cameras—but he wouldn't anyway, would he? Behind the front seats was a metal partition without a window. Bolted in there, aftermarket. Maybe truck full of PD he's driving around.

Van felt still, though. He opened the glove compartment, again using the rag. Gently, as if a gag snake might jump out at him, and the little light came on. Laid out inside was the ignition key, the parking garage ticket he needed to get out, and a manila envelope.

He looked inside the envelope and the first thing he saw was his pay. Five new $100 bills, which pleased and pissed him off at the same time. Pleased him because it was more than he had expected, and pissed him off because no one would break a century from him without a hassle, especially nowhere in the hood. Even a bank would scan the hell out of those bills, coming out of the pocket of an eighteen-year-old tatted-up Mexican.

Folded around the bills was another index card listing the destination address and a garage access code, GOOD FOR ONE USE ONLY.

He compared the cards side by side. Same handwriting.

Anxiety faded as excitement rose. *Sucker!* Trusting him with this vehicle. Gus knew, right off the top of his head, three different spots in the South Bronx to take this baby for *reconditioning*. And to quickly satisfy his curiosity as to what sort of contraband goodness he was carrying in back.

The last item in the larger envelope was a smaller, letter-size envelope. He withdrew a few sheets of paper, unfolded them, and a warm flame rose out of the center of his back and into his shoulders and neck.

AUGUSTIN ELIZALDE, headed the first one. It was Gus's rap sheet, his juvenile jacket leading up to the manslaughter conviction and his being kicked free with a clean slate on his eighteenth birthday, just three short weeks ago.

The second page showed a copy of his driver's license and, below that, his *mother's* driver's license with the same East 115th Street address. Then a small picture of the front door of their building at the Taft Houses.

He stared at that paper for two straight minutes. His mind raced back and forth between that missionary-looking dude and how much he knew, and his *madre* here, and what kind of bad shit Gus had gotten himself into this time.

Gus didn't take well to threats. Especially involving his *madre*: he had already put her through enough.

The third page was printed in the same handwriting as the index cards. It read: NO STOPS.

Gus sat at the window of the Insurgentes, eating his fried eggs doused with Tabasco sauce, looking at the white van double-parked out on Queens Boulevard. Gus loved breakfast, and, since getting out, had eaten breakfast at nearly every meal. He ordered specific now, because he could: bacon extra crispy, burn the toast.

Fuck them, NO STOPS. Gus didn't like this game, not once they included his *madre*. He watched the van, thinking over his options, waiting for something to happen. Was he being watched? If so, how close? And if they could watch him—why weren't they just driving the van themselves? What kind of shit had he gotten himself into here?

What was inside that van?

A couple of *cabrones* came sniffing around the front of the van. They ducked their heads and scattered when Gus emerged from the diner, his top-buttoned flannel shirt flaring out behind him in the late-day breeze, tats sleeving his bare forearms in bright accents of red around jailhouse black. The Latin Sultans' cred carried out of Spanish

Harlem north and east to the Bronx, and as far south into Queens. Their numbers were small, their shadow long. You didn't mess with one unless you wanted war with all.

He pulled out into the boulevard, continuing west toward Manhattan, one eye out for tails. The van bounced over some roadwork and he listened closely but heard nothing shift in back. Yet something was weighing down the suspension.

He got thirsty and pulled over again outside a corner market, picking up two twenty-four-ounce cans of Tecate. He jammed one of the red-and-gold cans into the cup holder and pulled out again, the city buildings coming up across the river now, the sun falling behind them. Night was coming. He thought about his brother at home, Crispin, that shitbag addict, showing up just as Gus was trying his best to be good to his mother. Sweating out chemicals on the living room sofa, and all Gus wanted to do was slide a rusty blade between his ribs. Bringing his disease into their crib. His older brother was a ghoul, a straight-up zombie, but she wouldn't put him out. She let him lay around and pretended he wasn't shooting smack in her bathroom, biding time until he would vanish again, along with some of her things.

Gus needed to put some of this *dinero sucio* aside for his *madre*. Give it to her *after* Crispin was gone. Stick some more in his hat and leave it there for her. Make her happy. Do something right.

Gus pulled out his phone before the tunnel. "Felix, man. Come get me."

"Where you at, bro?"

"I'll be down Battery Park."

"Battery Park? All the way down there, Gusto?"

"So roll over to Ninth and drop straight down, bitch. We're going out. Have ourselves a party, man. That money I owe you—I made me some flash today. Bring me out a jacket or something to wear, clean shoes. Get me into a club."

"Fuckin'—anything else?"

"Just pull your fingers out of your sister's *concha* and come get me—*comprende?*"

He came out of the tunnel into Manhattan and drove across town before turning south. He maneuvered onto Church Street, south of Canal, and started checking street signs. The address was a loft building fronted with scaffolding, its windows plastered with building permits, but without any construction trucks around. The street was quiet, residential. The garage worked as advertised, the access code raising a steel door under which the van just fit, rolling down a ramp beneath the building.

Gus parked and sat still a moment, listening. The garage was dingy and underlit, looking to him like a good trap, the kicked-up dust swirling in the fading light through the open doorway. His impulse was to beat a hasty retreat, but he needed to be sure he was out clean. He waited as the garage door rolled shut.

Gus folded the pages and envelope from the glove compartment and stuffed them inside his pockets, draining the last of the first beer and crushing the can to an aluminum pick, then stepping out of the van. After a moment's deliberation, he went back in with his hand rag and wiped down the steering wheel, the radio knobs, the glove compartment, the door handles inside and out, and anything else he thought he might have touched.

He looked around the garage, the only light now coming in between the blades of an exhaust fan, dust drifting like a mist in its faint rays. Gus wiped off the ignition key, then went around to the side and back doors of the van. He tried the handles, just to see. They were locked.

He thought about it a moment, and then curiosity got the better of him. He tried the key.

The locks were different from the ignition. Part of him was relieved.

Terrorists, he thought. *Could be I'm a fucking terrorist now. Driving a van full of explosives.*

What he could do was drive the van back out of here. Park it outside the nearest police precinct, leave a note on the windshield. Have them see if it's anything or nothing.

But these fuckers had his address. His *madre*'s address. Who were they?

He got angry, a heat flare of shame shooting up his back. He pounded the meat of his fist once against the side of the white van, demonstrating his dissatisfaction with the arrangement. A satisfying sound resounded within, breaking the silence. He gave up then, tossing the key onto the front seat and slamming the driver's door with his elbow—another satisfying bang.

But then—instead of getting quiet quickly again—he heard something. Or thought he did: something inside. With the last of the light eking in through the fan grate, Gus got right up to the locked back doors to listen, his ear almost touching the van.

Something. Almost . . . like a stomach rumbling. That same kind of empty, roiling hunger. A stirring.

Ah, what the fuck, he decided, stepping back. *The deed is done. So long as the bomb goes off below 110th Street, what do I care?*

A dull but distinct *bang* from inside the van rocked Gus back a step. The paper bag containing the second cerveza slipped from underneath his arm, and the can burst and sprayed beer over the gritty floor.

The spraying faded to a dull foaming, and Gus bent to gather up the mess, then stopped, crouching, his hand on the soaked bag.

The van listed ever so slightly. Its undercarriage springs pinged once.

Something had moved or shifted inside.

Gus straightened, leaving the burst beer on the ground and moving backward, shoes scraping the grit. A few steps away, he reset himself, willing himself to relax. His trick was to think that someone was watching him lose his cool. He turned and walked calmly to the closed garage door.

The spring creaked again, putting a hitch in his step, but not halting him.

He reached the black panel with a red plunger switch next to the door. He hit it with the heel of his hand, and nothing happened.

He hit it two more times, first slow and easy, then hard and fast, the spring action on the plunger sticking as though from disuse.

The van creaked again, and Gus did not allow himself to look back.

The garage door was made of faceless steel, no grip handles. Nothing to pull. He kicked it once and the thing barely rattled.

Another *bang* from inside the van, almost answering his own, followed by a severe creak, and Gus rushed back to the plunger. He hit it again, rapid-fire, and then a pulley whirred and the motor clicked and the chain started running.

The door began lifting off the ground.

Gus was outside before it was halfway up, scuttling up onto the sidewalk like a crab and then quickly catching his breath. He turned and waited, watching the door open, hold there, and then go back down again. He made certain it closed tightly and that nothing emerged.

Then he looked around, shaking off his nerves, checking his hat—and walked to the corner, guilty fast, wanting to put another block between him and the van. He crossed to Vesey Street and found himself standing before the Jersey barriers and construction fences surrounding the city block that had been the World Trade Center. It was all dug out now, the great basin a gaping hole in the crooked streets of Lower Manhattan, with cranes and construction trucks building up the site again.

Gus shook off his chill. He unfolded his phone at his ear.

"Felix, where are you, amigo?"

"On Ninth, heading downtown. Whassup?"

"Nothing. Just get here pronto. I've done something I need to forget about."

Isolation Ward, Jamaica Hospital Medical Center

EPH ARRIVED AT the Jamaica Hospitel Medical Center, fuming. "What do you mean they're gone?"

"Dr. Goodweather," said the administrator, "there was nothing we could do to compel them to remain here."

"I told you to post a guard to keep that Bolivar character's slimy lawyer out."

"We did post a guard. An actual police officer. He looked at the legal order and told us there was nothing he could do. And—it wasn't the rock star's lawyer. It was Mrs. Luss the lawyer. Her firm. They went right over my head, right to the hospital board."

"Then why wasn't I told this?"

"We tried to get in touch with you. We called your contact."

Eph whipped around. Jim Kent was standing with Nora. He looked stricken. He pulled out his phone and thumbed back through his calls. "I don't see . . ." He looked up apologetically. "Maybe it was those sunspots from the eclipse, or something. I never got the calls."

"I got your voice mail," said the administrator.

He checked again. "Wait . . . there were some calls I might have missed." He looked up at Eph. "With so much going on, Eph—I'm afraid I dropped the ball."

This news hollowed out Eph's rage. It was not at all like Jim to make any mistake whatsoever, especially at such a critical time. Eph stared at his trusted associate, his anger fizzling out into deep disappointment. "My four best shots at solving this thing just walked out that door."

"Not four," said the administrator, behind him. "Only three."

Eph turned back to her. "What do you mean?"

Inside the isolation ward, Captain Doyle Redfern sat on his bed, inside the plastic curtains. He looked haggard; his pale arms were resting on a pillow in his lap. The nurse said that he had declined all food, claiming stiffness in his throat and persistent nausea, and had rejected even tiny sips of water. The IV in his arm was keeping him hydrated.

Eph and Nora stood with him, masked and gloved, eschewing full barrier protection.

"My union wants me out of here," said Redfern. "The airline industry policy is, 'Always blame pilot error.' Never the airline's fault, overscheduling, maintenance cutbacks. They're going to go after Captain Moldes on this one, no matter what. And me, maybe. But—something doesn't feel right. Inside. I don't feel like myself."

Eph said, "Your cooperation is critical. I can't thank you enough for staying, except to say that we'll do everything in our power to get you healthy again."

Redfern nodded, and Eph could tell that his neck was stiff. He probed the underside of his jaw, feeling for his lymph nodes, which were quite swollen. The pilot was definitely fighting off something. Something related to the airplane deaths—or merely something he had picked up over the course of his travels?

Redfern said, "Such a young aircraft, and an all-around beautiful machine. I just can't see it shutting down so completely. It's got to be sabotage."

"We've tested the oxygen mix and the water tanks, and both came back clean. Nothing to indicate why people died or why the plane went dark." Eph massaged the pilot's armpits, finding more jelly-bean-size lymph nodes there. "You still remember nothing about the landing?"

"Nothing. It's driving me crazy."

"Can you think of any reason the cockpit door would be unlocked?"

"None. Completely against FAA regulations."

Nora said, "Did you happen to spend any time up in the crew rest area?"

"The bunk?" Redfern said. "I did, yeah. Caught a few z's over the Atlantic."

"Do you remember if you put the seat backs down?"

"They were already down. You need the leg room if you're stretching out up there. Why?"

Eph said, "You didn't see anything out of the ordinary?"

"Up there? Not a thing. What's to see?"

Eph stood back. "Do you know anything about a large cabinet loaded into the cargo area?"

Captain Redfern shook his head, trying to puzzle it out. "No idea. But it sounds like you're on to something."

"Not really. Still as baffled as you are." Eph crossed his arms. Nora had switched on her Luma light and was going over Redfern's arms with it. "Which is why your agreeing to stay is so critical right now. I want to run a full battery of tests on you."

Captain Redfern watched the indigo light shine over his flesh. "If you think you can figure out what happened, I'll be your guinea pig."

Eph nodded their appreciation.

"When did you get this scar?" asked Nora.

"What scar?"

She was looking at his neck, the front of his throat. He tipped his head back so that she could touch the fine line that showed up deep blue under her Luma. "Looks almost like a surgical incision."

Redfern felt for it himself. "There's nothing."

Indeed, when she switched off the lamp, the line was all but invisible. She turned it back on and Eph examined the line. Maybe a half inch across, a few millimeters thick. The tissue growth over the wound appeared quite recent.

"We'll do some imaging later tonight. MRI should show us something."

Redfern nodded, and Nora turned off her light wand. "You know . . . there is one other thing." Redfern hesitated, his airline pilot's confidence fading for a moment. "I do remember something, but it won't be of any use to you, I don't think . . ."

Eph shrugged almost imperceptibly. "We'll take anything you can give us."

"Well, when I blacked out . . . I dreamed of something—something very old . . ." The captain looked around, almost ashamedly, then started talking in a very low voice. "When I was a kid . . . at night . . . I used to sleep in this big bed in my grandmother's home. And every night, at midnight, as the bells chimed in the church nearby, I used to see a thing come out from behind a big old armoire. Every night, without fail—it would poke out its black head and long arms and bony shoulders . . . and *stare* at me . . ."

"Stare?" asked Eph.

"It had a jagged mouth, with thin, black lips . . . and it would look at me, and just . . . smile."

Eph and Nora were both transfixed, the intimacy of the confession and its dreamlike tone both unexpected.

"And then I would start screaming, and my grandmother would turn on the light and take me to her bed. It went on for years. I called him Mr. Leech. Because his skin . . . that black skin looked just like the engorged leeches we used to pick up in a nearby stream. Child psychiatrists looked at me and talked to me and called it 'night terrors' and gave me reasons not to believe in him, but . . . every night he came back. Every night I would sink under my pillows, hiding from him—but it was useless. I knew he was there, in the room . . ." Redfern grimaced. "We moved out some years later and my grandmother sold the armoire and I never saw it again. Never dreamed of it again."

Eph had listened carefully. "You'll have to excuse me, Captain . . . but what does this have to do with . . . ?"

"I'm coming to that," he said. "The only thing I remember between our descent and waking up here—is that he came back. In my dreams. I saw him again, this Mr. Leech . . . and he was smiling."

THE BURNING HOLE

HIS NIGHTMARES WERE ALWAYS THE SAME: ABRAHAM, OLD or young, naked and kneeling before the huge hole in the ground, the bodies burning below as a Nazi officer moved down the row of kneeling prisoners, shooting them in the back of the head.

The burning hole was behind the infirmary in the extermination camp known as Treblinka. Prisoners too sick or too old to work were taken through the white-painted barracks with a red cross painted on it, and into the hole they went. Young Abraham saw many die there, but he himself came close to it only once.

He tried to avoid notice, worked in silence, and kept to himself. Each morning he pricked his finger and smeared a drop of blood on each cheek in order to appear as healthy as possible at roll call.

He first saw the hole while repairing some shelving in the infirmary. At age sixteen, Abraham Setrakian was a yellow patch, a craftsman. He curried no favor; he was no one's pet, merely a slave with a talent for woodwork that, in a death camp, was a talent for living. He had some value for the Nazi Hauptmann who used him without mercy, without regard, and without end. He raised barbed-wire fences, crafted a library set, repaired the railways. He carved elaborate pipes for the Ukrainian guard captain at Christmastime in '42.

It was his hands that kept Abraham away from the hole. At dusk he could see its glow, and sometimes from his workshop the smell of flesh and petrol mixed with sawdust. As his fear took hold of his heart, so did the hole take residence there.

To this day, Setrakian still felt it in him, every time fear took hold—whether crossing a dark street, closing his shop at night, or upon waking from the nightmares—the tatters of his memories revived. Himself kneeling, naked, praying. In his dreams he could feel the mouth of the gun pressing against his neck.

Extermination camps had no function other than killing. Treblinka was disguised to look like a train station, with travel posters and timetables, and greenery woven into the barbed wire. He arrived there in September 1942 and spent all of his time working. "Earning his breath," he called it. He was a quiet man, young but well raised, full of wisdom and compassion. He helped as many prisoners as he could and prayed in silence all the time. Even with the atrocities he witnessed daily, he believed that God was watching over all men.

But one winter night, in the eyes of a dead thing, Abraham saw the devil. And understood the ways of the world to be different from what he'd thought.

It was past midnight and the camp was as quiet as Setrakian ever saw it. The forest murmur had quieted down and the cold air was splitting his bones. He shifted quietly in his bunk and gazed blindly at the darkness surrounding him. And then he heard it—

Pick-pick-pick.

Exactly as his *bubbeh* had said . . . it sounded exactly as she'd said . . . and for some reason that made it all the more frightful . . .

His breath vanished and he felt in his heart the burning hole. In a corner of the barracks, the darkness moved. A *Thing*, a towering gaunt figure peeled off from the inky depths and glided over his sleeping comrades.

Pick-pick-pick.

Sardu. Or a Thing that once had been him. Its skin was shriveled and dark, blending with the fold of its dark, loose robes. Much like an animated blotch of ink. The Thing moved effortlessly, a weightless phantom gliding across the floor. Its talonlike toenails scraped the wood ever so softly.

But—it couldn't be. The world was real—evil was real, and surrounding him all the time—but this could not be real. This was a *bubbeh meiseh*. A *bubbeh*—

Pick-pick-pick . . .

In a matter of seconds, the long-dead Thing reached the bunk across from Setrakian. Abraham could smell it now: dried leaves and earth and mold. He could see hints of its blackened face as it emerged from the bundled darkness of the body—and leaned forward, smelling the neck of Zadawski, a young Pole, a hard worker. The Thing stood the height of the barracks, its head among the beams above, breathing hard and hollowly, excited, hungry. It moved along to the next bunk, where its face was briefly outlined by the light of a nearby window.

The darkened skin became translucent, like a sliver of dry meat against the light. It was all dry and matte—except for its eyes: two gleaming spheres that seemed to glow intermittently, like lumps of burning coal catching a reanimating breath. Its dry lips drew back to reveal mottled gums and two rows of small, yellowed teeth, impossibly sharp.

It paused above the frail form of Ladizlav Zajak, an old man from Grodno, a late arrival sickened with tuberculosis. Setrakian had supported Zajak since his arrival, showing him the ropes and shielding him from scrutiny. His disease alone was reason enough for instant execution—but Setrakian claimed him as his assistant, and kept him away from the SS overseers and Ukrainian guards at critical times. But Zajak was gone now. His lungs were giving out, and, more important, he had lost the will to live: shutting down, seldom speaking, constantly crying in silence. He had become a liability to Setrakian's survival, but his entreaties no longer inspired the old man—Setrakian hearing him shudder with silent coughing spasms and quietly sobbing until dawn.

But now, towering above him, the Thing observed Zajak. The arrhythmic breathing of the old man seemed to please it. Like the angel of death, it extended its darkness over the man's frail body and clucked its dry palate eagerly.

What the Thing did then . . . Setrakian could not see. There was noise, but his ears refused to hear it. This great, gloating Thing bent over the old man's head and neck. Something about its posture indicated . . . a feeding. Zajak's old body twitched and spasmed ever so lightly, but, remarkably, the old man never awoke.

And never did again.

Setrakian muffled a gasp with his hand. And the feeding Thing didn't seem to mind him. It spent time over the various sick and infirm. By night's end, three corpses were left behind, and the thing looked flushed—its skin suppler but equally dark.

Setrakian saw the Thing fade away into the darkness and leave. Cautiously, he got up and moved next to the bodies. He looked them over in the faint light, and there was no sign of any trauma—other than a thin slit in the neck. A breach so thin as to be nearly imperceptible. If he hadn't witnessed the horror himself . . .

Then it dawned on him. This Thing. It would return again—and soon. This camp was a fertile feeding ground, and it would graze on the unnoticed, the forgotten, the inconsequential. It would feed on them. All of them.

Unless someone rose up to stop it.

Someone.

Him.

Coach

Flight 753 survivor Ansel Barbour huddled with his wife, Ann-Marie, and his two children, eight-year-old Benjy and five-year-old Haily, on a blue chintz sofa in the back sunroom of their three-bedroom home in Flatbush, New York. Even Pap and Gertie got into the act, the two big Saint Bernards allowed inside the house for this special occasion, so happy to see him home, their man-size paws leaning on his knees and patting gratefully at his chest.

Ansel had been seated in aisle seat 39G, in coach, returning home from an employer-paid database security training session in Potsdam, southwest of Berlin. He was a computer programmer embarking on a four-month contract with a New Jersey–based retailer following the electronic theft of millions of customers' credit card numbers. He had never been out of the country before, and had missed his family intensely. Downtime and sightseeing tours were built into the four-day conference, but Ansel never ventured outside his hotel, preferring to remain inside his room with his laptop, talking to the kids via Webcam and playing hearts over the Internet with strangers.

His wife, Ann-Marie, was a superstitious, sheltered woman, and Flight 753's tragic end only confirmed her closely held fears of air travel and new experiences in general. She did not drive a car. She lived in the grip of dozens of borderline obsessive-compulsive routines, including touching and repetitively cleaning every mirror in the house, which reliably warded off bad luck. Her parents had died in an automobile accident when she was four—she'd survived the crash—and she was raised by an unmarried aunt who passed away just one week before Ann-Marie and Ansel's wedding. The births of her children had only intensified Ann-Marie's isolation, amplifying her fears, to the point where she would often go days without leaving the safety of her own house, relying exclusively on Ansel for anything involving a transaction with the outside world.

The news of the crippled airplane had brought her to her knees. Ansel's subsequent survival revived her with the power of an exultation that she could define only in religious terms, a deliverance confirming and consecrating the absolute necessity of her redundant, life-preserving routines.

Ansel, for his part, was intensely relieved to be back home. Both Ben and Haily tried to pile on top of him, but he had to hold them off due to the lingering pain in his neck. The tightness—his muscles felt like ropes being torturously twisted—was centralized in his throat, but extended past the hinges of his jaw up to his ears. When you twist a rope, it shortens, and that was how his muscles felt. He stretched his neck, hoping for some chiropractic relief—

SNAP . . . CRACKLE . . . POP . . .

—which nearly doubled him over. The pain wasn't worth the effort.

Later, Ann-Marie walked in on him in the kitchen as he was replacing her economy-size bottle of ibuprofen in the high cabinet over the stove. He popped six at once, the daily recommended dosage—and was barely able to get them down.

Her fearful eyes drained of all cheer. "What is it?"

"Nothing," he said, though he was in too much discomfort to shake his head. But best not to worry her. "Just stiffness from the plane. The way my head hung, probably."

She remained in the doorway, pulling at her fingers. "Maybe you shouldn't have left the hospital."

"And how would you have been able to get by?" he shot back, being shorter with her than he'd planned.

SNAP, CRACKLE, AND POP—

"But what if . . . what if you have to go back in? What if, this time, they want you to stay?"

It was exhausting, having to dismiss her fears at the expense of his own. "I can't miss any work as it is. You know we're right on the edge with our finances."

They were a one-income household in an America of two-income households. And Ansel couldn't take a second job, because then who would do the grocery shopping?

She said, "You know I . . . I couldn't get along without you." They never discussed her illness. At least, never in terms of it *being* an illness. "I need you. *We* need you."

Ansel's shoulder nod was more like a bow, dipping at his waist instead of his neck. "My God, when I think about all those people." He pictured his seatmates from the long flight. The family with three grown children two rows in front of him. The older couple sitting across the aisle, sleeping most of the way, white-haired heads sharing the same travel pillow. The bleached-blond flight attendant who dripped diet soda on his lap. "Why me, you know? Is there some reason I survived?"

"There *is* a reason," she said, her hands flat against her chest. "Me."

Later, Ansel took the dogs back out to their backyard shed. The yard was the main reason they'd bought this house: plenty of play room for the kids and the dogs. Ansel had Pap and Gertie before he'd ever met Ann-Marie, and she had fallen in love with them at least as much as she had him. They loved her back, no conditions. As did Ansel, and as did the kids—although Benjy, the older one, was starting to question her eccentricities here and there. Especially when they caused a conflict with an eight-year-old's schedule of baseball practices and play dates. Already Ansel could sense Ann-Marie pulling back from him a bit. But Pap and Gertie would never challenge her, so long as she kept overfeeding them. He feared for the kids as they grew up, feared that they might outgrow their mother at too early an age, and never truly understand why she might appear to favor the dogs over them.

Inside the old garden shed, a metal fence pole was driven into the center floorboards, with two chains attached to it. Gertie had run off earlier that year, coming back with switch marks all over her back and legs, somebody having taken a whipping stick to her. So they chained up the dogs at night now, for their own protection. Ansel slowly— keeping his neck and head aligned, minimizing discomfort—set down their food and water, then ran his hand over the tufts of their enormous heads as they ate, just making them real, appreciating them for what they were at the end of this lucky day. He went out and closed the door after chaining them to the pole, and stood looking at his house from the back, trying to imagine this world without him in it. Ansel had seen his children weep today, and he had wept with them. His family needed him more than anything.

A sudden, piercing pain in his neck shook him. He grabbed for the corner of the dog shed in order to keep from falling over, and for several moments stood frozen like that, doubled over to one side, shivering and riding out this flaring, knifing pain. It passed finally, leaving him with a seashell-like roaring in one ear. He probed his neck gently with his fingers, too tender to touch. He tried to stretch it, to improve his mobility, tipping his head back as far as he could toward the night sky. Airplane lights up there, stars.

I survived, he thought. *The worst is over. This soon will pass.*

That night he had a horrifying dream. His children were being chased through the house by some rampaging beast, but when Ansel ran to save them, he found he had monster claws for hands. He woke up with his half of the bed soaked in sweat, and climbed out quickly—only to be gripped by another seizure of pain.

SNAP

His ears, jaw, and throat were fused together by the same taut ache, leaving him unable to swallow.

CRACKLE

The pain of that basic esophageal retraction was nearly crippling.

And then there was the thirst. Like nothing he had ever felt—an urge that would not stop.

When he could move again, he walked across the hall and into the dark kitchen. He opened the fridge and poured himself a tall glass of lemonade, then another, and another . . . and soon he was drinking straight from the pitcher. But nothing would quench the thirst. Why was he sweating so much?

The stains on his nightshirt had a heavy odor—vaguely musky—and the sweat had an amber tint. So hot in here . . .

As he placed the pitcher back in the fridge, he spotted a plate with marinating meat. He saw the sinuous strands of blood mixing lazily with oil and vinegar, and his mouth watered. Not at the prospect of grilling it, but at the idea of biting it—of sinking his teeth into it and tearing it and draining it. At the idea of drinking the blood.

POP

He wandered into the main hallway and took a peek at the kids. Benjy was balled up under Scooby-Doo sheets; Haily was snoring softly with her arm dangling off the side of her mattress, reaching for picture books that had fallen there. Seeing them allowed him to relax his shoulders and catch his breath a bit. He stepped out into the backyard to cool off, the night air chilling the dried sweat on his skin. Being home, he felt, being with his family, could cure him of anything. They would help him.

They would provide.

Office of the Chief Medical Examiner, Manhattan

THERE WAS NO BLOOD on the medical examiner who met Eph and Nora. That alone was a strange sight. Normally it ran down their waterproof gowns and stained their plastic sleeves up to the elbows. But not today. The M.E. might as well have been a Beverly Hills gynecologist.

He introduced himself as Gossett Bennett, a brown-skinned man with browner eyes, a purposeful face behind a plastic shield. "We're just getting under way here," he said, waving at the tables. The autopsy room was a noisy place. Whereas an operating room is sterile and silent, the morgue is its direct opposite: a bustling space hectic with whining saws, running water, and dictating doctors. "We've got eight going from your airplane."

Bodies lay upon eight guttered tables of cold stainless steel. The airline fatalities were in various stages of autopsy, two of them fully "canoed": that is, their chests had already been eviscerated, the removed organs laid out on an open plastic bag on their shins, a pathologist paring away samples on a cutting board like a cannibal preparing a platter of human sashimi. The wounded necks had been dissected and the tongues pulled through, the faces folded halfway down like latex masks, exposing the skullcaps, which had been opened with the circular saw. One brain was in the process of being severed from its attachment to the spinal cord, whereupon it would be placed in a formalin solution to harden, the last step of an autopsy. A morgue attendant was standing by with wadding, and a large curved needle threaded with heavy waxed twine, to refill the emptied skull.

A long-handled pair of hardware-store pruning shears was being passed from one table to the next, where another attendant stood on a metal footstool over an open-chested body and began cracking ribs one at a time, so that the entire rib cage and sternum could be lifted out whole. The smell was an absorbing stew of Parmesan cheese, methane, and rotten eggs.

"After you called, I began checking their necks," said Bennett. "All the bodies so far present the same laceration you spoke of. But no scar. An open wound, as precise and clean as any I've ever seen."

He showed them to an undissected female body laid out on a table. A six-inch metal block beneath her neck made her head fall back, arching her chest, extending her neck. Eph probed the skin over the woman's throat with his gloved fingers.

He noticed the faint line—as thin as a paper cut—and gently parted the wound. He was shocked by its neatness as well as its apparent depth. Eph released her skin, and the breach closed lazily, like a sleepy eyelid or a timid smile.

"What could have caused this?" he asked.

"Nothing in nature, not that I know of," said Bennett. "Notice the scalpel-like precision. Almost calibrated, you might say, both in aim and length. And yet—the edges are rounded, which is to say, almost organic in appearance."

"How deep?" asked Nora.

"A clean breach, straight in, puncturing the wall of the common carotid, but stopping there. Not going out the other side, not rupturing the artery."

"In every case?" gasped Nora.

"Every one I've looked at so far. Every body bears the laceration, though if you hadn't alerted me, I have to admit I might not have noticed it. Especially with everything else going on with these bodies."

"What else?"

"We'll get there in a moment. Each laceration is on the neck, either front or side. Excluding one female who had hers on the chest, high above her heart. And one male we had to search, and eventually found the breach on the upper inside thigh, over the femoral artery.

Each wound perforated skin and muscle, ending exactly inside a major artery."

"A needle?" ventured Eph.

"But finer than that. I . . . I need to do more research into it, we're just at the beginning here. And there's plenty of other freaky shit going down. You're aware of this, I assume?" Bennett led them to the door of a walk-in refrigerator. Inside, it was wider than a two-car garage. There were fifty or so gurneys, most containing a crash bag unzipped down to the corpse's chest. A handful were fully unzipped, those bodies nude—having already been weighed, measured, and photographed—and ready for the autopsy table. There were also eight or so corpses unrelated to Flight 753, lying on bare gurneys without crash bags, bearing standard yellow toe tags.

Refrigeration slows decomposition, in the same way it preserves fruits and vegetables and delays cold cuts from spoiling. But the airplane bodies hadn't spoiled at all. Thirty-six hours out, and they looked nearly as fresh as when Eph had first boarded the plane. As opposed to the yellow-tagged corpses, which were bloating, effluvium oozing from every orifice like a black purge, flesh going dark green and leatherlike from evaporation.

"These are some pretty good-looking dead people," said Bennett.

Eph felt a chill that had nothing to do with the temperature in the cooler. He and Nora both waded in, three rows deep. The bodies looked—not healthy, for they were shrunken and bloodlessly wan—but not long dead. They bore the characteristic mask of the deceased, but it was as though they had just passed over, not thirty minutes ago.

They followed Bennett back out into the autopsy room, to the same female corpse—a woman in her early forties with no distinguishing marks other than a decade-old cesarean scar below the bikini line—being prepped for incision. But instead of a scalpel, Bennett reached for a tool never used inside a morgue. A stethoscope.

"I noticed this earlier," he said, offering the scope to Eph. Eph put in the ear plugs, and Bennett called for everyone else in the room to stop, for silence. A pathology assistant rushed around turning off the running water.

Bennett laid the acoustic end of the stethoscope against the corpse's chest, just below her sternum. Eph listened with trepidation, afraid of what he was to hear. But he heard nothing. He looked at Bennett again, who showed no expression, waiting. Eph closed his eyes and focused.

Faint. Very faint. A squirming sound, almost like that of something wriggling in mud. A slow sound, so maddeningly slight he couldn't be altogether certain he wasn't imagining it.

He gave the scope to Nora to have a listen.

"Maggots?" she said, straightening.

Bennett shook his head. "In fact there is no infestation at all, accounting in part for the lack of decay. But there *are* some other intriguing abnormalities . . ."

Bennett waved everyone else to return to their work, selecting, from a side tray, a big number 6 blade scalpel. But instead of starting in on the chest with the usual Y-shaped incision, he took a large-mouthed stock jar from the enameled counter and placed it beneath the corpse's left hand. He drew the scalpel blade abruptly across the underside of the wrist, slicing it open like the rind of an orange.

A pale, opalescent liquid sprayed at first, some of it spurting out onto his gloves and his hip on the initial cut, then sluicing steadily out of the arm, singing into the bottom of the jar. Flowing fast, but then, lacking any circulatory pressure from its stilled heart, losing force after about three ounces or so. Bennett lowered the arm to draw out more.

Eph's shock at the callousness of the cut was quickly overcome by his amazement at the sight of the flow. This couldn't be blood. Blood settles and congeals after death. It doesn't drain out like engine oil.

Nor does it turn white. Bennett returned the arm to the corpse's side and held up the jar for Eph to see.

Lieutenant—the corpses—they're . . .

"At first I thought maybe the proteins were separating, the way oil sits on top of water," Bennett said. "But it's not quite that either."

The issue was pasty white, almost as though sour milk had been introduced into the bloodstream.

Lieutenant . . . oh, Jesus—

Eph could not believe what he was seeing.

Nora said, "They're all like this?"

Bennett nodded. "Exsanguinated. They have no blood."

Eph eyed the white matter in the jar, and his taste for whole milk turned his stomach.

Bennett said, "I've got some other things. Core temperature is elevated. Somehow these bodies are still generating heat. Additionally, we've found dark spots on some organs. Not necrosis, but almost more like . . . like bruising."

Bennett set the jar of opalescent fluid back down on the counter and called over a pathology assistant. She brought with her an opaque plastic tub of the same sort that take-out soup comes in. She peeled off the top and Bennett reached inside, removing an organ, setting it on a cutting board like a small, fresh-from-the-butcher roast. It was an undissected human heart. He pointed a gloved finger at where it would have joined the arteries. "See the valves? Almost as if they have grown open. Now, they couldn't have operated like this in life. Not closing and opening and pumping blood. So this can't have been congenital."

Eph was aghast. This abnormality was a fatal defect. As every anatomist knows, people look just as different on the inside as they do on the outside. But no human being could conceivably have survived to adulthood with this heart.

Nora asked, "Do you have medical records for the patient? Anything we can check this against?"

"Nothing yet. Probably not until morning. But it's made me slow this process down. *Way* down. I'm stopping in a little while, shutting down for the night so I can get some more support in here tomorrow. I want to check every little thing. Such as—this."

Bennett walked them down to a fully anatomized body, that of a midweight adult male. His neck had been dissected back to the throat, exposing the larynx and trachea, so that the vocal folds, or vocal cords, were visible just above the larynx.

Bennett said, "See the vestibular folds?"

They were also known as "false vocal cords": thick mucous membranes whose only function is to sit above and protect the true vocal folds. They are a true anatomical oddity in that they can regenerate themselves completely, even after surgical removal.

Eph and Nora leaned in closer. Both saw the outgrowth from the vestibular folds, a pinkish, fleshy protuberance—not disruptive or malformed like a tumorous mass, but branching from and within the inner throat, below the tongue. A novel, seemingly spontaneous augmentation of the soft lower mandible.

They scrubbed up outside, more diligently than usual. Both were deeply shaken by what they had seen inside the morgue.

Eph spoke first. "I'm wondering when things are going to start making sense again." He dried his hands completely, feeling the open air against his gloveless hands. Then he felt his own neck, over the throat, approximately where the incisions were all located. "A straight, deep puncture wound in the neck. And a virus that slows antemortem decomposition on the one hand, yet apparently causes spontaneous antemortem tissue growth on the other?"

Nora said, "This is something new."

"Or—something very, very old."

They started out the delivery door, to Eph's illegally parked Explorer, his EMERGENCY BLOOD DELIVERY pass on the dash. The last streaks of daytime warmth were leaving the sky. Nora said, "We need to check out the other morgues, see if they are finding the same deviations."

The alarm went off on Eph's cell phone. A text message from Zack:

whre R U ???? Z

"Shit," said Eph. "I forgot . . . the custody hearing . . ."

"Now?" Nora said, before catching herself. "Okay. You go. I'll meet you after—"

"No, I'll call them—it will be fine." He looked around, feeling himself splitting in two. "We need to take another look at the pilot. Why did his puncture close up, but not the others'? We need to get on top of the physiopathology of this thing."

"And the other survivors."

Eph frowned, reminded that they were gone. "It's not like Jim to screw up like that."

Nora wanted to defend Jim. "If they're getting sick, they'll come back."

"Only—it might be too late. For them, and for us."

"What do you mean, for us?"

"To get to the bottom of this thing. There's got to be an answer somewhere, an explanation. A rationale. Something impossible is happening, and we need to find out why and stop it."

Up on the sidewalk at the main entrance on First Street, news crews were set up for live remotes from the medical examiner's office. That attracted a sizable crowd of onlookers, whose nervousness was palpable from around the corner. Lots of uncertainty in the air.

But one man broke from the crowd, a man Eph had noticed on the way in. An old man with birch white hair, holding a walking stick that was too tall for him, gripping it, like a staff, below its high silver handle. Like a dinner-theater Moses, except that he was impeccably dressed, formal and old-fashioned, in a light black overcoat over a gabardine suit, with a gold watch chain looped on his vest. And—oddly for the otherwise distinguished wardrobe—gray wool gloves with the fingertips cut off.

"Dr. Goodweather?"

The old man knew his name. Eph gave him another look, and said, "Do I know you?"

The man spoke with an accent, maybe Slavic. "I saw you on the box. The TV. I knew you would have to come here."

"You've been waiting here for me?"

"What I have to say, Doctor, it is very important. Critical."

Eph was distracted by the handle on top of the old man's tall walking stick: a silver wolf's head. "Well, not now . . . call my office, make an appointment . . ." He moved away, dialing rapidly on his cell phone.

The old man appeared anxious, an agitated man striving to speak calmly. He put on his best gentlemanly smile, including Nora in his introduction. "Abraham Setrakian is my name. Which should mean nothing to you." He gestured, with his walking stick, at the morgue. "You saw them in there. The passengers from the airplane."

Nora said, "You know something about that?"

"Indeed," he said, sending a grateful smile her way. Setrakian glanced at the morgue again, like a man who, having waited so long to speak, was uncertain where to start. "You found them not much changed in there, no?"

Eph turned off his cell phone before it rang through. The old man's words echoed his own irrational fears. "Not changed how?" he said.

"The dead. Bodies not breaking down."

Eph said, more out of concern than intrigue, "So that is what people are hearing out here?"

"No one had to tell me anything, Doctor. I know."

"You 'know,'" said Eph.

"Tell us," said Nora. "What else do you know?"

The old man cleared his throat. "Have you found a . . . coffin?"

Eph felt Nora rise up almost three inches off the sidewalk. Eph said, "What did you say?"

"A coffin. If you have it, then you still have him."

Nora said, "*Him* who?"

"Destroy it. Right away. Do not keep it for study. You must destroy the coffin, without delay."

Nora shook her head. "It's gone," she said. "We don't know where it is."

Setrakian swallowed with bitter disappointment. "It is as I feared."

"Why destroy it?" asked Nora.

Eph cut in then, saying to Nora, "If this kind of talk is getting around, people will panic." He looked at the old man. "Who are you? How did you hear these things?"

"I am a pawnbroker. I heard nothing. These things I *know*."

"You know?" said Nora. "How do you know?"

"Please." He focused on Nora now, the more receptive one. "What I am about to say, I do not say lightly. I say it desperately and with utter honesty. Those bodies in there?" He pointed at the morgue. "I tell you, before this night falls, they must be destroyed."

"Destroyed?" said Nora, reacting negatively to him for the first time. "Why?"

"I recommend incineration. Cremation. It is simple and sure."

"*That's him*," came a voice from the side doors, a morgue official leading a uniformed New York City patrolman toward them. Toward Setrakian.

The old man ignored them, speaking faster now. "Please. It is almost too late."

"Right there," said the morgue official, marching over, pointing out Setrakian to the cop. "That's the guy."

The cop, amiable and bored, said to Setrakian, "Sir?"

Setrakian ignored him, pleading his case directly to Nora and Eph. "A truce has been broken. An ancient, sacred pact. By a man who is no longer a man, but an abomination. A walking, devouring abomination."

"Sir," said the cop. "May I have a word with you, sir?"

Setrakian reached out and grasped Eph's wrist, to command his attention. "He is here now, here in the New World, this city, this very day. This night. Do you understand? He must be stopped."

The wool-covered fingers of the old man's hand were gnarled, claw-like. Eph pulled away from him, not roughly but enough to jostle the old man backward. His walking stick whacked the cop on the shoulder, almost in the face—and suddenly the cop's disinterest turned to anger.

"Okay, that's it," said the cop, twisting the walking stick out of his hands and bracing the old man's arm. "Let's go."

"You must stop him here," Setrakian continued, being led away.

Nora turned to the morgue official. "What's this about? What are you doing?"

The official glanced at the laminated identification cards hanging from their necks—the red letters reading CDC—before answering. "He tried to get inside earlier, claiming to be a family member. Insisting on viewing the dead bodies." The official looked at him being taken away. "Some kind of ghoul."

The old man continued to plead his case. "Ultraviolet light," he called over his shoulder. "Go over the bodies with ultraviolet light . . ."

Eph froze. Had he just heard that?

"Then you will see I am right," yelled the old man, being folded into the backseat of a cruiser. "Destroy them. Now. Before it is too late . . ."

Eph watched them slam the door on the old man, the cop climbing behind the wheel and pulling away.

Excess Baggage

EPH'S CALL RANG through forty minutes late to his, Kelly's, and Zack's fifty-minute session with Dr. Inga Kempner, their court-appointed family therapist. He was relieved not to be sitting inside her first-floor office in a prewar brownstone in Astoria, the place where the final custody issues were to be decided.

Eph pled his case through the doctor's speakerphone. "Let me explain—I've been dealing all weekend with the most extreme of circumstances. This dead-airplane situation out at Kennedy. It couldn't be helped."

Dr. Kempner said, "This isn't the first time you've failed to present yourself at an appointment."

"Where's Zack?" he said.

"Out in the waiting area," said Dr. Kempner.

She and Kelly had been talking without him. Things had already been decided. It was all over before it had even begun.

"Look, Dr. Kempner—all I ask is that you reschedule our appointment . . ."

"Dr. Goodweather, I am afraid that—"

"No—wait—please, hold on." He cut right to it. "Look, am I the perfect father? No, I'm not. I admit that. Points for honesty, right? In fact, I'm not even sure I'd want to be the 'perfect' father, and raise some plain vanilla kid who's not going to make a difference in this world. But I do know that I want to be the best father I can be. Because that is what Zack deserves. And that is my only goal right now."

"All appearances to the contrary," said Dr. Kempner.

Eph gave his phone the finger. Nora stood just a few feet away. He felt angry, yet strangely exposed and vulnerable.

"Listen to me," said Eph, fighting hard to keep his cool. "I know that you know I have rearranged my life around this situation, around Zack. I established this office in New York City specifically so that I could be here, near his mother, so that he would have the benefit of us both. I—usually—have very regular hours during the week, a dependable schedule, with established off-call times. I'm working doubles on weekends in order to have two off for every one I'm on."

"Did you attend an AA meeting this weekend?"

Eph grew silent. All the air went out of his tires. "Were you even listening?"

"Have you felt the need to drink?"

"No," he grunted, making a supreme effort to keep his cool. "I've been sober twenty-three months, you know that."

Dr. Kempner said, "Dr. Goodweather, this isn't a question of who loves your son more. It never is, in these situations. Wonderful, that you both care *so* much, *so* deeply. Your dedication to Zack is plainly evident. But, as is so often the case, there seems to be no way to prevent this from turning into a contest. The state of New York issues guidelines I must follow in my recommendation to the judge."

Eph swallowed bitterly. He tried to interrupt, but she kept on talking.

"You've resisted the court's original custodial inclination, you've fought it every step of the way. And I consider that a measure of your affection for Zachary. You have also made great personal strides, and that is both evident and admirable. But now we find that you have reached your court of last resort, if you will. In the formulas we use for arbitrating custody. Visitation rights, of course, have never been in question . . ."

"No, no, no," murmured Eph, like a man about to be rammed by an oncoming car. It was this same sinking feeling he'd had all weekend. He tried reaching back—to he and Zack sitting in his apartment, eating Chinese food and playing video games. The entire weekend stretched out before them. What a glorious feeling that had been.

"My point, Dr. Goodweather," said Dr. Kempner, "is that I can't see much purpose in going any further."

Eph turned to Nora, who looked up at him, understanding in an instant what he was going through.

"You can tell me it's over," Eph whispered into the phone. "But it's not over, Dr. Kempner. It never will be." And with that, he hung up.

He turned away, knowing Nora would respect him in this moment and not try to approach. And for that he was grateful, because there were tears in his eyes that he did not want her to see.

THE FIRST
NIGHT

J ust a few hours later, inside the basement morgue of the Office of the Chief Medical Examiner in Manhattan, Dr. Bennett was finishing up after a very long day. He should have been exhausted, but in fact he was exhilarated. Something extraordinary was happening. It was as though the normally reliable rules of death and decomposition were being rewritten, right in this room. This shit went beyond established medicine, beyond human biology itself . . . perhaps even into the realm of the miraculous.

As planned, he had halted all autopsies for the night. Some work continued on other matters, the medico-legal investigators operating out of the cubicles upstairs, but the morgue was Bennett's. He had noticed something during the CDC doctors' visit, something about the blood sample he had drawn, the opalescent fluid he had collected in a specimen jar. He had stored it in the back of one of the specimen coolers, stashing it behind some glassware like the last good dessert inside a community refrigerator.

He unscrewed the cap and looked at it now, seated on a stool at the examination counter near the sink. After a few moments, the surface of the six or so ounces of white blood rippled, and Bennett shivered. He took a deep breath in order to collect himself. He thought about what to do, and then pulled an identical jar down from the shelf above. He filled it with the same amount of water and set the jars down side by side. He needed to make certain that the disturbance was not the result of vibrations from a passing truck or some such.

He watched and waited.

There it was again. The viscous white fluid rippled—he saw it—while the considerably less dense water surface did not undulate at all.

Something was moving inside the blood sample.

Bennett thought for a moment. He poured the water down the sink drain, and then slowly poured the oily blood from one jar into the other. The fluid was syrupy and poured slowly but neatly. He saw nothing pass through the thin stream. The bottom of the first jar remained lightly coated with the white blood, but he saw nothing there.

He set the new jar down, and again he watched and waited.

He did not have to watch very long. The surface undulated and Bennett nearly leaped out of his stool.

He heard a noise behind him then, a scratching or a rustling sound. He turned, made jumpy by his discovery. Overhead lamps shone down on the empty stainless-steel tables behind him, every surface wiped down, the floor drains mopped clean. The Flight 753 victims locked away inside the walk-in cooler across the morgue.

Rats, maybe. There was nothing they could do to keep the vermin out of the building—and they had tried everything. In the walls. Or beneath the floor drains. He listened for a moment longer, then returned to the jar.

He poured the liquid from jar to jar again, this time stopping halfway. The amounts in each jar were roughly even. He set them underneath the overhead lamp and watched the milky surface for a sign of life.

There it was. In the first jar. A *plip* this time, almost like that of a small fish nibbling at the surface of a cloudy pond.

Bennett watched the other jar until he was satisfied, and then poured its contents down the drain. He then started over, again dividing the contents between the two glass vessels.

A siren in the street outside made him sit up. It passed, and in what should have been the ensuing silence, he heard sounds again. Movement-type sounds, behind him. Again he turned, feeling equal parts paranoid and foolish now. The room was empty, the morgue sterilized and still.

Yet . . . something was making that noise. He stood from his stool, silently, turning his head this way and that in order to get a fix on its source.

His divining directed his attention to the steel door of the walk-in refrigerator. He took a few steps toward it, all his senses attuned.

A rustling. A stirring. As though from inside. He had spent more than enough time down here not to be spooked by the mere proximity to the dead . . . but then he remembered the antemortem growth these corpses had exhibited. Clearly, these anxieties had prompted him to revert to the usual human taboos regarding the dead. Everything about his job flew in the face of normal human instinct. Cutting open corpses. Defiling cadavers, peeling faces back from skulls. Excising organs and flaying genitals. He smiled at himself in the empty room. So he was basically normal after all.

His mind playing tricks on him. Probably a glitch in the cooling fans or something. There was a safety switch inside the cooler, a big red button, in the event anyone ever got himself stuck in there accidentally.

He turned back to the jars. Watching them, waiting for more movement. He was wishing he had brought his laptop down in order to record his thoughts and impressions.

Plip.

He had been ready for it this time, his heart leaping but his body staying put. Still in the first jar. He poured out the other one and split the fluid a third time, approximately one ounce in each.

As he did this, he thought he saw something ride the spill from the first jar to the second. Something very thin, no more than an inch and a half in length—if indeed he saw what he thought he saw . . .

A worm. A fluke. Was this a parasitic disease? There were various examples of parasites reshaping hosts in order to serve their own reproductive aspects. Was this the explanation for the bizarre after-death changes he had seen on the autopsy table?

He held up the jar in question, swishing around the thinning white fluid underneath the lamplight. He eyed the contents carefully, closely . . . and yes . . . not once but twice, something slithered inside. Wriggled. Wire thin and as white as its surroundings, moving very fast.

Bennett had to isolate it. Dip it in formalin, and then study it, and identify it. If he had this one, he had dozens, maybe hundreds, maybe . . . who knows how many, circulating inside the other bodies in the—

A sharp *bang* from the cooler shocked him, made him jerk up, jostling the jar from his hand. It fell to the counter, but did not shatter—bouncing instead, clattering into the sink, spilling and splattering its contents. Bennett let loose a string of obscenities, searching the stainless-steel basin for the worm. Then he felt warmth on the back of his left hand. Some of the white blood had spattered on him, and was now stinging his flesh. Not burning, but mildly caustic, enough to hurt. He quickly ran cold water over it and wiped it off on his lab coat before it could damage his skin.

He whirled around then, facing the cooler. The bang he had heard was certainly no electrical malfunction, but more like a wheeled stretcher banging into another wheeled stretcher. Impossible . . . and his ire rose again. His worm had just gone down the drain. He would get another blood sample, and isolate this parasite. This discovery was his.

Still wiping his hand on the flap of his jacket, he went to the door and pulled on the handle, releasing the chamber's seal. A hiss of stale, refrigerated air breathed over him as the door opened wide.

Joan Luss, after having released herself and the others from the isolation ward, hired a car to take her straight to the weekend home in New Canaan, Connecticut, of one of the founding partners of her law firm. She'd had the driver pull over twice so she could retch out the window. A combination of flu and nerves. But no matter. She was victim class and advocate now. Aggrieved party and crusading counselor. Fighting for restitution for the families of the dead and for the four fortunate survivors. The white-shoe firm of Camins, Peters, and Lilly could be looking at 40 percent of the largest corporate-claim payout ever, bigger than Vioxx, bigger even than WorldCom.

Joan Luss, partner.

You think you're doing all right in Bronxville until you drive out into New Canaan. Bronxville, Joan's home, is a leafy village in Westchester County, fifteen miles north of midtown Manhattan, twenty-eight minutes by Metro-North train. Roger Luss worked in international finance for Clume and Fairstein, and traveled out of the country most weeks.

Joan had traveled quite a bit, but had to pull back after the children were born, because it didn't look good. But she missed it, and had thoroughly enjoyed her previous week in Berlin, at the Ritz-Carlton on the Potsdamer Platz. She and Roger, having grown so accustomed to hotel living, had emulated that very lifestyle in their home, with heated bathroom floors, a downstairs steam room, twice-weekly fresh flower deliveries, seven-day-a-week landscaping, and of course their house-keeper and laundress. Everything but turn-down service and a sweet on their pillows at night.

Buying into Bronxville several years before, with its lack of new construction and forbiddingly high tax rate, had been a big step up for them. But now, having had a taste of New Canaan—where lead partner Dory Camins lived like a feudal lord on a three-house estate complete with a fishing pond, horse stables, and an equestrian track—Bronxville, on her way back, had struck her as quaint, provincial, even a little . . . tired.

Now home, she had just awakened after suffering through a tremulous late-afternoon nap. Roger was still in Singapore, and she kept hearing noises in the house, noises that finally scared her awake. Restless anxiety. She attributed it to the meeting, perhaps the biggest meeting of her life.

Joan emerged from her study, holding the wall on her way downstairs, coming into the kitchen as Neeva, the children's wonderful nanny, was clearing away the dinner mess, running a damp cloth over the table crumbs. "Oh, Neeva, I could have done that," said Joan, not meaning a word of it, walking right to the tall glass cabinet where she kept their medicine. Neeva was a Haitian grandmother who lived in Yonkers, one town over. She was sixty-something, but looked basically ageless, always wearing a long ankle-length floral dress and comfortable Converse sneakers. Neeva was a much-needed calming influence in the Luss home. They were a busy bunch, what with Roger's traveling and Joan's long hours in the city and the children's school and programs in between, everyone going in sixteen different directions. Neeva was the family rudder, and Joan's secret weapon in keeping the household running right.

"Joan, you don't look so good."

"Joan" and "don't" came out sounding like "Jon" and "don" in Neeva's island lilt.

"Oh, I'm just a little run-down." She popped some Motrin and two Flexerils and sat down at the kitchen island, opening *House Beautiful*.

"You should eat," said Neeva.

"Hurts to swallow," said Joan.

"Soup, then," decreed Neeva, and set about getting it for her.

Neeva was a mother figure for all of them, not just the children. And why shouldn't Joan have some mothering too? God knows, her real mother—twice divorced, living in an apartment in Hialeah, Florida—wasn't up to the task. And the best part? When Neeva's doting ways became too annoying, Joan could simply send her away on an errand with the kiddies. Best. Arrangement. Ever.

"I hear about that air-o-plane." Neeva looked back at Joan from the can opener. "No good. An evil thing."

Joan smiled at Neeva and her adorable little tropical superstitions—the smile cut abruptly short by a sharp pain in her jaw.

While the soup bowl rotated in the whirring microwave, Neeva came back to look at Joan, laying her roughened brown hand against Joan's forehead, exploring the glandular region of Joan's neck with gray-nailed fingers. Joan pulled back in pain.

"Swollen bad," Neeva said.

Joan closed the magazine. "Maybe I should go back to bed."

Neeva stood back, looking at her strangely. "You should go back to hospital."

Joan would have laughed if she knew it wouldn't hurt. Back to Queens? "Trust me, Neeva. I am much better off here in your hands. Besides—take it from one who knows. That whole hospital thing was an insurance ploy on the airline's behalf. All for their benefit—not mine."

As she rubbed her sore, swollen neck, Joan envisioned the impending lawsuit, and once again her spirits soared. She glanced around the kitchen. Funny how a house she had spent so much time and money redecorating and re-renovating could appear so suddenly . . . shabby.

Camins, Peters, Lilly . . . and Luss.

The children entered the kitchen then, Keene and Audrey, whining about some toy-related incident. Their voices worked their way inside Joan's head such that she was seized by a commanding urge to backhand them each hard enough to send them flying halfway across the kitchen. But she managed to do what she always did, channeling her aggression toward her children into false enthusiasm, thrown up like a wall around her angry self. She closed the magazine and raised her voice in order to silence theirs.

"How would you each like a pony, and your very own pond?"

She believed it was her generous bribe that had silenced the children, but it was in fact her smile, gargoylelike and glaring, baring an expression of utter hatred, that frightened them into stillness.

For Joan, the momentary silence was bliss.

The 911 call came in for a naked man at the Queens-Midtown Tunnel exits. The dispatch went out as a 10–50, a low-priority disorderly person call. A unit from the 1–7 arrived within eight minutes, and found a bad jam-up, worse than usual for a Sunday night. A few drivers honked and pointed them uptown. The suspect, they yelled, a fat guy wearing nothing but a red tag on his toe, had already moved on.

"I got kids here!" howled one guy in a dinged-up Dodge Caravan.

Officer Karn, the driver, said to his partner, Officer Lupo, "I'm gonna say Park Avenue type. Sex club regular. Took too much X before his weekend kink session."

Officer Lupo unbuckled and opened his door. "I'm on traffic duty. Loverboy's all yours."

"Thanks a lot," said Officer Karn to the slamming of the door. He lit up his rack and waited patiently—he wasn't paid extra to rush—for the traffic snarl to part for him.

He cruised up past Thirty-eighth, eyeballing cross streets. A fat naked guy on the loose shouldn't be too hard to find. People on the sidewalks seemed okay, not freaked. One helpful citizen smoking outside a bar saw the slow-rolling cruiser and stepped forward, pointing him up the street.

A second and third call came in, both for a naked man marauding outside the United Nations headquarters. Officer Karn hit the gas, looking to end this. He cruised past the lit-up flags of all the member nations flying out front, to the visitors' entrance at the north end. Blue NYPD sawhorses everywhere, as well as car-bomb deterring cement planters.

Karn rolled up on a detail of bored cops near the sawhorses. "I'm looking for a fat naked man."

One cop shrugged. "I could give you a few phone numbers."

Gabriel Bolivar returned by limousine to his new home in Manhattan, two town houses undergoing extensive renovations on Vestry Street, in Tribeca. When finished, the home would encompass thirty-one rooms and fourteen thousand total square feet, including a mosaic-lined swimming pool, servants' quarters for a staff of sixteen, a basement recording studio, and a twenty-six-seat movie theater.

Only the penthouse was finished and furnished, rushed into completion while Bolivar was away on his European tour. The rest of the rooms in the lower floors were roughed out, some of them plastered, others still dressed in plastic wrap and insulation. Sawdust had worked its way onto every surface and into every crevice. Bolivar's business manager had briefed him on the developments, but Bolivar wasn't much interested in the journey, only the destination of his soon-to-be lavish and decadent palace.

The "Jesus Wept" tour had ended on a down note. The promoters had had to work hard to fill the arenas so that Bolivar could truthfully claim to have played to sold-out audiences everywhere—but he had. Then the tour charter crapped out in Germany, and rather than wait behind with the others, Bolivar had consented to hop a commercial flight home. He was still feeling the aftereffects of that big mistake. In fact, it was getting worse.

He moved inside the front entrance with his security detail and three young ladies from the club. A few of his larger treasures had been moved in, including twin black marble panthers poised on either side of the twenty-foot-high foyer. Two blue industrial-waste drums said to have belonged to Jeffrey Dahmer and several rows of framed paintings: Mark Ryden, Robert Williams, Chet Zar—big, expensive stuff. The loose light switch on the wall activated a string of construction lights winding up the marble staircase, beyond a great, winged, weeping angel of uncertain provenance, having been "rescued" from a Romanian church during the Ceauşescu regime.

"He's beautiful," said one of the girls, looking up into the angel's shadowed, time-worn features.

Bolivar stumbled near the great angel, seized by a pain in his gut that was more than a cramp, that was like a punch from an adjoining organ. He gripped the angel's wing to steady himself, and the girls converged on him.

"Baby," they cooed, helping him to stand, and he tried to shake off the pain. Had someone slipped him something at the club? It had happened before. Christ, girls had drugged him before, so desperate were they to have their way with Gabriel Bolivar—to get the legend underneath the makeup. He pushed the three of them away, waving off his bodyguards as well, standing erect despite the ache. His detail remained below while he used his silver-encrusted walking stick to shoo the girls up the curling flights of blue-veined white marble to the penthouse.

He left the girls to mix themselves more drinks and fix themselves up in the other bathroom. Bolivar locked himself inside the master bath and dug out his Vicodin stash and self-medicated with two pretty white pills chased with a gulp of scotch. He rubbed his neck, massaging the rawness of his throat, worried about his voice. He wanted to run water through the raven's-head faucet and splash some on his face to cool down, but he still had his makeup on. Nobody would know him in the clubs without it. He stared at the sickly pallor it gave him, the gaunt shadowing of his cheeks, the dead black pupils of his contact lenses. He was in fact a beautiful man, and no amount of makeup could hide it, and this, he knew, was part of the secret of his success. His entire career consisted of taking beauty and corrupting it. Seducing the ear with moments of transcendent music only to subvert it with gothic screams and industrial distortion. That was what the young responded to. Defacing beauty. Subverting good.

Beautiful Corruption. Possible title for his next CD.

The Lurid Urge had moved 600,000 copies in the first week of its U.S. release. Huge for the post-mp3 era, but still down almost a full half million units from *Lavish Atrocities*. People were becoming inured to his antics, both onstage and off. He was no longer the anti-everything Wal-Mart had loved to ban and religious America—including his own father—had sworn to oppose. Funny how his father was in agreement with Wal-Mart, proving his thesis about how dull everything was. Nonetheless, with the exception of the religious right, it was getting difficult to shock people anymore. His career was hitting a wall and he knew it. Bolivar was not exactly considering a switch to coffeehouse folk—though that would indeed shock the world—but the theatrical autopsies and onstage biting and cutting were no longer fresh. They were anticipated, like encores. He was playing to his audience instead of playing against them. He had to run ahead of them, because if they ever caught up, he'd be trampled.

But hadn't he taken his act as far as he could? Where could it possibly go from here?

He heard the voices again. Like an unrehearsed chorus, voices in pain, pain that echoed his own. He spun around in the bathroom to make certain he was alone. He shook his head hard. The sound was like that when you put seashells to your ears, only, instead of hearing an echo of the ocean, he heard the moaning of souls in limbo.

When he came out of the bathroom, Mindy and Sherry were kissing, and Cleo lay on the big bed with a drink in hand, smiling at the ceiling. All of them started when he appeared, and turned in anticipation of his advance. He crawled up onto the bed, his gut doing kayak rolls, thinking that this was just what he needed. A vigorous pipe cleaning to clear the system. Blond Mindy came at him first, running her fingers through his silky black hair, but Bolivar chose Cleo, something about her, running his pale hand over the brown flesh of her neck. She removed her top for easier access and slipped her own hands down over the fine leather sheathing his hips.

She said, "I've been a fan of yours ever since—"

"Shhhh," he told her, hoping to cut through the usual acolyte's back-and-forth. The Vikes must have acted on the voices in his head, because they had dulled to a thrumming noise, almost like an electrical current, but with some throbbing mixed in.

The other two crawled up around him now, their hands like crabs, touching him, exploring him. Starting to peel off his clothes to reveal the man beneath. Mindy again ran her fingers through his hair, and he pulled away, as if there was something clumsy in her touch. Sherry squealed playfully, undoing the buttons of his fly. He knew the whispers that went around about him, from conquest to conquest, about his prodigious size and skill. She slid her hand across his leather pants and over his crotch, and while there was no groan of disappointment, there was no gasp of astonishment either. Nothing doing down there yet. Which was baffling, even given his illness. He had proven himself in much more adverse conditions, over and over and over again.

He returned his focus to the girl Cleo's shoulders, her neck, her throat. Lovely—but it was more than that. He felt a bucking sensation in his mouth. Not a sensation of nausea, but perhaps its opposite:

a need somewhere on the continuum between the longing for sex and the necessity of nourishment. But—bigger. A compulsion. A craving. An urge to violate, to ravish, to consume.

Mindy nibbled on his neck, and Bolivar turned on her finally, pushing her back down against the sheets—first in a fury, but then with a forced tenderness. He eased back her jaw, extending her neck, running his warm fingers over her fine, firm throat. He felt the strength of her young muscles inside—and he wanted them. More than he wanted her breasts, her ass, her loins. The thrumming that obsessed him was coming from her.

He brought his mouth to her throat. He tried with his lips, kissing, but that didn't quite do it. He tried nibbling on her, and the instinct seemed correct but the method . . . something about it was all wrong.

He wanted—somehow—more.

The thrumming vibrated throughout his own body now, his skin like that of a drum being pounded in an ancient ceremony. The bed was twirling a bit and his neck and thorax were bucking with need and repulsion. He went away for a little while, mentally. Like the amnesia of great sex, only, when he came back, it was to a woman's squealing. He had the girl's neck in his hands and was sucking on it with an intensity that went beyond the realm of the teenage hickey. He was drawing her blood to the surface of her skin, and she was screaming and the other two half-naked girls were trying to pull her away from him.

Bolivar straightened, first chastened by the sight of the florid bruising along her throat—then, remembering his stature as the maypole of this foursome, he asserted his authority.

"Get out!" he railed, and they did, clothes clutched to their bodies, the blond Mindy whimpering and sniffling all the way down the stairs.

Bolivar staggered off the bed and back into his bathroom and his makeup case. He sat down on the leather stool and went through his nightly ministrations. The makeup came off—he knew this because he saw it on the tissues—and yet his flesh looked much the same in the mirror. He rubbed harder, scraping at his cheeks with his fingernail, but nothing more came off. Had the makeup adhered to his skin? Or was he this sick, this gaunt?

He ripped off his shirt and examined himself: white as marble and crisscrossed with greenish veins and purplish blotches of settled blood.

He went to his contact lenses, carefully pinching out the cosmetic gels and depositing them in the fluid baths of their holding cases. He blinked a few times in relief, swiping at his eyes with his fingers, then feeling something weird. He leaned closer to the glass, blinking, examining his own eyes.

The pupils were dead black. Almost as though he still had the lenses in, only more textured now—more real. And—when he blinked, he noticed further activity within the eye. He got right up against the mirror, eyes wide now, almost afraid to close them.

A nictitating membrane had formed underneath his eyelid, a translucent second eyelid closing beneath the outer eyelid, gliding horizontally across the eyeball. Like a filmy cataract eclipsing his black pupil, closing upon his wild and horrified stare.

Augustin "Gus" Elizalde sat slumped in the back of the dining area with his pinch-front hat on the seat next to him. It was a narrow storefront eatery, one block east of Times Square. Neon burgers shining in the window, and red-and-white-checkered tablecloths on the tables. Budget eating in Manhattan. You walk in and order at the counter up front—sandwiches, pizza, something on the grill—pay for it, and take it in back, to a windowless room of tables jammed in tight. Wall murals of Venice and gondolas surrounded them. Felix scarfed down a plate of goopy macaroni and cheese. It was all he ate, mac and cheese, the more disgustingly orange the better. Gus looked down at his half-eaten greaseburger, suddenly more interested in his Coke, in the caffeine and sugar, getting some jolt back into him.

He still didn't feel right about that van. Gus turned over his hat underneath the table and checked the inside band again. The original five $10 bills he had gotten from that dude, plus the $500 he had earned for driving the van into the city, were still tucked in there. Tempting him. He and Felix could have a hell of a lot of fun on half that amount. Take home half for his *madre*, money she *needed*, money she could *use*.

Problem was, Gus knew himself. Problem was *stopping* at half. Problem was walking around with unspent money on his person.

He should get Felix to run him home right now. Unburden himself of half this haul. Slip it to his *madre* without his dirtbag brother Crispin knowing. Crackhead could sniff out dollars like a fiend.

Then again, this was dirty money. He had done something wrong to get it—clearly, though he didn't know what he'd done—and handing the money over to his *madre* was like passing on a curse. Best thing to do with dirty money is spend it quick, get rid of it—easy come, easy go.

Gus was torn. He knew that, once he started drinking, he lost all impulse control. And Felix was the gasoline to his flame. The two of them would burn through $550 before sunup, and then, instead of bringing something beautiful home to his *madre,* instead of bringing home something good, he would come in dragging his own hungover ass, hat all dented to hell, empty pockets turned inside out.

"Penny for your thoughts, Gusto," said Felix.

Gus shook his head. "I'm my own worst enemy, *'mano.* I'm like a fucking mutt sniffing in the street who don't know what tomorrow means. I got a dark side, amigo, and sometimes it takes me over."

Felix sipped his giant-ass Coke. "So what are we doing in this greasy spoon? Let's get out and meet some young ladies tonight."

Gus ran his thumb along the leather rim inside his hat, over the folded cash Felix knew nothing about—so far. Maybe just a hundred. Two hundred, half for each. Pull out exactly that much, that was his limit, no more. "Gotta pay to play, right, *'mano*?"

"Fuck yeah."

Gus looked away and saw a family next to him, dressed for the theater, rising and leaving with their desserts unfinished. Because of Felix's language, Gus guessed. By the looks of these Midwestern kids, they had never heard hard talk. Well, fuck them. You come into this town, you keep your kids out past nine o'clock, you risk them seeing the full show.

Felix finally finished his slop and Gus eased his cash-filled hat onto his head and they sauntered out into the night. They were walking on Forty-fourth Street, Felix sucking on a cigarette, when they heard screams. It didn't quicken their pace any, hearing screams in Midtown Manhattan. Not until they saw the fat, naked guy shuffling across the street at Seventh and Broadway.

Felix nearly spit out his cigarette laughing. "Gusto, you see that shit?" He started to jog ahead, like a bystander called by a barker to a show.

Gus wasn't into it. He followed slowly after him.

People in Times Square were making way for this guy and his pasty, floppy ass. Women screamed at the sight, half laughing, covering their eyes or their mouths or both. A young bachelorette party group snapped photos with their phones. Every time the guy turned, a new group got a look at his shriveled, flesh-buried junk, and howled.

Gus wondered where the cops were. This was America for you: a brown brother couldn't even duck into a doorway for a discreet piss without getting hassled, yet a white guy can parade naked through the crossroads of the world and get a free pass.

"Wasted off his *ass*," hooted Felix, following the fool, along with a loose bunch of others, many drunk themselves, savoring the street theater. The lights of the brightest intersection in the world—Times Square is a slashing X of avenues, walled with eye-popping advertisements and word crawls, a pinball game run through with never-ending traffic—dazzled the fat man, set him spinning. He lunged about, lurching like a circus bear on the loose.

Felix's crowd of carousers laughed and reared back when the man turned and staggered toward them. He was getting bolder now, or a little panicked, like a frightened animal, and more confused and seemingly—sometimes he pressed a hand to his throat, as though choking—more pained. Everything was really lively until the pale, fat man lashed out at a laughing woman, grabbing her by the back of her head. The woman screamed and twisted and a part of her head came off in his hand—for a moment it looked as though he had ripped open her skull—but it was just her frizzy black extensions.

The attack crossed the line from fun into fright. The fat man stumbled out into traffic with the fistful of fake hair still in his hand, and the crowd followed, pursuing him now, growing angry, yelling. Felix took the lead, crossing to the traffic island after this guy. Gus went along, but away from the crowd, threading through the honking cars. He was calling to Felix to come away, to be done with this. This was not going to end well.

The fat man was advancing toward a family gathered in the island to take in Times Square at night. He had them backed up against the traffic shooting past, and when the father tried to intervene he got knocked back hard. Gus recognized them as the theatergoing family from the restaurant. The mother seemed more concerned about shielding her kids' eyes from the sight of the naked man than protecting herself. She got grabbed by the back of the neck, pulled close up against his sagging belly and pendulous man breasts. The crazy man's mouth opened as though he wanted a kiss. But then it kept opening, like a snake's mouth—clearly dislocating the jaw with a soft *pop.*

Gus had no love for tourists, but he didn't even think before coming up behind the guy and hook-arming him in a headlock. He choked back on him strong, the guy's neck surprisingly muscular beneath the loose folds of flesh. Gus had the advantage, though, and the guy released the mother, falling against her husband in front of her screaming kids.

Now Gus was stuck. He had the naked man locked up, the big bear's arms pinwheeling. Felix came up in front to help . . . but then stopped. He was staring at the naked guy's face as if there was something really wrong there. A few people behind him reacted the same, others turned away in horror, but Gus couldn't see why. He did feel the guy's neck undulate under his forearm, very unnaturally—almost as though he were swallowing sideways. Felix's look of disgust made him think the fat guy was maybe suffocating under his choke hold, so Gus relaxed his grip a bit—

—just enough for the guy, with the animal strength of the insane, to hurl Gus off with a hairy elbow.

Gus fell to the sidewalk hard and his hat popped off. He turned in time to see it roll off the curb and into traffic. Gus jumped up and started after his hat and his money—but Felix's yell spun him back. The guy had Felix wrapped up in some kind of maniacal embrace, the big man's mouth going at Felix's neck. Gus saw Felix's hand pull something from his back pocket, flicking it open with a wrist flip.

Gus ran toward Felix before Felix could use the knife, dropping a shoulder into the fat man's side, feeling ribs crack, sending the tub of flesh sprawling. Felix fell too, Gus seeing blood spilling down the front of Felix's neck, and—more shockingly—a look of outright terror on his *compadre's* face. Felix sat up, dropping the knife in order to grip his neck, and Gus had never seen Felix look that way. Gus knew then that something bizarre had happened—*was happening*—he just didn't know what. All he knew was that he had to act in order to make his friend right again.

Gus reached for the knife, taking its burled black grip in his hand as the naked man got to his feet. The guy stood with his hand covering his mouth, almost as though trying to contain something in there. Something squirming. Blood rimmed his fat cheeks and stained his chin—Felix's blood—as he started toward Gus with his free hand outstretched.

He came fast—faster than a man of his size should have—shoving Gus down backward, before he could react. Gus's bare head smacked against the sidewalk—and for a moment everything was silent. He saw the Times Square billboards flashing above him in a kind of liquid slow motion . . . a young model staring down at him, wearing only a bra and panties . . . then the big man. Looming over him. Something undulating inside his mouth as he stared at Gus with empty, dark eyes . . .

The man dropped to one knee, choking out this thing in his throat. Pinkish and hungry, it shot out at Gus with the greedy speed of a frog's darting tongue. Gus slashed at the thing with his knife, cutting and stabbing like a dreamer fighting some creature in a nightmare. He didn't know what it was—only that he wanted it away from him, wanted to kill it. The fat man reeled back, making a noise like squealing. Gus kept up his slashing, cutting the man's neck, slicing his throat to ribbons.

Gus kicked away and the guy got to his feet, hands over his mouth and throat. He was bleeding white—not red—a creamy substance thicker and brighter than milk. He stumbled backward off the curb and fell into the moving traffic.

The truck tried to stop in time. That was the worst of it. After rolling over his face with the front tires, the rear set stopped right on the fat man's crushed skull.

Gus staggered to his feet. Still dizzy from his fall, he looked down at the blade of Felix's knife in his hand. It was stained white.

He was hit from behind then, his arms wrapped up, his shoulder driven into the pavement. He reacted as though it were the fat man still attacking him, writhing and kicking.

"Drop the knife! Drop it!"

He got his head around and saw three red-faced cops on him, two more behind him aiming guns.

Gus released the knife. He allowed his arms to be wrenched behind him, where they were cuffed. His adrenaline exploded. He said, "*Fucking now you're here?*"

"Stop resisting!" said the cop, cracking Gus's face into the pavement.

"He was attacking this family here—ask them!"

Gus turned.

The tourists were gone.

Most of the crowd was gone. Only Felix remained, seated on the edge of the island in a daze, gripping his throat—as a blue-gloved cop shoved him down, dropping a knee into his side.

Beyond Felix, Gus saw a small black thing rolling farther out into traffic. His hat, with all his dirty money still inside the brim—a slow-rolling taxi crushing it flat, Gus thinking, *This was America for you.*

Gary Gilbarton poured himself a whiskey. The family—the extended family, both sides—and friends were all gone finally, leaving behind stacks of take-out food cartons in the refrigerator and wastebaskets full of tissues. Tomorrow they'd be back to their lives, and with a story to tell.

My twelve-year-old niece was on that plane . . .

My twelve-year-old cousin was on that plane . . .

My neighbor's twelve-year-old daughter was on that plane . . .

Gary felt like a ghost walking through his nine-room home in the leafy suburb of Freeburg. He touched things—a chair, a wall—and felt nothing. Nothing mattered anymore. Memories could console him, but were more likely to drive him mad.

He had disconnected all the telephones after reporters started calling, wanting to know about the youngest casualty on board. To humanize the story. Who was she? they asked him. It would take Gary the rest of his life to work on a paragraph about his daughter, Emma. It would be the longest paragraph in history.

He was more focused on Emma than he was Berwyn, his wife, because children are our second selves. He loved Berwyn, and she was gone. But his mind kept circling around his lost little girl like water circling an ever-emptying drain.

That afternoon, a lawyer friend—a guy Gary hadn't had over to the house in maybe a year—pulled him aside in the study. He sat Gary down and told him that he was going to be a very rich man. A young victim like Em, with a much longer timeline of life lost, guaranteed a huge settlement payout.

Gary did not respond. He did not see dollar signs. He did not throw the guy out. He truly did not care. He felt nothing.

He had spurned all the offers from family and friends to spend the night so that he would not be alone. Gary had convinced one and all that he was fine, though thoughts of suicide had already occurred to him. Not just thoughts: a silent determination; a certainty. But later. Not now. Its inevitability was like a balm. The only sort of "settlement" that would mean anything to him. The only way he was getting through all this now was knowing that there would be an end. After all the formalities. After the memorial playground was erected in Emma's honor. After the scholarship was funded. But before he sold this now-haunted house.

He was standing in the middle of the living room when the doorbell rang. It was well after midnight. If it was a reporter, Gary would attack and kill him. It was as simple as that. To violate this time and place? He would tear the interloper apart.

He whipped open the door . . . and then all at once the pent-up mania went out of him.

A girl stood barefoot on the welcome mat. His Emma.

Gary Gilbarton's face crumpled in disbelief, and he slipped to his knees in front of her. Her face showed no reaction, no emotion. Gary reached out to his daughter—then hesitated. Would she pop like a soap bubble and disappear again forever?

He touched her arm, gripping her thin biceps. The fabric of her dress. She was real. She was there. He grasped her and pulled her to him, hugging her, wrapping her up in his arms.

He pulled back and looked at her again, pushing the stringy hair off her freckled face. How could this be? He looked around outside, scanning his misty front yard to see who had brought her.

No car in the driveway, no sound of an automobile engine pulling away.

Was she alone? Where was her mother?

"Emma," he said.

Gary got to his feet and led her inside, closing the front door, switching on the light. Em looked dazed. She wore the dress her mother had bought her for the trip, that made her look so grown up as she twirled around when she'd first tried it on for him. There was dirt on one sleeve—and perhaps blood. Gary spun her around, looking her over and finding more blood on her bare feet—no shoes?—and dirt all over, and scrapes on her palms and bruises on her neck.

"What happened, Em?" he asked her, holding her face in his palms. "How did you . . . ?"

The wave of relief struck him again, nearly knocking him over, and he grasped her tight. He picked her up and carried her over to the sofa, sitting her there. She was traumatized, and oddly passive. So unlike his smiling, headstrong Emma.

He felt her face, the way her mother always did when Emma acted strangely, and it was hot. So hot that her skin felt sticky, and she was terribly pale, nearly translucent. He saw veins beneath the surface, prominent red veins he had never seen before.

The blue in her eyes seemed to have faded. A head wound, probably. She was in shock.

Thoughts of hospitals ran through his head, but he wasn't letting her out of this house now, never again.

"You're home now, Em," he said. "You're going to be fine."

He took her hand and tugged on it to get her to stand, leading her into the kitchen. Food. He installed her in her chair at the table, watching her from the counter as he toasted two chocolate chip waffles, her favorite. She sat there with her hands at her sides, watching him, not staring exactly, but not alive to the room either. No silly stories, no school-day chatter.

The toaster jumped and he slathered the waffles with butter and syrup and set the plate down in front of her. He sat in his seat to watch. The third chair, Mommy's place, was still empty. Maybe the doorbell would ring again . . .

"Eat," he told her. She hadn't picked up her fork yet. He cut off a corner of the stack and held it before her mouth. She did not open it.

"No?" he said. He showed her himself, putting the waffles in his mouth, chewing. He tried her again, but her response was the same. A tear slipped from Gary's eye and rolled down his cheek. He knew by now that something was terribly wrong with his daughter. But he shoved all that aside.

She was here now, she was back.

"Come."

He walked her upstairs to her bedroom. Gary entered first, Emma stopping inside the doorway. Her eyes looked on the room with something akin to recognition, but more like distant memory. Like the eyes of an old woman returned miraculously to the bedroom of her youth.

"You need sleep," he said, rummaging through her chest of drawers for pajamas.

She remained by the door, her hands at her sides.

Gary turned with the pajamas in his hand. "Do you want me to change you?"

He got down on his knees and lifted off her dress, and his very modest preteen daughter offered no protest. Gary found more scratches, and a big bruise on her chest. Her feet were filthy, the crevices of her toes crusted with blood. Her flesh hot to the touch.

No hospital. He was never letting her out of his sight again.

He ran a cool bath and sat her in it. He knelt by the edge and gently worked a soapy facecloth over her abrasions, and she did not even squirm. He shampooed and conditioned her dirty, flat hair.

She looked at him with her dark eyes but there was no rapport. She was in some sort of trance. Shock. Trauma.

He could make her better.

He dressed her in her pajamas, taking the big comb from the straw basket in the corner and combing her blond hair down straight. The comb snagged in her hair and she did not flinch or utter a complaint.

I am hallucinating her, Gary thought. *I have lost my bearings on reality.*

And then, still combing her hair: *I don't goddamn care.*

He flipped back her sheets and quilted comforter and laid his daughter down in her bed, just as he used to when she was still a toddler. He pulled the covers up around her neck, tucking her in, Emma lying still and sleeplike but with her black eyes wide open.

Gary hesitated before leaning over to kiss her still-hot forehead. She was little more than a ghost of his daughter. A ghost whose presence he welcomed. A ghost he could love.

He wet her brow with his grateful tears. "Good night," he said, to no response. Emma lay still in the pinkish spray of her night-light, staring at the ceiling now. Not acknowledging him. Not closing her eyes. Not waiting for sleep. Waiting . . . for something else.

Gary walked down the hallway to his bedroom. He changed and climbed into bed alone. He did not sleep either. He was waiting also, though he didn't know what for.

Not until he heard it.

A soft creak on the threshold of his bedroom. He rolled his head and saw Emma's silhouette. His daughter standing there. She came to him, out of the shadows, a small figure in the night-darkened room. She paused near his bed, opening her mouth wide, as though for a gusty yawn.

His Emma had returned to him. That was all that mattered.

Zack had trouble sleeping. It was true what everyone said: he was very much like his father. Obviously too young to have an ulcer, but already with the weight of the world on his shoulders. He was an intense boy, an earnest boy, and he suffered for it.

He had always been that way, Eph had told him. He would stare back from the crib with a little grimace of worry, his intense dark eyes always making contact. And his little worried expression made Eph laugh—for he reminded him of himself so much—the worried baby in the crib.

For the last few years, Zack had felt the burden of the separation, divorce, and custody battle. It took some time to convince himself that all that was happening was not his fault. Still, his heart knew better: knew that somehow, if he dug deep enough, all the anger would connect with him. Years of angry whispers behind his back . . . the echoes of arguments late at night . . . being awakened by the muffled pounding on walls . . . It had all taken its toll. And Zack was now, at the ripe old age of eleven, an insomniac.

Some nights he would quiet the house noises with his iPod and stare out his bedroom window. Other nights he would crack open his window and listen to every little noise the night had to offer, listening so hard his ears buzzed as the blood rushed in.

He enacted that age-old hope of many a boy, that his street, at night, when it believed itself unwatched, would yield its mysteries. Ghosts, murder, lust. But all he ever saw, until the sun rose again on the horizon, was the hypnotic blue flicker of the distant TV in the house across the street.

The world was devoid of heroes or monsters, though in his imagination Zack sought both. A lack of sleep took its toll on the boy, and he kept dozing off during the daytime. He zoned out at school, and the other kids, never kind enough to let a difference go unnoticed, immediately found nicknames for him. They ranged from the common "Dickwad" to the more inscrutable "Necro-boy," every social clique choosing its favorite.

And Zack faded through the days of humiliation until the time came for his dad to visit him again.

With Eph he felt comfortable. Even in silence—*especially* in silence. His mom was too perfect, too observant, too kind—her silent standards, all for his "own good," were impossible to meet, and he knew, in a strange way, that from the moment he was born, he had disappointed her. By being a boy—by being too much like his dad.

With Eph he felt alive. He would tell his dad the things Mom always wanted to know about: out-of-boundaries things that she was eager to learn. Nothing critical—just private. Important enough not to reveal. Important enough to save for his father, and that was what Zack did.

Now, lying awake on the top of his bedcovers, Zack thought of the future. He was certain now that they would never again be together as a family. No chance. But he wondered how much worse it would get. That was Zack in a nutshell. Always wondering: *how much worse can it get?*

Much worse was always the answer.

At least, he hoped, now the army of concerned adults would finally screw out of his life. Therapists, judges, social workers, his mother's boyfriend. All of them keeping him hostage to their own needs and stupid goals. All of them "caring" for him, for his well-being, and none of them really giving a shit.

My Bloody Valentine grew quiet in the iPod and Zack popped the earphones out. The sky was still not yet brightening outside, but he finally felt tired. He loved feeling tired now. He loved not thinking.

So he readied himself for sleep. But as soon as he got settled, he heard the footsteps.

Flap-flap-flap. Like bare feet out on the asphalt. Zack looked out his window and saw a guy. A naked guy.

Walking down the street, skin pale as moonlight, shining stretch marks glowing in the night, crisscrossing the deflated belly. Obvious that the man had been fat once—but had since lost so much weight that now his skin folded in all different ways and different directions, so much so that it was almost impossible to figure out his exact silhouette.

It was old but appeared ageless. The balding head with badly tinted hair and varicose veins on the legs pinned him at around seventy, but there was a vigor to his step and a tone to his walk that made you think of a young man. Zack thought all these things, noticed all these things, because he was so much like Eph. His mother would have told him to move away from the window and called 911, while Eph would have pointed out all the details that formed the picture of that strange man.

The pale creature circled the house across the street. Zack heard a soft moan, and then the rattle of a backyard fence. The man came back and moved toward the neighbor's front door. Zack thought of calling the police, but that would raise all sorts of questions for him with Mom: he'd had to hide his insomnia from her, or else suffer days and weeks of doctor's appointments and tests, never mind her worrying.

The man walked out into the middle of the street and then stopped. Flabby arms hanging at his side, his chest deflated—was he even breathing?—hair ruffling in the soft night wind. Exposing the roots to a bad "Just for Men" reddish brown.

It looked up toward Zack's window, and for one weird moment they locked eyes. Zack's heart raced. This was the first time he saw the guy frontally. During the whole time, he had been able to see only a flank or the man's skin-draped back, but now he saw his full thorax—and the pale Y-shaped scar that crossed it whole.

And his eyes—they were dead tissue, glazed over, opaque even in the gentle moonlight. But worst of all, they had a frenzied energy, darting back and forth and then fixing on him—looking up at him with a feeling that was hard to pinpoint.

Zack shrank back, peeling away from the window, scared to death by the scar and those vacant eyes that had looked back at him. What was that expression . . . ?

He knew that scar, knew what it meant. An autopsy scar. But how could that be?

He risked another peek over the window's edge, so carefully, but the street was empty now. He sat up to see better, and the man was gone.

Had he ever even been there? Maybe the lack of sleep was *really* getting to him now. Seeing naked male corpses walking in the street: not something a child of divorce wants to share with a therapist.

And then it came to him: hunger. That was it. The dead eyes looked at him with intense *hunger* . . .

Zack dove into his sheets and buried his face in his pillow. The man's absence did not ease his mind, but instead did the contrary. The man was gone, but he was everywhere now. He could be downstairs, breaking in through the kitchen window. Soon it would be on the steps, climbing ever so slowly—*could he hear his footsteps already?*—and then in the corridor outside his door. Softly rattling his lock—the busted lock that would not catch. And soon it would reach Zack's bed and then—what? He feared the man's voice and its dead stare. Because he had the horrible certainty that, even though it moved, the man was no longer alive.

Zombies . . .

Zack hid under his pillow, mind and heart racing, full of fear and praying for dawn to come and save him. Much as he dreaded school, he begged the morning to come.

Across the street, in the neighboring house, window glass was broken and the TV light snapped off.

Ansel Barbour whispered to himself as he wandered about the second floor of his house. He wore the same T-shirt and boxer shorts he had tried to sleep in, and his hair darted up at odd angles from continuous squeezing and pulling. He didn't know what was happening to him. Ann-Marie suspected a fever, but when she came to him with the thermometer, he could not bear to think of that steel-tipped probe being stuck in under his inflamed tongue. They had an ear thermometer, for the kids, but he couldn't even sit still long enough to get an accurate reading. Ann-Marie's practiced palm against his forehead detected heat—lots of heat—but then, he could have told her that.

She was petrified, he could tell. She made no effort to hide it. To her, any illness whatsoever was an assault on the sanctity of their family unit. The kids' throw-up bugs were met with the same dark-eyed fear another might reserve for, say, a bad blood test or the appearance of an unexplained lump. *This is it.* The beginning of the terrible tragedy she was certain would one day befall her.

His tolerance for Ann-Marie's eccentricities was at low ebb. He was dealing with something serious here, and he needed her help, not her added stress. Now he couldn't be the strong one. He needed her to take charge.

Even the kids were staying away from him, startled by the not-there look in their father's eyes, or perhaps—he was vaguely aware of this—the odor of his sickness, which to his nose resembled the smell of congealed cóoking grease stored too long in a tin can rusting beneath the sink. He saw them from time to time hiding behind the balusters at the bottom of the staircase, watching him cross the second-floor landing. He wanted to allay their fears, but worried he might lose his temper trying to explain this to them, and in doing so make things worse. The surest way to set their minds at ease was to get better. To outlast this surge of disorientation and pain.

He stopped inside his daughter's bedroom, found the purple walls too purple, then doubled back into the hallway. He stood very still on the landing—as still as he could—until he could hear it again. That thumping. A beating—quiet and close. Wholly separate from the head-ache pounding in his skull. Almost . . . like in small-town movie the-aters, where you can hear, during quiet moments in movies, the clicking of the film running through the projector in the back. Which distracts you, and keeps pulling you back to the reality that *this is not real*, as though you and you alone realize this truth.

He shook his head hard, grimacing from the pain that went with it . . . trying to use that pain like bleach, to clean his thoughts . . . but the thumping. The *throbbing*. It was everywhere, all around him.

The dogs too. Acting strange around him. Pap and Gertie, the big, bumbling Saint Bernards. Growling as they would when some strange animal came into the yard.

Ann-Marie came up later, alone, finding him sitting at the foot of their bed, his head in his hands like a fragile egg. "You should sleep," she said.

He gripped his hair like the reins of a mad horse and fought down the urge to berate her. Something was wrong in his throat, and whenever he lay down for any length of time, his epiglottis seized up, cutting off his airway, suffocating him until he choked himself back to breathing. He was terrified now of dying in his sleep.

"What do I do?" she asked, remaining in the doorway, her palm and fingers pressing against her own forehead.

"Get me some water," he said. His voice hissed through his raw throat, burning like steam. "Lukewarm. Dissolve some Advil in it, ibuprofen—anything."

She didn't move. She stood there staring, worrying. "Aren't you even a little better . . . ?"

Her timidity, which normally aroused strong protective instincts in him, now moved him only to rage. "Ann-Marie, get me some goddamn water, and then take the kids outside or something but *keep them the hell away from me!*"

She scurried away in tears.

When Ansel heard them go outside into the darkened backyard, he ventured downstairs, walking with one hand clamped on the handrail. She had left the glass on the counter next to the sink, set on a folded napkin, dissolved pills clouding the water. He brought the glass to his lips two-handedly and forced himself to drink. He poured the water into his mouth, giving his throat no choice but to swallow. He got some of it down before gagging on the rest of the contents, coughing onto the sink window overlooking the backyard. He gasped as he watched the splatter drip down the glass pane, distorting his view of Ann-Marie standing behind the kids on the swings, staring off into the darkened sky, breaking her crossed arms only occasionally to push low-swinging Haily.

The glass slipped from his hand, spilling into the sink. He left the kitchen for the living room, dropping onto the sofa there in a kind of a stupor. His throat was engorged and he felt sicker than ever.

He had to return to the hospital. Ann-Marie would just have to make it on her own for a little while. She could do it if she had no choice. Maybe it would even end up being good for her . . .

He tried to focus, to determine what needed to be done before he left. Gertie came into the doorway, panting softly. Pap entered behind her, stopping near the fireplace, settling down into a crouch. Pap started a low, even growl, and the thumping noise surged in Ansel's ears. And Ansel realized: the noise was coming from them.

Or was it? He got down off the sofa, moving over toward Pap on his hands and knees, getting closer to hear. Gertie whimpered and retreated to the wall, but Pap held his unrelaxed crouch. The growl intensified in the dog's throat, Ansel grasping his collar just as the dog tried to back up onto its feet and get away.

Thrum . . . Thrum . . . Thrum . . .

It was *in* them. Somehow. Somewhere. Some*thing*.

Pap was pulling and whimpering, but Ansel, a big man who rarely had to use his strength, curled his free arm around the Saint Bernard's neck, holding him in a canine headlock. He pressed his ear to the dog's neck, the hair of its fur tickling the inside of his auditory canal.

Yes. A thrumming pulse. Was it the animal's circulating blood?

That was the noise. The yelping dog strained to get away, but Ansel pressed his ear harder against the dog's neck, needing to know.

"Ansel?"

He turned fast—too fast, a blinding shot of white pain—and saw Ann-Marie at the door, Benjy and Haily behind her. Haily was hugging her mother's leg, the boy standing alone, both of them staring. Ansel's grip relaxed and the dog pulled away.

Ansel was still on his knees. "What do you want?" he yelled.

Ann-Marie stayed frozen in the doorway, in a trance of fear. "I'm . . . I don't . . . I'm taking them for a walk."

"Fine," he said. He wilted a little under the gaze of his children, another choke from his throat making him rasp. "Daddy's fine," he told them, wiping off spit with the back of his hand. "Daddy's going to be fine."

He turned his head toward the kitchen, where the dogs were. All the make-nice thoughts faded under the resurgent thrumming. Louder than before. Pulsating.

Them.

A nauseous shame rose up within him, and he shuddered, then put a fist to his temple.

Ann-Marie said, "I'll let the dogs out."

"*No!*" He caught himself, holding out an open palm to her from where he knelt on the living room floor. "No," he said, more evenly. He tried to catch his breath, to *seem* normal. "They're fine. Leave them in."

She hesitated, wanting to say more. To do something, anything. But in the end, she turned and went out, pulling Benjy after her.

Ansel used the wall to get to his feet and walk to the first-floor bathroom. He pulled the string light on over the mirror, wanting to stare into his own eyes. Glowering, red-veined eggs of sallow ivory. He swiped perspiration from his forehead and upper lip and opened his mouth to try and look down his own throat. He expected to see inflamed tonsils, or some kind of white-bump rash, but it only looked dark. It hurt to raise his tongue, but he did, looking underneath. The pad beneath was scarlet and sore, and angry red, glowing hot the way a charcoal glows. He touched it and the pain was brain-splittingly raw, riding out along both sides of his jaw, straining the cords in his neck. His throat bucked in protest, issuing a harsh, barking cough that hacked dark specks onto the mirror. Blood, mixed with something white, maybe phlegm. Some spots were closer to black than others, as though he had brought up some solid residue, like rotten bits of himself. He reached for one of those dark nuggets, smearing the chunk off the glass and onto the tip of his middle finger. He brought it to his nose, sniffing it, then rubbed it with his thumb. It was like a discolored clot of blood. He brought it to the tip of his tongue, and before he knew it, he was tasting it. He swirled the small, soft mass inside his mouth, and then, once it dissipated, swiped another spot off the glass, tasting that one too. Not much taste, but there was something about the sensation on his tongue that was almost healing.

He leaned forward, licking the bloody stains off the cool glass. It should have hurt his tongue to do this, but, on the contrary, the soreness in his mouth and throat had abated. Even that most tender part underneath his tongue—the pain was reduced to a tingle. The thrumming sound also faded, though never completely went away. He looked at his reflection in the red-smeared mirror and tried to understand.

This respite was maddeningly brief. The tightness, like having his throat wrung by powerful hands, resurged, and he pulled his gaze away from the mirror, lurching out into the hallway.

Gertie whined and back-stepped down the hall, away from him, trotting into the living room. Pap was scratching at the back door, wanting to get out. When he saw Ansel coming into the kitchen, he scooted away. Ansel stood there, his throat throbbing, then reached into the dogs' cabinet, pulling down the box of Milk-Bone treats. He jammed one between his fingers, as he usually did, and went into the living room.

Gertie was lying on the wood landing at the bottom of the stairs, paws out, ready to spring away. Ansel sat down on his footstool and waved the treat. "Come on, baby," he said, in a heartless whisper that grated against his soul.

Gertie's leathery nostrils flared, sniffing at the scent in the air.

Thrum . . . thrum. . .

"Come on, girl. Get your treat."

She pushed up slowly onto all fours. She took one small step forward, then stopped again and sniffed. She knew instinctively that there was something wrong with this bargain.

But Ansel held the cookie still, which seemed to reassure her. She padded slowly over the rug, head low, eyes alert. Ansel nodded his encouragement, the thrumming intensifying in his head as she approached.

He said, "Come on, Gertie, old girl."

Gertie came up and swiped the cookie once with her thick tongue, catching some of his finger. She did this again, wanting to trust him, wanting the treat. Ansel brought out his other hand and laid it on top of her head, stroking her as she liked him to. Tears sprang out of his eyes as he did this. Gertie leaned forward to close her teeth on the treat, taking it from his fingers, and that was when Ansel grabbed her collar and fell upon her with all his weight.

The dog struggled beneath him, snarling and trying to bite him, her panic giving his rage a focus. He forced back her lower jaw with his hand, effectively shutting her mouth by raising her head, then brought his mouth to her furry neck.

He tore in. He bit through her silky, slightly greasy coat, opening a wound. The dog howled as he tasted her fur, the texture of her thick soft flesh vanishing quickly under a hot surge of blood. The pain of his biting pushed Gertie into a frenzy beneath him, but Ansel held his grip, forcing the dog's big head even higher, fully exposing the neck.

He was drinking the dog. Somehow drinking without swallowing. Ingesting. As though there were some new mechanism of which he was not aware working in his throat. He could not understand it; he only understood the satisfaction he felt. A palliative pleasure in the act. And power. Yes—power. As that of drawing life from one being into another.

Pap came into the room howling. A mournful bassoon sound,

and Ansel had to stop this sad-eyed Saint Bernard from spooking the neighbors. With Gertie twitching limply beneath him, he sprang up, and with renewed speed and strength, raced across the room after Pap, knocking a floor lamp down as he lunged and tackled the big, clumsy dog in the hall.

The pleasure of the sensation, in drinking the second dog, was rapturous. He felt within him that tipping point, as when suction catches inside a siphoning tube and the desired change in pressure is achieved. Fluid flowed without effort, replenishing him.

Ansel sat back when he was done, numb for a while, dazed, slow to return to the here and now of the room. He looked down at the dead dog on the floor at his feet and felt suddenly wide awake, and cold. Remorse came all at once.

He got to his feet and saw Gertie, then looked down at his own chest, clawing at his T-shirt, wet with dog blood.

What is happening to me?

The blood on the checkered rug made a nasty black stain. Yet there wasn't much of it. And that was when he remembered that he had drunk it.

Ansel went first to Gertie, touching her coat, knowing that she was dead—that he had killed her—and then, setting aside his disgust, rolled her up inside the ruined rug. He lifted the bundle into his arms with a great grunt and carried it through the kitchen, outside and down the steps to the backyard dog shed. Inside, he dropped to his knees, unrolled the rug and the heavy Saint Bernard, and left Gertie to go back for Pap.

He laid them together against the wall of the shed, underneath his pegboard of tools. His revulsion was distant, foreign. His neck was tight but not sore, his throat cool suddenly, his head calm. He looked at his bloody hands and had to accept what he could not understand.

What he had done had made him better.

He went back inside the house, to the bathroom upstairs. He stripped off his bloody shirt and boxers and pulled on an old sweat suit, knowing Ann-Marie and the kids would return at any moment. As he searched the bedroom for sneakers, he felt the thrumming return. He didn't hear it: he felt it. And what it meant terrified him.

Voices at the front door.

His family was home.

He made it back downstairs and just out the back door, unseen, his bare feet hitting the backyard grass, running from the pulsating sense filling his head.

He turned toward the driveway, but there were voices in the dark street. He had left the shed doors open, and so, in his desperation, ducked inside the doghouse to hide, shutting both doors behind him. He didn't know what else to do.

Gertie and Pap lay dead against the side wall. A cry nearly escaped Ansel's lips.

What have I done?

New York winters had warped the shed doors, so they no longer hung perfectly flush. He could still see through the seam, spying Benjy getting a glass of water from the kitchen sink, his head in the window, Hailey's little hand reaching up.

What is happening to me?

He was like a dog who had turned. A rabid dog.

I have caught some form of rabies.

Voices now. The kids coming down the back-porch steps, lit by the security light over the deck, calling the dogs. Ansel looked around him fast and seized a rake from the corner, sliding it through the interior door handles as quickly and quietly as he could. Locking the children out. Locking himself inside.

"*Ger-tie! Pa-ap!*"

No true concern in their voices, not yet. The dogs had gotten away a few times in the past couple of months, which was why Ansel had dug the iron stake into the ground here in the shed, so they could be chained up securely at night.

Their calling voices faded in his ears as the thrum took over his head: the steady rhythm of blood circulating through their young veins. Little hearts pumping hard and strong.

Jesus.

Haily came to the doors. Ansel saw her pink sneakers through the gap at the bottom and shrank back. She tried the doors. They rattled but wouldn't give.

She called to her brother. Benjy came and shook the doors with all his eight-year-old might. The four walls shivered, but the rake handle held.

Thrummity . . . thrummity . . . thrum. . .

Their blood. Calling to him. Ansel shuddered and let his focus fall on the dog's stake in front of him. Buried six feet deep, set in a solid block of concrete. Strong enough to keep two Saint Bernards leashed during a summer thunderstorm. Ansel looked to the wall shelves and saw an extra chain collar, price tag still attached. He felt certain he had an old shackle lock in here somewhere.

He waited until they were a safe distance away before he reached up and pulled down the steel collar.

Captain Redfern was laid out in his johnny on the stretcher bed inside the clear plastic curtains, his lips open in a near-grimace, his breathing deep and labored. Having grown increasingly uncomfortable as night approached, Redfern had been administered enough sedatives to put him out for hours. They needed him still for imaging. Eph dimmed the light inside the bay and switched on his Luma light, again aiming the indigo glow at Redfern's neck, wanting another look at the scar. But now, with the other lights dimmed, he saw something else as well. A strange rippling effect along Redfern's skin—or, rather, *beneath* his skin. Like a mottling, or a subcutaneous psoriasis, blotching that appeared just below the surface of the flesh in shades of black and gray.

When he brought the Luma light closer for further examination, the shading beneath the skin reacted. It swirled and squirmed, as though trying to get away from the light.

Eph backed off, pulled the wand away. With the black light removed from Redfern's skin, the sleeping man appeared normal.

Eph returned, this time running the violet lamplight over Redfern's face. The image revealed beneath it, the mottled subflesh, formed a kind of mask. Like a second self lurking behind the airline pilot's face, aged and malformed. A grim visage, an evil awake within him while the sick man slept. Eph brought the lamp even closer . . . and again the interior shadow rippled, almost forming a grimace, trying to shy away.

Redfern's eyes opened. As though awakened by the light. Eph jerked back, shocked by the sight. The pilot had enough secobarbital in him for two men. He was too heavily sedated to reach consciousness.

Redfern's staring eyes were wide in their sockets. He stared straight at the ceiling, looking scared. Eph held the lamp away and moved into his line of sight.

"Captain Redfern?"

The pilot's lips were moving. Eph leaned closer, wanting to hear what Redfern was trying to say.

The man's lips moved dryly, saying, "He is here."

"Who is here, Captain Redfern?"

Redfern's eyes stared, as though witnessing a terrible scene being played out before him.

He said, "Mr. Leech."

Much later, Nora returned, finding Eph down the hallway from radiology. They spoke standing before a wall covered with crayon artwork from thankful young patients. He told her about what he had seen under Redfern's flesh.

Nora said, "The black light of our Luma lamps—isn't that low-spectrum ultraviolet light?"

Eph nodded. He too had been thinking about the old man outside the morgue.

"I want to see it," said Nora.

"Redfern's in radiology now," Eph told her. "We had to further sedate him for MRI imaging."

"I got the results from the airplane," said Nora, "the liquid sprayed around there. Turns out you were right. There's ammonia and phosphorous—"

"I knew it—"

"But also oxalic and iron and uric acids. Plasma."

"What?"

"Raw plasma. And a whole load of enzymes."

Eph held his forehead as though taking his own temperature. "As in digestion?"

"Now what does that remind you of?"

"Excretions. Birds, bats. Like guano. But how . . ."

Nora shook her head, feeling in equal parts both excited and bewildered. "Whoever, whatever was on that airplane . . . took a giant shit in the cabin."

While Eph was trying to wrap his mind around that one, a man in hospital scrubs came hustling down the hallway, calling his name. Eph recognized him as the technician from the MRI room.

"Dr. Goodweather—I don't know what happened. I just stepped out to get some coffee. I wasn't gone five minutes."

"What do you mean? What is it?"

"Your patient. He's gone from the scanner."

Jim Kent was downstairs near the closed gift shop, away from the others, talking on his mobile phone. "They are imaging him now," he told the person on the other end. "He seems to be going downhill pretty fast, sir. Yes, they should have the scans in just a few hours. No—no word on the other survivors. I thought you'd want to know. Yes, sir, I am alone—"

He became distracted by the sight of a tall, ginger-haired man wearing a hospital johnny, walking unsteadily down the hallway, trailing along the floor IV tubes from his arm. Unless Jim was mistaken, it was Captain Redfern.

"Sir, I . . . something's happening . . . let me call you back."

He hung up and plucked the wire from his ear, stuffing it into his jacket pocket and following the man a few dozen yards away. The patient slowed for just a moment, turning his head as though aware of his pursuer.

"Captain Redfern?" said Jim.

The patient continued around a corner and Jim followed, only to find, when he turned the same corner, the hallway empty.

Jim checked door signs. He tried the one marked STAIRS and looked down the narrow well between half flights. He caught sight of an IV tube trailing down the steps.

"Captain Redfern?" said Jim, his voice echoing in the stairwell. He fumbled out his phone as he descended, wanting to call Eph. The display said NO SERVICE because he was underground now. He pushed through the door into the basement hallway and, distracted by his phone, never saw Redfern running at him from the side.

When Nora, searching the hospital, went through the door from the stairwell into the basement hallway, she found Jim sitting against the wall with his legs splayed. He had a sleepy expression on his face.

Captain Redfern was standing barefoot over him, his johnny-bare back to her. Something hanging from his mouth spilled driblets of blood to the floor.

"Jim!" she yelled, though Jim did not react in any way to her voice. Captain Redfern stiffened, however. When he turned to her, Nora saw nothing in his mouth. She was shocked by his color, formerly quite pale, now florid and flushed. The front of his johnny was indeed blood-stained, and blood also rimmed his lips. Her first thought was that he was in the grip of some sort of seizure. She feared he had bitten off a chunk of his tongue and was swallowing blood.

Closer, her diagnosis became less certain. Redfern's pupils were dead black, the sclera red where it should have been white. His mouth hung open strangely, disjointedly, as though his jaw had been reset on a lower hinge. And there was a heat coming off him that was extreme, beyond the warmth of any normal, natural fever.

"Captain Redfern," she said, calling him over and over, trying to snap him out of it. He advanced on her with a look of vulturelike hunger in his filmy eyes. Jim remained slumped on the floor, not moving. Redfern was obviously violent, and Nora wished she had a weapon. She looked around, seeing only a hospital phone, 555 the alert code.

She grabbed the receiver off the wall, barely getting it into her hand before Redfern attacked, throwing her to the floor. Nora kept hold of the receiver, its cord pulling right out of the wall. Redfern had maniacal strength, descending on her and pinning her arms hard to the polished floor. His face strained and his throat bucked. She thought he was about to vomit on her.

Nora was screaming when Eph came flying from the stairwell door, throwing his weight into Redfern's torso, sending him sprawling, off her. Eph righted himself and held out a cautionary hand toward his patient, dragging himself up from the floor now. "Hold on—"

Redfern emitted a hissing sound. Not snakelike, but throaty. His black eyes were flat and vacant as he started to smile. Or seemed to smile, using those same facial muscles—only, when his mouth opened, it kept on opening.

His lower jaw descended and out wriggled something pink and fleshy that was not his tongue. It was longer, more muscular and complex . . . and squirming. As though he had swallowed a live squid, and one of its tentacles was still thrashing about desperately inside his mouth.

Eph jumped back. He grabbed the IV tree to keep from falling, and then upended it, using it like a prod to keep Redfern and that thing in his mouth at bay. Redfern grabbed the steel stand and then the thing in his mouth lashed out. It extended the six-foot distance of the IV tree, Eph spinning out of the way just in time. He heard the *flap* of the end of the appendage—narrowed, like a fleshy stinger—strike the wall. Redfern flung the stand to the side, cracking it in half, Eph tumbling with it backward into a room.

Redfern entered after him, still with that hungry look in his black-and-red eyes. Eph searched around wildly for anything that would help him keep this guy away from him, finding only a trephine in a charger on a shelf. A trephine is a surgical instrument with a spinning cylindrical blade generally used for cutting open the human skull during autopsy. The helicopter-type blade whirred to life, and Redfern advanced, his stinger mostly retracted yet still lolling, with flanking sacs of flesh pulsing at its sides. Before Redfern could attack again, Eph tried to cut it.

He missed, slicing a chunk out of the pilot's neck. White blood kicked out, just as he had seen in the morgue, not spraying out arterially but spilling down his front. Eph dropped the trephine before its whirring blades could spit the substance at him. Redfern grabbed at his neck, and Eph picked up the nearest heavy object he could find, a fire extinguisher. He used the butt end of it to batter Redfern in the face—his hideous stinger Eph's prime target. Eph smashed him twice more, Redfern's head snapping back with the last blow, his spine emitting an audible crack.

Redfern collapsed, his body giving out. Eph dropped the tank and stumbled back, looking in horror at what he had done.

Nora came rushing in wielding a broken piece of the IV tree, then saw Redfern lying in a heap. She dropped the shaft and rushed to Eph, who caught her in his arms.

"Are you okay?" he said.

She nodded, her hand over her mouth. She pointed at Redfern and

Eph looked down and saw the worms wriggling out of his neck. Reddish worms, as though blood filled, spilling out of Redfern's neck like cockroaches fleeing a room when a light is turned on. Eph and Nora backed up to the open doorway.

"What the hell just happened?" said Eph.

Nora's hand came away from her mouth. "Mr. Leech," she said.

They heard a groan from the hallway—Jim—and rushed out to tend to him.

INTERLUDE III

REVOLT, 1943

AUGUST WAS SEARING THROUGH THE CALENDAR AND ABRAHAM Setrakian, laying out beams for a suspended roof, felt its burden more than most. The sun was baking him, every day it was like this. But even more than that, he had come to loathe the night—his bunk and his dreams of home, which had formerly been his only respite from the horror of the death camp—and was now a hostage to two equally merciless masters.

The Dark Thing, Sardu, now spaced his visits to a regular pattern of twice-a-week feedings in Setrakian's barracks, and probably the same in the other barracks as well. The deaths went completely unnoticed by guards and prisoners alike. The Ukrainian guards wrote the corpses off as suicides, and to the SS it meant only a change in a ledger entry.

In the months since the Sardu-Thing's first visit, Setrakian—obsessed with the notion of defeating such evil—learned as much as he could from other local prisoners about an ancient Roman crypt located somewhere in the outlying forest. There, he was now certain, the Thing had made its lair, from whence it emerged each night to slake its ungodly thirst.

If Setrakian ever understood true thirst, it was that day. Water carriers circulated among the prisoners constantly, though many of them themselves fell prey to heat seizures. The burning hole was well fed that day. Setrakian had managed to collect what he needed: a length of raw white oak, and a bit of silver for the tip. That was the old way to dispose of the *strigoi*, the vampire. He had sharpened the tip for days before treating it with the silver. Smuggling it into his barracks alone took the better part of two weeks of planning. He had lodged it in an empty space directly behind his bed. If the guards ever found it, they would execute him on the spot, for there was no mistaking the shape of the hardwood as a weapon.

The night before, Sardu had entered the camp late, later than usual. Setrakian had lain very still, waiting patiently for it to begin feeding on an infirm Romani. He felt revulsion and remorse, and prayed for forgiveness—but it was a necessary part of his plan, for the half-gorged creature would be less alert.

The blue light of impending dawn filtered through the small grated windows at the east end of the barracks. Just what Setrakian had been waiting for. He pricked his index finger, drawing a perfect crimson pearl out of his dry flesh. Yet he was completely unprepared for what happened next.

He had never heard the Thing utter a sound. It conducted its unholy repast in utter silence. But now, at the smell of young Setrakian's blood, the Thing *groaned*. The sound reminded Setrakian of the creaking sound of dry wood when twisted, or the sputter of water down a clogged drain.

In a matter of seconds, the Thing was at Setrakian's side.

As the young man cautiously slid his hand back, reaching for the stake, the two locked eyes. Setrakian couldn't help but turn toward it when it moved near his bed.

The Thing smiled at him.

"Ages since we fed looking into living eyes," the Thing said. "Ages . . ."

Its breath smelled of earth and of copper, and its tongue clicked in its mouth. Its deep voice sounded like an amalgam of many voices, poured forth as though lubricated by human blood.

"Sardu . . . ," whispered Setrakian, unable to keep the name to himself.

The beady, burnished eyes of the Thing opened wider, and for a fleeting moment they looked almost human.

"He is not alone in this body," it hissed. "How dare you call to him?"

Setrakian gripped the stake behind his bed, slowly sliding it out . . .

"A man has the right to be called by his own name before meeting God," said Setrakian, with the righteousness of youth.

The Thing gurgled with joy. "Then, young thing, you may tell me yours . . ."

Setrakian made his move then, but the silver tip of the stake made a tiny scraping noise, revealing its presence a mere instant before it flew toward the Thing's heart.

But that instant was enough. The Thing uncoiled its claw and stopped the weapon an inch from its own chest.

Setrakian tried to free himself, striking out with his other hand, but the Thing stopped that too. It lacerated the side of Setrakian's neck with the tip of its stinger—just a gash, coming as fast as the blink of an eye, enough to inject him with the paralyzing agent.

Now it held the young man firmly by both hands. It raised him up from the bed.

"But you will not meet God," the Thing said. "For I am personally acquainted with him, and I know him to be *gone* . . ."

Setrakian was on the verge of fainting from the vicelike pressure the claws exerted upon his hands. The hands that had kept him alive for so long in that camp. His brain was bursting with pain, mouth gaping, lungs gasping for breath, but no scream would surge from within.

The Thing looked deep into Setrakian's eyes then, and saw his soul.

"Abraham Setrakian," it purred. "A name so soft, so sweet, for a boy so full of spirit . . ." It moved close to his face. "But why destroy me, boy? Why am I so deserving of your wrath, when around you you find even more death in my absence. I am not the monster here. It is God. Your God and mine, the absent Father who left us all so long ago . . . In your eyes I see what you fear most, young Abraham, and it is not me . . . It is the pit. So now you shall see what happens when I feed you to it and God does nothing to stop it."

And then, with a brutal cracking noise, the Thing shattered the bones in the hands of young Abraham.

The boy fell to the floor, curled in a ball of pain, his crushed fingers near his chest. He had landed in a faint pool of sunlight.

Dawn.

The Thing hissed, attempting to move close to him one more time.

But the prisoners in the barracks began to stir, and as young Abraham lost consciousness, the Thing vanished.

Abraham was discovered bleeding and injured before roll call. He was dispatched to the infirmary from which wounded prisoners never returned. A carpenter with broken hands served no purpose in the camp, and the head overseer immediately approved his disposal. He was dragged out to the burning hole with the rest of the roll-call failures, made to kneel in a line. Thick, greasy, black smoke occluded the sun above, searing hot and merciless. Setrakian was stripped and dragged to the very edge, cradling his destroyed hands, shivering in fear as he gazed into the pit.

The searing pit. The hungry flames twisting, the greasy smoke lifting away in a kind of hypnotic ballet. And the rhythm of the execution line—gunshot, gun carriage clicking, the soft bouncing tinkle of the bullet casing against the dirt ground—lulled him into a death trance. Staring down into the flames stripping away flesh and bone, unveiling man for what he is: mere matter. Disposable, crushable, flammable sacks of meat—easily revertible to carbon.

The Thing was an expert in horror, but this human horror indeed exceeded any other possible fate. Not only because it was without mercy, but because it was acted upon rationally and without compulsion. It was a choice. The killing was unrelated to the larger war, and served no purpose other than evil. Men chose to do this to other men and invented reasons and places and myths in order to satisfy their desire in a logical and methodical way.

As the Nazi officer mechanically shot each man in the back of the head and kicked them forward into the consuming pit, Abraham's will eroded. He felt nausea, not at the smells or the sights but at the knowledge—the certainty—that God was no longer in his heart. Only this pit.

The young man wept at his failure and the failure of his faith as he felt the muzzle of the Luger press against the bare skin—

Another mouth at his neck—

And then he heard the shots. From across the yard, a work crew of prisoners had taken the observation towers and were now overriding the camp, shooting every uniformed officer in sight.

The man at his back went away. Leaving Setrakian poised at the edge of that pit.

A Pole next to him in line stood and started to run—and the will seeped back into young Setrakian's body. Hands clutched to his chest, he found himself up and running, naked, toward the camouflaged barbed-wire fence.

Gunfire all around him. Guards and prisoners bursting with blood and falling. Smoke now, and not just from the pit: fires starting all across the camp. He made it to the fence, near some others and somehow, with anonymous hands lifting him to the top, doing what his broken hands could not, he fell to the other side.

He lay on the ground, rifle rounds and machine-gun fire ripping into the dirt around him—and again, helping hands and arms raised him up, lifting him to his feet. And as his unseen helpers were torn apart by bullets, Setrakian ran and ran and found himself crying . . . for in the absence of God he had found Man. Man killing man, man helping man, both of them anonymous: the scourge and the blessing.

A matter of choice.

For miles he ran, even as Austrian reinforcements closed in. His feet were sliced open, his toes shattered by rocks, but nothing could stop him now that he was beyond the fence. His mind was of a single purpose as he finally reached the woods and collapsed in the darkness, hiding in the night.

Setrakian shifted his weight, trying to get comfortable on the bench against the wall inside the precinct house holding tank. He had waited in a glass-walled prebooking area all night, stuck with many of the same thieves, drunks, and perverts he was caged in with now. During the long wait, he had had sufficient time to consider the scene he had made outside the coroner's office, and realized he had spoiled his best chance at reaching the federal disease control agency in the person of Dr. Goodweather.

Of course he had come off like a crazy old man. Maybe he was slipping. Going wobbly like a gyroscope at the end of its revolutions. Maybe the years of waiting for this moment, lived on that line between dread and hope, had taken their toll.

Part of getting old is checking oneself constantly. Keeping a good firm grip on the handrail. Making sure you're still you.

No. He knew what he knew. The only thing wrong with him now was that he was being driven mad by desperation. Here he was, being held captive in a police station in Midtown Manhattan, while all around him . . .

Be smart, you old fool. Find a way out of here. You've worked your way out of far worse places than this.

He replayed the scene from the booking area in his mind. In the middle of his giving his name and address and having the charges of disturbing the peace and criminal trespass explained to him, and signing a property form for his walking stick ("It is of immense personal significance," he had told the sergeant) and his heart pills, a Mexican youth of eighteen or nineteen was brought in, wrists handcuffed behind him. The youth had been roughed up, his face scratched, his shirt torn.

What caught Setrakian's eye were the burn holes in his black pants and across his shirt.

"This is *bullshit*, man!" said the youth, arms pulled tight behind him, leaning back as he was pushed ahead by detectives. "That *puto* was crazy. Dude was *loco*, he was naked, running in the streets. Attacking people. He came at *us*!" The detectives dropped him, hard, into a chair. "You didn't see him, man. That fucker bled *white*. He had this fucking . . . this *thing* in his mouth! It wasn't fucking *human*!"

One of the detectives came over to Setrakian's booking sergeant's cubicle, wiping sweat off his face with a paper towel. "Crazy-ass Mex. Two-time juvie loser, just turned eighteen. Killed a man this time, in a fight. Him and a buddy, must have jumped the guy, stripped off his clothes. Tried to roll him right in the middle of Times Square."

The booking sergeant rolled his eyes and continued pecking at his keyboard. He asked Setrakian another question, but Setrakian didn't hear him. He barely felt the seat beneath him, or the warped fists his old, broken hands made. Panic nearly overtook him at the thought of facing the unfaceable again. He saw the future. He saw families torn apart, annihilation, an apocalypse of agonies. Darkness reigning over light. Hell on earth.

At that moment Setrakian felt like the oldest man on the planet.

Suddenly, his dark panic was supplanted by an equally dark impulse: revenge. A second chance. The resistance, the fight—the coming war—it had to begin with him.

Strigoi.

The plague had started.

Isolation Ward, Jamaica Hospital Medical Center

Jim Kent, still in his street clothes, lying in the hospital bed, sputtered, "This is ridiculous. I feel fine."

Eph and Nora stood on either side of the bed. "Let's just call it a precaution, then," said Eph.

"Nothing happened. He must have knocked me down as I went through the door. I think I blacked out for a minute. Maybe a low-grade concussion."

Nora nodded. "It's just that . . . you're one of us, Jim. We want to make sure everything checks out."

"But—why in isolation?"

"Why not?" Eph forced a smile. "We're here already. And look—you've got an entire wing of the hospital to yourself. Best bargain in New York City."

Jim's smile showed that he wasn't convinced. "All right," he said finally. "But can I at least have my phone so I can feel like I'm contributing?"

Eph said, "I think we can arrange that. After a few tests."

"And—please tell Sylvia I'm all right. She's going to be panicked."

"Right," said Eph. "We'll call her as soon as we get out of here."

They left shaken, pausing before exiting the isolation unit. Nora said, "We have to tell him."

"Tell him what?" said Eph, a little too sharply. "We have to find out what we're dealing with first."

Outside the unit, a woman with wiry hair pulled back under a wide headband stood up from the plastic chair she had pulled in from the lobby. Jim shared an apartment in the East Eighties with his girlfriend, Sylvia, a horoscope writer for the *New York Post*. She brought five cats to the relationship, and he brought one finch, making for a very tense household. "Can I go in?" said Sylvia.

"Sorry, Sylvia. Rules of the isolation wing—only medical personnel. But Jim said to tell you that he's feeling fine."

Sylvia gripped Eph's arm. "What do *you* say?"

Eph said, tactfully, "He looks very healthy. We want to run some tests, just in case."

"They said he passed out, he was a bit woozy. Why the isolation ward?"

"You know how we work, Sylvia. Rule out all the bad stuff. Go step by step."

Sylvia looked to Nora for female reassurance.

Nora nodded and said, "We'll get him back to you as soon as we can."

Downstairs, in the hospital basement, Eph and Nora found an administrator waiting for them at the door to the morgue. "Dr. Goodweather, this is completely irregular. This door is never to be locked, and the hospital insists on being informed of what is going on—"

"I'm sorry, Ms. Graham," said Eph, reading her name off her hospital ID, "but this is official CDC business." He hated pulling rank like a bureaucrat, but occasionally being a government employee had its advantages. He took out the key he had appropriated and unlocked the door, entering with Nora. "Thank you for your cooperation," he said, locking it again behind him.

The lights came on automatically. Redfern's body lay underneath a sheet on a steel table. Eph selected a pair of gloves from the box near the light switch and opened up a cart of autopsy instruments.

"Eph," said Nora, pulling on gloves herself. "We don't even have a death certificate yet. You can't just cut him open."

"We don't have time for formalities. Not with Jim up there. And besides—I don't even know how we're going to explain his death in the first place. Any way you look at it, I murdered this man. My own patient."

"In self-defense."

"I know that. You know that. But I certainly don't have the time to waste explaining that to the police."

He took the large scalpel and drew it down Redfern's chest, making the Y incision from the left and right collarbones down on two diagonals to the top of the sternum, then straight down the center line of the trunk, over the abdomen to the pubis bone. He then peeled back the skin and underlying muscles, exposing the rib cage and the abdominal apron. He didn't have time to perform a full medical autopsy. But he did need to confirm some things that had shown up on Redfern's incomplete MRI.

He used a soft rubber hose to wash away the white, bloodlike leakage and viewed the major organs beneath the rib cage. The chest cavity was a mess, cluttered with gross black masses fed by spindly feeders, veinlike offshoots attached to the pilot's shriveled organs.

"Good God," said Nora.

Eph studied the growths through the ribs. "It's taken him over. Look at the heart."

It was misshapen, shrunken. The arterial structure had been altered also, the circulatory system grown more simplified, the arteries themselves covered over with a dark, cancerous blight.

Nora said, "Impossible. We're only thirty-six hours out from the plane landing."

Eph flayed Redfern's neck then, exposing his throat. The new construct was rooted in the midneck, grown out of the vestibular folds. The protuberance that apparently acted as a stinger lay in its retracted state. It connected straight into the trachea, in fact fusing with it, much like a cancerous growth. Eph elected not to anatomize further just yet, hoping instead to remove the muscle or organ or whatever it was in its entirety at a later time, to study it whole and determine its function.

Eph's phone rang then. He turned so that Nora could pull it from his pocket with her clean gloves. "It's the chief medical examiner's office," she said, reading the display. She answered it for him, and after listening for a few moments, told the caller, "We'll be right there."

Office of the Chief Medical Examiner, Manhattan

DIRECTOR BARNES ARRIVED at the OCME at Thirtieth and First at the same time as Eph and Nora. He stepped from his car, unmistakable in his goatee and navy-style uniform. The intersection was jammed with police cars and TV news crews set up outside the turquoise front of the morgue building.

Their credentials got them inside, all the way to Dr. Julius Mirnstein, the chief medical examiner for New York. Mirnstein was bald but for tufts of brown hair on the sides and back of his head, long faced, dour by nature, wearing the requisite white doctor's coat over gray slacks.

"We think we were broken into overnight—we don't know." Dr. Mirnstein looked at an overturned computer monitor and pencils spilled from a cup. "We can't get any of the overnight staff on the phone." He double-checked that with an assistant who had a telephone to her ear, and who shook her head in confirmation. "Follow me."

Down in the basement morgue, everything appeared to be in order, from the clean autopsy tables to the countertops, scales, and measuring devices. No vandalism here. Dr. Mirnstein led the way to the walk-in refrigerator and waited for Eph, Nora, and Director Barnes to join him.

The body cooler was empty. The stretchers were all still there, and a few discarded sheets, as well as some articles of clothing. A handful of dead bodies remained along the left wall. All the airplane casualties were gone.

"Where are they?" said Eph.

"That's just it," said Dr. Mirnstein. "We don't know."

Director Barnes stared at him for a moment. "Are you telling me that you believe someone broke in here overnight and *stole* forty-odd corpses?"

"Your guess is as good as mine, Dr. Barnes. I was hoping your people could enlighten me."

"Well," said Barnes, "they didn't just walk away."

Nora said, "What about Brooklyn? Queens?"

Dr. Mirnstein said, "I have not heard from Queens yet. But Brooklyn is reporting the same thing."

"The same thing?" said Nora. "The airline passengers' corpses are *gone*?"

"Precisely," said Dr. Mirnstein. "I called you here in the hopes that perhaps your agency had claimed these cadavers without our knowledge."

Barnes looked at Eph and Nora. They shook their heads.

Barnes said, "Christ. I have to get on the phone with the FAA."

Eph and Nora caught him before he did, away from Dr. Mirnstein. "We need to talk," said Eph.

The director looked from face to face. "How is Jim Kent?"

"He looks fine. He says he feels fine."

"Okay," said Barnes. "What?"

"He has a perforation wound in his neck, through the throat. The same as we found on the Flight 753 victims."

Barnes scowled. "How can that be?"

Eph briefed him on Redfern's escape from imaging and the subsequent attack. He pulled an MRI scan from an oversize X-ray envelope and stuck it up on a wall reader, switching on the backlight. "This is the pilot's 'before' picture."

The major organs were in view, everything looked sound. "Yes?" said Barnes.

Eph said, "This is the 'after' picture." He put up a scan showing Redfern's torso clouded with shadows.

Barnes put on his half-glasses. "Tumors?"

Eph said, "It's—uh—hard to explain, but it is new tissue, feeding off organs that were completely healthy just twenty-four hours ago."

Director Barnes pulled down his glasses and scowled again. "New tissue? What the hell do you mean by that?"

"I mean this." Eph went to a third scan, showing the interior of Redfern's neck. The new growth below the tongue was evident.

"What is it?" asked Barnes.

"A stinger," answered Nora. "Of some sort. Muscular in construction. Retractable, fleshy."

Barnes looked at her as if she was crazy. "A stinger?"

"Yes, sir," said Eph, quick to back her up. "We believe it's responsible for the cut in Jim's neck."

Barnes looked back and forth between them. "You're telling me that one of the survivors of the airplane catastrophe grew a stinger and attacked Jim Kent with it?"

Eph nodded and referred to the scans again as proof. "Everett, we need to quarantine the remaining survivors."

Barnes checked Nora, who nodded rigorously, with Eph on this all the way.

Director Barnes said, "The inference is that you believe this . . . this tumorous growth, this biological transformation . . . is somehow transmissible?"

"That is our supposition and our fear," said Eph. "Jim may well be infected. We need to determine the progression of this syndrome, whatever it is, if we want to have any chance at all of arresting it and curing him."

"Are you telling me you saw this . . . this retractable stinger, as you call it?"

"We both did."

"And where is Captain Redfern now?"

"At the hospital."

"His prognosis?"

Eph answered before Nora could. "Uncertain."

Barnes looked at Eph, now starting to sense that something wasn't kosher.

Eph said, "All we are requesting is an order to compel the others to receive medical treatment—"

"Quarantining three people means potentially panicking three hundred million others." Barnes checked their faces again, as though for final confirmation. "Do you think this relates in any way to the disappearance of these bodies?"

"I don't know," said Eph. What he almost said was, *I don't want to know.*

"Fine," said Barnes. "I will start the process."

"*Start* the process?"

"This will take some doing."

Eph said, "We need this now. Right now."

"Ephraim, what you have presented me with here is bizarre and unsettling, but it is apparently isolated. I know you are concerned for the health of a colleague, but securing a federal order of quarantine means that I have to request and receive an executive order from the president, and I don't carry those around in my wallet. I don't see any indication of a potential pandemic just yet, and so I must go through normal channels. Until that time, I do not want you harassing these other survivors."

"Harassing?" said Eph.

"There will be enough panic without our overstepping our obligations. I might point out to you, if the other survivors have indeed become ill, why haven't we heard from them by now?"

Eph had no answer.

"I will be in touch."

Barnes went off to make his calls.

Nora looked at Eph. She said, "Don't."

"Don't what?" She could see right through him.

"Don't go looking up the other survivors. Don't screw up our chance of saving Jim by pissing off this lawyer woman or scaring off the others."

Eph was stewing when the outside doors opened. Two EMTs wheeled in an ambulance gurney with a body bag set on top, met by two morgue attendants. The dead wouldn't wait for this mystery to play itself out. They would just keep coming. Eph foresaw what would happen to New York City in the grip of a true plague. Once the municipal resources were overwhelmed—police, fire, sanitation, morticians—the entire island, within weeks, would degenerate into a stinking pile of compost.

A morgue attendant unzipped the bag halfway—and then emitted an uncharacteristic gasp. He backed away from the table with his gloved hands dripping white, the opalescent fluid oozing from the black rubber bag, down the side of the stretcher, onto the floor.

"What the hell is this?" the attendant asked the EMTs, who stood by the doorway looking particularly disgusted.

"Traffic fatality," said one, "following a fight. I don't know . . . must have been a milk truck or something."

Eph pulled gloves from the box on the counter and approached the bag, peering inside. "Where's the head?"

"In there," said the other EMT. "Somewhere."

Eph saw that the corpse had been decapitated at the shoulders, the remaining mass of its neck splattered with gobs of white.

"*And* the guy was naked," added the EMT. "Quite a night."

Eph drew the zipper all the way down to the bottom seam. The headless corpse was overweight, male, roughly fifty. Then Eph noticed its feet.

He saw a wire wound around the bare big toe. As though there had been a casualty tag attached.

Nora saw the toe wire also, and blanched.

"A fight, you say?" said Eph.

"That's what they told us," said the EMT, opening the door to the outside. "Good day to you, and good luck."

Eph zipped up the bag. He didn't want anyone else seeing the tag wire. He didn't want anyone asking him questions he couldn't answer.

He turned to Nora. "The old man."

Nora nodded. "He wanted us to destroy the corpses," she remembered.

"He knew about the UV light." Eph stripped off his latex gloves, thinking again of Jim, lying alone in isolation—with who could say what growing inside him. "We have to find out what else he knows."

17th Precinct Headquarters, East Fifty-first Street, Manhattan

SETRAKIAN COUNTED thirteen other men inside the room-size cage with him, including one troubled soul with fresh scratches on his neck, squatting in the corner and rubbing spit vigorously into his hands.

Setrakian had seen worse than this, of course—much worse. On another continent, in another century, he had been imprisoned as a Romanian Jew in World War II, in the extermination camp known as Treblinka. He was nineteen when the camp was brought down in 1943, still a boy. Had he entered the camp at the age he was now, he would not have lasted a few days—perhaps not even the train ride there.

Setrakian looked at the Mexican youth on the bench next to him, the one he had first seen in booking, who was now roughly the same age Setrakian had been when the war ended. His cheek was an angry blue and dried black blood clogged the slice beneath his eye. But he appeared to be uninfected.

Setrakian was more concerned about the youth's friend, lying on the bench next to him, curled up on his side, not moving.

For his part, Gus, feeling angry and sore, and jittery now that his adrenaline was gone, grew wary of the old man looking over at him. "Got a problem?"

Others in the tank perked up, drawn by the prospect of a fight between a Mexican gangbanger and an aged Jew.

Setrakian said to him, "I have a very great problem indeed."

Gus looked at him darkly. "Don't we all, then."

Setrakian felt the others turning away, now that there would be no sport to interrupt their tedium. Setrakian took a closer look at the Mexican's curled-up friend. His arm lay over his face and neck, his knees were pulled up tight, almost into a fetal position.

Gus was looking over at Setrakian, recognizing him now. "I know you."

Setrakian nodded, used to this, saying, "118th Street."

"Knickerbocker Loan. Yeah—shit. You beat my brother's ass one time."

"He stole?"

"Tried to. A gold chain. He's a druggie shitbag now, nothing but a ghost. But back then, he was tough. Few years older than me."

"He should have known better."

"He *did* know better. Why he tried it. That gold chain was just a trophy, really. He wanted to defy the street. Everybody warned him, 'You don't fuck with the pawnbroker.'"

Setrakian said, "The first week I took over the shop, someone broke my front window. I replaced it—and then I watch, and I wait. Caught the next bunch who came to break it. I gave them something to think about, and something to tell their friends. That was more than thirty years ago. I haven't had a problem with my glass since."

Gus looked at the old man's crumpled fingers, outlined by wool gloves. "Your hands," he said. "What happened, you get caught stealing once?"

"Not stealing, no," said the old man, rubbing his hands through the wool. "An old injury. One I did not receive medical attention for until much too late."

Gus showed him the tattoo on his hand, making a fist so that the webbing between his thumb and forefinger swelled up. It showed three black circles. "Like the design on your shop sign."

"Three balls is an ancient symbol for a pawnbroker. But yours has a different meaning."

"Gang sign," said Gus, sitting back. "Means thief."

"But you never stole from me."

"Not that you knew, anyway," said Gus, smiling.

Setrakian looked at Gus's pants, the holes burned into the black fabric. "I hear you killed a man."

Gus's smile went away.

"You were not wounded? The cut on your face, you received from the police?"

Gus stared at him now, like the old man might be some kind of jailhouse informer. "What's it to you?"

Setrakian said, "Did you get a look inside his mouth?"

Gus turned to him. The old man was leaning forward, almost in prayer. Gus said, "What do you know about that?"

"I know," said the old man, without looking up, "that a plague has been loosed upon this city. And soon the world beyond."

"This wasn't no plague. This was some crazy psycho with kind of a . . . a crazy-ass tongue coming up out of his . . ." Gus felt ridiculous saying this aloud. "So what the fuck *was* that?"

Setrakian said, "What you fought was a dead man, possessed by a disease."

Gus remembered the look on the fat man's face, blank and hungry. His white blood. "What—like a *pinche* zombie?"

Setrakian said, "Think more along the lines of a man with a black cape. Fangs. Funny accent." He turned his head so that Gus could hear him better. "Now take away the cape and fangs. The funny accent. Take away anything funny about it."

Gus hung on the old man's words. He had to know. His somber voice, his melancholy dread, it was contagious.

"Listen to what I have to say," the old man continued. "Your friend here. He has been infected. You might say—bitten."

Gus looked over at unmoving Felix. "No. No, he's just . . . the cops, they knocked him out."

"He is changing. He is in the grip of something beyond your comprehension. A disease that changes human people into nonpeople. This person is no longer your friend. He is turned."

Gus remembered seeing the fat man on top of Felix, their maniacal embrace, the man's mouth going at Felix's neck. And the look on Felix's face—a look of terror and awe.

"You feel how hot he is? His metabolism, racing. It takes great energy to change—painful, catastrophic changes are taking place inside his body now. The development of a parasitic organ system to accommodate his new state of being. He is metamorphosing into a feeding organism. Soon, twelve to thirty-six hours from the time of infection, but most likely tonight, he will arise. He will thirst. He will stop at nothing to satisfy his craving."

Gus stared at the old man as though in a state of suspended animation.

Setrakian said, "Do you love your friend?"

Gus said, "What?"

"By 'love,' I mean honor, respect. If you love your friend—you will destroy him before he is completely turned."

Gus's eyes darkened. "Destroy him?"

"Kill him. Or else he will turn you."

Gus shook his head in slow motion. "But . . . if you say he's already dead . . . how can I kill him?"

"There are ways," said Setrakian. "How did you kill the one who attacked you?"

"A knife. That thing coming out of his mouth—I cut up that shit."

"His throat?"

Gus nodded. "That too. Then a truck hit him, finished the job."

"Separating the head from the body is the surest way. Sunlight also works—direct sunlight. And there are other, more ancient methods."

Gus turned to look at Felix. Lying there, not moving. Barely breathing. "Why doesn't anybody know about this?" he said. He turned back to Setrakian, wondering which one of them was crazy. "Who are you really, old man?"

"*Elizalde! Torrez!*"

Gus was so absorbed in the conversation that he never saw the cops enter the cell. He looked up at hearing his and Felix's names and saw four policemen wearing latex gloves come forward, geared up for a struggle. Gus was pulled to his feet before he even knew what was happening.

They tapped Felix's shoulder, slapped at his knee. When that failed to rouse him, they lifted him up bodily, locking their arms underneath his. His head hung low and his feet dragged as they hauled him away.

"Listen, please." Setrakian got to his feet behind them. "This man—he is sick. Dangerously ill. He has a communicable disease."

"Why we wear these gloves, Pops," called back one cop. They wrenched up Felix's limp arms as they dragged him through the door. "We deal with STDs all the time."

Setrakian said, "He must be segregated, do you hear me? Locked up separately."

"Don't worry, Pops. We always offer preferential treatment to killers."

Gus's eyes stayed on the old man as the tank door was closed and the cops pulled him away.

Stoneheart Group, Manhattan

HERE WAS the bedroom of the great man.

Climate controlled and fully automated, the presets adjustable through a small console just an arm's reach away. The shushing of the corner humidifiers in concert with the drone of the ionizer and the whispering air-filtration system was like a mother's reassuring hush. Every man, thought Eldritch Palmer, should slumber nightly in a womb. And sleep like a baby.

Dusk was still many hours away, and he was impatient. Now that everything was in motion—the strain spreading throughout New York City with the sure exponential force of compound interest, doubling and doubling itself again every night—he hummed with the glee of a greedy banker. No financial success, of which there had been plenty, ever enlivened him as much as did this vast endeavor.

His nightstand telephone toned once, the handset flashing. Any calls to this phone had to be routed through his nurse and assistant, Mr. Fitzwilliam, a man of extraordinary good judgment and discretion. "Good afternoon, sir."

"Who is it, Mr. Fitzwilliam?"

"Mr. Jim Kent, sir. He says it is urgent. I am putting him through."

In a moment, Mr. Kent, one of Palmer's many well-placed Stoneheart Society members, said, "Yes, hello?"

"Go ahead, Mr. Kent."

"Yes—can you hear me? I have to talk quietly . . ."

"I can hear you, Mr. Kent. We were cut off last time."

"Yes. The pilot had escaped. Walked away from testing."

Palmer smiled. "And he is gone now?"

"No. I wasn't sure what to do, so I followed him through the hospital until Dr. Goodweather and Dr. Martinez caught up with him. They said Redfern is okay, but I can't confirm his status. I heard another nurse saying I was alone up here. And that members of the Canary project had taken over a locked room in the basement."

Palmer darkened. "You are alone up where?"

"In this isolation ward. Just a precaution. Redfern must have hit me or something, he knocked me out."

Palmer was silent for a moment. "I see."

"If you would explain to me exactly what I am supposed to be looking for, I could assist you better—"

"You said they have commandeered a room in the hospital?"

"In the basement. It might be the morgue. I will find out more later."

Palmer said, "How?"

"Once I get out of here. They just need to run some tests on me."

Palmer reminded himself that Jim Kent was not an epidemiologist himself, but more of a facilitator for the Canary project, with no medical training. "You sound as though you have a sore throat, Mr. Kent."

"I do. Just a touch of something."

"Mm-hmm. Good day, Mr. Kent."

Palmer hung up. Kent's exposure was merely an aggravation, but the report about the hospital morgue room was troubling. Though in any worthy venture, there are always hurdles to overcome. A lifetime of deal making had taught him that it was the setbacks and pitfalls that make final victory so sweet.

He picked up the handset again and pressed the star button.

"Yes, sir?"

"Mr. Fitzwilliam, we have lost our contact within the Canary project. You will ignore any further calls from his mobile phone."

"Yes, sir."

"And we need to dispatch a team to Queens. It seems there may be something in the basement of the Jamaica Hospital Medical Center that needs retrieving."

Flatbush, Brooklyn

ANN-MARIE BARBOUR checked again to make sure that she had locked all the doors, then went through the house twice—room by room, top to bottom—touching every mirror twice in order to calm herself down. She could not pass any reflective surface without reaching out to it with the first two fingers of her right hand, a nod following each touch, a rhythmic routine resembling genuflection. Then she went through a third time, wiping each surface clean with a fifty-fifty mix of Windex and holy water until she was satisfied.

When she felt in control of herself again, she phoned her sister-in-law, Jeanie, who lived in central New Jersey.

"They're fine," said Jeanie, referring to the children, whom she had come and picked up the day before. "Very well behaved. How is Ansel?"

Ann-Marie closed her eyes. Tears leaked out. "I don't know."

"Is he better? You gave him the chicken soup I brought?"

Ann-Marie was afraid her trembling lower jaw would be detected in her speech. "I will. I . . . I'll call you back."

She hung up and looked out the back window, at the graves. Two patches of overturned dirt. Thinking of the dogs lying there.

Ansel. What he had done to them.

She scrubbed her hands, then went through the house again, just the downstairs this time. She pulled out the mahogany chest from the buffet in the dining room and opened up the good silver, her wedding silver. Shiny and polished. Her secret stash, hidden there as another woman might hide candy or pills. She touched each utensil, her fingertips going back and forth from the silver to her lips. She felt that she would fall apart if she didn't touch every single one.

Then she went to the back door. She paused there, exhausted, her hand on the knob, praying for guidance, for strength. She prayed for knowledge, to understand what was happening, and to be shown the right thing to do.

She opened the door and walked down the steps to the shed. The shed from which she had dragged the dogs' corpses to the corner of the yard, not knowing what else to do. Luckily, there had been an old shovel underneath the front porch, so she didn't have to go back into the shed. She buried them in shallow soil and wept over their graves. Wept for them and for her children and for herself.

She stepped to the side of the shed, where orange and yellow mums were planted in a box beneath a small, four-pane window. She hesitated before looking inside, shading her eyes from the sunlight. Yard tools hung from pegboard walls inside, other tools stacked on shelves, and a small workbench. The sunlight through the window formed a perfect rectangle on the dirt floor, Ann-Marie's shadow falling over a metal stake driven into the ground. A chain like the one on the door was attached to the stake, the end of which was obscured by her angle of vision. The floor showed signs of digging.

She went back to the front, stopping before the chained doors. Listening.

"Ansel?"

No more than a whisper on her part. She listened again, and, hearing nothing, put her mouth right up to the half inch of space between the rain-warped doors.

"Ansel?"

A rustling. The vaguely animalistic sound terrified her . . . and yet reassured her at the same time.

He was still inside. Still with her.

"Ansel . . . I don't know what to do . . . please . . . tell me what to do . . . I can't do this without you. I need you, dearest. Please answer me. What will I do?"

More rustling, like dirt being shaken off. A guttural noise, as from a clogged pipe.

If she could just see him. His reassuring face.

Ann-Marie reached inside the front of her blouse, drawing out the stubby key that hung on a shoelace there. She reached for the lock that secured the chain through the door handles and inserted the key, turning it until it clicked, the curved top disengaging from the thick steel base. She unwound the chain and pulled it through the metal handles, letting it fall to the grass.

The doors parted, swinging out a few inches on their own. The sun was straight overhead now, the shed dark inside but for residual light from the small window. She stood before the opening, trying to see inside.

"Ansel?"

She saw a shadow stirring.

"Ansel . . . you have to keep quieter, at night . . . Mr. Otish from across the street called the police, thinking it was the dogs . . . the dogs . . ."

She grew teary, everything threatening to spill out of her.

"I . . . I almost told him about you. I don't know what to do, Ansel. What is the right thing? I am so lost here. Please . . . I need you . . ."

She was reaching for the doors when a moanlike cry shocked her. He drove at the shed doors—at her—attacking from within. Only the staked chain jerked him back, strangling an animal roar in his throat. But as the doors burst open, she saw—before her own scream, before she slammed the doors on him like shutters on a ferocious hurricane— her husband crouched in the dirt, naked but for the dog collar tight around his straining neck, his mouth black and open. He had torn away most of his hair just as he had torn off his clothes, his pale, blue-veined body filthy from sleeping—hiding—beneath the dirt like a dead thing that had burrowed into its own grave. He bared his bloodstained teeth, eyes rolling back inside his head, recoiling from the sun. A demon. She wound the chain back through the handles with wildly fluttering hands and fastened the lock, then turned and fled back into her house.

Vestry Street, Tribeca

THE LIMOUSINE took Gabriel Bolivar straight to his personal physician's office in a building with an underground garage. Dr. Ronald Box was the primary physician for many New York–based celebrities of film, television, and music. He was not a Rock Doc, or a Dr. Feelgood, a pure prescription-writing machine—although he was liberal with his electronic pen. He was a trained internist, and well versed in drug-rehabilitation centers, the treatment of sexually transmitted diseases, hepatitis C, and other fame-related maladies.

Bolivar went up the elevator in a wheelchair, clad only in a black robe, sunk into himself like an old man. His long, silken black hair had gone dry and was falling out in patches. He covered his face with thin, arthriticlike hands so that none would recognize him. His throat was so swollen and raw that he could barely speak.

Dr. Box saw him right away. He was looking through images transferred electronically from the clinic. The images came with a note of apology from the head clinician, who saw only the results and not the patient, promising to repair their machines and suggesting another round of tests in a day or two. But, looking at Bolivar, Dr. Box didn't think it was their equipment that was corrupt. He went over Bolivar with his stethoscope, listening to his heart, asking him to breathe. He tried to look into Bolivar's throat, but the patient declined, wordlessly, his black-red eyes glaring in pain.

"How long have you had those contact lenses in?" asked Dr. Box.

Bolivar's mouth curled into a jagged snarl and he shook his head.

Dr. Box looked at the linebacker standing by the door, wearing a driver's uniform. Bolivar's bodyguard, Elijah—six foot six, two hundred and sixty pounds—looked very nervous, and Dr. Box was becoming frightened. He examined the rock star's hands, which appeared aged and sore yet not at all fragile. He tried to check the lymph nodes under his jaw, but the pain was too great. The temperature reading from the clinic had read 123° F, a human impossibility, and yet, standing near enough to feel the heat coming off Bolivar, Dr. Box believed it.

Dr. Box stood back.

"I don't really know how to tell you this, Gabriel. Your body, it seems, is riddled with malignant neoplasms. That's cancer. I'm seeing carcinoma, sarcoma, and lymphoma, and all of it is wildly metastasized. There is no medical precedent for this that I am aware of, although I will insist on involving some experts in the field."

Bolivar just sat there, listening, a baleful look in his discolored eyes.

"I don't know what it is, but something has you in its grip. I do mean that literally. As far as I can tell, your heart has ceased beating on its own. It appears that the cancer is . . . manipulating the organ now. Beating it for you. Your lungs, the same. They are being invaded and . . . almost absorbed, transformed. As though . . ." Dr. Box was just realizing this now. "As though you are in the midst of a metamorphosis. Clinically, you could be considered deceased. It appears that the cancer is keeping you alive. I don't know what else to say to you. Your organs are all failing, but your cancer . . . well, your cancer is doing great."

Bolivar sat staring into the middle distance with those frightful eyes. His neck bucked slightly, as though he were trying to formulate speech but could not get his voice past an obstruction.

Dr. Box said, "I want to check you in to Sloan-Kettering right away. We can do so under an assumed name with a dummy social security number. It's the top cancer hospital in the country. I want Mr. Elijah to drive you there now—"

Bolivar emitted a rumbling chest groan that was an unmistakable *no*. He placed his hands on the armrests of the wheelchair and Elijah came forward to brace the rear handles as Bolivar rose to his feet. He took a moment regaining his balance, then picked at the belt of his robe with his sore hands, the knot falling open.

Revealed beneath his robe was his limp penis, blackened and shriveled, ready to drop from his groin like a diseased fig from a dying tree.

Bronxville

NEEVA, THE LUSSES' NANNY, still very much rattled by the events of the past twenty-four hours, left the children in the care of her nephew, Emile, while her daughter, Sebastiane, drove her back to Bronxville.

She had kept the Luss children, Keene and his eight-year-old sister, Audrey, eating Frosted Flakes for lunch, and cubed fruit, things Neeva had taken with her from the Luss house when she'd fled.

Now she was returning for more. The Luss children wouldn't eat her Haitian cooking, and—more pressingly—Neeva had forgotten Keene's Pulmicort, his asthma medication. The boy was wheezing and looking pasty.

They pulled in to find Mrs. Guild's green car in the Lusses' driveway, the sight of which gave Neeva pause. She told Sebastiane to wait for her there, then got out and straightened her slip beneath her dress, going with her key to the side entrance. The door opened without any tone, the house alarm not set. Neeva walked through the perfectly appointed mudroom with built-in cubbies and coat hooks and heated tile floor—a mudroom that had never seen any mud—and pushed through the French doors into the kitchen.

It did not appear that anyone had been in the room since she had left with the children. She stood still inside the doorway and listened with extraordinary attention, holding her breath for as long as she could before exhaling. She heard nothing.

"Hallo?" she called a few times, wondering if Mrs. Guild, with whom she had a largely silent relationship—the housekeeper, Neeva suspected, was a silent racist—would answer. Wondering if Joan—a mother so devoid of natural maternal instinct as to be, for all her lawyerly success, like a child herself—would answer. And knowing, in both cases, that they would not.

Hearing nothing, she crossed to the central island and laid her bag gently down on it, between the sink and the countertop range. She opened the snack cabinet, and quickly, a bit more like a thief than she had imagined, filled a Food Emporium bag with crackers and juice pouches and Smartfood popcorn—stopping once in a while to listen.

After raiding the paneled refrigerator of string cheese and yogurt drinks, she noticed Mr. Luss's number on the contact sheet taped to the wall near the kitchen phone. A bolt of uncertainty shot through her. What could she say to him? *Your wife is ill. She is not right. So I take the children.* No. As it was, she barely exchanged words with the man. There was something evil in this magnificent house, and her first and only duty—both as an employee and as a mother herself—was the safety of the children.

She checked the cabinet over the built-in wine cooler, but the box of Pulmicort was empty, just as she had dreaded. She had to go down to the basement pantry. At the top of the curling, carpeted stairs, she paused and pulled from her bag her black enameled crucifix. She descended with it at her side just in case. From the bottom step, the basement appeared very dark for that time of day. She flipped up every switch on the panel and stood listening after the lights came on.

They called it the basement, but it was actually another fully appointed floor of their home. They had installed a home theater downstairs, complete with theater chairs and a reproduction popcorn cart. Another subroom was jammed with toys and game tables; another was the laundry where Mrs. Guild kept up with the family's clothing and linens. There was also a fourth bathroom, the pantry, and a recently installed temperature-controlled wine cellar. It was European in style, the workers having broken through the basement foundation to create a pure dirt floor.

The heat came rumbling on with a sound like that of somebody kicking the furnace—the actual working guts of the basement were hidden behind a door somewhere—and the sound nearly sent Neeva through the ceiling. She turned back to the stairs, but the boy needed his nebulizer medicine, his color wasn't good.

She crossed the basement determinedly, and was between two leather theater chairs, halfway to the folding door of the pantry, when she noticed the stuff stacked up against the windows. Why it had seemed so dark down there in the middle of the day: toys and old packing cartons were arranged in a tower up the wall, obscuring the small windows, with old clothes and newspapers snuffing out every ray of the day's sun.

Neeva stared, wondering who had done this. She hurried to the pantry, finding Keene's asthma medicine stacked on the same steel-wire shelf as Joan's vitamins and tubs of candy-colored Tums. She pulled down two long boxes of the plastic vials, ignoring the rest of the food in her haste, rushing away without closing the door.

Starting back across the basement, she noticed that the door to the laundry room was ajar. Something about that door, which was never left open, represented the disruption of normal order that Neeva felt so palpably in this house.

She saw rich and dark dirt stains on the plush carpeting then, spaced almost like footprints. Her eye followed them to the wine cellar door she had to pass in order to reach the stairs. She saw soil smeared on the door handle.

Neeva felt it as she neared the wine cellar door. From that earthen room, a tomblike blackness. A soullessness. And yet—not a coldness. Instead, a contradictory warmth. A heat, lurking and seething.

The door handle began to turn as she rushed past it to the stairs. Neeva, a fifty-three-year-old woman with bad knees, her feet as much kicking at the steps as running up them. She stumbled, steadying herself against the wall with her hand, the crucifix gouging out a small chunk of plaster. Something was behind her, coming up the stairs at her. She yelled in Creole as she emerged into the sunlit first floor, running the length of the long kitchen, grabbing her handbag, knocking over the Food Emporium bag, snacks and drinks crashing to the floor, too scared to turn back.

The sight of her mother running screaming from the house in her ankle-length floral dress and black shoes brought Sebastiane out of her car. "No!" yelled her mother, motioning her back inside. She ran as if she was being chased, but in fact there was no one behind her. Sebastiane dropped back into her seat, alarmed.

"Mama, what happened?"

"Drive!" Neeva yelled, her large chest heaving, her eyes still wild, focused on the open side door.

"Mama," said Sebastiane, putting the car into reverse. "This is kidnapping. They have *laws*. Did you call the husband? You said you would call the husband."

Neeva opened her palm, finding it bloody. She had gripped the beaded crucifix so tightly the crosspiece had cut into her flesh. She let it fall to the floor of the car.

17th Precinct Headquarters, East Fifty-first Street, Manhattan

THE OLD PROFESSOR sat at the very end of the bench inside lockup, as far away as possible from a shirtless, snoring man who had just relieved himself without wishing to trouble anyone else for directions to the toilet in the corner of the room, or even removing his pants.

"Setraykeen . . . Setarkian . . . Setrainiak . . ."

"Here," he answered, rising and walking toward the remedial reader in the police officer's uniform by the open tank door. The officer let him out and closed the door behind him.

"Am I being released?" asked Setrakian.

"I guess so. Your son's here to pick you up."

"My—"

Setrakian held his tongue. He followed the officer to an unmarked interrogation room. The cop pulled open the door and motioned for him to walk inside.

It took Setrakian a few moments, just long enough for the door to close behind him, to recognize the person on the other side of the bare table as Dr. Ephraim Goodweather of the Centers for Disease Control and Prevention.

Next to him was the female doctor who had been with him before. Setrakian smiled appreciatively at their ruse, though he was not surprised by their presence.

Setrakian said, "So it has begun."

Dark circles—like bruises of fatigue and sleeplessness—hung under Dr. Goodweather's eyes as he looked the old man up and down. "You want out of here, we can get you out. First I need an explanation. I need information."

"I can answer many of your questions. But we have lost so much time already. We must begin now—this moment—if we have any chance at all of containing this insidious thing."

"That's what I'm talking about," said Dr. Goodweather, thrusting out one hand rather harshly. "*What* is this insidious thing?"

"The passengers from the plane," said Setrakian. "The dead have risen."

Eph did not know how to answer that. He couldn't say. He wouldn't say.

"There is much you will need to let go of, Dr. Goodweather," said Setrakian. "I understand that you believe you are taking a risk in trusting the word of an old stranger. But, in a sense, I am taking a thousandfold greater risk entrusting this responsibility to you. What we are discussing here is nothing less than the fate of the human race—though I don't expect you to quite believe that yet, or understand it. You think that you are drafting me into your cause. The truth of the matter is, I am drafting you into mine."

THE OLD
PROFESSOR

Knickerbocker Loans and Curios, East 118th Street, Spanish Harlem

Eph put up his EMERGENCY BLOOD DELIVERY windshield placard and parked in a marked loading zone on East 119th Street, following Setrakian and Nora one block south to his corner pawnshop. The doors were gated, the windows shuttered with locked metal plates. Despite the tilted CLOSED sign jammed in the door glass over the store hours, a man in a tattered black peacoat and a high knit hat—like the kind Rastafarians liked to wear, except that he lacked the ropy dreadlocks to fill it out, so it sagged off his head like a collapsed soufflé—stood at the door with a shoe box in his hand, shifting his weight from foot to foot.

Setrakian came out with keys dangling from a chain, busying himself with the locks up and down the door grates, making his gnarled fingers work. "No pawns today," he said, allowing himself a sidelong glance at the box in the man's hand.

"Look here." The man produced a bundle of linen from the shoe box, a dinner napkin he unwrapped to reveal nine or ten utensils. "Good silverware. You buy silver, I know that."

"I do, yes." Setrakian, having unlocked the grate, rested the handle of his tall walking stick against his shoulder and selected a knife, weighing it, rubbing the blade with his fingers. After patting his vest pockets, he turned to Eph. "Do you have ten dollars, Doctor?"

In the interest of hurrying this along, Eph reached for his money clip and peeled off a ten-dollar bill. He handed it to the man with the shoe box.

Setrakian then handed the man back his utensils. "You take," he said. "Not real silver."

The man accepted the handout gratefully and backed away with the shoe box under his arm. "God bless."

Setrakian said, entering his shop, "We'll soon see about that."

Eph watched his money hustle off down the street, then followed Setrakian inside.

"The lights are right on the wall there," said the old man, pulling the gate ends to meet again, locking up.

Nora threw all three switches at once, illuminating glass cabinets, display walls, and the entrance where they stood. It was a small corner shop, wedge-shaped, banged into the city block with a wooden hammer. The first word that came to Eph's mind was "junk." Lots and lots of junk. Old stereo systems. VCRs and other outdated electronics. A wall display of musical instruments, including a banjo and a Keytar guitarlike keyboard from the 1980s. Religious statues and collectible plates. A couple of turntables and small mixing boards. A locked glass countertop featuring cheap brooches and high-flash, low-quality bling. Racks of clothes, mostly winter coats with fur collars.

So much junk that his heart fell a little. Had he entrusted this precious time to a crazy person?

"Look," he told the old man, "we have a colleague, we believe he is infected."

Setrakian passed him, tapping his oversize walking stick. He lifted the hinged counter with his gloved hand and invited Eph and Nora through. "We go up here."

A back staircase led to a door on the second floor. The old man touched the mezuzah before entering, leaning his tall stick against the wall. It was an aged apartment of low ceilings and worn-out rugs. The furniture hadn't been moved in perhaps thirty years.

"You are hungry?" Setrakian asked. "Look around, you'll find something." Setrakian lifted the top of a fancy pastry container, revealing an open box of Devil Dogs. He lifted one out, tearing open its cellophane wrapper. "Don't let your energy run down. Keep up your strength. You'll need it."

The old man bit into the crème-filled cake on his way to a bedroom to change clothes. Eph looked around the small kitchen, and then at Nora. The place smelled clean despite its cluttered appearance. Nora lifted, from the table with only one chair, a framed black-and-white portrait of a young raven-haired woman in a simple dark dress, posed upon a great rock at an otherwise empty beach, fingers laced over one bare knee, pleasant features arranged in a winning smile. Eph returned to the hallway through which they had entered, looking into the old mirrors hanging from the walls—dozens of them, of all different sizes, time-streaked and imperfect. Old books were stacked along both sides of the floor, narrowing the passageway.

The old man reappeared, having changed into different articles of the same sort of clothing: an old tweed suit with vest, braces, a necktie, and brown leather shoes buffed until thin. He still wore wool tipless gloves over his damaged hands.

"I see you collect mirrors," Eph said.

"Certain kinds. I find older glass to be most revealing."

"Are you now ready to tell us what is going on?"

The old man dipped his head gently to one side. "Doctor, this isn't something one simply tells. It is something that must be revealed." He moved past Eph to the door through which they had entered. "Please—come with."

Eph followed him back down the stairs, Nora behind him. They passed the first-floor pawnshop, continuing through another locked door to another curling flight leading down. The old man descended, one angled step at a time, his gnarled hand sliding down the cool iron rail, his voice filling the narrow passageway. "I consider myself a repository of ancient knowledge, of persons dead and books long forgotten. Knowledge accumulated over a life of study."

Nora said, "When you stopped us outside the morgue, you said a number of things. You indicated that you knew the dead from the airplane were not decomposing normally."

"Correct."

"Based upon?"

"My experience."

Nora was confused. "Experience with other aircraft-related incidents?"

"The fact that they were on an airplane is completely incidental.

I have seen this phenomenon before, indeed. In Budapest, in Basra. In Prague and not ten kilometers outside Paris. I have seen it in a tiny fishing village on the banks of the Yellow River. I have seen it at a seven-thousand-feet elevation in the Altai Mountains of Mongolia. And yes, I have seen it on this continent as well. Seen its traces. Usually dismissed as a fluke, or explained away as rabies or schizophrenia, insanity, or, most recently, an occasion of serial murder—"

"Hold on, hold on. You yourself have seen corpses slow to decompose?"

"It is the first stage, yes."

Eph said, "The first stage."

The landing curled to an end at a locked door. Setrakian produced a key, separate from the rest, hanging from a chain around his neck. The old man's crooked fingers worked the key into two padlocks, one large, one small. The door opened inward, hot lights coming on automatically, and they followed him inside the humming basement room, bright and deep.

The first thing to catch Eph's eye was a wall of battle armor, ranging from full knight's wear to chain mail to Japanese samurai torso and neck plates, and cruder gear made of woven leather for protecting the neck, chest, and groin. Weapons also: mounted swords and knives, their blades fashioned of bright, cold steel. More modern-looking devices were arranged on an old, low table, their battery packs in chargers. He recognized night-vision goggles and modified nail guns. And more mirrors, mostly pocket-size, arranged so that he could see himself staring in bewilderment at this gallery of . . . of what?

"The shop"—the old man gestured to the floor above them—"gave me a fair living, but I did not come to this line of business because of an affinity for transistor radios and heirloom jewelry."

He closed the door behind them, the lights around the door frame going dark. The installed fixtures ran the height and length of the door—purple tubes Eph recognized as ultraviolet lamps—arranged around the door like a force field of light.

To prohibit germs from entering the room? Or to keep something else out?

"No," he continued, "the reason I chose it as my profession was because it afforded me ready access to an underground market of esoteric items, antiquities, and tomes. Illicit, though not usually illegal. Acquired for my personal collection, and my research."

Eph looked around again. This looked less like a museum collection than a small arsenal. "Your research?"

"Indeed. I was for many years a professor of Eastern European Literature and Folklore at the University of Vienna."

Eph appraised him again. He sure dressed like a Viennese professor. "And you retired to become a Harlem pawnbroker-slash-curator?"

"I did not retire. I was made to leave. Disgraced. Certain forces aligned against me. And yet, as I look back now, going underground at that time most certainly saved my life. It was in fact the best thing I could have done." He turned to face them, folding his hands behind his back, professorially. "This scourge we are now witnessing in its earliest stages has existed for centuries. Over millennia. I suspect, though cannot prove, it goes back to the most ancient of times."

Eph nodded, not understanding the man, only glad to finally be making some progress. "So we are talking about a virus."

"Yes. Of sorts. A strain of disease that is a corruption of both the flesh and the spirit." The old man was positioned in such a way that, from Eph's and Nora's perspective, the array of swords on the wall fanned out on either side of him like steel-bladed wings. "So, a virus? Yes. But I should also like to introduce you to another *v* word."

"What's that?" he said.

"Vampire."

A word like that, spoken in earnestness, hangs in the air for a while.

"You are thinking," said Setrakian, the former professor, "of a moody overactor in a black satin cape. Or else a dashing figure of power, with hidden fangs. Or some existential soul burdened with the curse of eternal life. Or—Bela Lugosi meets Abbott and Costello."

Nora was looking around the room again. "I don't see any crucifixes or holy water. No strings of garlic."

"Garlic has certain interesting immunological properties, and can be useful in its own right. So its presence in the mythology is biologically understandable, at any rate. But crucifixes and holy water?" He shrugged. "Products of their time. Products of one Victorian author's fevered Irish imagination, and the religious climate of the day."

Setrakian had expected their expressions of doubt.

"They have always been here," he continued. "Nesting, feeding. In secret and in darkness, because that is their nature. There are seven originals, known as the Ancients. The Masters. Not one per continent. They are not solitary beings as a rule, but clannish. Until very recently—'recently' considering their open-ended life span—they were all spread throughout the greatest landmass, what we know today as Europe and Asia, the Russian federation, the Arabian peninsula, and the African continent. Which is to say, the Old World. There was a schism, a clash among their kind. The nature of this disagreement, I do not know. Suffice it to say, this rift preceded the discovery of the New World by centuries. Then the founding of the American colonies opened the door to a new and fertile land. Three remained behind in the Old World, and three went ahead to the New. Both sides respected the other's domain, and a truce was agreed upon and upheld.

"The problem was that seventh Ancient. He is a rogue who turned his back on both factions. While I cannot prove it at this time, the abrupt nature of this act leads me to believe that he is behind this."

"This," said Nora.

"This incursion into the New World. Breaking the solemn truce. This upsetting of the balance of their breed's existence. An act, essentially, of war."

Eph said, "A war of vampires."

Setrakian's smile was for himself. "You simplify because you cannot believe. You reduce; you diminish. Because you were raised to doubt and debunk. To reduce to a small set of knowns for easy digestion. Because you are a doctor, a man of science, and because this is America—where everything is known and understood, and God is a benevolent dictator, and the future must always be bright." He clasped his gnarled hands, as best as he could, touching his bare fingertips to his lips in a pensive moment. "This is the spirit here, and it is beautiful. Truly—I don't mock. Wonderful to believe only in what you *wish* to believe in, and to discount all else. I do respect your skepticism, Dr. Goodweather. And I say this to you in the hope that you will in turn respect my experience in this matter, and allow my observations into your highly civilized and scientific mind."

Eph said, "So you're saying, the airplane . . . one of them was on it. This rogue."

"Exactly."

"In the coffin. In the cargo hold."

"A coffin full of soil. They are of the earth, and like to return to that from which they arose. Like worms. *Vermis.* They burrow to nest. We would call it sleep."

"Away from daylight," said Nora.

"From sunlight, yes. It is in transit that they are most vulnerable."

"But you said this is a war of vampires. But isn't it vampires against people? All those dead passengers."

"This too will be difficult for you to accept. But to them we are not enemies. We are not worthy foes. We don't even rise to that level in their eyes. To them we are prey. We are food and drink. Animals in a pen. Bottles upon a shelf."

Eph felt a chill, but then just as quickly rejected his own shivery response. "And to someone who would say this sounds like so much science fiction?"

Setrakian pointed to him. "That device in your pocket. Your mobile telephone. You punch in a few numbers, and immediately you are in conversation with another person halfway around the world. *That* is science fiction, Dr. Goodweather. Science fiction come true." Here Setrakian smiled. "Do you require proof?"

Setrakian went to a low bench set against the long wall. There was a thing there covered in a drape of black silk and he reached for it in an odd way, his arm outstretched, pinching the nearest edge of fabric while keeping his body as far away from it as possible, and then drawing the cover off.

A glass container. A specimen jar, available from any medical supply house.

Inside, suspended in a dusky fluid, was a well-preserved human heart.

Eph stooped to regard it from a few feet away. "Adult female, judging by the size. Healthy. Fairly young. A fresh specimen." He looked back at Setrakian. "Where'd you get it?"

"I cut it out of the chest of a young widow in a village outside Shkodër, in northern Albania, in the spring of 1971."

Eph smiled at the strangeness of the old man's tale, leaning in for a closer look at the jar.

Something like a tentacle shot out of the heart, a sucker at its tip grabbing the glass where Eph's eye was.

Eph straightened fast. He froze, staring at the jar.

Nora, next to him, said, "Um . . . what the hell was that?"

The heart began moving in the serum.

It was throbbing.

Beating.

Eph watched the flattened, mouthlike sucker head scour the glass. He looked at Nora, next to him, staring at the heart. Then he looked at Setrakian, who hadn't moved, hands resting inside his pockets.

Setrakian said, "It animates whenever human blood is near."

Eph stared in pure disbelief. He edged closer again, this time to the right of the sucker's pale, lipless receptor. The outgrowth detached from the interior surface of the glass—then suddenly thrust itself toward him again.

"*Jesus!*" exclaimed Eph. The beating organ floated in there like some meaty, mutant fish. "It lives on without . . ." There was no blood supply. He looked at the stumps of its severed veins, aorta, and vena cava.

Setrakian said, "It is neither alive nor dead. It is animate. Possessed, you might say, but in the literal sense. Look closely and you will see."

Eph watched the throbbing, which he found to be irregular, not like a true heartbeat at all. He saw something moving around inside it. Wriggling.

"A . . . worm?" said Nora.

Thin and pale, lip-colored, two or three inches in length. They watched it make its rounds inside the heart, like a lone sentry dutifully patrolling a long-abandoned base.

"A blood worm," said Setrakian. "A capillary parasite that reproduces in the infected. I suspect, though have no proof, that it is the conduit of the virus. The actual vector."

Eph shook his head in disbelief. "What about this . . . this sucker?"

"The virus mimics the host's form, though it reinvents its vital systems in order to best sustain itself. In other words, it colonizes and adapts the host for its survival. The host being, in this case, a severed organ floating in a jar, the virus has found a way to evolve its own mechanism for receiving nourishment."

Nora said, "Nourishment?"

"The worm lives on blood. Human blood."

"Blood?" Eph squinted at the possessed heart. "From whom?"

Setrakian pulled his left hand out of his pocket. The wrinkled tips of his fingers showed at the end of the glove. The pad of his middle finger was scarred and smooth.

"A few drops every few days is enough. It will be hungry. I've been away."

He went to the bench and lifted the lid off the jar—Eph stepping back to watch—and, with the point of a little penknife from his keychain, pricked the tip of his finger over the jar. He did not flinch, the act so routine that it no longer hurt him.

His blood dripped into the serum.

The sucker fed on the red drops with lips like that of a hungry fish.

When he was done, the old man dabbed a bit of liquid bandage on his finger from a small bottle on the bench, returning the lid to the jar.

Eph watched the feeder turn red. The worm inside the organ moved more fluidly and with increased strength. "And you say you've kept this thing going in here for . . . ?"

"Since the spring of 1971. I don't take many vacations . . ." He smiled at his little joke, looking at his pricked finger, rubbing the dried tip. "She was a revenant, one who was infected. Who had been *turned*. The Ancients, who wish to remain hidden, will kill immediately after feeding, in order to prevent any spread of their virus. One got away somehow, returned home to claim its family and friends and neighbors, burrowing into their small village. This widow's heart had not been turned four hours before I found her."

"Four hours? How did you know?"

"I saw the mark. The mark of the *strigoi*."

Eph said, "*Strigoi?*"

"Old World term for vampire."

"And the mark?"

"The point of penetration. A thin breach across the front of the throat, which I am guessing you have seen by now."

Eph and Nora were nodding. Thinking about Jim.

Setrakian added, "I should say, I am not a man who is in the habit of cutting out human hearts. This was a bit of dirty business I happened upon quite by accident. But it was absolutely necessary."

Nora said, "And you've kept this thing going ever since then, feeding it like a . . . a pet?"

"Yes." He looked down at the jar, almost fondly. "It serves as a daily reminder. Of what I am up against. What *we* are now up against."

Eph was aghast. "In all this time . . . why haven't you shown this to anyone? A medical school. The evening news?"

"Were it that easy, Doctor, the secret would have become known years ago. There are forces aligned against us. This is an ancient secret, and it reaches deep. Touches many. The truth would never be allowed to reach a mass audience, but would be suppressed, and myself with it. Why I've been hiding here—hiding in plain sight—all these years. Waiting."

This kind of talk raised the hair on the back of Eph's neck. The truth was right there, right in front of him: the human heart in a jar, housing a worm that thirsted for the old man's blood.

"I'm not very good with secrets that imperil the future of the human race. No one else knows about this?"

"Oh, someone does. Yes. Someone powerful. The Master—he could not have traveled unaided. A human ally must have arranged for his safeguarding and transportation. You see—vampires cannot cross bodies of flowing water unless aided by a human. A human inviting them in. And now the seal—the truce—has been broken. By an alliance between *strigoi* and human. That is why this incursion is so shocking. And so fantastically threatening."

Nora turned to Setrakian. "How much time do we have?"

The old man had already run the numbers. "It will take this thing less than one week to finish off all of Manhattan, and less than a month to overtake the country. In two months—the world."

"No way," said Eph. "Not going to happen."

"I admire your determination," said Setrakian. "But you still don't quite know what it is you are up against."

"Okay," Eph said. "Then tell me—where do we start?"

Park Place, Tribeca

VASILIY FET pulled up in his city-marked van outside an apartment building down in Lower Manhattan. It didn't look like much from the outside, but had an awning and a doorman, and this was Tribeca after all. He would have double-checked the address were it not for the health department van parked illegally out in front, yellow dash light twirling. Ironically, in most buildings and homes in most parts of the city, exterminators were welcomed with open arms, like police arriving at the scene of a crime. Vasiliy didn't think that would be the case here.

His own van said BPCS-CNY on the back, standing for Bureau of Pest Control Services, City of New York. The health department inspector, Bill Furber, met him on the stairs inside. Billy had a sloping blond mustache that rode out the face waves caused by his constant jawing of nicotine-replacement gum. "Vaz," he called him, which was short for Vasya, the familiar diminutive form of his given Russian name. Vaz, or, simply, V, as he was often called, second-generation Russian, his gruff voice all Brooklyn. He was a big man, filling most of the stairway.

Billy clapped him on the arm, thanked him for coming. "My cousin's niece here, got bit on the mouth. I know—not my kinda building, but what can I do, they married into real estate money. Just so you know—it's family. I told them I was bringing in the best rat man in the five boroughs."

Vasiliy nodded with the quiet pride characteristic of exterminators. An exterminator succeeds in silence. Success means leaving behind no indication of his success, no trace that a problem ever existed, that a pest had ever been present or a single trap laid. It means that order has been preserved.

He pulled his wheeled case behind him like a computer repairman's tool kit. The interior of the loft opened to high ceilings and wide rooms, an eighteen-hundred-square-foot condo that cost three million easily in New York real estate dollars. Seated on a short, firm, basketball-orange sofa inside a high-tech room done in glass, teak, and chrome, a young girl clutched a doll and her mother. A large bandage covered the girl's upper lip and cheek. The mother wore her hair buzzed short; eyeglasses with narrow, rectangular frames; and a nubby, green knee-length wool skirt. She looked to Vasiliy like a visitor from a very hip, androgynous future. The girl was young, maybe five or six, and still frightened. Vasiliy would have attempted a smile, but his was the sort of face that rarely put children at ease. He had a jaw like the flat back of an ax blade and widely spaced eyes.

A panel television hung on the wall like a wide, glass-framed painting. On it, the mayor was speaking into a bouquet of microphones. He was trying to answer questions about the missing dead from the airplane, the bodies that had disappeared from the city's morgues. The NYPD was on high alert, and actively stopping all refrigerated trucks at bridges and tunnels. A TIPS line had been set up. The victims' families were outraged, and funerals had been put on hold.

Bill led Vasiliy to the girl's bedroom. A canopy bed, a gem-encrusted Bratz television and matching laptop, and an animatronic butterscotch pony in the corner. Vasiliy's eyes went immediately to a food wrapper near the bed. Toasted crackers with peanut butter inside. He liked those himself.

"She was in here taking a nap," said Billy. "Woke up feeling something gnawing on her lip. The thing was up on her pillow, Vaz. A rat in her bed. Kid won't sleep for a month. You ever heard of this?"

Vasiliy shook his head. There were rats in and around every building in Manhattan—no matter what landlords say or tenants think—but they didn't like to make their presence known, especially in the middle of the day. Rat attacks generally involve children, most often around the mouth, because that's where the food smell is. Norway rats— *Rattus norvegicus*, city rats—have a highly defined sense of smell and taste. Their front incisors are long and sharp, stronger than aluminum, copper, lead, and iron. Gnawing rats are responsible for one-quarter of all electric-cable breaks in the city, and the likely culprit behind the same percentage of fires of unknown origin. Their teeth are comparable in pure hardness to steel, and the alligator-like structure of their jaw allows for thousands of pounds of biting pressure. They can chew through cement and even stone.

Vasiliy said, "Did she see the rat?"

"She didn't know what it was. She screamed and flailed and it ran off. The emergency room told them it was a rat."

Vasiliy went to the window that was open a few inches to let in a breeze. He pushed it open farther and looked down three stories to a narrow cobblestone alley. The fire escape was ten or twelve feet from the window, but the centuries-old brick facing was uneven and craggy. People think of rats as squat and waddling, when in fact they move with squirrel-like agility. Especially when motivated by food or by fear.

Vasiliy pulled the girl's bed away from the wall and shed its bedding. He moved a dollhouse, a bureau, and a bookcase in order to look behind them, but he did not expect to find the rat still in the bedroom. He was merely eliminating the obvious.

He stepped out into the hallway, pulling his wheeled cart along the smooth, varnished wood. Rats have poor eyesight and move largely by feel. They get about quickly by repetition, wearing paths along low walls, rarely traveling more than sixty feet from their nest. They don't trust unfamiliar settings. This rat would have found the door and turned the corner, hugging the right-hand wall, his coarse fur gliding against the floorboard. The next open door led into a bathroom, the young daughter's own, decorated with a strawberry-shaped bath mat, a pale pink shower curtain, and a basket of bath bubbles and toys. Vasiliy scanned the room for hiding places, then sniffed the air. He nodded to Billy, who then closed the door on him.

Billy lingered a minute, listening, then decided to head back out to reassure the mother. He was almost there when he heard, from the hallway bathroom, a terrific *BANG!*—the sound of bottles falling into the bathtub—and a loud grunt and Vasiliy's voice, grown fierce, spurting Russian invective.

The mother and daughter looked stricken. Billy held out a hand to them in a gesture of patience—having accidentally swallowed his gum—then rushed back down the hall.

Vasiliy opened the bathroom door. He was wearing Kevlar-sleeved trapping gloves and holding a large sack. Something in the sack was writhing and pawing. And that something was big.

Vasiliy nodded once and handed the sack to Billy.

Billy couldn't do anything other than take it, otherwise the sack would fall and the rat would escape. He hoped the fabric was as sturdy as it seemed, the big rat twisting and fighting inside. Billy held the sack out as far from his body as his arm would reach while still allowing him to hold the flailing rat aloft. Vasiliy was, meanwhile, calmly—but too slowly—opening his cart. He removed a sealed package, a sponge prepared with halothane. Vasiliy took back the sack, and Billy was only too happy to relinquish it. He opened the top just long enough to drop the anesthetic inside, then closed it again. The rat struggled just as violently at first. Then it began to slow down. Vasiliy shook the sack to speed up the process.

He waited a few more moments after the fighting stopped, then opened the sack and reached inside, pulling the rat out tail first. It was sedated but not unconscious, its pink-digited front paws still digging their sharp nails into the air, its jaw snapping, its shiny black eyes open. This was a good-size one, maybe eight inches of body, the tail another eight. Its tough fur was dark gray on top, dirty white below. Nobody's escaped pet, this was a wild city rat.

Billy had moved many steps back. He had seen plenty of rats in his day, yet he never got used to them. Vasiliy seemed to be okay with it.

"She's pregnant," he said. Rats gestate for just twenty-one days and can birth a litter of up to twenty pups. One healthy female can breed two hundred and fifty pups each year—with half of that litter more females ready to mate. "Want me to bleed her for the lab?"

Billy shook his head, showing almost as much disgust as though Vasiliy had asked if he wanted to eat it. "The girl had her shots at the hospital. Look at the size, Vaz. In the good name of Christ. I mean, this isn't"—Billy lowered his voice—"this isn't some tenement in Bushwick, you catch my drift?"

Vasiliy did catch his drift. Intimately. Vasiliy's parents had first settled in Bushwick after they came over. Bushwick had seen waves of émigrés since the mid-1800s: the Germans, the English, the Irish, the Russians, the Polish, the Italians, the African Americans, the Puerto Ricans. Now it was Dominicans, Guyanese, Jamaicans, Ecuadorians, Indians, Koreans, Southeast Asians. Vasiliy spent a lot of time in the poorest neighborhoods of New York. He knew of families who used couch cushions, books, and furniture to wall off parts of their apartments every night, trying to keep out rats.

But this attack, indeed, was different. Daylight. The boldness. Usually it is only the weakest rats, forced out of the colony, who surface in search of food. This was a strong, healthy female. Highly unusual. Rats coexist in a fragile balance with man, exploiting the vulnerabilities of civilization, living off the larger breed's waste and refuse, lurking just out of sight, behind the walls or beneath the floorboards. The appearance of a rat symbolizes human anxiety and fear. Any incursion beyond the usual nocturnal scavenging indicates an alteration in the environment. Like man, rats are not accustomed to taking unnecessary risks: they have to be forced from the underground.

"Want me to comb it for fleas?"

"Christ, no. Just bag it and get rid of it. Whatever you do, don't show it to the girl. She's traumatized enough as it is."

Vasiliy pulled a large plastic bag from his kit and sealed the rat inside it with another sponge of halothane, this one a fatal dose. He stuffed the bag inside the sack to hide the evidence, then continued about his business, starting in the kitchen. He pulled out the heavy, eight-burner stove and the dishwasher. He checked the pipe holes under the sink. He saw no droppings, no burrows, but he seeded a little bait behind the cabinets anyway, because he was there. He did so without telling the occupants. People get nervous about poison, especially parents, but the truth is that rat poison is all over every building and street in Manhattan. Anything you see that resembles berry blue Pop Rocks or green kibble, you know rats have been spotted nearby.

Billy followed him down into the basement. It was neat and orderly, with no evident trash or soft refuse for nesting. Vasiliy scanned the space, sniffing for droppings. He had a good nose for rats, just as rats had a good nose for humans. He switched off the light, much to Bill's discomfort, and switched on the flashlight he wore clipped to the belt of his light blue overalls, shining purple instead of white. Rodent urine shows up indigo blue under black light, but here he saw none. He baited the crawl spaces with rodenticide and put down corner "motel"-type traps, just in case, then followed Billy back up to the lobby.

Billy thanked Vasiliy and told him he owed him one, and they went their separate ways at the door. Vasiliy was still puzzled though, and, after returning his kit and the dead rat to the back of his van, lit a Dominican corona and started walking. He went down the street and around to the cobblestone alley he had looked down upon from the girl's window. Tribeca was the sole remaining neighborhood in Manhattan with any alleys left.

Vasiliy hadn't gone more than a few steps before he saw his first rat. Skittering along the edge of a building, feeling its way around. He then saw another on the branch of a small, struggling tree grown up alongside a short brick wall. And a third, squatting in the stone gutter, drinking brown effluent flowing from some unseen garbage or sewage source.

As he stood there watching, rats started appearing out of the cobblestones. Literally, clawing up from between the worn-down stones, surfacing from the underground. Rats' skeletons are collapsible, allowing them to squeeze through holes no larger than the size of their skulls, about three-quarters of an inch in width. They were coming up through the gaps in twos and threes, and quickly scattering. Using the twelve-by-three stones as a ruler, Vasiliy estimated that these rats ranged from eight to ten inches in body length, doubled by their tail. In other words, fully grown adults.

Two garbage bags near him were twitching and bulging, rats eating their way through their insides. A small rat tried to dart past him to a trash barrel, and Vasiliy kicked out with his work boot, punting the muncher back fifteen feet. It landed in the middle of the alley, not moving. Within seconds, the other rats were greedily upon it, long, yellow incisors biting through fur. The most effective and efficient way to exterminate rats is to remove the food source from their environment and then let them eat one another.

These rats were hungry, and they were on the run. Such daytime surface activity was practically unheard of. This kind of mass displacement only happened in the wake of an event such as an earthquake or a building collapse.

Or, occasionally, a large construction project.

Vasiliy continued another block south, crossing Barclay Street to where the city opened up to the sky above, a sixteen-acre job site.

He stepped up to one of the viewing platforms overlooking the location of the former World Trade Center. They were nearing completion of the deep underground basin meant to support the new construction, the cement and steel columns now starting to rise out of the ground. The site existed like a gouge in the city—like the gnaw in the little girl's face.

Vasiliy remembered that apocalyptic September of 2001. A few days after the Twin Towers' collapse, he had gone in with the health department, starting with the shuttered restaurants around the perimeter of the site, clearing away abandoned food. Then down into the basements and underground rooms, never once seeing a live rat, but plenty of evidence of their presence, including miles of rat tracks enshrined in the settled dust. He remembered most vividly a Mrs. Fields cookie shop, almost entirely eaten through. The rat population was exploding at the site, the concern being that the rats would spill out of the ruins in search of new food sources, swarming into the surrounding streets and neighborhoods. So a massive, federally funded containment program was undertaken. Thousands of bait stations and steel-wire traps were set down in and around Ground Zero, and, thanks to Vasiliy's vigilance and that of others like him, the feared invasion never did materialize.

Vasiliy remained on a government contract to this day, his department overseeing a rat-control study in and around Battery Park. So he was pretty well caught up on local infestations, and had been throughout the beginnings of the construction project. And until now everything had been business as usual.

He looked down at the trucks pouring cement and the cranes moving rubble. He waited three minutes for a young boy to finish with one of the mounted viewfinders—the same kind they have on the top of the Empire State Building—then dropped in his two quarters and scanned the work site.

In a moment, he saw them, their little brown bodies scuttling out from corners, racing around stone piles, a few scampering hell bent for leather up the access road toward Liberty Street. Racing around rebar spikes marking the foundation of the Freedom Tower as though running a goddamned obstacle course. He looked for the breaks where the new construction would connect underground with the PATH subway. Then he turned the viewfinder higher and followed a line of them scrambling up the underpinnings of a steel platform along the east corner, clambering out onto strung wires. They were racing out of the basin, a mass exodus, following any escape route they could find.

Isolation Ward, Jamaica Hospital Medical Center

BEHIND THE SECOND DOOR of the isolation ward, Eph pulled on latex gloves. He would have insisted that Setrakian do the same, but another look at his crooked fingers made Eph wonder if it would even be possible.

They walked inside Jim Kent's bay, the only occupied station in the otherwise empty ward. Jim lay sleeping now, still in his street clothes, wires from his chest and hand leading to machines whose readings were quiet. The attending nurse had said his levels were dipping so low that all the automatic alarms—low heart rate, blood pressure, respiration, oxygen levels—had to be muted, because they kept going off.

Eph pushed past the hanging curtains of clear plastic, feeling Setrakian grow tense beside him. As they got close, Kent's vitals rose on all the readout screens—which was highly irregular.

"Like the worm in the jar," said Setrakian. "He senses us. He senses that blood is near."

"Can't be," said Eph.

He advanced farther. Jim's vitals and brainwave activity increased.

"Jim," said Eph.

His face was slack in sleep, his dark skin turning a putty gray color. Eph could see his pupils moving fast beneath his eyelids in a kind of manic REM sleep.

Setrakian drew back the last intervening layer of clear curtain with the silver wolf's head of his tall walking staff. "Not too close," he warned. "He is turning." Setrakian reached into his coat pocket. "Your mirror. Take it out."

The inside-front pocket of Eph's jacket was weighed down by a four-inch-by-three-inch silver-framed mirror, one of the many items the old man had collected from his basement vampire armory.

"You see yourself in there?"

Eph saw his reflection in the old glass. "Sure."

"Please use it to look at me."

Eph turned it at an angle, so as to view the old man's face. "Okay."

Nora said, "Vampires have no reflection."

Setrakian said, "Not quite. Please now—with caution—use it to look at his face."

Because the mirror was so small, Eph needed to step closer to the bed, his arm outstretched, holding the glass at an angle over Jim's head.

He couldn't pick up Jim's reflection at first. The image looked as though Eph's hand were violently shaking. But the background, the pillow and bed frame, were still.

Jim's face was a blur. It looked as though his head was shaking with tremendous speed, or vibrating with such force that his features were imperceptible.

He pulled his arm back fast.

"Silver backing," said Setrakian, tapping his own mirror. "That is the key. Today's mass-produced mirrors, with their chrome-sprayed backing, they won't reveal anything. But silver-backed glass always tells the truth."

Eph looked at himself in the mirror again. Normal. Except for the slight trembling of his own hand.

He angled the glass over Jim Kent's face again, trying to hold it still—and saw the tremulous blur that was Jim's reflection. As though his body were in the throes of something furious, his being vibrating too hard and too fast to be visibly rendered.

Yet to the naked eye he lay still and serene.

Eph handed it to Nora, who shared his astonishment, and his fear. "So this means . . . he's turning into a thing . . . a thing like Captain Redfern."

Setrakian said, "Following normal infection, they can complete their transformation and activate to feeding after just one day and night. It takes seven nights for one to fully turn, for the disease to consume the body and reshape it to its own end—its new parasitic state. Then about thirty nights to total maturity."

Nora said, "Total maturity?"

The old man said, "Pray we don't see that phase." He gestured toward Jim. "The arteries of the human neck offer the quickest access point, though the femoral artery is another direct route into our blood supply."

The neck breach was so neat it was not visible at the moment. Eph said, "Why blood?"

"Oxygen, iron, and many other nutrients."

"Oxygen?" asked Nora.

Setrakian nodded. "Their host bodies change. Part of the turning is that the circulatory and digestive systems merge, becoming one. Similar to insects. Their own blood substance lacks the iron-and-oxygen combination that accounts for the red color of human blood. Their product turns white."

"And the organs," Eph said. "Redfern's looked almost like cancers."

"The body system is being consumed and transformed. The virus takes over. They no longer breathe. They respire, merely as a vestigial reflex, but they don't oxygenate anymore. The unneeded lungs eventually shrivel and are readapted."

Eph said, "Redfern, when he attacked, exhibited a highly developed growth in his mouth. Like a well-developed muscular stinger underneath the tongue."

Setrakian nodded as though agreeing with Eph about the weather. "It engorges as they feed. Their flesh flushes almost crimson, their eyeballs, their cuticles. This stinger, as you call it, is in fact a reconversion, a repurposing of the old pharynx, trachea, and lung sacs with the newly developed flesh. Something like the sleeve of a jacket being reversed. The vampire can expel this organ from its own chest cavity, shooting out well over four and up to even six feet. If you anatomize a mature victim, you would find a muscular tissue, a sack that propels this for feeding. All they require is the regular ingestion of pure human blood. They are maybe like diabetics in that way. I don't know. You are the doctor."

"I thought I was," mumbled Eph. "Until now."

Nora said, "I thought vampires drank virgin blood. They hypnotize . . . they turn into bats . . . "

Setrakian said, "They are much romanticized. But the truth is more . . . how should I say?"

"Perverse," said Eph.

"Disgusting," said Nora.

"No," said Setrakian. "Banal. Did you find the ammonia?"

Eph nodded.

"They have a very compact digestive system," Setrakian continued. "No room for storing the food. Any undigested plasma and any other residues have to be expelled to make room for incoming nourishment. Much like a tick—excreting as it feeds."

Suddenly the temperature inside the bay changed. Setrakian's voice dropped to an icy whisper.

"*Strigoi*," he hissed. "Here."

Eph looked at Jim. Jim's eyes were open, his pupils dark, the sclera around them turning grayish orange, almost like an uncertain sky at dusk. He was staring at the ceiling.

Eph felt a spike of fear. Setrakian stiffened, his gnarled hand poised near the wolf's-head handle of his walking stick—ready to strike. Eph felt the electricity of his intent, and was shocked by the deep, ancient hatred he saw in the old man's eyes.

"Professor . . ." said Jim, on a slight groan escaping from his lips.

Then his eyelids fell closed again, Jim lapsing back into a REM-like trance.

Eph turned to the old man. "How did he . . . know you?"

"*He* doesn't," said Setrakian, still on alert, poised to strike. "He is like a drone now, becoming part of a hive. A body of many parts but one single will." He looked at Eph. "This thing must be destroyed."

"What?" said Eph. "No."

"He is no longer your friend," said Setrakian. "He is your enemy."

"Even if that is true—he is still my patient."

"This man is not ill. He has moved into a realm beyond illness. In a matter of hours, no part of him will remain. Apart from all that—it is supremely dangerous, keeping him here. As with the pilot, you will be placing the people in this building at great risk."

"What if . . . what if he doesn't get blood?"

"Without nourishment, he will begin caving. After forty-eight hours without feeding, his body will begin to fail, his system cannibalizing his body's human muscle and fat cells, slowly and painfully consuming itself. Until only the vampiric systems prevail."

Eph was shaking his head, hard. "What I need to do is formulate some protocol for treatment. If this disease is caused by a virus, I need to work toward finding a cure."

Setrakian said, "There is only one cure. Death. Destruction of the body. A merciful death."

Eph said, "We're not veterinarians here. We can't just put down people who are too ill to survive."

"You did so with the pilot."

Eph stuttered, "That was different. He attacked Nora and Jim—he attacked me."

"Your philosophy of self-defense, if truly applied, absolutely holds in this situation."

"So would a philosophy of genocide."

"And if that is their goal—total subjugation of the human race— what is your answer?"

Eph didn't want to get tangled up in abstractions here. He was looking at a colleague. A friend.

Setrakian saw that he was not going to change their minds here, not just yet. "Take me to the pilot's remains, then. Perhaps I can convince you."

No one spoke on the elevator ride down to the basement. There, instead of finding the locked morgue room, they found the door open and the police and the hospital administrator huddling around it.

Eph went up to them. "What do you think you're doing . . . ?"

He saw that the doorjamb was scratched, the metal door frame dented and jimmied, the lock broken from the outside.

The administrator hadn't opened the door. Someone else had broken in.

Eph quickly looked inside.

The table was bare. Redfern's body was gone.

Eph turned to the administrator, wanting more information, but to his surprise found her retreating a few steps down the hall, glancing back at him as she spoke with the cops.

Setrakian said, "We should go now."

Eph said, "But I have to find out where his remains are."

"They are gone," said Setrakian. "They will never be recovered." The old man gripped Eph's arm with surprising strength. "I believe they have served their purpose."

"Their purpose? What is that?"

"Distraction, ultimately. For they are no more dead than their fellow passengers who once lay in the morgues."

Sheepshead Bay, Brooklyn

NEWLY WIDOWED Glory Mueller, while searching online about what to do when a spouse dies without leaving a will, noticed a news report about the missing corpses from Flight 753. She followed the link, reading a dispatch labeled DEVELOPING. The Federal Bureau of Investigation was due to hold a press conference within the hour, it said, to announce a new and larger reward for any information about the disappearance from the morgue of the bodies of the victims of the Regis Air tragedy.

This story struck a deep note of fear. For some reason she now remembered, that previous night, awaking from a dream and hearing sounds in her attic.

Of the dream that had awakened her, she remembered only that Hermann, her newly deceased husband, had come back to her from the dead. There had been a mistake, and the strange tragedy that was Flight 753 had never actually occurred, and Hermann had arrived at the back door of their home in Sheepshead Bay with a you-thought-you-were-rid-of-me smile, wanting his supper.

In public, Glory had played the part of the quietly grieving widow, as she would continue to do so throughout whatever inquest and court cases might come her way. But she was perhaps alone in considering the tragic circumstances that claimed the life of her husband of thirteen years a great gift.

Thirteen years of marriage. Thirteen years of unrelenting abuse. Escalating throughout their years together, occurring more and more in front of their boys, ages nine and eleven. Glory lived in constant fear of his mood swings, and had even allowed herself—a daydream only, too risky to attempt in reality—to consider what it would be like to pack up the boys and leave while he was away this past week, visiting his dying mother in Heidelberg. But where could she go? And, more important—what would he do to her and the boys if he caught up with them, as she knew he would?

But God was good. He had finally answered her prayers. She—and her boys—had been delivered. This dark pall of violence had been lifted from their home.

She went to the bottom of the stairs, looking up to the second floor and the trapdoor in the ceiling there, its rope pull hanging down.

The raccoons. They were back. Hermann, he'd first trapped one in the attic. He'd taken the fear-crazed intruder out into the backyard and made an example of it in front of her boys . . .

No more. She had nothing to be afraid of now. The boys wouldn't be home for at least another hour, and she decided to go up there now. She had planned to start going through Hermann's things anyway. Trash day was Tuesday, and she wanted to have it all gone by then.

She needed a weapon, and the first one that came to mind was Hermann's own machete. He had brought it home some years ago, and kept it wrapped in oilcloth in the locked plastic toolshed against the side of the house. When she asked him why he would ever want such a thing—a jungle tool here in Sheepshead Bay, of all places—he'd just sneered at her, "You never know."

These constant little insinuated threats were part of his daily menacing. She pulled the key from the hook behind the pantry door, and went outside and sprang the lock. She found the oilcloth buried under yard tools and an old, splintered croquet set they had received as a wedding gift (which she would use for kindling now). She took the package into the kitchen and set it on the table, pausing before she unwrapped it.

She had always ascribed evil to this object. Had always imagined it would be somehow significant in the fate of this household, possibly as an instrument of Glory's own demise at Hermann's hands. Accordingly, she unwrapped it with great care, as though unswaddling a sleeping baby demon. Hermann had never liked her touching his special things.

The blade was long, wide, and flat. The grip was formed of wrapped leather straps worn to a soft brown by the hand of the former owner. She lifted it, turning it over, feeling the weight of this strange object in her hand. She caught sight of her reflection in the microwave door, and it scared her. A woman standing with a machete in her kitchen.

He had made her crazy.

She walked upstairs with it in her hand. She stopped beneath the ceiling door and reached for the bottom knot of the dangling white rope handle. It opened down to a forty-five-degree angle on groaning springs. That noise should have scared any lurking critters. She listened for scattering sounds, but there were none.

She reached for the high wall switch, but no light came on above. She flicked it a couple of times, but still nothing. She hadn't been up here since after Christmas, and the bulb could have burned out at any time between now and then. There was a small skylight cut into the rafters. That would provide enough light.

She unfolded the hinged stairs and started up. Three steps brought her eye line above the attic floor. It was unfinished, with foil-backed pink fiberglass insulating blankets unrolled between the exposed joists. Plywood was laid out north–south and east–west, in a cross pattern, creating a walking path to each of the four quadrants of storage space.

The space was darker than she had expected, and then she saw that two of her old clothes racks had been moved, effectively blocking the low skylight. Clothes from her life before Hermann, zipped up in plastic and left in storage for thirteen years. She followed the plywood and moved the racks to allow more light in, with the idea of maybe sorting through the clothes and revisiting her old self. But then she saw, beyond the plywood walkway, a bare lane of floor between two long joists where the insulation had, for some reason, been pulled up.

Then she noticed another bare lane.

And another.

She froze there. She sensed something at her back suddenly. She was afraid to turn—but then she remembered the machete in her hand.

Behind her, against the vertical edge of the attic, farthest from the skylight, the missing strips of insulation had been piled up into a lumpy mound. Some of the fiberglass had been shredded, as though by an animal feathering an enormous nest.

Not a raccoon. Something bigger. Much bigger.

The mound was completely still, arranged as though to hide something. Had Hermann been tending to some strange project without her knowing? What dark secret had he stored under here?

With the machete raised in her right hand, she pulled on the end of a strip, drawing it away from the mound in a long trail that revealed . . .

. . . nothing.

She dragged away a second strip then—stopping when it revealed a man's hairy arm.

Glory knew that arm. She also knew the hand it was connected to. Knew them both intimately.

She could not believe what she was seeing.

With the machete raised in front of her, she pulled away another length of insulation.

His shirt. One of the short-sleeved button-ups he favored, even in winter. Hermann was a vain man, proud of his hairy arms. His wristwatch and wedding ring were gone.

Glory stood riveted by the sight, melting with dread. Still, she had to see. She reached for another strip which, when drawn away, made most of the rest of the insulation slide off to the floor.

Her dead husband, Hermann, lay asleep in her attic. On a bed of shredded pink fiberglass, fully dressed except for his feet, which were filthy, as though from walking.

She could not process this shock. She could not deal with it. The husband she had thought she was rid of. The tyrant. The batterer. The rapist.

She stood over his sleeping body, the machete a sword of Damocles, ready to fall if he offered the slightest move.

Then, by degrees, she lowered her arm, the machete blade coming to rest at her side. He was a ghost now, she realized. A man returned from the dead, a presence, meaning to haunt her forever. She would never be free of him.

As she was thinking this, Hermann opened his eyes.

The lids rose on his eyeballs, staring straight up.

Glory froze. She wanted to run and she wanted to scream and she could do neither.

Hermann's head rotated until his staring eyes fixed on her. That same taunting look, as always. That sneer. The look that always preceded the bad things.

And then something clicked inside her head.

A t that same moment, four houses down the street, three-year-old Lucy Needham stood in her driveway feeding a doll named Baby Dear from a snack-size bag of Cheez-Its. Lucy stopped munching the loud crackers, and instead listened to the muffled screams and hard, chopping *thwacks* coming from . . . somewhere nearby. She looked up at her own house, then north, her nose scrunched up toward her eyes in innocent confusion. She stood very still, an orange tongue of half-chewed, cheese-baked crackers sticking out of her open mouth, listening to some of the strangest noises she had ever heard. She was going to tell Daddy when he came back outside with the telephone, but by then her bag of Cheez-Its had spilled and she was squatting and eating them off the driveway, and after getting yelled at she forgot the whole thing.

G lory stood there gasping in her attic, retching, the machete gripped in both hands. Hermann lay in pieces among the sticky pink insulation, the attic wall splattered in dripping white.

White?

Glory trembled, soul sick. She surveyed the damage she had done.

Twice, the blade had become lodged in the wood joist, and in her mind it was Hermann trying to wrench the machete away from her, and she'd had to rock it back and forth violently to get it free again and keep swinging at his flesh.

She backed away one step. She was experiencing an out-of-body sensation. It was shocking what she had done.

Hermann's sneering head had rolled off between two joists, face-down now, a fluffy pinch of pink fiberglass stuck to his cheek like cotton candy. His torso was gouged and gored, his thighs sliced to the femur, his groin bubbling up white.

White?

She felt something poking her slipper, tap-tap-tap. She saw blood there—red blood—and realized she had nicked herself somehow, her left arm, though she felt no pain. She raised it for inspection, dripping fat, red plops onto the plywood.

White?

She saw something dark and small, slithering. She was bleary-eyed and blinking, still in the grip of a homicidal rage. She couldn't trust her sight.

She felt an itch on her ankle, underneath her bloody slipper. The itch crawled up her leg and she swatted at her thigh with the flat side of the sticky white blade.

Then—another tickle on the front of her other leg. And—separately—her waist. She realized she was having some sort of hyster-ical reaction, as if bugs were attacking her. She stumbled back another step, and almost tumbled off the plywood walkway.

There was then a most unnerving wriggling sensation around her crotch—and then a sudden, twisting discomfort in her rectum. An intrusive slithering that made her jump and clench her buttocks, as though she were about to soil herself. Her sphincter dilated and she stood that way for a long moment, paralyzed, until the feeling started to fade. She allowed herself to unclench, to relax. She needed to get to a bathroom. Another wriggle distracted her, inside her blouse sleeve now. And she felt a burning itch over the cut in her arm.

Then a wrenching pain, from deep within her bowels, doubled her over fast. The machete fell to the plywood and a scream that was a shriek of anguish and violation came out of Glory's mouth. She felt something rippling up her arm—beneath her flesh now, her skin crawling—and while her mouth was open and still screaming, another thin capillary worm slithered from behind her neck and across her jaw to her lip, darting inside the wall of her cheek, wriggling down the back of her throat.

Freeburg, New York

NIGHT WAS FAST approaching as Eph drove east, over the Cross Island Parkway, into Nassau County.

Eph said, "So you're telling me that the passengers from the city morgues, the ones the entire city is looking for—they all just went home?"

The old professor sat in the backseat with his hat on his lap. "Blood wants blood," he said. "Once turned, the revenants first seek out family and friends still uninfected. They return, by night, to those with whom they share an emotional attachment. Their 'Dear Ones.' Like a homing instinct, I suppose. The same animal impulse that guides lost dogs hundreds of miles back to their owners. As their higher brain function falls away, their animal nature takes over. These are creatures driven by urges. To feed. To hide. To nest."

"Returning to the people who are mourning them," said Nora, sitting next to Eph in the front passenger seat. "To attack and infect?"

"To feed. It is the nature of the undead to torment the living."

Eph exited the highway in silence. This vampire business was the mental equivalent of eating bad food: his mind refused to digest it. He chewed and chewed but could not get it down.

When Setrakian had asked him to pick a passenger from the list of Flight 753 victims, the first one who came to mind was the young girl Emma Gilbarton. The one he had found still holding hands with her mother in the airplane. It seemed a good test for Setrakian's hypothesis. How could an eleven-year-old dead girl journey at night from a Queens morgue all the way out to her family home in Freeburg?

But now, as he pulled up outside the Gilbartons' address—a stately looking Georgian on a broad side street of widely spaced properties— Eph realized that, were they wrong, he was about to wake up a man grieving for the end of his family, the loss of his wife and only child.

This was something Eph knew a little bit about.

Setrakian stepped out of the Explorer, fixing his hat on his head, carrying the long walking stick that he did not need for support. The street was quiet at that evening hour, lights glowing inside some of the other houses, but no people out and about, no cars driving past. The windows of the Gilbartons' house were all dark. Setrakian handed them each a battery-powered light with dark bulbs that looked like their Luma lamps, only heavier.

They went to the door and Setrakian rang the doorbell by using the head of the walking stick. He tried the doorknob when no one answered, using the gloved part of his hand only, keeping his bare fingertips off the knob. Not leaving any fingerprints.

Eph realized that the old man had done this sort of thing before.

The front door was firmly locked. "Come," said Setrakian.

They went back down the stairs, and started around the house. The backyard was a wide clearing set on the edge of an old wood. The early moon provided decent light, enough to cast faint shadows of their bodies over the grass.

Setrakian stopped and pointed with his walking stick.

A bulkhead rose out at an angle from the cellar, its doors wide open to the night.

The old man continued to the bulkhead, Eph and Nora following. Stone steps led down into a dark cellar. Setrakian scanned the high trees buffering the backyard.

Eph said, "We can't just go inside."

"This is exceedingly unwise after sundown," Setrakian said. "But we do not have the luxury of waiting."

Eph said, "No, I mean—this is trespassing. We should call the police first."

Setrakian took Eph's lamp from him with a scolding look. "What we have to do here . . . they would not understand."

He switched on the lamp, two purple bulbs emitting black light. It was similar to the medical-grade wands Eph used, but brighter and hotter, and fitted with bigger batteries.

"Black light?" said Eph.

"Black light is merely long-wave ultraviolet, or UVA. Revealing, but harmless. UVB is medium wave, can cause sunburn or skin cancer. This"—he took care to aim the beam away from them, as well as himself—"is short-wave UVC. Germicidal, used for sterilization. Excites and smashes DNA bonds. Direct exposure is very harmful to human skin. But to a vampire—this is weapons grade."

The old man started down the steps with the lamp, his walking stick in his other hand. The ultraviolet spectrum provides little real illumination, the UVC light adding to the gloom of the situation rather than alleviating it. Over the stone walls on the sides of the stairs, as they passed from the chill of the night into the cool of a cement-foundation cellar, moss glowed a spectral white.

Inside, Eph made out the dark outline of stairs going up to the first floor. A laundry area and an old-fashioned pinball machine.

And a body lying on the floor.

A man laid out in plaid pajamas. Eph started toward him with the impulse of a trained physician—then stopped himself. Nora groped the wall opposite the inside door, flipping the switch there, but no light came on.

Setrakian moved toward the man, thrusting the lamp close to his neck. The weird indigo glow revealed a small, perfectly straight fissure in glowing blue, just left of the center of his throat.

"He is turned," said Setrakian.

The old man pushed the Luma lamp back into Eph's hands. Nora turned on hers and shone it over the man's face, revealing a mad subcutaneous being, a scowling, deathlike mask shifting and writhing, looking indefinably, yet undoubtedly, evil.

Setrakian went and found, leaning against a corner workbench, a new ax with a glossy wooden handle and a shiny red-and-silver steel blade. He returned with it in his gnarled hands.

"Wait," said Eph.

Setrakian said, "Please stand back, Doctor."

"He's just lying here," said Eph.

"He will soon arise." The old man gestured to the stone steps leading up to the open bulkhead doors, his eyes never leaving the man on the floor. "The girl is out there now. Feeding on others." Setrakian readied the ax. "I don't ask that you condone this, Doctor. All I ask right now is that you step aside."

Eph saw the determination in Setrakian's face and knew the old man would swing whether or not he was in his way. Eph stepped back. The blade was heavy for Setrakian's size and age, the old man bringing both arms up over his head, the flat of the blade almost at the back of his waist.

Then his arms relaxed. His elbows lowered.

His head turned toward the open bulkhead doors, listening.

Eph heard it then too. The crunching of dry grass being flattened.

He imagined it was an animal, at first. But no. The crunching had the simple cadence of a biped.

Footsteps. Human—or once-human. Approaching.

Setrakian lowered the ax. "Stand by the door. *Silently.* Close it behind her once she enters." He took the lamp back from Eph, pressing the ax into his hands in trade. "She must not escape."

He withdrew to where his walking stick stood against the wall, on the opposite side of the door—then switched off the hot lamp, disappearing into total darkness.

Eph stood beside the open cellar door, his back to the wall, flat up against it. Nora was next to him, both of them shivering in the basement of a stranger's house. The footsteps were closer, light and soft on the ground.

They stopped at the top of the steps. A faint shadow fell over the moonlight on the cellar floor: a head and shoulders.

The footsteps started coming down.

At the bottom, just before the door, they stopped. Eph—not three yards away, the ax hugged to his chest—was transfixed by the girl's profile. Small and short, blond hair falling over the shoulders of a modest, shin-length nightgown. Barefoot, arms hanging straight and loose, standing with a peculiar stillness. Her chest rose and fell, but no steam came out of her mouth into the moonlight.

Later, he would learn much more. That her senses of hearing and smell had become greatly enhanced. That she could hear blood pulsing through his and Nora's and the professor's bodies, and could smell the carbon dioxide emitted by their breath. He would learn that sight was the least acute of her senses. She was now at the stage where she was losing her color vision, and yet her thermal imaging—the ability to "read" heat signatures as monochromatic halos—had not yet fully matured.

She took a few steps forward, moving out of the rectangle of faint moonlight and into the full darkness of the cellar. A ghost had entered the room. Eph should have shut the door, but the girl's very presence here froze him.

She turned toward where Setrakian stood, fixing on his position. The old man switched on his lamp. The girl looked at it with no expression. Then he started toward her with it. She felt its heat, and turned toward the cellar door to escape.

Eph swung it shut. The heavy door slammed hard, reverberating throughout the entire foundation. Eph imagined that the house was going to fall in on them.

The young girl, Emma Gilbarton, saw them now. She was lit purple from the side, and Eph saw glowing traces of indigo along her lips and on her small, pretty chin. Odd, like a ravegoer wearing fluorescent paint.

He remembered: blood glows indigo under ultraviolet light.

Setrakian held the bright lamp in front of him, using it to drive her back. Her reaction was animalistic and confused, recoiling as though confronted with a flaming torch. Setrakian pursued her cruelly, backing her up against a wall. From deep in her throat came a low, guttural noise, a groan of distress.

"Doctor." Setrakian was calling to Eph. "Doctor, come. Now!"

Eph went closer to the girl, taking the Luma lamp from Setrakian and handing him the ax—all the while keeping the light trained on the girl.

Setrakian stepped back. He tossed the ax away, sending it clanking along the hard floor. He held his tall walking stick in his gloved hands, gripping it beneath the wolf's-head handle. With one firm twist of his wrist, he separated the top handle from the rest.

From its wooden sheath, Setrakian withdrew a sword blade fashioned of silver.

"Hurry," said Eph, watching the girl writhe against the wall, trapped there by the lamp's killing rays.

The girl saw the old man's blade, glowing nearly white, and something like fear came into her face. Then the fear went fierce.

"Hurry!" said Eph, wanting it to be over. The girl hissed and he saw the dark shade inside her, beneath her skin, a demon snarling to be let out.

Nora was watching the father, lying on the floor. His body began to stir, his eyes opening. "Professor?" said Nora.

But the old man was locked in on the girl.

Nora watched Gary Gilbarton sit up, then rise to his bare feet, a dead man standing in his pajamas, eyes open.

"Professor?" said Nora again, switching on her lamp.

The lamp crackled. She shook it, smacking the bottom, where the battery went. The purple light fizzled on, then off—then on again.

"Professor!" she yelled.

The fluttering lamplight had gotten Setrakian's attention. He turned on the revenant man, who looked confused and unsteady on his feet. With skill rather than agility, Setrakian doubled Gilbarton up with jabbing thrusts to the gut and chest, opening white-bleeding wounds in his pajama top.

Eph, alone with the girl now, watching this demon assert itself inside her, and not knowing what was happening behind him, said, "Professor Setrakian!"

Setrakian directed thrusts at the father's armpits in order to bring his hands down by his sides, then slashed at the tendons behind his knees, collapsing the revenant onto all fours. With Gilbarton's head up and his neck extended, Setrakian raised his sword and uttered some words in a foreign language—like a solemn pronouncement—and then his blade sang through the man's neck, separating his head from his trunk, the revenant's lower quarters collapsing to the floor.

"Professor!" said Eph, pressing the lamplight on the girl, torturing her—a girl about Zack's age, her wild eyes filling with indigo coloring—bloody tears—while the being inside her raged.

Her mouth opened as though to speak. Almost as though to sing. Her mouth kept opening and the thing emerged, the stinger from the soft palate beneath her tongue. The appendage swelled as the girl's eyes changed from sad to hungry, almost glowing in anticipation.

The old man returned to her, sword first. "Back, *strigoi!*" he said.

The girl turned to the old man, her eyes still flaring. Setrakian's silver blade was now slick with white blood. He intoned the same words as before, his sword poised two-handedly over one shoulder. Eph backed out of the way just as the blade swept through.

She had raised her hand in protest at the last moment, and the blade lifted it from her wrist before separating her head from her neck. The cut was clean and perfectly flat. White blood splattered against the wall—not in an arterial spray, but with more of a sickening *splatch*—

and her body collapsed to the floor, head and hand dropping against it, the head tumbling away.

Setrakian lowered his sword and pulled the lamp from Eph's hands, holding the fading beam close to the girl's open neck wound, almost in a gesture of triumph. But triumph it was not: Eph saw things wriggling in the seeping pool of thick white blood.

The parasitic worms. They curled tight and went still when the light hit them. The old man was irradiating the scene.

Eph heard footfalls on the stone steps. Nora, racing out through the bulkhead. He ran after her, nearly tripping over the decapitated body of the girl's father, surfacing onto the grass and the night air.

Nora was running to the swaying, dark trees. He caught up to her before she reached them, pulling her close, wrapping her up tight. She screamed into his chest, as though afraid to allow her cry to escape into the night, and he held her until Setrakian surfaced onto the yard.

The old man's breath steamed into the cool night, chest pumping from exertion. He pressed his fingers to his heart. His white hair was mussed and shiny in the moonlight, making him appear—as did everything to Eph, at that moment—quite mad.

He cleaned his blade on the grass before returning it to the sheath end of the walking stick. He fixed the two pieces together with a firm twist, and the overlong walking stick was as it had been before.

"She is released now," he said. "The girl and her father are at peace."

He was checking his shoes and pants cuffs for vampire blood in the moonlight. Nora viewed him through wild eyes. "Who are you?" she said.

"Just a pilgrim," he answered. "Same as you."

They walked back to Eph's Explorer. Eph felt all jittery and exposed out in the front yard. Setrakian opened the passenger door and pulled out a spare battery pack. He swapped batteries with the one in Eph's lamp, then checked the purple light briefly against the side of the truck.

Setrakian said, "You wait here please."

"For what?" said Eph.

"You saw the blood on her lips, her chin. She was flushed. She had fed. This is not done yet."

The old man set off toward the next house. Eph watched him, Nora leaving Eph's side in order to lean against the truck. She swallowed hard, as though about to be sick. "We just killed two people in the cellar of their own home."

"This thing is spread by people. By unpeople."

"Vampires, my God . . ."

Eph said, "Rule number one is always—fight the disease, not its victims."

"Don't demonize the sick," said Nora.

"But now . . . now the sick *are* demons. Now the infected are active vectors of the disease, and have to be stopped. Killed. Destroyed."

"What will Director Barnes say about that?"

Eph said, "We can't wait for him. We've already waited too long."

They fell silent. Soon Setrakian returned carrying his walking stick/vampire sword and the still warm lamp.

"It is done," he said.

"Done?" Nora said, still appalled by what she had seen. "Now what? You do realize there were some two hundred other passengers aboard that plane."

"It is much worse than that. The second night is upon us. The second wave of infection is happening now."

THE SECOND
NIGHT

P atricia ran a hand vigorously back through her hair, as though shaking out the lost hours of another day gone by. She found herself actually looking forward to Mark coming home, and not just for the satisfaction of throwing the kids at him and saying, "Here." She wanted to fill him in on the only real news of the day, the Lusses' nanny—who Patricia spied through the sheers of the front-facing dining room windows—racing out of the Lusses' house not five minutes after arriving, children nowhere in sight, the old black woman running as if she was being chased.

Oooh, the Lusses. How neighbors can get under your *skin*. Whenever she thought of skin-and-bones Joanie tossing off a description of her "European-style pure-soil wine cellar," Patricia shot an automatic middle finger in the general direction of the Luss house. She was *dying* to find out what Mark knew about Roger Luss, if he was still overseas. She wanted to compare notes. The only time she and her husband seemed to get on the same page was when they were tearing down friends, family, and neighbors. Maybe because savoring others' marital problems and family misfortunes somehow made hers and Mark's seem less troublesome.

Scandal always went better with a glass of pinot, and she finished off her second with a flourish. She checked the kitchen clock, with sincere thoughts of pacing herself, given Mark's predictable impatience whenever he arrived home to find her two drinks ahead of him. Screw him, snug in his office in the city all day, doing his lunches, walking about at his leisure, hobnobbing on the late train home. Meanwhile, she was stuck here with the baby and Marcus and the nanny and the gardener . . .

She poured herself another glass, wondering how long it would be until Marcus, that jealous little demon, went in to wake up his napping sister. The nanny had put Jacqueline down before she left, and the little baby hadn't woken up yet. Patricia checked the clock again, remarking at this extended period of quiet in the house. Wow—sleeping like a champ. Fortified with another swallow of pinot, and mindful of her impish little four-year-old terrorist, she pushed back the ad-crammed *Cookie* magazine and started up the back steps.

She looked in on Marcus first, finding him lying facedown on the New York Rangers rug next to his sleigh bed, his portable game-unit thingy still turned on near his outstretched hand. Worn *out*. Of course, they would pay dearly for this late nap when the whirling dervish wouldn't settle down at bedtime—but by then it would be Mark's turn to deal.

She went down the hall—puzzled by and frowning at a few clumps of dark soil on the runner (*that little demon*)—to the closed door with the SH-SH-SH!—ANGEL SLEEPING heart-shaped silk pillow hanging from the doorknob on a frilly lace ribbon. She eased it open on the dim, warm nursery, and was startled to see an adult sitting in the rocking chair next to the crib, swaying back and forth. A woman, holding a little bundle in her arms.

The stranger was cradling baby Jacqueline. But in the quiet warmth of the room, under the softness of the recessed lighting, and feeling the high pile of the rug underfoot, everything still seemed okay.

"Who . . . ?" As Patricia ventured in farther, something in the rocking woman's posture clicked. "Joan? Joan—is that you?" Patricia stepped closer. "What are you . . . ? Did you come in through the garage?"

Joan—it *was* her—stopped her slow rocking and stood up from the chair. With the pink-shaded lamp behind her, Patricia barely made out the odd expression on Joan's face—in particular, the strange twist of her mouth. She smelled dirty, and Patricia's mind went immediately to her own sister, and that horrible, horrible Thanksgiving last year. Was Joan having a similar breakdown?

And why was she here now, holding baby Jacqueline?

Joan extended her arms to hand the infant back to Patricia. Patricia cradled her baby, and in a moment knew that something wasn't right. Her daughter's stillness went beyond the limpness of infant sleep.

With two anxious fingers, Patricia pinched back the blanket covering Jackie's face.

The baby's rosebud lips were parted. Her little eyes were dark and fixed and staring. The blanket was wet around her little neck. Patricia's two fingers came away sticky with blood.

The scream that rose in Patricia's throat never reached its destination.

Ann-Marie Barbour was literally at her wits' end. Standing in her kitchen, whispering prayers and gripping the edge of the sink as though the house she had lived in all her married life were a small boat caught in a swirling black sea. Praying endlessly for guidance, for relief. For a glimmer of hope. She knew that her Ansel was not evil. He was not what he seemed. He was just very, very sick. (*But he killed the dogs.*) Whatever illness he had would pass like a bad fever and everything would return to normal.

She looked out at the locked shed in the dark backyard. It was quiet now.

The doubts returned, as they had when she saw the news report about the dead people from Flight 753 who had disappeared from the morgues. Something was happening, something awful (*He Killed the Dogs*)—and her overwhelming sensation of dread was alleviated only by repeated trips to the mirrors and her sink. Washing and touching, worrying and praying.

Why did Ansel bury himself under the dirt during the day? (*He killed the dogs.*) Why did he look at her with such craving? (*He killed them.*) Why wouldn't he *say* anything, but only grunt and yowl (*like the dogs he killed*)?

Night had again taken the sky—the thing she had dreaded all day.

Why was he so quiet out there now?

Before she could think about what she was doing, before she could lose her reserve, she went out the door and down the porch stairs. Not looking at the dogs' graves in the corner of the yard—not giving in to that madness. She had to be the strong one now. For just a little while longer . . .

The shed doors. The lock and the chain. She stood there, listening, her fist pressed hard against her mouth until her front teeth started to hurt.

What would Ansel do? Would he open the door if it were she inside? Would he force himself to face her?

Yes. He would.

Ann-Marie undid the lock with the key from around her neck. She threaded out the thick chain, and this time stepped back to where she knew he could not reach her—past the length of the runner leash fixed to the dog pole—as the doors fell open.

An awful stink. A godless fetor. The stench alone brought tears to her eyes. That was her Ansel in there.

She saw nothing. She listened. She would not be drawn inside.

"Ansel?"

Barely a whisper on her part. Nothing came in return.

"Ansel."

A rustling. Movement in the dirt. Oh, why hadn't she brought a flashlight?

She reached forward just enough to nudge one door open more widely. Enough to let in a little more of the moonlight.

There he was. Lying half in a bed of soil, his face raised to the doors, eyes sunken and fraught with pain. She saw at once that he was dying. Her Ansel was dying. She thought again of the dogs who used to sleep here, Pap and Gertie, the dear Saint Bernards she had loved more than mere pets, whom he had killed and whose place he had willingly taken . . . yes . . . in order to save Ann-Marie and the children.

And then she knew. He needed to hurt someone else in order to revive himself. In order to live.

She shivered in the moonlight, facing the suffering creature her husband had become.

He wanted her to give herself over to him. She knew that. She could feel it.

Ansel let out a guttural groan, voiceless, as though from deep in the pit of his empty stomach.

She couldn't do it. Ann-Marie wept as she closed the shed doors on him. She pressed her shoulder to them, shutting him up like a corpse neither quite alive nor yet quite dead. He was too weak to charge the doors now. She heard only another moan of protest.

She was running the first length of chain back through the door handles when she heard a step on the gravel behind her. Ann-Marie froze, picturing that police officer returning. She heard another step, then spun around.

He was an older man, balding, wearing a stiff-collared shirt, open cardigan, and loose corduroys. Their neighbor from across the street, the one who had called the police: the widower, Mr. Otish. The kind of neighbor who rakes his leaves into the street so that they blow into your yard. A man they never saw or heard from unless there was a problem that he suspected them or their children of having caused.

Mr. Otish said, "Your dogs have found increasingly creative ways to keep me awake at night."

His presence, like a ghostly intrusion upon a nightmare, mystified Ann-Marie. *The dogs?*

He was talking about Ansel, the noises he made in the night.

"If you have a sick animal, you need to take it to a veterinarian and have it treated or put down."

She was too stunned even to reply. He walked closer, coming off the driveway and onto the edge of the backyard grass, eyeing the shed with contempt.

A hoarse moan rose from inside.

Mr. Otish's face shriveled in disgust. "You are going to do something about those curs or else I am going to call the police again, right now."

"*No!*" Fear escaped before she could hold it in.

He smiled, surprised by her trepidation, enjoying the sense of control over her that it gave him. "Then what is it you plan to do?"

Her mouth opened, but she couldn't think of anything to say. "I . . . I'll take care of it . . . I don't know how."

He looked at the back porch, curious about the light on in the kitchen. "Is the man of the house available? I would prefer to speak with him."

She shook her head.

Another pained groan from the shed.

"Well, you had damn well better do something about those sloppy creatures—or else I will. Anybody who grew up on a farm will tell you, Mrs. Barbour, dogs are service animals and don't need coddling. Far better for them to know the sting of the switch than the pat of a hand. Especially a clumsy breed such as the Saint Bernard."

Something he'd said got through to her. Something about her dogs . . .

Sting of the switch.

The whole reason they'd built the chain-and-post contraption in the shed in the first place was because Pap and Gertie had run off a few times . . . and once, not too long ago . . . Gertie, the sweetheart of the two, the trusting one, came home with her back and legs all ripped up . . .

. . . as though someone had taken a stick to her.

The normally shy and retiring Ann-Marie Barbour forgot all of her fear at that moment. She looked at this man—this nasty little shriveled-up excuse for a man—as though a veil had been lifted from her eyes.

"You," she said. Her chin trembled, not from timidity anymore but from rage. "*You* did that. To Gertie. You *hurt* her . . ."

His eyes flickered for a moment, unused to being confronted—and simultaneously betraying his guilt.

"*If* I did," he said, regaining his usual condescension, "I am sure he had it coming."

Ann-Marie burst with hatred suddenly. Everything she had been bottling up over these past few days. Sending away her children . . . burying her dead dogs . . . worrying about her afflicted husband . . .

"*She,*" Ann-Marie said.

"What?"

"*She.* Gertie. Is a *she.*"

Another tremulous groan from within the shed.

Ansel's need. His craving . . .

She backed up, shaking. Intimidated, not by him, but by these new feelings of rage. "You want to see for yourself?" she heard herself say.

"What is that?"

The shed crouched behind her like some beast itself. "Go ahead, then. You want a chance to tame them? See what you can do."

He stared, indignant. Challenged by a woman. "You aren't serious?"

"You want to fix things? You want peace and quiet? Well, so do I!" She wiped a bit of saliva off her chin and shook her wet finger at him. *"So do I!"*

Mr. Otish looked at her for one long moment. "The others are right," he said. "You *are* crazy."

She flashed him a wild, nodding grin, and he walked to a low branch of the trees bordering their yard. He pulled at a thin switch, twisting it, tugging hard until it finally tore free. He tested it, listening for the rapierlike *swish* as he sliced it through the air, and, satisfied, stepped to the doors.

"I want you to know," said Mr. Otish, "I do this for your benefit more than mine."

Ann-Marie trembled as she watched him run the chain through the shed door handles. The doors started to swing open, Mr. Otish standing near enough to the opening for the pole chain to reach him.

"Now," he said, "where are these beasts?"

Ann-Marie heard the inhuman growl, and the chain leash moving fast, sounding like spilled coins. Then the doors flew open, Mr. Otish stepped up, and in an instant his stupefied cry was cut short. She ran and threw herself against the shed doors, fighting to close them as the struggling Mr. Otish batted against them. She forced the chain through and around the handles, clasping the lock tight . . . then fled into her house, away from the shuddering backyard shed and the merciless thing she had just done.

Mark Blessige stood in the foyer of his home with his BlackBerry in hand, not knowing which way to turn. No message from his wife. Her phone was in her Burberry bag, the Volvo station wagon in the driveway, the baby bucket in the mudroom. No note on the kitchen island, only a half-empty glass of wine abandoned on the counter. Patricia, Marcus, and baby Jackie were all gone.

He checked the garage, and the cars and strollers were all there.

He checked the calendar in the hallway—nothing was listed. Was she pissed at him for being late again and had decided to do a little passive-aggressive punishment? Mark tried to flip on the television and wait it out, but then realized his anxiety was real. Twice he picked up the telephone to call the police, but didn't think he could live down the public scandal of a cruiser coming to his house. He went out his front door and stood on the brick step overlooking his lawn and lush flower beds. He looked up and down the street, wondering if they could have slipped over to a neighbor's—and then noticed that almost every house was dark. No warm yellow glow from heirloom lamps shining on top of polished credenzas. No computer monitor lights or plasma TV screens flashing through hand-sewn lace.

He looked at the Lusses' house, directly across the street. Its proud patrician face and aged white brick. Nobody home there either, it seemed. Was there some looming natural disaster he didn't know about? Had an evacuation order been issued?

Then he saw someone emerge from the high bushes forming an ornamental fence between the Lusses' property and the Perrys'. It was a woman, and in the dappling shadow of the oak leaves overhead she appeared disheveled. She was cradling what looked to be a sleeping child of five or six in her arms. The woman walked straight across the driveway, obscured for a moment by the Lusses' Lexus SUV, then entered the side door next to the garage. Before entering, her head turned and she saw Mark standing out on his front step. She didn't wave or otherwise acknowledge him, but her glance—brief though it was—put a block of ice against his chest.

She wasn't Joan Luss, he realized. But she might have been the Lusses' housekeeper.

He waited for a light to come on inside. None did. Superstrange, but whatever the case, he hadn't seen anyone else out and about this fine evening. So he started out across the road—first down his walk to the driveway, avoiding stepping on the lawn grass—and then, hands slipped casually into his suit pants pockets, up the Lusses' drive to the same side door.

The storm door was shut but the interior door was open. Rather than ring the bell, he gave the glass a jaunty knock and entered, calling, "Hello?" He crossed the tiled mudroom to the kitchen, flipping on the light. "Joan? Roger?"

The floor was streaked all over with dirty footprints, apparently from bare feet. Some of the cabinets and the counter edges were marked with soil-smudged handprints. Pears were rotting in a wire bowl on their kitchen island.

"Anybody home?"

He wagered that Joan and Roger were gone, but he wanted to speak to the housekeeper anyway. She wouldn't go around blabbing how the Blessiges didn't know where their children were, or that Mark Blessige couldn't keep track of his boozy wife. And if he was wrong and Joanie *was* here, well then he'd ask her about his family as though he had a tennis racket on his shoulder. *The kids are sooo busy, how do you keep track?* And if he ever heard anything from anyone else about his wayward brood, he'd have to bring up the horde of barefoot peasants the Lusses' evidently had stampeding through their kitchen.

"It's Mark Blessige from across the street. Anybody home?"

He hadn't been in their house since the boy's birthday party in May. The parents had bought him one of those electric kiddie race cars, but because it didn't come with a pretend trailer hitch—the kid was obsessed with trailer hitches, apparently—he drove the car straight into the cake table just after the hired help in the SpongeBob SquarePants costume had filled all the cups with juice. "Well," Roger had said, "at least he knows what he likes." Cue forced laughter and a fresh round of juice.

Mark ducked through a swinging door into a sitting room where, through the front windows, he got a good look at his own house. He savored the view for a moment, as he didn't often get a neighbor's perspective. Damn fine house. Although that stupid Mexican had clipped the west hedges unevenly again.

Footsteps came up the basement stairs. More than one set—more even than a few sets. "Hello?" he said, wondering about those barefoot hordes, and supposing he had gotten too comfortable in the neighbors' house. "Hi, there. Mark Blessige, from across the way." No voices answered. "Sorry to barge in like this, but I was wondering—"

He pushed back the swinging door and stopped. Some ten people stood facing him. Two of them were children who stepped out from behind the kitchen island—neither of them were his. Mark recognized a few of the people by face, fellow Bronxville residents, people he saw at Starbucks or the train station or the club. One of them, Carole, was the mother of a friend of Marcus's. Another was just a UPS delivery man, wearing the trademark brown shirt and shorts. Quite a random assortment for a get-together. Among them was nary a Luss nor a Blessige.

"I'm sorry. Am I interrupting . . . ?"

Now he really started to see them, their complexions and their eyes as they stared at him without speaking. He had never been stared at like that by people before. He felt a heat from them that was separate from their gaze.

Behind them stood the housekeeper. She looked flushed, her complexion red and her staring eyes scarlet, and there was a red stain on the front of her blouse. Her hair was stringy and unwashed and her clothes and skin couldn't have been dirtier if she had been sleeping in real dirt.

Mark flipped a forelock of hair out of his eyes. He felt his shoulders come up against the swinging door and realized he was backing up. The rest of them moved toward him, with the exception of the housekeeper, who merely stood and watched. One of the children, a twitchy boy with jagged black eyebrows, stepped up on an open drawer to climb onto the kitchen island, so that he stood a head taller than anyone else. He took a running start off the granite countertop and launched himself into the air toward Mark Blessige, who had no choice but to put out his arms and catch him. The boy's mouth opened as he leaped, and by the time he grabbed Mark's shoulders his little stinger was out. Like a scorpion's tail, it flexed up before shooting straight out, piercing Mark's throat. It split skin and muscle to anchor in his carotid artery, and the pain was like that of a hot skewer rammed halfway into his neck.

He fell backward through the door, crashing to the floor with the boy holding fast, tethered to his throat, sitting astride his chest. Then the pulling began. The drawing out. The sucking. The draining.

Mark tried to speak, tried to scream, but the words clotted in his throat and he choked on them. He was paralyzed. Something in his pulse changed—was interrupted—and he couldn't utter a sound.

The boy's chest pressed against his, and he could feel the faint thumping of its heart—or something—against his own. As the blood rushed out of Mark's body, he felt the boy's rhythm accelerate and become stronger—*thump-thump-thump*—reaching a frenzied, intimate gallop that was close to pleasure.

The boy's stinger engorged as he fed, and the whites of his eyes, as he stared at Mark, flushed crimson. Methodically, the boy kept twining his crooked, bony fingers through Mark's hair. Tightening his grip on his prey . . .

The others burst through the door, setting upon the victim, tearing at his clothes. As their stingers pierced his flesh, Mark felt a renewed pressure change inside his body, not decompression but *compression*. Vacuum collapse, like a juice pack being consumed.

And at the same time, a scent overpowered him, rising into his nose and eyes like a cloud of ammonia. He felt an eruption of wetness over his chest, warm, like freshly made soup, and his hands gripping the little fiend's body felt a sudden, hot dampness. The boy had soiled himself, defecating over Mark as he fed—though the excretion seemed more chemical than human.

Pain like a motherfucker. Corporeal, all over, his fingertips, his chest, his brain. The pressure went away from his throat, and Mark hung there like a bright white star of effulgent pain.

Neeva pushed open the bedroom door just a sliver, to see that the children were finally asleep. Keene and Audrey Luss lay in sleeping bags on the floor next to her own granddaughter Narushta's bed. The Luss children were all right most of the time—Neeva, after all, had been their sole daytime caretaker since Keene was four months old—but they had both cried tonight. They missed their beds. They wanted to know when they could go home, when Neeva would take them back. Sebastiane, Neeva's daughter, was constantly asking how long until the police came and knocked down their door. But it was not the police coming for them that concerned Neeva.

Sebastiane had been born in the United States, educated in United States schools, stamped with an American arrogance. Neeva took her daughter back to Haiti once each year, but it was not home to her. She rejected the old country and its old ways. She rejected old knowledge because new knowledge was so shiny and neat. But Sebastiane making her mother out to be a superstitious fool was almost more than Neeva could take. Especially since, by acting as she had, saving these two spoiled yet potentially redeemable children, she had placed the members of her own family at risk.

Though she had been raised a Roman Catholic, Neeva's maternal grandfather was Vodou and a village *bokor*, which is a kind of *houngan*, or priest—some call them sorcerers—who practices magic, both the benevolent kind and the dark kind. Though he was said to bear a great *ashe* (wield much spiritual power), and dabbled often with healing *zombi* astrals—that is, capturing a spirit in a fetish (an inanimate object)—he never attempted the darkest art, that of reanimating a corpse, raising a zombie from a dead body whose soul has departed. He never did so because he said he had too much respect for the dark side, and that crossing that infernal border was a direct affront to the *loa*, or the spirits of the Vodou religion, akin to saints or angels who act as intermediaries between man and the indifferent Creator. But he had participated in services that were a kind of back-country exorcism, righting the wrongs of other wayward *houngan*, and she had accompanied him, and had seen the face of the undead.

When Joan had shut herself away in her room that first night—her richly appointed bedroom as nice as any of the hotel suites Neeva used to clean in Manhattan when she first arrived in America—and the moaning finally stopped, Neeva had peeked in to check on her. Joan's eyes looked dead and faraway, her heart was racing, the sheets were soaked and putrid with sweat. Her pillow was stained with whitish, coughed-up blood. Neeva had nursed the ill and the dying alike, and she knew, looking at Joan Luss, that her employer was sinking not merely into sickness but into evil. That was when she took the children and left.

Neeva went around checking the windows again. They lived on the first floor of a three-family house and could view the street and the neighbors' houses only through iron bars. Security bars were a good deterrent for burglars, but beyond that, Neeva wasn't sure. That afternoon, she had gone around the outside of the house, pulling on them, and they felt strong. As an extra precaution, she had (without Sebastiane's knowledge, saving Neeva a lecture on fire safety) nailed the frames to the sills, and then blocked the children's window view with a bookshelf as a makeshift barricade. She had also (smartly telling no one) smeared garlic on each of the iron bars. She kept a quart bottle of holy water from her church, consecrated by the parish priest—though she remained mindful of how ineffectual her crucifix had been inside the Lusses' basement.

Nervous but confident, she drew all the shades and put on every light, then took to her chair and put up her feet. She left her thick-heeled black shoes on (they were orthopedic—bad arches) in case she had to rush somewhere, had to be ready to stand watch for another night. She put the TV on low, just for company. It drew more electricity out of the wall than attention from Neeva.

She was more bothered by her daughter's condescension than perhaps she should have been. It is the concern of every immigrant that their offspring will grow to embrace their adoptive culture at the expense of their natural heritage. But Neeva's fear was much more specific: she was afraid that her Americanized daughter's overconfidence would end up hurting her. To Sebastiane, the dark of night was merely an inconvenience, a deficient amount of light, which immediately went away when you flipped a switch. Night was leisure time to her, playtime, time to relax. When she let her hair down, and her guard. To Neeva, electricity existed as little more than a talisman against the dark. Night is real. Night is not an absence of light, but in fact, it is daytime that is a brief respite from the looming darkness . . .

The faint sound of scratching awoke her with a start. Her chin bobbed off her chest and she saw that the television was showing an infomercial for a sponge mop that was also a vacuum. She froze and listened. It was a clicking coming from the front door. At first she thought Emile was coming home—her nephew drove a taxi nights—but if he had forgotten his key again, he would have rung the bell.

Somebody was outside the front door. But they didn't knock or press the bell.

Neeva got to her feet as quickly as she could. She crept down the hallway and stood before the door, listening, only a slab of wood separating her from whoever—whatever—was on the outside.

She felt a presence. She imagined that, if she touched the door—which she did not—she would feel heat.

It was a plain exterior door with a security dead-bolt lock, no screen outside, no windows in the wood. Only an old-fashioned mail slot was centered near the bottom, one foot above the floor.

The hinge on the mail slot creaked. The brass flap moved—and Neeva rushed back down the hall. She stood there for a moment—out of sight, in a panic—then rushed to the bathroom and the basket of bath toys. She grabbed her granddaughter's water gun and uncapped the bottle of holy water and poured it into the tiny aperture, spilling much of it as she filled the plastic barrel.

She took the toy to the door. It was quiet now, but she felt the presence. She knelt down clumsily on her swollen knee, snagging her stocking on the roughened wood of the floor. She was near enough to feel the whisper of cool night air through the brass flap—and see a shadow along its edge.

The toy gun had a long front nozzle. Neeva remembered to slide back the underside pump action to prime the pressure, then used the very end of the muzzle to tip up the flap. When the hinge emitted a plaintive squeak, she put the gun in, thrusting the nozzle through and squeezing the trigger.

Neeva aimed blindly, up, down, and from side to side, squirting holy water in all directions. She imagined Joan Luss being burned, the acidlike water cutting through her body like Jesus' own golden sword— yet she heard no wailing.

Then a hand came through the slot. It grabbed at the gun muzzle, trying to take it away. Neeva pulled it back, reflexively, and got a good look at the fingers. They were gravedigger dirty. The nail beds were bloodred. The holy water spilled down the skin, merely smearing the dirt, with no steaming or burning.

No effect at all.

The hand pulled hard on the muzzle, jamming it inside the mail slot. Now Neeva realized the hand was trying to get at her. So she let go of the gun, the hand pulling and twisting until the plastic toy cracked, loosening a final splash of water. Neeva pushed away from the slot, on her hands and her bottom, as the visitor began ramming the door. Throwing her entire body against it, rattling the knob. The hinges trembled and the adjoining walls shook, the picture of the man and the boy hunting fell off its nail, shattering the protective glass. Neeva kicked her way to the end of the short entrance hall. Her shoulder knocked over the umbrella stand with the baseball bat in it, and Neeva grabbed the bat and gripped the black-taped handle, sitting there on the floor.

The wood held. The old door she hated for swelling and sticking to the frame in the summer heat was solid enough to withstand the blows, as was the dead bolt and even the smooth iron doorknob. The presence behind the door eventually went silent. Maybe even went away altogether.

Neeva looked at the puddle of Christ's tears on the floor. When the power of Jesus fails you, then you know you truly are shit out of luck.

Wait for daylight. That was all she could do.

"Neeva?"

Keene, the Luss boy, stood behind her in sweatpants and a T-shirt. Neeva moved faster than she imagined she ever could, clamping a hand over the young boy's mouth and sweeping him away around the corner. Neeva stood there with her back against the wall, the boy wrapped in her arms.

Had the thing at the door heard its son's voice?

Neeva tried to listen. The boy squirmed against her, trying to speak.

"*Hush, child.*"

Then she heard it. The squeak again. She grasped the boy even more tightly as she leaned to her left, risking a look around the corner.

The mail slot was propped open by a dirty finger. Neeva whipped back around the corner again, but not before she glimpsed a pair of glowing red eyes looking inside.

Gabriel Bolivar's manager, Rudy Wain, cabbed over to his town house from Hudson Street after a late dinner meeting at Mr. Chow's with the BMG people. He hadn't been able to get Gabe on the phone, but there were whispers about his health now, following the Flight 753 thing and a paparazzi picture of him in a wheelchair and Rudy had to see for himself. When he showed up at the door on Vestry Street, there were no paparazzi in sight, only a few dopey-looking Goth fans sitting around on the sidewalk smoking.

They stood up rather expectantly when Rudy walked up the front-stoop stairs. "What's up?" asked Rudy.

"We heard he's been letting people in."

Rudy looked straight up, but there were no lights on anywhere in the twin town houses, not even in the penthouse. "Looks like the party's over."

"It's no party," said one chubby kid with colored elastic bands hanging from a pin through his cheek. "He let the paparazzi in too."

Rudy shrugged and punched in his key code, entered, and closed the door behind him. At least Gabe was feeling better. Rudy entered, past the black marble panthers and into the dark foyer. The construction lights were all dark, and the light switches still weren't connected to anything. Rudy thought for a moment, then brought out his Black-Berry, changing the display to ALWAYS ON. He shone the blue light around, noticing, at the foot of the winged angel by the stairs, a heap of high-end digital SLRs and video cameras, weapons of the paparazzi. All piled there like shoes outside a swimming pool.

"Hello?"

His voice echoed dully through the unfinished first few floors. Rudy started up the curling marble stairs, following his BlackBerry's pool of electronic blue light. He needed to motivate Gabe for his Rose-land show next week, and there were scattered U.S. dates around Hal-loween to prepare for.

He reached the top floor, Bolivar's bedroom suite, and all the lights were off.

"Hey, Gabe? It's me, man. Don't let me walk in on anything."

Too quiet. He pushed into the master bedroom, scanning it with his phone light, finding the bedsheets tossed but no hungover Gabe. Probably out night crawling as usual. He wasn't here.

Rudy popped into the master bathroom to take a leak. He saw an open prescription bottle of Vicodin on the counter, and a crystal cocktail glass that smelled of booze. Rudy deliberated a moment, then dealt himself two Vikes, rinsing out the glass in the sink and washing the pills down with tap water.

As he was replacing the glass on the counter, he caught sight of movement somewhere behind him. He turned fast, and there was Gabe, coming out of the darkness and into the bathroom. The mirrored walls on both sides made it seem as though there were hundreds of him.

"Gabe, Jesus, you scared me," said Rudy. His genial smile faded as Gabe stood there staring at him. The blue phone light was indirect and faint, but Gabe's skin looked dark, his eyes tinged red. He wore a thin black robe, to his knees, with no shirt underneath. His arms hung straight, and he offered his manager no indication of greeting. "What's wrong, man?" His hands and chest were dirty. "You spend the night in a coal bin?"

Gabe just stood there, multiplied in the mirrors out to infinity.

"You really stink, man," said Rudy, holding his hand to his nose. "What the hell you been into?" Rudy felt a strange heat coming off Gabe. He held his phone closer to Gabe's face. His eyes didn't do anything in the light. "Dude, you left your makeup on way too long."

The Vikes were starting to kick in. The room, with its facing mirrors, expanded like an unpacked accordion. Rudy moved the phone light, and the entire bathroom flickered.

"Look, man," said Rudy, unnerved by Gabe's lack of reaction, "if you're tripping, I can come back."

He tried to glide out on Gabe's left, but Gabe didn't stand aside. He tried again, but Gabe would not give way. Rudy stood back, holding his phone light out on his longtime client. "Gabe, man, what the—?"

Bolivar opened his robe then, spreading his arms wide, like wings, before allowing the garment to fall to the floor.

Rudy gasped. Gabe's body was gray and gaunt throughout, but the sight that made him dizzy was Gabe's groin.

It was hairless and doll-smooth, lacking any genitalia.

Gabe's hand covered Rudy's mouth, hard. Rudy started to struggle, but much too late. Rudy saw Gabe grinning—and then that grin fell away, something like a whip writhing inside his mouth. By the trembling blue light of his phone—as he frantically and blindly felt for the numerals 9, 1, and 1—he saw the stinger emerge. Vaguely defined appendages inflated and deflated along its sides, like twin spongy sacs of flesh, flanked by gill-like vents that flared open and closed.

Rudy saw all of this in the instant before it shot into his neck. His phone fell to the bathroom floor beneath his kicking feet, the SEND button never pressed.

Nine-year-old Jeanie Millsome wasn't tired at all on her way home with her mother. Seeing *The Little Mermaid* on Broadway was so awesome, she believed she was the most awake she had ever been in her life. Now she truly knew what she wanted to be when she grew up. No more ballet school instructor (after Cindy Veeley broke two toes on a leap). No more Olympic gymnast (pommel horse too scary). She was going to be (drumroll, please . . .) a *Broadway Actress!* And she was going to dye her hair coral red and star in *The Little Mermaid* in the lead role of Ariel, and at the end take the biggest and most graceful curtain curtsy of all time, and after the thunderous applause she was going to greet her young theatergoing fans after the show and sign all their programs and smile for camera-phone pictures with them—and then, one very special night, she was going to select the most polite and sincere nine-year-old girl in the audience and invite her to be her understudy *and* Best Friend Forever. Her mother was going to be her hairstylist, and her dad, who stayed home with Justin, would be her manager, just like Hannah Montana's dad. And Justin . . . well, Justin could just stay home and be himself.

And so she sat, chin in hand, turned around in the seat on the subway running south underneath the city. She saw herself reflected in the window, saw the brightness of the car behind her, but the lights flickered sometimes, and in one of those dark blinks she found herself looking out into an open space where one tunnel fed into another. Then she saw something. No more than a subliminal flash of an image, like a single disturbing frame spliced into an otherwise monotonous strip of film. So fast that her nine-year-old conscious mind didn't have time to process it, this image she did not understand. She couldn't even say why she burst into tears, which woke up her nodding mother, so pretty in her theater coat and dress next to her, who comforted her and tried to draw out what had prompted the sobbing. Jeanie could only point to the window. She rode the rest of the way home cuddled beneath her mother's arm.

But the Master had seen her. The Master saw everything. Even—especially—while feeding. His night vision was extraordinary and nearly telescopic, in varying shades of gray, and registered heat sources in a glowing spectral white.

Finished, though not satiated—never satiated—he let his prey slide limply down his body, his great hands releasing the turned human to the gravel floor. The tunnels around him whispered with winds that fluttered his dark cloak, trains screaming in the distance, iron clashing against steel, like the scream of a world suddenly aware of his coming.

Canary Headquarters, Eleventh Avenue and Twenty-seventh Street

On the third morning following the landing of Flight 753, Eph took Setrakian to the office headquarters of the CDC Canary project on the western edge of Chelsea, one block east of the Hudson. Before Eph started Canary, the three-room office had been the local site for the CDC's World Trade Center Worker and Volunteer Medical Screening Program, investigating links between the 9/11 recovery effort and persistent respiratory ailments.

Eph's heart lifted as they pulled up at Eleventh Avenue. Two police cars and a pair of unmarked sedans with government license plates were parked outside the entrance. Director Barnes had come through finally. They were going to get the help they needed. There was no way Eph, Nora, and Setrakian could fight this scourge on their own.

The third-floor office door was open when they got there, and Barnes was conferring with a plainclothes man who identified himself as an FBI special agent. "Everett," said Eph, relieved to find him personally involved. "Your timing is perfect. Just the man I wanted to see." He moved to a small refrigerator near the door. Test tubes clinked as he reached for a quart of whole milk, uncapping it and drinking it down fast. He needed the calcium the same way he had once needed booze. We trade off our dependencies, he realized. For instance, just last week

Eph had been fully dependent upon the laws of science and nature. Now his fix was silver swords and ultraviolet light.

He brought the half-empty bottle away from his lips with the realization that he had just slaked his thirst with the product of another mammal.

"Who is this?" asked Director Barnes.

"This," said Eph, swiping the milk mustache from his upper lip, "is Professor Abraham Setrakian." Setrakian was holding his hat, his alabaster hair bright under the low ceiling lights. "So much has happened, Everett," said Eph, swallowing more milk, putting out the fire in his belly. "I don't even know where to begin."

Barnes said, "Why don't we start with the bodies missing from the city morgues."

Eph lowered the bottle. One of the cops had edged closer to the door behind him. A second FBI man was sitting at Eph's laptop, pecking away. "Hey, excuse me," said Eph.

Barnes said, "Ephraim, what do you know about the missing corpses?"

Eph was a moment trying to read the CDC director's face. He glanced back at Setrakian, but the old man offered him nothing, standing very still with his hat in his gnarled hands.

Eph turned back to his boss. "They have gone home."

"Home?" said Barnes, turning his head as though trying to hear him better. "To heaven?"

"To their families, Everett."

Barnes looked at the FBI agent who kept looking at Eph.

"They are dead," said Barnes.

"They aren't dead. At least, not in the way we understand it."

"There is only one way to be dead, Ephraim."

Eph shook his head. "Not anymore."

"Ephraim." Barnes took one sympathetic step forward. "I know you have been under a keen amount of stress recently. I know you have had family troubles . . ."

Eph said, "Hold on. I don't think I understand what the hell this is."

The FBI agent said, "This is about your patient, Doctor. One of the pilots of Regis Air Flight 753, Captain Doyle Redfern. We have a few questions about his care."

Eph hid a chill. "Get a court order and I'll answer your questions."

"Maybe you'd like to explain this."

He opened a portable video player on the edge of the desk and pressed play. It showed a security-camera view of a hospital room. Redfern was seen from behind, staggering, his johnny open in back. He looked wounded and confused rather than predatory and enraged. The camera angle did not show the stinger swirling out of his mouth.

It did however show Eph facing him with the whirling trephine, jabbing at Redfern's throat with the circular blade.

There was the flicker of a jump cut, and now Nora was in the background, covering her mouth as Eph stood by the doorway with his chest heaving, Redfern in a heap on the floor.

Then another sequence began. A different camera farther along the same basement hallway, set at a higher angle. It showed two people, a man and a woman, forcing their way into the locked morgue room where Redfern's body was being held. Then it showed them leaving with a heavy body bag.

The two people looked very much like Eph and Nora.

Playback stopped. Eph looked at Nora—who was shocked—and then at the FBI agent and Barnes. "That was . . . that attack was edited to look bad. There was a cut there. Redfern had—"

"Where are Captain Redfern's remains?"

Eph couldn't think. He couldn't get past the lie he had just seen. "That wasn't us. The camera was too high to—"

"So are you saying that was not you and Dr. Martinez?"

Eph looked at Nora, who was shaking her head, both of them too mystified to mount any immediate coherent defense.

Barnes said, "Let me ask you one more time, Ephraim. Where are the missing bodies from the morgues?"

Eph looked back to Setrakian, standing near the door. Then at Barnes. He couldn't come up with anything to say.

"Ephraim, I am shutting Canary down. As of this moment."

"What?" said Eph, coming around. "Wait, Everett—"

Eph moved fast, toward Barnes. The other cops started toward him as though he was dangerous, their reaction stopping Eph, alarming him even more.

"Dr. Goodweather, you have to come with us," said the FBI agent. "All of you . . . hey!"

Eph turned. Setrakian was gone.

The agent sent two cops out to get him.

Eph looked back toward Barnes. "Everett. You know me. You know who I am. Listen to what I am about to tell you. There is a plague spreading throughout this city—a scourge unlike anything we've ever seen."

The FBI agent said, "Dr. Goodweather, we want to know what you injected into Jim Kent."

"What I . . . *what?*"

Barnes said, "Ephraim, I have made a deal with them. They will spare Nora if you agree to cooperate. Spare her the scandal of arrest and preserve her professional reputation. I know that you two . . . are close."

"And how exactly do you know that?" Eph looked around at his persecutors, moving past bewilderment and into anger. "This is bullshit, Everett."

"You are on video attacking and murdering a patient, Ephraim. You have been reporting fantastic test results, unexplained by any rational measurement, unsubstantiated and most likely doctor-manipulated. Would I be here if I had a choice? If you had a choice?"

Eph turned to Nora. She would be spared. She could perhaps fight on.

Barnes was right. For the moment at least, in a room full of lawmen, he had no choice.

"Don't let this slow you down," Eph told Nora. "You may be the only one left who knows what's really happening."

Nora shook her head. She turned to Barnes. "Sir, there is a conspiracy here, whether you are willingly a part of it or not—"

"Please, Dr. Martinez," said Barnes. "Don't embarrass yourself any further."

The other agent packed up Eph's and Nora's laptops. They started walking Eph down the stairs.

At the second-floor hallway, they met the two cops who had gone after Setrakian. They were standing side by side, almost back to back. Handcuffed together.

Setrakian appeared behind the group with his sword drawn. He held its point at the lead FBI agent's neck. There was a smaller dagger in his other hand, also fashioned of silver. He held that one near Director Barnes's throat.

The old professor said, "You gentlemen are pawns in a scheme well beyond your comprehension. Doctor, take this dagger."

Eph took the weapon's handle, holding the point at his boss's throat.

Barnes said, breathlessly, "Good *Christ*, Ephraim. Have you lost your *mind*?"

"Everett, this is bigger than you can know. This goes beyond the CDC—beyond regular law enforcement even. There is a catastrophic disease outbreak in this city, the likes of which we have never seen. And that's just the half of it."

Nora came up beside him, reclaiming hers and Ephraim's laptops from the other FBI agent. She said, "I got everything else we need from the office. Looks like we won't be coming back."

Barnes said, "For God's sake, Ephraim, come to your senses."

"This is the job you hired me to do, Everett. To sound the alarm when a public health crisis warrants. We are on the verge of a worldwide pandemic. An extinction event. And somebody somewhere is pulling out all the stops to make damn sure it succeeds."

Stoneheart Group, Manhattan

ELDRITCH PALMER switched on a bank of monitors, showing six television news channels. The one in the lower-left-hand box interested him most. He angled his chair up a few degrees and isolated the channel, raising its volume.

The reporter was posted outside the 17th Precinct headquarters on East Fifty-first Street, getting a "No comment" from a police official concerning a rash of missing persons reports being filed throughout the New York area in the past few days. They showed the line of people waiting outside the precinct house, too many to be allowed inside, filling out forms on the sidewalk. The reporter noted that other seemingly unexplained incidents, such as house break-ins in which nothing appeared to have been stolen and no one appeared to have been home, were being reported also. Strangest of all was the fact of the failure of modern technology to assist in the search for the missing persons: mobile phones, almost all of which contain traceable GPS technology, had apparently gone missing with their owners. This led some to speculate that people were perhaps willfully abandoning families and jobs, and noted that the spike in disappearances seemed to have coincided with the recent lunar occultation, suggesting a link between the two occurrences. A psychologist then commented on the potential for low-grade mass hysteria in the wake of certain startling celestial events. The story ended with the reporter giving airtime to a teary woman holding up a JCPenney portrait of a missing mother of two.

The program then went to a commercial for an "age-defying" cream designed to "help you live longer and better."

The congenitally ill tycoon then switched off the audio, so that the only sound, other than the dialysis machine, was the humming behind his avaricious smile.

On another screen was a graphic showing the financial markets declining while the dollar continued its fall. Palmer himself was moving the markets, steadily divesting himself of equities and buying into metals: gold, silver, palladium, and platinum bullion.

The commentator went on to suggest that the recent recession represented opportunities in futures trading. Palmer strongly disagreed. He was shorting futures. Everybody's except his own.

A telephone call was forwarded to his chair through Mr. Fitzwilliam. A sympathetic member of the Federal Bureau of Investigation, calling to inform him that the epidemiologist with the Canary project, Dr. Ephraim Goodweather, had escaped.

"Escaped?" said Palmer. "How is that possible?"

"He had an elderly man with him who apparently was more wily than he'd seemed. He carried a long silver sword."

Palmer was silent for one full respiration. Then, slowly, he smiled.

Forces were aligning against him. All well and good. Let them come together. It would be easier to clear them all away.

"Sir?" said the caller.

"Oh—nothing," said Palmer. "I was just thinking of an old friend."

Knickerbocker Loans and Curios, East 118th Street, Spanish Harlem

EPH AND NORA stood with Setrakian behind the locked doors of his pawnshop, the two epidemiologists still shaken up.

"I gave them your name," said Eph, looking outside the window.

"The building is in my late wife's name. We should be safe here for the moment."

Setrakian was anxious to get downstairs to his basement armory, but the two doctors were still rattled. "They are coming after us," said Eph.

"Clearing the way for infection," said Setrakian. "The strain will move faster through an orderly society than one on high alert."

"*They* who?" said Nora.

"Whoever had the influence to get that coffin loaded onto a transatlantic flight in this age of terrorism," said Setrakian.

Eph said, pacing, "They're framing us. Sending someone in there to steal Redfern's remains . . . who *looked* like us?"

"As you said, you are the lead authority to sound the general alarm for disease control. Be thankful they only tried to discredit you."

Nora said, "Without the CDC behind us, we have no authority."

Setrakian said, "We must continue on our own now. This is disease control at its most elemental."

Nora looked over at him. "You mean—murder."

"What would you want? To become like that . . . or to have someone release you?"

Eph said, "It's still a polite euphemism for murder. And easier said than done. How many heads do we have to cut off? There are three of us here."

Setrakian said, "There are ways other than severing the spinal column. Sunlight, for example. Our most powerful ally."

Eph's phone trembled inside his pocket. He pulled it out, wary, checking the display.

An Atlanta exchange. CDC headquarters. "Pete O'Connell," he said to Nora, and took the call.

Nora turned to Setrakian. "So where are they all right now, during the day?"

"Underground. Cellars and sewers. The dark bowels of buildings, such as maintenance rooms, in the heating and cooling systems. In the walls sometimes. But usually in dirt. That is where they prefer to make their nests."

"So—they sleep during the day, right?"

"That would be most convenient, wouldn't it? A handful of coffins in a basement, full of dozing vampires. But no, they don't sleep at all. Not as we understand it. They will shut down for a while if they are sated. Too much blood digestion fatigues them. But never for long. They go underground during daylight hours solely to escape the killing rays of the sun."

Nora appeared quite pale and overwhelmed, like a little girl who'd been told that dead people do not in fact grow wings and fly straight up to heaven to be angels, but instead stay on earth and grow stingers under their tongues and turn into vampires.

"That thing you said," she said. "Before you cut them down. Something in another language. Like a pronouncement, or a kind of curse."

The old man winced. "Something I say only to calm myself. To steady my hand for the final blow."

Nora waited to hear what it was. Setrakian saw that, for whatever reason, she needed to know.

"I say, '*Strigoi*, my sword sings of silver.'" Setrakian winced again, uncomfortable saying this now. "Sounds better in the old language."

Nora saw that this old vampire killer was essentially a modest man. "Silver," she said.

"Only silver," he said. "Renowned throughout the ages for its antiseptic and germicidal properties. You can cut them with steel or shoot them with lead, but only silver really *hurts* them."

Eph had his free hand over his other ear, trying to hear Pete, who was driving in a car just outside Atlanta. Pete said, "What's going on up there?"

"Well . . . what have you heard?"

"That I'm not supposed to be talking to you. That you're in trouble. That you've gone off the reservation or some such."

"It's a mess here, Pete. I don't know what to tell you."

"Well, I had to call anyway. I've been putting in time on the samples you sent me."

Eph felt another stone fall into his gut. Dr. Peter O'Connell was one of the heads of the Unexplained Deaths Project at the CDC's National Center for Zoonotic, Vector-Borne, and Enteric Diseases. UNEX was an interdisciplinary group made up of virologists, bacteriologists, epidemiologists, veterinarians, and clinicians from inside and outside the CDC. A great many naturally occurring deaths go unexplained in the United States each year, and a fraction of these—about seven hundred per annum—are referred to UNEX for further investigation. Of those seven hundred, merely 15 percent are satisfactorily resolved, with samples from the rest being banked for possible future reexamination.

Every UNEX researcher holds another position within the CDC, and Pete was the chief of Infectious Disease Pathology, an expert on how and why a virus affects its host. Eph had forgotten sending him early biopsies and blood samples from Captain Redfern's preliminary examination.

"It's a viral strain, Eph. No doubt about that. A remarkable bit of genetic acid."

"Pete, wait, listen to me—"

"The glycoprotein has amazing binding characteristics. I'm talking skeleton key. Astonishing. This little bugger doesn't merely hijack the host cell, tricking it into reproducing more copies of itself. No—it fuses to the RNA. *Melds* with it. Consumes it . . . yet somehow doesn't use it up. What it's doing is, it's making a copy of itself *mated with* the host cell. And taking only the parts it needs. I don't know what you're seeing with your patient, but theoretically, this thing could replicate and replicate and replicate, and many millions of generations later—and this thing is *fast*—it could reproduce its own organ structure. Systemically. It could change its host. Into what, I don't know—but I sure would like to find out."

"Pete." Eph's head was swimming. It made too much sense. The virus overwhelmed and transformed the cell—just as the vampire overwhelmed and transformed the victim.

These vampires were viruses incarnate.

Pete said, "I'd like to do the genetics on this one myself, really see what makes it tick—"

"Pete, listen to me. I want you to destroy it."

Eph heard Pete's windshield wipers working in the silence. "What?"

"Save your findings, hang on to those, but destroy that sample right away."

More windshield wipers, metronomes of Pete's uncertainty. "Destroy the one I was working on, you mean? Because you know that we always bank some, just in case—"

"Pete, I need you to drive straight to the lab and destroy that sample."

"Eph." Eph heard Pete's blinker, Pete pulling off the road to finish the conversation. "You know how careful we are with any potential pathogens. We're clean and we're safe. And we have a very strict laboratory protocol that I can't just break for your—"

"I made a terrible mistake letting it out of New York City. I didn't know then what I know now."

"Exactly what kind of trouble are you in, Eph?"

"Bleach it. If that doesn't work, use acid. Set it on fire if you have to, I don't care. I'll take full responsibility—"

"It's not about responsibility, Eph. It's about good science. You need to be straight with me now. Someone said they saw something about you on the news."

Eph had to end this. "Pete, do as I ask—and I promise I will explain everything to you when I can."

He hung up. Setrakian and Nora had listened to the end of his conversation.

Setrakian said, "You sent the virus somewhere else?"

"He's going to destroy it. Pete will err on the side of caution—I know him too well." Eph looked at the televisions for sale along the wall. *Something about you on the news* . . . "Any of these work?"

They found one that did. It wasn't long before the story rolled around.

They showed Eph's photograph from his CDC identification card. Then a blurry snippet of his encounter with Redfern, and one of the two look-alikes carrying a body bag from the hospital room. It said that Dr. Ephraim Goodweather was being sought as "a person of interest" in the disappearance of the corpses of the Flight 753 airline passengers.

Eph stood motionless. He thought of Kelly watching this. Of Zack.

"Those bastards," he hissed.

Setrakian switched off the television. "The only good news about this is that they still consider you a threat. That means there is still time. Still hope. A chance."

Nora said, "You sound like you have a plan."

"Not a plan. A strategy."

Eph said, "Tell us."

"Vampires have their own laws, both savage and ancient. One such commandment that endures is that a vampire cannot cross moving water. Not without human assistance."

Nora shook her head. "Why not?"

"The reason perhaps lies in their very creation, so long ago. The lore has existed in every known culture on the planet, for all time. Mesopotamians, Ancient Greeks and Egyptians, Hebrews, the Romans. Old as I am, I am not old enough to know. But the prohibition holds even today. Giving us something of an advantage here. Do you know, what is New York City?"

Nora got it right away. "An island."

"An archipelago. We are surrounded on all sides by water right now. The airline passengers, they went to morgues in all five boroughs?"

"No," said Nora. "Only four. Not Staten Island."

"Four, then. Queens and Brooklyn are both separated from the mainland, by the East River and the Long Island Sound respectively. The Bronx is the only borough connected to the United States."

Eph said, "If only we could seal off the bridges. Set up fire lines north of the Bronx, east of Queens at Nassau . . ."

"Wishful thinking at this point," said Setrakian. "But, can you see, we do not have to destroy every one of them individually. They are all of one mind, operating in a hive mentality. Controlled by a single intelligence. Who is very likely landlocked somewhere here in Manhattan."

"The Master," said Eph.

"The one who came over in the belly of the airplane. The owner of the missing coffin."

Nora said, "How do you know he's not back near the airport? If he can't cross the East River on his own."

Setrakian smiled flatly. "I feel very confident that he did not journey all the way to America to hide out in Queens." He opened the rear door, the steps leading to his basement armory. "What we have to do now is hunt him down."

Liberty Street,
the World Trade Center Site

VASILIY FET, the exterminator with the New York City Bureau of Pest Control, stood at the construction fence above the great "bathtub" foundation at the site of the former World Trade Center complex. He had left his handcart in his van, parked over on West Street, in a Port Authority lot with the other construction vehicles. In one hand he carried rodenticide and light tunnel gear in a red-and-black Puma sport bag. In his other he held his trusty length of rebar, found at a job site once, a one-meter-long steel rod perfect for probing rat burrows and pushing bait inside—and occasionally beating back aggressive or panicked vermin.

He stood between the Jersey barriers and the construction fence at the corner of Church and Liberty, among the orange-and-white caution barrels along the wide pedestrian walkway. People walked past, striding toward the temporary subway entrance at the other end of the block. There was a sense of new hope in the air here, warm, like the abundant sunshine that blessed this destroyed part of the city. The new buildings were starting to go up now, after years of planning and excavation, and it was as though this terrible black bruise was finally starting to heal.

Only Fet noticed the oily smears discoloring the vertical edges of the curb. The droppings around the parking barriers. The gnaw marks scoring the lid of the corner garbage can. Telltale signs of surface rat presence.

One of the sandhogs took him down the haul road and into the basin. He pulled up at the foot of the structure that would become the new underground WTC PATH station, with five tracks and three underground platforms. For now, the silver trains entered through daylight and open air as they made their way along the bottom of the bathtub toward the temporary platforms.

Vasiliy stepped out of the pickup, down among the concrete footings, looking up seven stories to the street above him. He was in the pit where the towers had fallen. It was enough to take his breath away.

Vasiliy said, "This is a holy place."

The sandhog had a bushy, gray-flecked mustache, and wore a loose flannel shirt over a tucked-in flannel shirt—both heavy with soil and sweat—and blue jeans with muddy gloves tucked into the belt. His hard hat was covered with stickers. "I always thought so," he said. "Recently I'm not so sure."

Fet looked at him. "Because of the rats?"

"There's that, sure. Gushing out of the tunnels the past few days, like we've struck rat oil. But that's fallen off now." He shook his head, looking up at the slurry wall erected beneath Vesey Street, seventy sheer feet of concrete studded with tiebacks.

Fet said, "Then what?"

The guy shrugged. Sandhogs are a proud lot. They built New York City, its subways and sewers, every tunnel, pier, skyscraper, and bridge foundation. Every glass of clean water comes out of the tap thanks to a sandhog. A family job, different generations working together on the same sites. Dirty work done right. So the guy was reluctant to sound reluctant. "Everyone's in kind of a funk. We had two guys walk off, disappear. Clocked in for a shift, went down into the tunnels, but never clocked out. We're twenty-four/seven here, but nobody wants night shifts anymore. Nobody wants to be underground. And these are young guys, my daredevils."

Fet looked ahead to the tunnel openings where the subterranean structures would be joined beneath Church Street. "So no new construction these past few days? Breaking new ground?"

"Not since we got the basin hollowed out."

"And all this started with the rats?"

"Around then. Something's come over this place, just in the past few days." The sandhog shrugged, shaking it off. He had a plain white hard hat for Vasiliy. "And I thought I had a dirty job. What makes someone want to become a rat catcher anyway?"

Vasiliy put on the hat, feeling the wind change near the mouth of the underground passage. "I guess I'm addicted to the glamour."

The sandhog looked at Vasiliy's boots, his Puma bag, the steel rod. "Done this before?"

"Gotta go where the vermin are. There's a lot of city under this city."

"Tell me about it. You got a flashlight, I hope? Some bread crumbs?"

"Think I'm good."

Vasiliy shook the sandhog's hand, then started inside.

The tunnel was clean at first, where it had been shored up. He followed it out of the sunlight, yellow lights strung every ten or so yards, marking his way. He was under where the original concourse had been located. This big burrow would, when all was said and done, connect the new PATH station to the WTC transportation hub located between towers two and three, a half block away. Other feed tunnels connected to city water, power, and sewer.

Deeper in, he couldn't help but notice fine, powdery dust still coating the walls of the original tunnel. This was a hallowed place, still very much a graveyard. Where bodies and buildings were pulverized, reduced to atoms.

He saw burrows, he saw tracks and scat, but no rats. He picked away at the burrows with his rod, and listened. He heard nothing.

The strung-up work lights ended at a turn, a deep, velvety blackness lying ahead. Vasiliy carried a million-candlepower spot lamp in his bag—a big yellow Garrity with a bullhorn grip—as well as two backup mini Maglites. But artificial light in a dark enclosure wiped out one's night vision altogether, and for rat hunting he liked to stay dark and quiet. He pulled out a night-vision monocular instead, a handheld unit with a strap that attached nicely to his hard hat, coming down over his left eye. Closing his right eye turned the tunnel green. Rat vision, he called it, their beady eyes glowing in the scope.

Nothing. Despite all the evidence to the contrary, the rats were gone. Driven off.

That stumped him. It took a lot to displace rats. Even once you removed their food source, it could be weeks before seeing a change. Not days.

The tunnel was joined by older passages, Vasiliy coming across filth-covered rail tracks unused for many years. The quality of the ground soil had changed, and he could tell by its very texture that he had crossed over from "new" Manhattan—the landfill that had been brought in to build up Battery Park out of sludge—into "old" Manhattan, the original dry island bedrock.

He stopped at a junction to make certain he had his bearings. As he looked down the length of the crossing tunnel, he saw, in his rat vision, a pair of eyes. They glowed back at him like rat eyes, but bigger, and high off the ground.

The eyes were gone in a flash, turning out of sight.

"Hey?" yelled Vasiliy, his call echoing. "Hey up there!"

After a moment, a voice answered him, echoing back off the walls. "Who goes there?"

Vasiliy detected a note of fear in the voice. A flashlight appeared, its source down at the end of the tunnel, well beyond where Vasiliy had seen the eyes. He flipped up the monocular just in time, saving his retina. He identified himself, pulling out a little Maglite to shine back as a signal, then moved forward. At the point where he estimated seeing the eyes, the old access tunnel ran up alongside another tunnel track that appeared to be in use. The monocular showed him nothing, no glowing eyes, so he continued around the bend to the next junction.

He found three sandhogs there, in goggles and sticker-covered hard hats, wearing flannels, jeans, and boots. A sump pump was running, channeling out a leak. The halogen bulbs of their high-powered work-light tripods lit up the new tunnel like a space-creature movie. They stood close together, tense until they could fully see Vasiliy.

"Did I just see one of you back there?" he asked.

The three guys looked at one another. "What'd you see?"

"Thought I saw someone." He pointed. "Cutting across the track."

The three sandhogs looked at one another again, then two of them started packing up. The third one said, "You the guy looking for rats?"

"Yeah."

The groundhog shook his head. "No more rats here."

"I don't mean to contradict you, but that's almost impossible. How come?"

"Could be they've got more sense than us."

Vasiliy looked down the lit tunnel, in the direction of the sump hose. "The subway exit down there?"

"That's the way out."

Vasiliy pointed in the opposite direction. "What's this way?"

The sandhog said, "You don't want to go that way."

"Why not?"

"Look. Forget about rats. Follow us out. We're done here."

Water was still trickling into the troughlike puddle. Vasiliy said, "I'll be right along."

The guy dead-eyed him. "Suit yourself," he said, switching off a tripod lamp and then hoisting a pack onto his back, starting after the others.

Vasiliy watched them go, lights playing far down the tunnel, darkening along a gradual turn. He heard the screeching of subway car wheels, near enough to concern him. He went on, crossing to the newer track, waiting for his eyes to acclimate themselves to the darkness again.

He switched on his monocular, everything going subterranean green. The echoing of his footfalls changed as the tunnel broadened to a trash-strewn exchange near a convergence of tracks. Rivet-studded steel beams stood at regular intervals, like pillars in an industrial ballroom. An abandoned maintenance shack stood to Vasiliy's right, defaced by vandalism. The shack's crumbling brick walls featuring some artless graffiti tags around a depiction of the twin towers in flames. One was labeled "Saddam," the other "Gamera."

On an old support, an ancient track sign had once warned workers:

WARNING
LOOK OUT FOR TRAINS

It had since been defaced, the T and the N in TRAINS blotted out, and electric tape stuck atop the I to turn it into a T, so that it now read:

WARNING
LOOK OUT FOR RAT S

Indeed, this godforsaken place should have been rat central. He decided to go to black light. He pulled the small wand from his Puma bag and switched it on, the bulb burning cool blue in the dark. Rodent urine fluoresces under black light, due to its bacterial content. He ran it over the ground near the supports, a moonlike landscape of dry trash and filth. He noticed some duller, older, piddling stains but nothing fresh. Not until he waved it near a rusted oil barrel lying on its side. The barrel and the floor beneath it lit up bigger and brighter than any rat piss he had ever seen. A huge splash. Factored out from what he normally found, this trace would indicate a six-foot rat.

It was the recent bodily waste of some larger animal, possibly a man.

The *drip-dripping* of the water over the old track echoed down the breezy tunnels. He sensed rustling, some distant movement, or else maybe this place was getting to him. He put away the black light and scanned the area with his monocular. Behind one of the steel supports, he again saw a pair of shining eyes reflecting back at him—then turning away and vanishing.

He couldn't tell how near. Given his one-eyed view scope and the geometrical pattern of the identical beams, his depth perception was shot.

He did not call out a hello this time. He did not say anything but gripped his rebar a bit more tightly. The homeless, when you encountered them, were rarely combative—but this felt like something different. Put it down to an exterminator's sixth sense. The way he could sniff out rat infestations. Vasiliy suddenly felt outnumbered.

He pulled out his bright bullhorn spot lamp and scanned the chamber. Before retreating, he reached back into his bag, broke open the cardboard spout on a box of tracking powder, and shook out a fair amount of rodenticide over the area. Tracking powder worked more slowly than pure edible bait, but also more surely. It had the added advantage of showing the intruders' tracks, making follow-up nest baiting easier.

Vasiliy hastily emptied three cartons, then turned with his lamp and made his way back through the tunnels. He came across active tracks with the boxed-over third rail, and then the sump pump, and followed the long hose. At one point he felt the tunnel wind change, and turned to see the curve brightening behind him. He quickly stepped back into a wall recess, bracing himself, the roar deafening. The train squealed past and Vasiliy glimpsed commuters in the windows before shielding his eyes from the smoky swirl of grit and dust.

It passed, and he followed the tracks until he reached a lighted platform. He surfaced with bag and rod, pulling himself up off the track onto the mostly empty platform, next to a sign that read, IF YOU SEE SOMETHING, SAY SOMETHING. Nobody did. He walked up the mezzanine stairs and moved through the turnstiles, resurfacing on the street into the warming sun. He moved to a nearby fence and found himself back above the World Trade Center construction site. He lit a cheroot with his blue flame butane Zippo and sucked in the poison, chasing the fear he'd felt under the streets. He walked back across the street to the World Trade Center site, coming upon two handmade fliers stapled to the fence. They were scanned color photographs of two sandhogs, one with his helmet still on and dirt on his face. The blue heading over both photographs read: MISSING.

FINAL INTERLUDE

THE RUINS

In the intervening days after the fall of Treblinka, most of the escapees were tracked down and executed. Yet Setrakian managed to survive in the woods, remaining within range of the stench of the death camp. He gobbled up roots and whatever small prey he could catch with his broken hands, while from the bodies of other corpses he scavenged an imperfect wardrobe and raggedy, mismatched shoes.

He avoided the search patrols and the barking dogs by the day—while at night, he searched.

He had heard of the Roman ruins through camp hearsay from native Poles. It took him almost a week of roaming, until late one afternoon, in the dying light of dusk, he found himself at the mossy steps at the top of the ancient rubble.

Most of what remained was underground, with only a few overgrown stones visible from the outside. A large pillar still stood at the top of a mound of stones. He could make out a few letters, but they had faded so long ago that it was impossible to discern any meaning.

It was also impossible to stand there at the dark mouth of these catacombs and not shudder.

Abraham was certain: down there was the lair of Sardu. He knew. Fear overcame him, and he felt the burning hole growing in his chest.

But purpose was stronger in his heart. Because he knew that it was his calling to find that thing, that hungry thing, and kill it. Make it cease. The camp rebellion had scuttled his killing plan—after weeks and months of procuring raw white oak for shaping—but not his need for vengeance. Of everything that was wrong in the world, this was the thing he could do right. That could give his existence meaning. And now he was about to do it.

Using a broken rock, he had fashioned a crude new stake, chosen from the hardest branch he could find, not pure white oak, but it would have to do. He did this with mangled fingers, further ruined his aching hands for all time. His footsteps echoed in the stone chamber that formed the catacomb. Its ceiling was quite low—surprising, given the Thing's unnatural height—and roots had upset the stones that precariously held the structure together. The first chamber led to a second, and, amazingly, a third. Each one smaller than the other.

Setrakian had nothing with which to light his way, but the crumbling structure allowed for faint columns of late-day light to seep through the darkness. He moved cautiously through the chambers, pulse racing, stricken at the threshold of murder. His crude wooden stake seemed wholly inadequate as a weapon to fight with in the dark, with the hungry Thing. Especially with broken hands. What was he doing? How would he kill this monster?

As he entered the last chamber, an acid pang of surging fear burned his throat. For the rest of his life, he would be afflicted by acid reflux. The room was vacant, but there, at its center, Setrakian the woodworker saw clearly in the dirt floor—as though inscribed there—the outline marking of a coffin. A huge box, two and a half yards by one and a quarter yards, and one that could only have been removed from this lair by the hands of a Thing with monstrous will.

Then—from behind him—he heard the scratch of footsteps along the stony floor. Setrakian whirled with the wooden stake outstretched, trapped within the Thing's innermost chamber. The beast had come home to nest, only to find prey lurking in its sleeping place.

The faintest shadow preceded it, but the footfalls were light and dragging. It was not the Thing who appeared at the stone turn to menace Setrakian, but a man of normal human size. A German officer, his uniform tattered and soiled. Its eyes were crimson and watery, brimming with a hunger that had grown into pure manic pain. Setrakian recognized him: Dieter Zimmer, a young officer not much older than he, a true sadist, a barracks officer who bragged of polishing his boots every night in order to scrub away the crust of Jewish blood.

Now it longed for it—for Setrakian's blood. Any blood. To gorge itself.

Setrakian would not be taken here. He was outside the camp walls now, and so resolved that he had not endured such hell only to fall here, to succumb to the unholy might of this cursed Nazi-Thing.

He ran at it with the point of his stake, but the Thing was faster than anticipated, grasping the wooden weapon and wrenching it from Setrakian's useless hands, snapping the radius and the ulna in Setrakian's forearm. He cast the stick aside, and it clacked against a stone wall and fell to the dirt.

The Thing started for Setrakian, wheezing with excitement. He backed up until he realized he was in the center of the rectangular coffin impression. Then, with unexplained strength, he ran at the Thing, forcing it hard against the wall. Dirt crumbled out from around the exposed stones, falling like wisps of smoke. The Thing tried to grab for his head, but Setrakian again lunged at him, shoving his broken arm up under the demon's chin, forcing its sneering face upward so that it could not sting him and drink.

The Thing improved its leverage and flung Setrakian aside. He landed next to his stake. He gripped it, but the Thing stood smiling, ready to take it away again. Setrakian jabbed it beneath the supporting wall stones instead. He wedged it beneath a loose stone and used his legs to pry out the stone, just as the Thing's mouth began to open.

Stones gave way, the side wall of the chamber entrance collapsing as Setrakian crawled away. The roar was loud but brief, the chamber filling with dust, smothering the remaining light. Setrakian crawled blindly over the stones, and a hand grabbed him, its grip strong. The dust parted enough for Setrakian to see that a large stone had crushed the Thing's head from crown to jaw—and yet it was still functioning. Its dark heart, or whatever it was, still throbbed hungrily. Setrakian kicked at its arm until he escaped the Thing's grip, and in doing so dislodged the stone. The top half of the head was split, the skull slightly cracked, like a soft-boiled egg.

Setrakian grabbed a leg and dragged the body with his one good arm. He hauled it back to the surface and out of the ruins, into the very last vestiges of daylight filtering in through the tree cover. The dusk was orange and dim—but it was enough. The Thing writhed in pain as it quickly cooked, settling into the ground.

Setrakian raised his face to the dying sun and let loose an animal howl. An unwise act, as he was still on the run from the fallen camp—an outpouring of his anguished soul, from the slaughter of his family, to the terrors of his captivity, to the new horrors he had found . . . and, finally, to the God who had abandoned him and his people.

Next time he met one of these creatures, he would have the proper tools at his disposal. He would give himself better than a fighting chance. He knew then, as surely as he was still alive, that he would follow the tracks of that vanished coffin for years to come. For decades, if necessary. It was this certainty that gave him a newfound direction and sent him forward in the quest that would occupy him for the rest of his life.

REPLICATION

Jamaica Hospital Medical Center

Eph and Nora swept their badges through security and got Setrakian through the emergency room entrance without attracting any undo attention. On the stairs going up to the isolation ward, Setrakian said, "This is unreasonably risky."

Eph said, "This man, Jim Kent—he and Nora and I have worked side by side for a year now. We can't just abandon him."

"He is turned. What can you do for him?"

Eph slowed. Setrakian was huffing and puffing behind them, and appreciated the stop, leaning on his walking stick. Eph looked at Nora, and they were agreed.

"I can release him," said Eph.

They exited the stairwell and eyed the isolation ward entrance down the hallway.

"No police," Nora said.

Setrakian was looking around. He was not so sure.

"There is Sylvia," said Eph, noticing Jim's frizzy-haired girlfriend sitting in a folding chair near the ward entrance.

Nora nodded to herself, ready. "Okay," she said.

She went to Sylvia alone, who rose out of her chair when she saw her coming. "Nora."

"How is Jim?"

"They haven't told me anything." Sylvia looked past her. "Eph isn't with you?"

Nora shook her head. "He went away."

"It isn't true what they say, is it?"

"Never. You look worn out. Let's get you something to eat."

While Nora was asking for directions to the cafeteria, distracting the nurses, Eph and Setrakian slipped inside the doors to the isolation ward. Eph passed the glove-and-gown station like a reluctant assassin, moving through layers of plastic to Jim's bay.

His bed was empty. Jim was gone.

Eph quickly checked the other bays. All vacant.

"They must have moved him," said Eph.

Setrakian said, "His lady friend would not be outside if she knew he was gone."

"Then . . . ?"

"They have taken him."

Eph stared at the empty bed. "They?"

"Come," said Setrakian. "This is very dangerous. We have no time."

"Wait." He went to the bedside table, seeing Jim's earpiece hanging from the drawer below. He found Jim's phone and checked to make sure that it was charged. He pulled out his own phone and realized it was like a homing device now. The FBI could close in on his location through GPS.

He dropped his phone into the drawer, swapping it for Jim's.

"Doctor," said Setrakian, growing impatient.

"Please—call me Eph," he said, slipping Jim's phone into his pocket on the way out. "I don't feel much like a doctor these days."

West Side Highway, Manhattan

Gus Elizalde sat in the back of the NYPD prisoner transport van, his hands cuffed around a steel bar behind him. Felix sat diagonally across from him, head down, rocking with the motion, growing paler by the minute. They had to be on the West Side Highway to be moving this fast in Manhattan. Two other prisoners sat with them, one across from Gus, one to his left, across from Felix. Both asleep. The stupid can sleep through anything.

Gus smelled cigarette smoke from the cab of the windowless van, through the closed partition. It had been near dusk when they were loaded in. Gus kept his eye on Felix, sagging forward off the handcuff bar. Thinking about what the old pawnbroker had said. And waiting.

He didn't have to wait long. Felix's head started to buck, then turn to the side. At once he sat erect and surveyed his surroundings. Felix looked at Gus, stared at him, but nothing in Felix's eyes showed Gus that his lifelong *compadre* recognized him.

A darkness in his eyes. A void.

A blaring car horn woke up the dude next to Gus then, startling him awake. "Shit," said the guy, rattling his cuffs behind him. "Fuck we headed?" Gus didn't answer. The dude was looking across at Felix, who was looking at him. He kicked Felix's foot. "I said where the fuck we headed, junior?"

Felix looked at him for an instant with a vacant, almost idiotic stare. His mouth opened as though to answer—and the stinger shot out, piercing the helpless guy's throat. Right across the entire width of the van, and the dude couldn't do anything about it except stomp and kick. Gus started to do the same, trapped as he was in back there with the former Felix, yelling and rattling and waking up the prisoner across from him. They all yelled and screamed and stomped as the dude next to Gus went limp, Felix's stinger flushing from translucent to bloodred.

The partition opened between the prisoner area and the front cab. A head with a cop hat on it twisted around from the passenger's seat. "Shut the fuck up back there or else I will—"

He saw Felix drinking the other prisoner. Saw the engorging appendage reaching across the van, the first messy feeding, Felix disengaging and his stinger coming back into his mouth. Blood spilling out of the dude's neck and dribbling down Felix's front.

The passenger cop yelped and turned away.

"What is it?" yelled the driver, trying to get a look in the back.

Felix's stinger shot out through the partition, latching onto the van driver's throat. Screaming rang from the cab as the van lurched, out of control. Gus grabbed the handcuff rail with his fingers just in time to keep his hands from being broken at the wrists, and the van veered right and then left, hard—before crashing on its side.

The van scraped along until it hit a guardrail, bouncing off, spinning to a stop. Gus was on his side, the prisoner across from him now dangling from broken arms, yelping in pain and fear. Felix's bar latch had broken, his stinger hanging down and twitching like a live electrical cable dripping human blood.

His dead eyes came up and looked at Gus.

Gus found his pole broken and slid his manacles fast along its length, kicking at the crumpled door until it opened. He tumbled out fast, onto the side of the road, ears roaring as though a bomb had exploded.

His hands were still cuffed behind him. Headlights went past, cars slowing to inspect the wreckage. Gus rolled away fast, quickly bringing his wrists underneath his feet, getting his hands in front of him. He eyed the busted-open cargo door of the van, waiting for Felix to climb out after him.

Then Gus heard a scream. He looked around for some kind of weapon, and had to settle for a dented hubcap. He went up with it, edging to the open door of the tipped-over van.

There was Felix, drinking the wide-eyed prisoner still strung up on the handcuff bar.

Gus swore, sickened by the sight. Felix disengaged and without any hesitation, shot his stinger at Gus's neck. Gus just got the hubcap up in time, deflecting the blow before spinning away, out of sight of the rear of the van.

Again, Felix did not follow him. Gus stood there a moment, regaining his senses—wondering why—and then noticed the sun. It was floating between two buildings across the Hudson, bloodred and almost gone, sinking fast.

Felix was hiding in the van, waiting for sundown. In three minutes he was going to be free.

Gus looked around wildly. He saw broken windshield glass on the road, but that wouldn't do it. He climbed up the chassis of the van, onto the side that was the top now. He scooted over to the driver's-side door and kicked at the hinge of the side mirror. It cracked off, and he was pulling at the wires to get it free when the cop inside yelled at him.

"Hold it!"

Gus looked at him, the driver cop, bleeding from the neck, holding on to the top handle of the roof, his gun out. Then Gus pulled the mirror free with one hard yank and jumped back down onto the road.

The sun was melting away like a punctured egg yolk. Gus went to figure out the angle, holding the mirror over his head to catch its last rays. He saw the reflection shimmer on the ground. It looked vague, too dim to do anything. So he cracked the planar glass with his knuckles, breaking it up but keeping the pieces adhered to the mirror backing. He tried it again and the reflected rays now had some distinction.

"I said hold it!"

The cop came down from the van with his gun still out. His free hand was holding his neck where Felix had gotten him, his ears bleeding from the impact. He came around and looked in the van.

Felix was crouched inside, handcuffs dangling from one hand. The other hand was gone, severed at the wrist by the cuffs at the force of impact. Its absence didn't seem to bother him. Nor did the white blood spilling from the open stump.

Felix smiled and the cop opened up on him. Rounds pierced Felix's chest and legs, ripping away flesh and chips of bone. Seven, eight shots, and Felix fell backward. Two more shots into his body. The cop lowered the gun and then Felix sat upright, still smiling.

Still thirsty. Forever thirsty.

Gus shoved the cop aside then, and held up his mirror. The last vestiges of the dying orange sun were just poking over the building across the river. Gus called Felix's name one last time, as though saying his name would snap him out of it, would miraculously bring Felix back . . .

But Felix was no longer Felix. He was a vampire motherfucker. Gus reminded himself of this as he angled the mirror so that the blazing orange shafts of reflected sunlight shot into the overturned van.

Felix's dead eyes went to horror as the beams of sun shot through him. They impaled him with the force of lasers, burning holes and igniting his flesh. An animal howl arose from deep inside him, like the cry of a man shattered at the atomic level, as the rays ravaged his body.

The sound etched itself into Gus's mind, but he kept working the reflection around until all that was left of Felix was a charred mass of smoking ash.

The light rays faded and Gus lowered his arm.

He looked across the river.

Night.

Gus felt like crying—all kinds of anguish and pain mixed together in his heart—and his pain was turning into rage. Fuel was pooled beneath the van, almost at his feet. Gus went to the cop who was still staring from the roadside at what had happened. He riffled through his pockets, finding a Zippo lighter. Gus popped the top and scratched the wheel and the flame jumped up dutifully.

"*Lo siento, 'mano.*"

He touched off the fuel spill and the van went up with a boom, knocking back both Gus and the cop.

"*Chingado*—he stung you," Gus said to the cop who still held his neck. "You'll become one of them now."

He took the cop's gun and pointed it at him. Now the sirens were coming.

The cop looked up at Gus, and then a second later his head was gone. Gus kept the smoking gun aimed at the body until he was off the side of the highway. Then he tossed away the gun and thought about the handcuff keys, but too late. Flashing lights were approaching. He turned and ran off the side of the highway, into the new night.

Kelton Street, Woodside, Queens

KELLY WAS STILL in her teaching clothes, a dark tank shirt beneath a soft wraparound top and a long, straight skirt. Zack was up in his room, supposedly doing his homework, and Matt was home, having only worked a half day because he had a store inventory that night.

This news about Eph on the television had Kelly horrified. And now she couldn't get him on his cell phone.

"He finally did it," said Matt, the tails of his denim Sears shirt pulled out for the time being. "He finally cracked."

"Matt," said Kelly, only half scolding. But—had Eph cracked? And what did this mean for her?

"Delusions of grandeur, the big virus hunter," said Matt. "He's like those firefighters who set blazes in order to be the hero." Matt sank deeply into his easy chair. "Wouldn't surprise me if he was doing all this for you."

"Me?"

"The attention, or whatnot. 'Look at me, I'm important.'"

She shook her head fast, as if he was wasting her time. Sometimes it confounded her that Matt could be so wrong about people.

The doorbell rang, and Kelly stopped her pacing. Matt sprang up from his chair, but Kelly was at the door first.

It was Eph, with Nora Martinez behind him, and an old man in a long tweed coat behind her.

"What are you doing here?" said Kelly, looking up and down the street.

Eph pushed inside. "I'm here to see Zack. To explain."

"He doesn't know."

Eph looked around, completely ignoring Matt, who was standing right there. "Is he upstairs doing homework on his laptop?"

"Yes," said Kelly.

"If he has Internet access, then he knows."

Eph went to the stairs, taking the steps two at a time.

Leaving Nora there at the door with Kelly. Nora exhaled, soaking in awkwardness. "Sorry," she said. "Barging in on you like this."

Kelly shook her head gently, looking her over with just a hint of appraisal. She knew that there was something going on between Nora and Eph. For Nora, Kelly Goodweather's house was the last place she wanted to be.

Kelly then turned her attention to the old man with the wolf-head walking stick. "What is going on?"

"The ex–Mrs. Goodweather, I presume?" Setrakian offered his hand with the courtly manners of a lost generation. "Abraham Setrakian. A pleasure to make your acquaintance."

"The same," said Kelly, taken aback, casting an uncertain glance at Matt.

Nora said, "He needed to see you guys. To explain."

Matt said, "Doesn't this little visit make us criminal accomplices to something?"

Kelly had to counter Matt's rudeness. "Would you like a drink?" she asked Setrakian. "Some water?"

Matt said, "Jesus—we could both get twenty years for that glass of water . . ."

Eph sat on the edge of Zack's bed, Zack at his desk with his laptop open.

Eph said, "I'm caught up in something I don't really understand. But I wanted you to hear it from me. None of it is true. Except for the fact that there are people after me."

Zack said, "Won't they come here looking for you?"

"Maybe."

Zack looked down, troubled, working through it. "You gotta get rid of your phone."

Eph smiled. "Already did." He clasped his conspiratorial son on the shoulder. He saw, next to the boy's laptop, the video recorder Eph had bought him for Christmas.

"You still working on that movie with your friends?"

"We're kind of in the editing stage."

Eph picked it up, the camera small and light enough to fit into his pocket. "Think I could borrow this for a little while?"

Zack nodded slowly. "Is it the eclipse, Dad? Turning people into zombies?"

Eph reacted with surprise—realizing the truth was not much more plausible than that. He tried to see this thing from the point of view of a very perceptive and occasionally sensitive eleven-year-old. And it drew something up in him, from a deep reservoir of feeling. He stood and hugged his boy. An odd moment, fragile and beautiful, between a father and son. Eph felt it with absolute clarity. He ruffled the boy's hair, and there was nothing more to be said.

Kelly and Matt were having a whispered conversation in the kitchen, leaving Nora and Setrakian alone in the glassed-in sunroom off the back of the house. Setrakian stood with his hands in his pockets, looking out at the glowing sky of early night, the third since the landing of the accursed airplane, his back to her.

A clock on the shelf went *tick-tick-tick*.

Setrakian heard *pick-pick-pick*.

Nora sensed his impatience. She said, "He, uh, he's got a lot of issues with his family. Since the divorce."

Setrakian moved his fingers into the small pocket on his vest, checking on his pillbox. The pocket was near his heart, as there were circulatory benefits to be gleaned just from placing nitroglycerin close to his aged pump. It beat steadily if not robustly. How many more beats did he have in him? Enough, he hoped, to get the job done.

"I have no children," he said. "My wife, Anna, gone seventeen years now, and I were not so blessed. You would assume that the ache for children fades over time, but in fact it deepens with age. I had much to teach, yet no student."

Nora looked at his walking stick, stood up against the wall near her chair. "How did you . . . how did you first come to this?"

"When did I discover their existence, you mean?"

"And devote yourself to this, over all these years."

He was silent for a moment, summoning the memory. "I was a young man then. During World War Two, I found myself interred in occupied Poland, very much against my own wishes. A small camp northeast of Warsaw, named Treblinka."

Nora shared the old man's stillness. "A concentration camp."

"Extermination camp. These are brutal creatures, my dear. More brutal than any predator one could ever have the misfortune of encountering in this world. Rank opportunists who prey on the young and the infirm. In the camp, myself and my fellow prisoners were a meager feast set unknowingly before him."

"Him?"

"The Master."

The way he said the word chilled Nora. "He was German? A Nazi?"

"No, no. He has no affiliation. He is loyal to no one and nothing, belonging not to one country or another. He roams where he likes. He feeds where there is food. The camp to him was like a fire sale. Easy prey."

"But you . . . you survived. Couldn't you have told someone . . . ?"

"Who would have believed an emaciated man's ravings? It took me weeks to accept what you are processing now, and I was a witness to this atrocity. It is more than the mind will accept. I chose not to be judged insane. His food source interrupted, the Master simply moved on. But I made a pledge to myself in that camp, one I have never forgotten. I tracked the Master for many years. Across central Europe and the Balkans, through Russia, central Asia. For three decades. Close on his heels at times, but never close enough. I became a professor at the

University of Vienna, I studied the lore. I began to amass books and weapons and tools. All the while preparing myself to meet him again. An opportunity I have waited more than six decades for."

"But . . . then who is he?"

"He has had many forms. Currently, he has taken the body of a Polish nobleman named Jusef Sardu, who went missing during a hunting expedition in the north country of Romania, in the spring of 1873."

"1873?"

"Sardu was a giant. At the time of the expedition, he already stood nearly seven feet tall. So tall that his muscles could not support his long, heavy bones. It was said that his pants pockets were the size of turnip sacks. For support, he had to lean heavily on a walking stick whose handle bore the family heraldic symbol."

Nora looked over again at Setrakian's oversize walking stick, its silver handle. Her eyes widened. "A wolf's head."

"The remains of the other Sardu men were found many years later, along with young Jusef's journal. His account detailed their stalking of their hunting party by some unknown predator, who abducted and killed them, one by one. The final entry indicated that Jusef had discovered the dead bodies inside the opening to an underground cave. He buried them before returning to the cave to face the beast, to avenge his family."

She could not take her eyes off the wolf's-head grip. "How ever did you get it?"

"I tracked this walking stick to a private dealer in Antwerp in the summer of 1967. Sardu eventually returned to his family's estate in Poland, many weeks later, though alone and much changed. He carried his cane, but no longer leaned on it, and in time ceased carrying it altogether. Not only had he apparently been cured of the pain of his gigantism, he was now rumored to possess great strength. Villagers soon began to go missing, the town was said to be cursed, and eventually it died away. The house of Sardu fell into ruin and the young master was never seen again."

Nora sized up the walking stick. "At fifteen he was that tall?"

"And still growing."

"The coffin . . . it was at least eight by four."

Setrakian nodded solemnly. "I know."

She nodded. Then she said, "Wait—how do you know?"

"I saw, once—at least, the marks it left in the dirt. A long time ago."

Kelly and Eph stood across from each other in the modest kitchen. Her hair was lighter and shorter, more businesslike now. Maybe more Mom-like. She gripped the edge of the countertop, and he noticed little paper cuts on her knuckles, a hazard of the classroom.

She had gotten him an unopened pint of milk from the fridge. "You still keep whole milk?" he said.

"Z likes it. Wants to be like his father."

Eph drank some, and the milk cooled him but didn't give him that usual calming sensation. He saw Matt lurking on the other side of the pass-through, sitting in a chair, pretending not to look their way.

"He is so much like you," she said. She was referring to Zack.

"I know," said Eph.

"The older he gets. Obsessive. Stubborn. Demanding. Brilliant."

"Tough to take in an eleven-year-old."

Her face broke into a broad smile. "I'm cursed for life, I guess."

Eph smiled also. It felt strange, exercise his face hadn't gotten in days.

"Look," he said, "I don't have much time. I just . . . I want things to be good. Or at least, to be okay between us. The custody thing, that whole mess—I know it did a job on us. I'm glad it's over. I didn't come here to make a speech, I just . . . now seems like a good time to clear the air."

Kelly was stunned, searching for words.

Eph said, "You don't have to say anything, I just—"

"No," she said, "I want to. I am sorry. You'll never know just how sorry I am. Sorry that everything has to be this way. Truly. I know you never wanted this. I know you wanted us to stay together. Just for Z's sake."

"Of course."

"You see, I couldn't do that—I *couldn't*. You were sucking the life out of me, Eph. And the other part of it was . . . I wanted to hurt you. I did. I admit it. And that was the only way I knew I could."

He exhaled deeply. She was finally admitting to something he'd always known. But there was no victory for him in that.

"I need Zack, you know that. Z is . . . he's it. I think, without him, there would be no me. Unhealthy or not, that's just the way it is. He's *everything* to me . . . as you once were." She paused to let that sink in, for both of them. "Without him, I would be lost, I would be . . ."

She gave up on her rambling.

Eph said, "You would be like me."

That froze her. They stood there looking at each other.

"Look," Eph said, "I'll take some blame. For us, for you and me. I know I'm not the . . . the whatever, the easiest guy in the world, the ideal husband. I went through my thing. And Matt—I know I've said some things in the past . . ."

"You once called him my 'consolation life.'"

Eph winced. "You know what? Maybe if I managed a Sears, if I had a job that was just that, a job, and not another marriage entirely . . . maybe you wouldn't have felt so left out. So cheated. So . . . second place."

They were quiet for a bit then, Eph realizing how bigger issues tended to crowd out the little ones. How true strife caused personal problems to be set aside with alacrity.

Kelly said, "I know what you're going to say. You're going to say we should have had this talk years ago."

"We should have," he agreed. "But we couldn't. It wouldn't have worked. We had to go through all this shit first. Believe me, I'd have paid any amount *not* to—not to have gone through one second of it— but here we are. Like old acquaintances."

"Life doesn't go at all the way you think it will."

Eph nodded. "After what my parents went through, what they put me through, I always told myself, never, never, never, never."

"I know."

He folded in the spout on the milk carton. "So forget who did what. What we need to do now is make it up to him."

"We do."

Kelly nodded. Eph nodded. He swirled the milk around in the carton, feeling the coldness brush up against his palm.

"Christ, what a day," he said. He thought again about the little girl in Freeburg, the one who had been holding hands with her mother on Flight 753. The one who was Zack's age. "You know how you always told me, if something hit, some biological threat, that if I didn't let you know first you'd divorce me? Well—too late for that."

She came forward, reading his face. "I know you're in trouble."

"This isn't about me. I just want you to listen, okay, and not flip out. There is a virus moving through the city. It's something . . . extraordinary . . . easily the worst thing I've ever seen."

"The worst?" She blanched. "Is it SARS?"

Eph almost smiled at the grand absurdity of it all. The insanity.

"What I want you to do is to take Zack and get out of the city. Matt too. As soon as possible—tonight, right now—and as far away as you can possibly go. Away from populated areas, I mean. Your parents . . . I know how you feel about taking things from them, but they have that place up in Vermont still, right? On top of that hill?"

"What are you saying?"

"Go there. For a few days at least. Watch the news, wait for my call."

"Wait," she said. "I'm the head-for-the-hills paranoiac, not you. But . . . what about my classroom? Zack's school?" She squinted. "Why won't you tell me what it is?"

"Because then you would not go. Just trust me, and go," he said. "Go, and hope we can turn it back somehow, and this all passes quickly."

"'Hope?'" she said. "Now you're really scaring me. What if you can't turn it back? And—and what if something happens to you?"

He couldn't stand there with her and address his own doubts. "Kelly—I gotta go."

He tried to walk out, but she grabbed his arm, checking his eyes to see if it was okay, then put her arms around him. What started as just a make-up hug turned into something more, and by the end of it she was gripping him tightly. "*I'm sorry,*" she whispered into his ear, then left a kiss on the bristly side of his unshaven neck.

Vestry Street, Tribeca

ELDRITCH PALMER sat waiting on an uncushioned chair on the rooftop patio, bathed in night. The only direct light was that of an outdoor gas lamp burning in the corner. The terrace was on the top of the lower of the two adjoining buildings. The floor was made of square clay tiles, aged and blanched by the elements. One low step preceded a high brick wall at the northern end, with two door-size archways hung with ironwork. Fluted terra-cotta tiling topped the wall and the overhangs on each side. To the left, through wider decorative archways, were oversize doorways to the residence. Behind Palmer, centered before the southern white cement wall, was a headless statue of a woman in swirling robes, her shoulders and arms darkly weathered. Ivy slithered up the stone base. Though a few taller buildings were visible both north and east, the patio was reasonably private, as concealed a rooftop as one might hope to find in lower Manhattan.

Palmer sat listening to the sounds of the city rising off the streets. Sounds that would end so soon. If only they knew this down there, they would embrace this night. Every mundanity of life grows infinitely more precious in the face of impending death. Palmer knew this intimately. A sickly child, he had struggled with his health all his life. Some mornings he had awakened amazed to see another dawn. Most people didn't know what it was to mark existence one sunrise at a time. What it was like to depend on machines for one's survival. Good health was the birthright of most, and life a series of days to be tripped through. They had never known the nearness of death. The intimacy of ultimate darkness.

Soon Eldritch Palmer would know their bliss. An endless menu of days stretched out before him. Soon he would know what it was not to worry about tomorrow, or tomorrow's tomorrow . . .

A breeze fluttered the patio trees and rustled through some of the plantings. Palmer, seated facing the taller residence, at an angle, next to a small smoking table, heard a rustling. A rippling, like the hem of a garment on the floor. A black garment.

I thought you wanted no contact until after the first week.

The voice—at once both familiar and monstrous—sent a dark thrill racing up Palmer's crooked back. If Palmer hadn't purposely been facing away from the main part of the patio—both out of respect as well as sheer human aversion—he would have seen that the Master's mouth never moved. No voice went out into the night. The Master spoke directly into your mind.

Palmer felt the presence high above his shoulder, and kept his gaze trained on the arched doors to the residence. "Welcome to New York."

This came out as more of a gasp than he would have liked. Nothing can unman you like an un-man.

When the Master said nothing, Palmer tried to reassert himself. "I have to say, I disapprove of this Bolivar. I don't know why you should have selected him."

Who he is matters not to me.

Palmer saw instantly that he was right. So what if Bolivar had been a makeup-wearing rock star? Palmer was thinking like a human, he supposed. "Why did you leave four conscious? It has created many problems."

Do you question me?

Palmer swallowed. A kingmaker in this life, subordinate to no man. The feeling of abject servility was as foreign to him as it was overwhelming.

"Someone is on to you," Palmer said quickly. "A medical scientist, a disease detective. Here in New York."

What does one man matter to me?

"He—his name is Dr. Ephraim Goodweather—is an expert in epidemic control."

You glorified little monkeys. Your kind is the epidemic—not mine.

"This Goodweather is being advised by someone. A man with detailed knowledge of your kind. He knows the lore and even a bit of the biology. The police are looking for him, but I think that more decisive action is warranted. I believe that this could mean the difference between a quick, decisive victory or a protracted struggle. We have many battles to come, on the human front as well as others—"

I will prevail.

As to that, Palmer harbored no doubts. "Yes, of course." Palmer wanted the old man for himself. He wanted to confirm his identity before divulging any information to the Master. So he was actively trying not to think about the old man—knowing that, in the presence of the Master, one must protect one's thoughts . . .

I have met this old man before. When he was not quite so old.

Palmer went cold with astonished defeat. "You will remember, it took me a long time to find you. My travels took me to the four corners of the world, and there were many dead ends and side roads—many people I had to go through. He was one of them." He tried to make his change in topic fluid, but his mind felt clouded. Being in the presence of the Master was like being oil in the presence of a burning wick.

I will meet this Goodweather. And tend to him.

Palmer had already prepared a bulleted sheet containing background information on the CDC epidemiologist. He unfolded the sheet from his jacket pocket, laying it flat on the table. "Everything is there, Master. His family, known associates . . ."

There was a scrape along the tile top of the table, and the piece of paper was taken. Palmer glimpsed the hand only peripherally. The middle finger, crooked and sharp-nailed, was longer and thicker than the others.

Palmer said, "All we need now is a few more days."

An argument, of sorts, had begun inside the rock star's residence, the unfinished twin town houses that Palmer had had the unfortunate pleasure of walking through in order to get to the patio rendezvous. He showed particular distaste for the only finished part of the household, the penthouse bedroom, garishly overdecorated and reeking of primate lust. Palmer himself had never been with a woman. When he was young, it was because of illness, and the preaching of the two aunts who had raised him. When he was older, it was by choice. He came to understand that the purity of his mortal self should never be tainted by desire.

The interior argument grew louder, into the unmistakable clatter of violence.

Your man is in trouble.

Palmer sat forward. Mr. Fitzwilliam was inside. Palmer had expressly forbidden him to enter the patio area. "You said his safety here was guaranteed."

Palmer heard the pounding of running feet. He heard grunting. A human yell.

"Stop them," said Palmer.

The Master's voice was, as ever, languid and unperturbed.

He is not the one they want.

Palmer rose in a panic. Did the Master mean him? Was this some sort of trap? "We have an agreement!"

For as long as it suits me.

Palmer heard another yell, close at hand—followed by two quick gun reports. Then one of the interior arched doors was thrown open, inward, and the ornamental gate was pushed out. Mr. Fitzwilliam, 260 pounds of ex-marine in a Savile Row suit, came racing through, his sidearm gripped in his right hand, eyes bright with distress. "Sir—they are right behind me . . ."

It was then that his vision moved from Palmer's face to the impossibly tall figure standing behind him. The gun slipped from Mr. Fitzwilliam's grip, clunking to the tile. Mr. Fitzwilliam's face drained of color and he swayed there for a moment like a man swaying from a wire, then dropped to his knees.

Behind him came the turned. Vampires in various modes of civilian dress, from business suits to Goth wear to paparazzi casual. All stinking and scuffed from nesting in the dirt. They rushed onto the patio like creatures beckoned by an unheard whistle.

Leading them was Bolivar himself, gaunt and nearly bald, wearing a black robe. As a first-generation vampire, he was more mature than the rest. His flesh had a bloodless, alabaster-like pallor that was almost glowing and his eyes were dead moons.

Behind him was a female fan who had been shot in the face by Mr. Fitzwilliam in the midst of his panic. Her cheekbone was split open back to her lopsided ear, leaving her with one half of a garish, teeth-baring smile.

The rest staggered out into the new night, excited into action by the presence of their Master. They stopped, staring at him in black-eyed awe.

Children.

Palmer—standing right before them, between them and the Master—was completely ignored. The force of the Master's presence held them in abeyance. They gathered before him like primitives before a temple.

Mr. Fitzwilliam remained on his knees, as though struck down.

The Master spoke in a way that Palmer believed exclusive to his own ears.

You brought me all this way. Aren't you going to look?

Palmer had beheld the Master once before, in a darkened cellar on another continent. Not clearly, and yet—clearly enough. The image had never left him.

No way to avoid him now. Palmer closed his eyes to steel himself, then opened them and forced himself to turn. Like risking blindness by staring into the sun.

His eyes traveled up from the Master's chest to . . .

. . . his face.

The horror. And the glory.

The impious. And the magnificent.

The savage. And the holy.

Unnatural terror stretched Palmer's face into a mask of fear, eventually turning the corners of it into a triumphant, teeth-clenching smile.

The hideous transcendent.

Behold the Master.

Kelton Street, Woodside, Queens

KELLY WALKED FAST across the living room with clean clothes and batteries in her hands, past Matt and Zack, who were watching the television news.

"We're going," said Kelly, dumping the load into a canvas bag on a chair.

Matt turned to her with a smile but Kelly wanted none of it. "Come on, babe," he said.

"Haven't you been listening to me?"

"Yes. Patiently." He stood up from his chair. "Look, Kel, your ex-husband is doing his thing again. Lobbing a grenade into our happy home life here. Can't you see that? If this was something really serious, the government would tell us."

"Oh. Yes, of course. Elected officials never lie." She stomped off to the front closet, pulling out the rest of the luggage. Kelly kept a go bag also, as recommended by the New York City Office of Emergency Management, in the event of an emergency evacuation. It was a sturdy canvas bag packed with bottled water and granola bars, a Grundig hand-crank AM/FM/shortwave radio, a Faraday flashlight, a first-aid kit, $100 in cash, and copies of all their important documents in a waterproof container.

"This is a self-fulfilling prophesy with you," continued Matt, following her. "Don't you see? He knows you. He knows exactly which button to push. This is why you two were no good for each other."

Kelly dug to the back of the closet, tossing out two old tennis rackets in her way, hitting Matt on the feet for talking like that in front of Zack. "It's not like that. I believe him."

"He's a wanted man, Kel. He's having some sort of breakdown, a collapse. All these so-called geniuses are basically fragile. Like those sunflowers you're always trying to grow out along the back fence—heads too big, collapsing underneath their own weight." Kelly sent a winter boot out, flying near his shins, but this one he dodged. "This is all about you, you know. He's pathological. Can't let go. This whole thing is about keeping you close."

She stopped, turning on all fours, staring at him through the bottom of the coats. "Are you really that clueless?"

"Men don't like to lose. They won't give in."

She backed out hauling her big American Tourister. "Is that why you won't leave now?"

"I won't leave because I have to go to work. If I thought I could use your daffy husband's end-of-the-world excuse to get out of this floor-to-computer inventory, I would, believe me. But in the real world, when you don't show up at your job, you lose it."

She turned, burning at his obstinacy. "Eph said to go. He's never acted that way before, never talked like that. This is real."

"It's eclipse hysteria, they were talking about it on TV. People freaking out. If I was going to flee New York because of all the crazies, I'd have been out of here years ago." Matt reached for her shoulders. She shook him off at first, then let him hold her for a moment. "I'll check in with the electronics department now and then, the TVs there, to see if anything's happening. But the world keeps turning, all right? For those of us with real jobs. I mean—you're just going to leave your classroom?"

Her students' needs pulled on her, but everybody and everything else came second to Zack. "Maybe they'll cancel school for a few days. Come to think of it, I had a lot of unexplained absences today—"

"These are kids, Kel. Flu."

"I think it's actually the eclipse," said Zack, from across the room. "Fred Falin told me in school. Everyone who looked at the moon without glasses? It cooked their brains."

Kelly said, "What is this fascination with you and zombies?"

"They're out there," he said. "Gotta be prepared. I'll bet you don't even know the two most important things you need in order to survive a zombie invasion."

Kelly ignored him. Matt said, "I give up."

"A machete and a helicopter."

"Machete, huh?" Matt shook his head. "I think I'd rather have a shotgun."

"Wrong," said Zack. "You don't have to reload a machete."

Matt conceded the point, turning to Kelly. "This Fred Falin kid really knows his stuff."

"Guys—I've HAD it!" Being ganged up on by them wasn't something she was used to. Any other time, she might have been happy seeing Zack and Matt pulling together. "Zack—you're talking nonsense. This is a virus, and it's real. We need to get out of here."

Matt stood there while Kelly carried the empty suitcase to the other bags. "Kel, relax. Okay?" He pulled his car keys out of his pocket, twirling them around his finger. "Take a bath, catch your breath. Be rational about this—please. Taking into account the source of your 'inside' info." He went to the front door. "I'll check in with you later."

He went out. Kelly stood staring at the closed door.

Zack came over to her with his head cocked slightly to one side, the way he used to when he'd ask what death meant or why some men held hands. "What did Dad say to you about this?"

"He just . . . he wants the best for us."

Kelly rubbed her forehead in a way that hid her eyes. Should she alarm Zack too? Could she pack up Zack and leave here solely on Eph's word, without Matt? Should she? And—if she believed Eph, didn't she have a moral obligation to warn others in turn?

The Heinsons' dog started barking next door. Not her usual angry yipping, but a high-pitched noise, sounding almost scared. It was enough to bring Kelly into the back sunroom, where she found that the motion light over the backyard deck had come on.

She stood there with arms crossed, watching the yard for movement. Everything looked still. But the dog kept going, until Mrs. Heinson went out and brought it—still barking—inside.

"Mom?"

Kelly jumped, scared by her son's touch, totally losing her cool.

"You okay?" Zack said.

"I hate this," she said, walking him back into the living room. "Just hate it."

She would pack, for her and for Zack and for Matt.

And she would watch.

And she would wait.

Bronxville

THIRTY MINUTES NORTH of Manhattan, Roger Luss sat poking at his iPhone inside the oak-paneled bar room of the Siwanoy Country Club, awaiting his first martini. He had instructed the Town Car driver to let him off at the club rather than take him straight home. He needed a little reentry time. If Joan was sick, as the nanny's voice mail message seemed to indicate, then the kids probably had it by now, and he could be walking into a real mess. More than enough reason to extend his business trip by one or two more hours.

The dining room overlooking the golf course was completely empty at the dinner hour. The server came with his three-olive martini on a tray covered in white linen. Not Roger's usual waiter. He was Mexican, like the fellows who parked cars out in front. His shirt was shrugged up out of his waistband in the back, and he wore no belt. His nails were dirty. Roger would have a talk with the club manager first thing in the morning. "There she is," said Roger, the olives sunk at the bottom of the V-shaped cocktail glass, like beady little eyeballs preserved in a pickling vinegar. "Where is everyone tonight?" he asked in his usual booming voice. "What is it, a holiday? The market closed today? President died?"

Shrug.

"Where are all the regular staff?"

He shook his head. Roger realized now that the man looked scared.

Then Roger recognized him. The barman's uniform had thrown Roger off. "Groundskeeper, right? Usually out trimming the greens."

The groundskeeper in the barman's uniform nodded nervously and shambled off to the front lobby.

Damn peculiar. Roger lifted his martini glass and looked around, but there was nobody to toast or nod to, no town politicking to be done. And so, with no eyes on him, Roger Luss slurped the cocktail, downing half of it in two great swallows. It hit his stomach and he let go a low purr in greeting. He speared one of the olives, tapping it dry on the edge of the glass before popping it into his mouth, swishing it around for a thoughtful moment, then squishing it between his back molars.

On the muted television built into the wood above the bar mirror, he saw clips from a news conference. The mayor flanked by other grim-faced city officials. Then—file footage of the Regis Air Flight 753 plane on the tarmac at JFK.

The silence of the club made him look around again. *Where in the hell was everyone?*

Something was going on here. Something was happening and Roger Luss was missing out.

He took another quick sip of the martini—and then one more—then set down the glass and stood. He walked to the front, checking the pub room off to the side—also empty. The kitchen door was just to the side of the pub bar, padded and black with a porthole window in the upper center. Roger peeked inside and saw the barman/groundskeeper all alone, smoking a cigarette and grilling himself a steak.

Roger went out the front doors, where he had left his luggage. No valets were there to call him a taxi, so he reached for his phone, searched online, found the listing that was closest, and called for a car.

While waiting under the high lights of the pillared carport entrance, the taste of the martini going sour in his mouth, Roger Luss heard a scream. A single, piercing cry into the night, from not so far away. On the Bronxville side of things, as opposed to Mount Vernon. Perhaps coming from somewhere on the golf course itself.

Roger waited without moving. Without breathing. Listening for more.

What spooked him more than the scream was the silence that followed.

The taxi pulled up, the driver a middle-aged Middle Eastern man wearing a pen behind his ear, who smilingly dumped Roger's luggage into the trunk and drove off.

On the long private road out from the club, Roger looked out onto the course and thought he saw someone out there, walking across the fairway in the moonlight.

Home was a three-minute drive away. There were no other cars on the road, the houses mostly dark as they passed. As they turned onto Midland, Roger saw a pedestrian coming up the sidewalk—an odd sight at night, especially without a dog to walk. It was Hal Chatfield, an older neighbor of his, one of the two club members who had sponsored Roger into Siwanoy when Roger and Joan first bought into Bronxville. Hal was walking funny, hands straight down at his sides, dressed in an open, flapping bathrobe and a T-shirt and boxer shorts.

Hal turned and stared at the taxi as it passed. Roger waved. When he turned back to see if Hal had recognized him, he saw that Hal was running, stiff-legged, after him. A sixty-year-old man with his bathrobe trailing like a cape, chasing a taxi down the middle of the street in Bronxville.

Roger turned to see if the driver saw this also, but the man was scribbling on a clipboard as he drove.

"Hey," said Roger. "Any idea what's going on around here?"

"Yes," said the driver, with a smile and a curt nod. He had no idea what Roger was saying.

Two more turns brought them to Roger's house. The driver popped the trunk and jumped out with Roger. The street was quiet, Roger's house as dark as the rest.

"You know what? Wait here. Wait?" Roger pointed at the cobblestone curb. "Can you wait?"

"You pay."

Roger nodded. He wasn't even sure why he wanted him there. It had something to do with feeling very alone. "I have cash in the house. You wait. Okay?"

Roger left his luggage in the mudroom by the side entrance and moved into the kitchen, calling out, "Hello?" He reached for the light switch but nothing happened when he flipped it. He could see the microwave clock glowing green, so the power was still on. He felt his way forward along the counter, feeling for the third drawer and rooting around inside for the flashlight. He smelled something rotting, more pungent than leftovers moldering in the trash, heightening his anxiety and quickening his hand. He gripped the shaft of the flashlight and switched it on.

He swept the long kitchen with the beam, finding the island counter, the table beyond, the range and double oven. "Hello?" he called again, the fear in his voice shaming him, prompting him to move faster. He saw a dark spatter on the glass-front cabinets and trained his beam on what looked like the aftermath of a ketchup and mayonnaise fight. The mess brought a surge of anger. He saw the overturned chairs then, and dirty footprints (*footprints?*) on the center island granite.

Where was the housekeeper, Mrs. Guild? Where was Joan? Roger went closer to the spatter, bringing the light right up to the cabinet glass. The white stuff, he didn't know—but the red was not ketchup. He couldn't be certain . . . but he thought it might be blood.

He saw something moving in the reflection of the glass and whipped around with the flashlight. The back stairs behind him were empty. He realized he had just moved the cabinet door himself. He didn't like his imagination taking over, and so ran upstairs, checking each room with the flashlight. "Keene? Audrey?" Inside Joan's office, he found handwritten notes pertaining to the Regis Air flight. A timeline of sorts, though her penmanship failed over the last couple of incomprehensible sentences. The last word, scrawled in the bottom-right corner of the legal pad, read, "hummmmmm."

In the master bedroom, the bedsheets were all kicked down, and inside the master bath, floating unflushed in the toilet, was what looked to him like curdled, days-old vomit. He picked a towel up off the floor and, letting it fall open, discovered dark clots of staining blood, as though the plush cotton had been used as a coughing rag.

He ran back down the front stairs. He picked up the wall phone in the kitchen and dialed 911. It rang once before a recording played, asking him to hold. He hung up and dialed again. One ring and the same recording.

He dropped the phone from his ear when he heard a thump in the basement beneath him. He threw open the door, about to call down into the darkness—but something made him stop. He listened, and heard . . . something.

Shuffling footsteps. More than one set, coming up the stairs, approaching the halfway point where the steps hooked ninety degrees and turned toward him.

"Joan?" he said. "Keene? Audrey?"

But he was already backpedaling. Falling backward, striking the door frame, then scrambling back through the kitchen, past the gunk on the walls and into the mudroom. His only thought was to get out of there.

He slammed through the storm door and out into the driveway, running to the street, yelling at the driver sitting behind the wheel, who didn't understand English. Roger opened the back door and jumped inside.

"Lock the doors! Lock the doors!"

The driver turned his head. "Yes. Eight dollar and thirty."

"Lock the goddamn doors!"

Roger looked back at the driveway. Three strangers, two women and one man, exited his mudroom and started across his lawn.

"Go! Go! Drive!"

The driver tapped the pay slot in the partition between the front and back seats. "You pay, I go."

Four of them now. Roger stared, stupefied, as a familiar-looking man wearing a ripped shirt knocked the others aside to get to the taxi first. It was Franco, their gardener. He looked through the passenger-door window at Roger, his staring eyes pale in the center but red around the rims, like a corona of bloodred crazy. He opened his mouth as though to roar at Roger—and then this thing came out, punched the window with a solid *whack*, right at Roger's face, then retracted.

Roger stared. *What the hell did I just see?*

It happened again. Roger understood—on a pebble level, deep beneath many mattresses of fear, panic, mania—that Franco, or this thing that was Franco, didn't know or had forgotten or misjudged the properties of glass. He appeared confused by the transparency of this solid.

"Drive!" screamed Roger. *"Drive!"*

Two of them stood close, in front of the taxi now. A man and a woman, headlights brightening their waists. There were seven or eight in total, all around them, others coming out of the neighbors' houses.

The driver yelled something in his own language, leaning on the horn.

"Drive!" screamed Roger.

The driver reached for something on the floor instead. He pulled up a small bag the size of a toiletry case and ran back the zipper, spilling out a few Zagnut bars before getting his hand on a tiny silver revolver. He waved the weapon at the windshield and hollered in fear.

Franco's tongue was exploring the window glass. Except that the tongue wasn't a tongue at all.

The driver kicked open his door. Roger yelled, *"No!"* through the partition glass, but the driver was already outside. He fired the hand-gun from behind the door, shooting it with a flick of his wrist, as though throwing bullets from it. He fired again and again, the pair in front of the car doubling up, struck by small-caliber rounds, but not dropping.

The driver kicked off two more wild shots and one of them struck the man in the head. His scalp flew backward and he stumbled to the ground.

Then another grabbed the driver from behind. It was Hal Chatfield, Roger's neighbor, his blue bathrobe hanging off his shoulders.

"No!" Roger shouted, but too late.

Hal spun the driver to the road. The thing came out of his mouth and pierced the driver's neck. Roger watched the howling driver through his window.

Another one rose up into the headlights. No, not another one—the same man who had been shot in the head. His wound was leaking white, running down the side of his face. He used the car to hold himself up, but he was still coming.

Roger wanted to run, but he was trapped. To the right, past Franco the gardener, Roger saw a man in UPS brown shirt and shorts come out of the garage next door with the head of a shovel on his shoulder, like the baseball bat of an on-deck hitter.

The head-wound man pulled himself around the driver's open door and climbed into the front seat. He looked through the plastic partition at Roger, the front-right lobe of his head raised like a forelock of flesh. White ooze glazed his cheek and jaw.

Roger turned just in time to see the UPS guy swing the shovel. It clanged off the rear window, leaving a long scrape in the reinforced glass, light from the streetlamps glinting in the spiderweb cracks.

Roger heard the scrape on the partition. The head-wound man's tongue came out, and he was trying to slip it through the ashtray-style pay slot. The fleshy tip poked through, straining, almost sniffing at the air as it tried to get at Roger.

With a scream, Roger kicked at the slot in a frenzy, slamming it shut. The man in front let out an ungodly squeal, and the severed tip of his . . . whatever it was, fell directly into Roger's lap. Roger swatted it away as, on the other side of the partition, the man spurted white all over, gone wild either in pain or in pure castration hysteria.

Whamm! Another swing of the shovel crashed against the back window behind Roger's head, the antishatter glass cracking and bending but still refusing to break.

Pown-pown-pown. Footsteps leaving craters on the roof now.

Four of them on the curb, three on the street side, and more coming from the front. Roger looked back, saw the deranged UPS man rear back to swing the shovel at the broken window again. Now or never.

Roger reached for the handle and kicked the street-side door open with all his might. The shovel came down and the back window was smashed away, raining chips of glass. The blade just missed Roger's head as he slid out into the street. Someone—it was Hal Chatfield, his eyes glowing red—grabbed his arm, spinning him around, but Roger shed his suit jacket like a snake wriggling out of its skin and kept on going, racing up the street, not looking back until he reached the corner.

Some came in a hobbling jog, others moved faster and with more coordination. Some were old, and three of them were grinning children. His neighbors and friends. Faces he recognized from the train station, from birthday parties, from church.

All coming after him.

Flatbush, Brooklyn

EPH PRESSED THE DOORBELL at the Barbour residence. The street was quiet, though there was life in the other homes, television lights, bags of trash at the curb. He stood there with a Luma lamp in his hand and a Setrakian-converted nail gun hanging on a strap from his shoulder.

Nora stood behind him, at the foot of the brick steps, holding her own Luma. Setrakian brought up the rear, his staff in hand, its silver head glowing in the moonlight.

Two rings, no answer. Not unexpected. Eph tried the doorknob before looking for another entrance, and it turned.

The door opened.

Eph went in first, flicking on a light. The living room looked normal, slipcovered furniture and throw pillows set just so.

He called out, "Hello," as the two others filed in behind him. Strange, letting himself into the house. Eph trod softly on the rug, like a burglar or an assassin. He wanted to believe he was still a healer, but that was becoming more difficult to believe by the hour.

Nora started up the stairs. Setrakian followed Eph into the kitchen. Eph said, "What do you think we will learn here? You said the survivors were distractions—"

"I said that was the purpose they served. As to the Master's intent—I don't know. Perhaps there is some special attachment to the Master. In any event, we must start somewhere. These survivors are our only leads."

A bowl and spoon sat in the sink. A family Bible lay open on the table, stuffed with mass cards and photographs, turned to the final chapter. A passage was underlined in red ink with a shaky hand, Revelations 11:7–8:

> **. . . the beast that ascends from the bottomless pit will make war upon them and conquer them and kill them, and their dead bodies will lie in the street of the great city which is allegorically called Sodom . . .**

Next to the open Bible, like instruments set out upon an altar, were a crucifix and a small glass bottle Eph presumed to be holy water.

Setrakian nodded at the religious articles. "No more reasonable than duct tape and Cipro," he said. "And no more effective."

They proceeded into the back room. Eph said, "The wife must have covered for him. Why wouldn't she call a doctor?"

They explored a closet, Setrakian tapping the walls with the bottom of his staff. "Science has made many advances in my lifetime, but the instrument has yet to be invented that can see clearly into the marriage of a man and a woman."

They closed the closet. Eph realized they were out of doors to open. "If there's no basement?"

Setrakian shook his head. "Exploring a crawl space is many times worse."

"Up here!" It was Nora, calling down from upstairs, urgency in her voice.

Ann-Marie Barbour was slumped over from a sitting position on the floor between her nightstand and her bed, dead. Between her legs was a wall mirror that she had shattered on the floor. She had selected the longest, most daggerlike shard and used it to sever the radial and ulnar arteries of her left arm. Wrist cutting is one of the least effective methods of suicide, with a success rate of less than 5 percent. It is a slow death, due to the narrowness of the lower arm, and the fact that only one wrist cut is possible: a deep slice severs nerves, rendering that hand useless. It is also extremely painful, and as such, generally successful only among the profoundly depressed or the insane.

Ann-Marie Barbour had cut very deeply, the severed arteries as well as the dermis pulled back, exposing both bones in the wrist. Tangled in the curled fingers of her immobilized hand was a bloodied shoelace, upon which was strung a round-headed padlock key.

Her spilled blood was red. Still, Setrakian produced his silver-backed mirror and held it at an angle to her down-turned face, just to be sure. No blurring—the image was true. Ann-Marie Barbour had not been turned.

Setrakian stood slowly, bothered by this development. "Strange," he said.

Eph stood over her in such a way that her down-turned face—her expression one of bewildered exhaustion—was reflected in the pieces of shattered glass. He noticed, tucked beneath a twin frame containing photographs of a young boy and girl on the nightstand, a folded piece of notebook paper. He slid it out, paused a moment with it in his hand, then opened it carefully.

Her handwriting was shaky, in red ink, just like the notation in the kitchen Bible. Her lower case *i*'s were dotted with circles, giving the penmanship a juvenile appearance.

"'To my dearest Benjamin and darling Haily,'" he began reading.

"Don't," interrupted Nora. "Don't read it. It's not for us."

She was right. He scanned the page for pertinent information—"The children are with the father's sister in Jersey, safe"—skipping down to the final passage, reading just that bit. "'I am so sorry, Ansel . . . this key I hold I cannot use . . . I know now that God has cursed you to punish me, he has forsaken us and we are both damned. If my death will cure your soul, then He can have it . . .'"

Nora knelt, reaching for the key, drawing the bloody shoelace away from Ann-Marie's lifeless fingers. "So . . . where is he?"

They heard a low moan that almost passed for a growl. It was bestial, glottal, the kind of throaty noise that can only be made by a creature with no human voice. And it came from outside.

Eph went to the window. He looked down at the backyard and saw the large shed.

They went out silently into the backyard, to stand before the chained handles of the twin shed doors. There, they listened.

Scratching inside. Guttural noises, quiet and choked.

Then the doors *bang*ed. Something shoved against them. Testing the chain.

Nora had the key. She looked to see if anyone else wanted it, and then walked to the chain herself, inserting the key in the padlock and turning it gingerly. The lock clicked and the shackle popped free.

Silence inside. Nora lifted the lock out of the links, Setrakian and Eph ready behind her—the old man drawing his silver sword from its wooden sheath. She began unwinding the heavy chain. Threading it through the wooden handles . . . expecting the doors to burst open immediately . . .

But nothing happened. Nora pulled the last length free and stepped back. She and Eph powered on their UVC lamps. The old man was locked in on the doors, so Eph sucked in a brave breath and reached for the handles, pulling open the doors.

It was dark inside. The only window was covered with something, and the outward-opening doors blocked most of the light coming down from the house porch.

It was a few airless moments before they perceived the form of something crouching.

Setrakian stepped forward, stopping within two paces of the open door. He appeared to be showing the occupant of the shed his silver blade.

The thing attacked. It charged, running at Setrakian, leaping for him, and the old man was ready with his sword—but then the leash chain caught, snapping the thing back.

They saw it now—saw its face. It sneered, its gums so white it appeared at first that its bared teeth went all the way up into the jaw. Its lips were pale with thirst, and what was left of its hair had whitened at the roots. It crouched on all fours on a bed of soil, a chain collar locked tight around its neck, dug into the flesh.

Setrakian said, never taking his eyes off it, "This is the man from the airplane?"

Eph stared. This thing was like a demon that had devoured the man named Ansel Barbour and half-assumed his form.

"It *was* him."

"Somebody caught it," said Nora. "Chained it here. Locked it away."

"No," said Setrakian. "He chained himself."

Eph then understood. How the wife had been spared, and the children.

"Stay back," warned Setrakian. And just then the vampire opened its mouth and struck, the stinger lashing out at Setrakian. The old man did not flinch, as the vampire did not have the reach, despite his stinger being many feet long. It retracted in failure, the disgusting outgrowth drooping just past the vampire's chin, flicking around its open mouth like the blind pink feeler of some deep-sea creature.

Eph said, "Jesus God . . ."

The vampire Barbour turned feral. It backed up on its haunches, hissing at them. The unbelievable sight shocked Eph into remembering Zack's camera in his pocket, and he handed Nora his lamp, taking out the recorder.

"What are you doing?" asked Nora.

He fumbled on the power, capturing this thing in the viewfinder. Then, with his other hand, he switched off the safety on his nail gun and aimed it at the beast.

Snap-chunk. Snap-chunk. Snap-chunk.

Eph fired three silver needles from his nail gun, the long-barreled tool bucking with recoil. The projectiles ripped into the vampire, burning into his diseased muscle, bringing forth a hoarse howl of pain that tipped him forward.

Eph kept recording.

"Enough," said Setrakian. "Let us remain merciful."

The beast's neck extended as he strained from the pain. Setrakian repeated his refrain about his singing sword—and then swung right through the vampire's neck. The body collapsed, arms and legs shivering. The head rolled to a stop, eyes blinking a few times, the stinger flailing like a cut snake, then going still. Hot white effluent bled out of the trunk of the neck, steaming faintly into the cool night air. The capillary worms slithered into the dirt, like rats fleeing a sinking ship, looking for a new vessel.

Nora caught whatever sort of cry was rising in her throat with a hand clamped fast over her open mouth.

Eph stared, revolted, forgetting to look through the viewfinder.

Setrakian stepped back, sword pointed down, white spatter steaming off the silver blade, dripping to the grass. "In the back there. Under the wall."

Eph saw a hole dug beneath the rear of the shed.

"Something else was in here with him," said the old man. "Something crawled out, escaped."

Houses lined the street on either side. It could be in any one of them. "But no sign of the Master."

Setrakian shook his head. "Not here. Maybe the next."

Eph looked deep into the shed, trying to make out the blood worms in the light of Nora's lamps. "Should I go in and irradiate them?"

"There is a safer way. That red can on the back shelf?"

Eph looked. "The gasoline can?"

Setrakian nodded, and at once Eph understood. He cleared his throat and brought the nail gun up again, aiming it, squeezing the trigger twice.

The weaponized tool was accurate from that distance. Fuel glugged out of the punctured canister, spilling down off the wooden shelf to the dirt below.

Setrakian swept open his light topcoat and fished a small box of matches from a pocket in the lining. With a very crooked finger he picked out one wooden match and struck it against the strip on the box, bringing it flaring orange into the night.

"Mr. Barbour is released," he said.

Then he threw in the lit match and the woodshed roared.

Rego Park Center, Queens

MATT GOT THROUGH an entire rack of juniors' separates, and then holstered his bar code collection unit—the inventory gun—and set off downstairs for a snack. After-hours inventory actually wasn't all that bad. As the Sears store manager, he was comped the overtime, applicable toward his regular weekday hours. And the rest of the mall was closed and locked, the security grates down, meaning no customers, no crowds. And he didn't have to wear a necktie.

He took the escalator to the merchandise pickup bay, where the best vending machines were. He was coming back through the first-floor jewelry counters eating jelly Chuckles (in ascending order of preference: licorice, lemon, lime, orange, cherry) when he heard something out in the mall proper. He went to the wide steel gate and saw one of the security guards crawling on the floor, three stores down.

The guard was holding his hand to his throat, as though choking, or badly hurt.

"Hey!" called Matt.

The guard saw him and reached out, not a wave but a plea for help. Matt dug out his key ring and turned the longest one in the wall slot, raising the gate just four feet, high enough to duck under, and ran down to the man.

The security guard gripped his arm and Matt got him up onto a nearby bench next to the wishing fountain. The man was gasping. Matt saw blood on his neck between his fingers, but not enough to indicate a stabbing. There were bloodstains on his uniform shirt also, and the guy's lap was damp where he had peed himself.

Matt knew the guy by sight only, recognizing him as kind of a douche. A big-armed guy who patrolled the mall with his thumbs in his belt like some southern sheriff. With his hat off now, Matt saw the guy's receding hairline, black strands straggly and greasy, over his pate like oil. The guy was rubber limbed and clinging to Matt's arm, painfully and not very manfully.

Matt kept asking what had happened, but the guard was hyperventilating and looking all around. Matt heard a voice and realized it was the guard's hip radio. Matt lifted the receiver off his belt. "Hello? This is Matt Sayles, manager of Sears. Hey, one of your guys here, on the first level—he's hurt. He's bleeding from the neck, and he's all gray."

The voice on the other end said, "This is his supervisor. What's happening there?"

The guard was fighting to spit something out but only air wheezed from his ravaged throat.

Matt relayed, "He was attacked. He's got bruises on the sides of his neck, and wounds . . . he's pretty scared. But I don't see anybody else . . . "

"I'm coming down the utility stairs now," said the supervisor. Matt could hear his footfalls over the radio broadcast. "Where did you say you—"

He cut out there. Matt waited for him to come back on, then pressed the call button. "Where did we say we what?"

Finger off, he listened. Nothing again.

"Hello?"

A burst of transmission came through, less than one second long. A voice yelling, muffled: "*GARGAHRAH*—"

The guard pitched forward off the bench, crawling away on all fours, dragging himself toward Sears. Matt got to his feet, radio in hand, turning toward the restrooms sign next to which was the door to the utility stairs.

He heard thumping, like kicking coming down.

Then a familiar whirring. He turned back toward his store and saw the steel security gate lowering to the floor. He had left his keys hanging in the control.

The terrified guard was locking himself in.

"Hey—*hey!*" yelled Matt.

But before he could run there, Matt felt a presence behind him. He saw the guard back off, big-eyed, knocking over a rack of dresses and crawling away. Matt turned and saw two kids in baggy jeans and oversize cashmere hoodies coming out of the corridor to the restrooms. They looked drugged out, their brown skin yellowed, their hands empty.

Junkies. Matt's fear spiked, thinking they might have hit the guard with a dirty syringe. He pulled out his wallet, tossing it to one of them. The kid didn't move to catch it, the wallet smacking him in the gut and falling to the floor.

Matt backed up against the store grate as the two guys closed in.

Vestry Street, Tribeca

EPH PULLED UP across the street from Bolivar's residence, a pair of conjoined town houses fronted by three stories of scaffolding. They crossed to the door and found it boarded up. Not haphazardly or temporarily, but covered with thick planking bolted over the door frame. Sealed.

Eph looked up the front face of the building to the night sky beyond. "What's this hiding?" he said. He put a foot up on the scaffolding, starting to climb. Setrakian's hand stopped him.

There were witnesses. On the sidewalk of the neighboring buildings. Standing and watching in the darkness.

Eph went to them. He found the silver-backed mirror in his jacket pocket and grabbed one of them to check his reflection. No shaking. The kid—no older than fifteen, done up in sad-eyed Goth paint and black lipstick—shook away from Eph's grip.

Setrakian checked the others with his glass. None of them was turned.

"Fans," said Nora. "A vigil."

"Get out of here," snarled Eph. But they were New York kids, they knew they didn't have to move.

Setrakian looked up at Bolivar's building. The front windows were darkened but he could not tell, at night, if they were blacked out or just in the process of renovation.

"Let's climb up that scaffolding," said Eph. "Break in a window."

Setrakian shook his head. "No way we can get inside now without the police being called and you being taken away. You're a wanted man, remember?" Setrakian leaned on his walking stick, looking up at the dark building before starting away. "No—we have no choice but to wait. Let's find out some more about this building, and its owner. It might help to know first what we are getting into."

Bushwick, Brooklyn

Vasiliy Fet's first stop the next morning was a house in Bushwick, not far from where he had grown up. Inspection calls were coming in from all over, the normal two- to three-week wait time easily doubling. Vasiliy was still working off his backlog from last month, and he had promised this guy he'd come through for him today.

He pulled up behind a silver Sable and got his gear out of the back of his truck, his length of rebar and magician's cart of traps and poisons. First thing he noticed was a rivulet of water running along the gangway between the two row houses, a clear, slow trickle, as from a broken pipe. Not as appetizing as creamy brown sewage, but more than enough to hydrate an entire rat colony.

One basement window was broken, plugged up with rags and old towels. It could have been simple urban blight, or it could have been the handiwork of "midnight plumbers," a new breed of copper thieves ripping out pipe to sell at salvage yards.

The bank owned both houses now, neighboring investment properties that, thanks to the subprime mortgage meltdown, flipped back on their owners, who lost them to foreclosure. Vasiliy was meeting a property manager there. The door to the first house was unlocked, and Vasiliy knocked and called out a hello. He poked his head into the first room before the staircase, checking baseboards for runs and droppings. A broken, half-fallen shade hung from one window, casting a slanting shadow onto the gouged wood floor. But no manager in sight.

Vasiliy was in too much of a rush to be kept waiting here. On top of his backlog, he hadn't been able to sleep right last night, and wanted to get back to the World Trade Center site that morning to talk to somebody in charge. He found a metal clipboard case stuck between balusters on the third step of the stairs. The company name on the business cards in the clip matched the one on Vasiliy's work order.

"Hello!" he called again, then gave up. He found the door to the basement stairs, deciding to get started anyway. The basement was dark below—the stuffed window frame he had glimpsed from the outside—and the electricity had long ago been turned off. It was doubtful there was even a bulb in the ceiling fixture. Vasiliy left his handcart behind to prop open the door, and walked down carrying his poker.

The staircase hooked left. He saw loafers first, then khaki-clad legs: the property manager sitting against the side stone wall in a crackhouse slump, his head to one side, his eyes open but staring, dazed.

Vasiliy had been in enough abandoned houses in enough rough neighborhoods to know better than to rush right over to the guy. He looked around from the bottom step, eyes slow to adjust to the darkness. The basement was unremarkable except for two lengths of cut copper piping lying on the floor.

To the right of the stairs was the base of the chimney, adjacent to the furnace that vented into it. Vasiliy saw, curled low around the far corner of the chimney mortar, four dirty fingers.

Somebody was crouched there, hiding, waiting for him.

He had turned to go back up the stairs to call the police when he saw the light around the bend in the steps disappear. The door had been closed. By someone else at the top of the stairs.

Vasiliy's first impulse was to run, and run he did, racing off the stairs and right at the chimney where the owner of the dirty hand crouched. With a cry of attack, he swung his length of rebar at the knuckles, crushing bone against mortar.

The attacker came up at him fast, without regard to pain. *Crack has a way of doing that,* he thought. It was a girl, no older than her teens, and she was filthy all over, with blood down her chest and around her mouth. All of this he saw in a dim flash as she threw herself at him with weird speed, and even weirder strength, propelling him back, hard, against the far wall despite being half his size. She made an airless raging noise, and when she opened her mouth a freakishly long tongue slithered out. Vasiliy's boot came up instantly, striking her in the chest and putting her down on the floor.

He heard footsteps coming down the stairs and knew he could not win a fight in the dark. He reached up to the blocked window with his rebar and snagged the dirty rags jammed in there, twisting and pulling them down, falling like a plug out of a dyke with light instead of water flooding through.

He turned back just in time to see her eyes go to horror. She lay fully within the frame of sunlight, her body emitting a kind of anguished howl and breaking down all at once, smashed and steaming. It was as he imagined nuclear radiation might work on a person, cooking and dissolving them at the same time.

It happened almost all at once. The girl—or whatever she was—lay desiccated on the filthy floor of the basement.

Vasiliy stared. Horrified wasn't even the word. He completely forgot about the one coming off the stairs until the guy moaned, reacting to the light. The guy backed away, stumbling near the property manager, then regaining his footing and starting for the stairs.

Vasiliy recovered just in time to go underneath the stairs. He jabbed the rod through the step planks, tripping the man, making him fall back down hard to the floor. Vasiliy went around him, his poker raised, as the man got to his feet. His formerly brown skin was a sickly jaundiced yellow. His mouth opened, and Vasiliy saw that it was not a tongue but something much worse.

Vasiliy cracked him across the mouth with the rebar. It sent the man spinning and dropped him to his knees. Vasiliy reached forward and grasped the back of his neck, as he would a hissing snake or a snapping rat, keeping that mouth thing away from him. He looked back to the rectangle of light, swirling with the dust of the annihilated girl. He felt the guy buck and fight to get away. Vasiliy brought the rod down hard against the thing's knees and forced it toward the light.

Fear-maddened Vasiliy Fet realized he wanted to see it again. This slaying trick of the light. With a boot to the lower back, he sent the guy flailing into the sun—and watched him break and crumble all at once, shredded by the burning rays, sinking into ash and steam.

South Ozone Park, Queens

ELDRITCH PALMER'S limousine eased into a warehouse in a weedy industrial park less than one mile from the old Aqueduct Racetrack. Palmer traveled in a modest motorcade, his own car followed by a second, empty limousine, in the event that his broke down, followed by a third vehicle, a customized black van that was in fact a private ambulance equipped with his dialysis machine.

A door opened on the side of the warehouse to admit the vehicles, then closed behind them. Waiting to greet him were four members of the Stoneheart Society, a subset of his powerful international investment conglomerate, the Stoneheart Group.

Palmer's door was opened for him by Mr. Fitzwilliam, and he stepped out to their awe. An audience with the chairman was a rare privilege.

Their dark suits emulated his. Palmer was accustomed to awe in his presence. His group investors regarded him as a messianic figure whose foreknowledge of market turns had enriched them. But his society disciples—they would follow him into hell.

Palmer felt invigorated today, and stood with only the aid of his mahogany cane. The former box-company warehouse was mostly empty. The Stoneheart Group used it occasionally for vehicle storage, but its value today lay in its old-fashioned, precode, underground incinerator, accessed by a large oven-size door in the wall.

Next to the Stoneheart Society members was a Kurt isolation pod on top of a wheeled stretcher. Mr. Fitzwilliam stood at his side.

"Any problems?" said Palmer.

"None, Chairman," they replied. The two who resembled Doctors Goodweather and Martinez handed over their forged Centers for Disease Control and Prevention credentials to Mr. Fitzwilliam.

Palmer looked in through the transparent isolation pod at the decrepit form of Jim Kent. The blood-starved vampire's body was shriveled, like the form of a demon whittled out of diseased birch. His muscular and circulatory features showed through his disintegrated flesh except at his swollen, blackened throat. His eyes were open and staring out of the hollows of his drawn face.

Palmer felt for this vampire starved into petrifaction. He knew what it was for a body to crave simple maintenance while the soul suffers and the mind waits.

He knew what it was to be betrayed by one's maker.

Now Eldritch Palmer found himself on the cusp of deliverance. Unlike this poor wretch, Palmer was on the verge of liberation, and immortality.

"Destroy him," he said, and stood back as the pod was wheeled to the open door of the incinerator, and the body was fed into the flames.

Pennsylvania Station

THEIR TRIP TO Westchester to find Joan Luss, the third Flight 753 survivor, was cut short by the morning news. The village of Bronxville had been closed off by New York State Police and HAZMAT teams due to a "gas leak." Aerial news helicopter recordings showed the town nearly still at daybreak, the only cars on the road being state police cruisers. The next story showed the Office of the Chief Medical Examiner building at Thirtieth and First being boarded up, with speculation about more people disappearing from the area, and incidents of panic among local residents.

Penn Station was the only place they could think of guaranteed to have old-fashioned pay telephones. Eph stood at a bank of them with Nora and Setrakian off to the side as morning commuters moved through the station.

Eph thumbed through Jim's phone, the RECENT CALLS list, looking for Director Barnes's direct mobile line. Jim rolled close to one hundred calls each day, and Eph kept scrolling through them while, on the landline, Barnes answered his phone.

Eph said, "Are you really going with the 'gas leak' gambit, Everett? How long do you think that's going to hold in this day and age?"

Barnes recognized Eph's voice. "Ephraim, where are you?"

"Have you been to Bronxville? Have you seen it now?"

"I have been there . . . we don't know what we have quite yet . . ."

"Don't know! Give me a break, Everett."

"They found the police station empty this morning. The entire town appears to have been abandoned."

"Not abandoned. They're all still there, just hiding. Come sundown, in Westchester County it's going to be like Transylvania. What you need are strike teams, Everett. Soldiers. Going house to house through that town, as if it's Baghdad. It's the only way."

"What we don't want is to create a panic—"

"The panic is already starting. Panic is an appropriate response to this thing, more so than denial."

"The New York DOH Syndromic Surveillance Systems show no indication of any emerging outbreak."

"They monitor disease patterns by tracking ER visits, ambulance runs, and pharmacy sales. None of which figures into this scenario. This whole city is going to go the way of Bronxville if you don't get going on it."

Director Barnes said, "I want to know what you have done with Jim Kent."

"I went to go see him and he was already gone."

"I'm told you had something to do with his disappearance."

"What am I, Everett—the Shadow? I'm everywhere at once. I'm an evil genius. Yes I am."

"Ephraim, listen—"

"You listen to me. I am a doctor—a doctor you hired to do a job. To identify and contain emerging diseases in the United States. I am calling to tell you that it's still not too late. This is the fourth day since the arrival of the plane and the start of the spread—but there is still a chance, Everett. We can hold them here in New York City. Listen—vampires can't cross bodies of moving water. So we quarantine the island, seal off every bridge—"

"I don't have that kind of control here—you know that."

A train announcement broadcast from overhead speakers. "I'm in Penn Station, by the way, Everett. Send the FBI if you like. I'll be gone well before they arrive."

"Ephraim . . . come back in. I promise you a fair shot at convincing me, at convincing everyone. Let's work on this together."

"No," said Eph. "You just said you don't have that kind of control. These vampires—and that's what they are, Everett—they are viruses incarnate, and they are going to burn through this city until there are none of us left. Quarantine is the one and only answer. If I see news that you're moving in that direction, then maybe I'll consider coming back in to help. Until then, Everett—"

Eph hung the receiver up on its hook. Nora and Setrakian waited for him to say something, but an entry on Jim's phone log had piqued Eph's interest. Each one of Jim's contacts was entered last name first, all except one. A local exchange, to which Jim had made a series of calls within the past few days. Eph picked up the landline and pressed zero and waited through the computer responses until he got a real Verizon operator.

"Yes, I have a number in my phone and I can't remember who it connects to, and I'd like to save myself some embarrassment before placing a call. It's a 212 exchange, so I believe it is a landline. Can you do a reverse lookup?"

He read her the number and heard fingers clicking on a keyboard.

"That number is registered to the seventy-seventh floor of the Stoneheart Group. Would you like the building address?"

"I would."

He covered the mouthpiece and said to Nora, "Why was Jim calling someone at the Stoneheart Group?"

"Stoneheart?" said Nora. "You mean that old man's investment company?"

"Investment guru," said Eph. "Second-richest man in the country, I think. Something Palmer."

Setrakian said, "Eldritch Palmer."

Eph looked at him. He saw consternation on the professor's face. "What about him?"

"This man, Jim Kent," said Setrakian. "He was not your friend."

Nora said, "What do you mean? Of course he was . . ."

Eph hung up after getting the address. He then highlighted the number on the screen of Jim's phone and pressed send.

The number rang. No answer, no voice-mail recording.

Eph hung up, still staring at the phone.

Nora said, "Remember the administrator for the isolation ward, after the survivors left isolation? She said she had called, Jim said she hadn't—then he said he just missed some calls?"

Eph nodded. It didn't make any sense. He looked at Setrakian. "What do you know about this guy Palmer?"

"Many years ago he came to me for help in finding someone. Someone I was also keenly interested in finding."

"Sardu," guessed Nora.

"He had the funding, I had the knowledge. But the arrangement ended after only a few months. I came to understand that we were searching for Sardu for two very different reasons."

Nora said, "Was he the one who ruined you at the university?"

Setrakian said, "I always suspected."

Jim's phone buzzed in Eph's hand. The phone did not recognize the number, but it was a local New York exchange. A callback from someone at Stoneheart, maybe. Eph answered it.

"Yeah," said the voice, "is this the CDC?"

"Who is calling?"

The voice was gruff and deep. "I'm looking for the disease guy from the Canary project who's in all that trouble. Any way you can put me through to him?"

Eph suspected a trap. "What do you want him for?"

"I'm calling from outside a house in Bushwick, here in Brooklyn. I've got two dead eclipse hysterics in the basement. Who didn't like the sun. This mean anything to you?"

Eph felt a tingle of excitement. "Who is this?"

"My name is Fet. Vasiliy Fet. I'm with the city's pest control, an exterminator who's also working a pilot program for integrated pest management in lower Manhattan. It's funded by a seven hundred and fifty thousand dollar grant from the CDC. How I have this phone number. Am I right in guessing that this is Goodweather?"

Eph hesitated a moment. "It is."

"I guess you could say that I work for you. Nobody else I could think to bring this to. But I'm seeing signs all over the city."

Eph said, "It's not the eclipse."

"I think I know that. I think you need to get over here. Because I've got something you need to see."

Stoneheart Group, Manhattan

EPH HAD TWO STOPS to make on the way. One alone, and one with Nora and Setrakian.

Eph's CDC credentials got him through a security checkpoint in the main lobby of the Stoneheart Building, but not past a second checkpoint on the seventy-seventh floor, where an elevator change was necessary to gain access to the top ten floors of the Midtown building.

Two immense bodyguards stood upon the massive brass Stoneheart Group logo, inlaid in the onyx floor. Behind them, movers in overalls crossed the lobby, rolling large pieces of medical equipment on dollies.

Eph asked to see Eldritch Palmer.

The larger of the two bodyguards almost smiled. A shoulder holster bulged conspicuously beneath his suit jacket. "Mr. Palmer does not accept visitors without an appointment."

Eph recognized one of the machines being dismantled and crated. It was a Fresenius dialysis machine. An expensive piece of hospital-grade equipment.

"You're packing up," said Eph. "Moving house. Getting out of New York while the getting's good. But won't Mr. Palmer need his kidney machine?"

The bodyguards didn't answer, didn't even turn to look.

Eph understood it then. Or thought he did.

They met up again outside Jim and Sylvia's place, a high-rise on the Upper East Side.

Setrakian said, "It was Palmer who brought the Master into America. Why he is willing to risk everything—even the future of the human race—in order to further his own ends."

"Which are?" said Nora.

Setrakian said, "I believe Eldritch Palmer intends to live forever."

Eph said, "Not if we can do anything about it."

"I applaud your determination," said Setrakian. "But with his wealth and influence, my old acquaintance has every advantage. This is his endgame, you realize. There is no going back for him. He will do whatever it takes to achieve his goal."

Eph couldn't afford to think in big-picture terms or else he might discover that he was fighting a losing battle. He focused on the task at hand. "What did you find out?"

Setrakian said, "My brief visit to the New York Historical Society bore fruit. The property in question was completely rebuilt by a boot-legger and smuggler who made his fortune during Prohibition. His home was raided numerous times but never more than a pint of illicit brew was seized, due, it was said, to a web of tunnels and underground breweries—some of those tunnels were expanded later to accommodate underground subway lines."

Eph looked at Nora. "What about you?"

"The same. And that Bolivar bought the property expressly because it was an old bootlegger's pad, and because it was said that the owner before that was a Satanist who held black masses on the rooftop altar around the turn of the twentieth century. Bolivar's been renovating that building and combining it with the one next to it on and off for the past year, constructing one of the largest private residences in New York."

"Good," said Eph. "Where did you go, the library?"

"No," she said, handing over a printout featuring photos of the original town house interior and current photos of Bolivar in stage makeup. "*People* magazine online."

They were buzzed in and rode up to Jim and Sylvia's small ninth-floor unit. Sylvia answered the door in a flowing linen dress befitting a horoscope columnist, her hair pulled back with a wide headband. She was surprised to see Nora, and doubly shocked to see Eph.

"What are you doing—?"

Eph moved inside. "Sylvia, we have some very important questions, and we only have a little time. What do you know about Jim and the Stoneheart Group?"

Sylvia held her hand to her chest as if she didn't understand. "The who?"

Eph saw a desk in the corner, a tabby cat snoozing on top of a closed laptop. He crossed to it and started opening drawers. "Do you mind if we take a quick look through his things?"

"No," she said, "if you think it will help. Go ahead."

Setrakian remained near the door while Eph and Nora searched the contents of the desk. Sylvia apparently received a strong vibration from the old man's presence. "Would anyone like anything, a drink?"

"No," said Nora, smiling briefly, then getting back to the search.

"I'll be right back." Sylvia went to the kitchen.

Eph stood back from the cluttered desk, mystified. He didn't even know what he was looking for. Jim working for Palmer? How far back in time did this reach? And what was Jim's motive anyway? Money? Would he have turned on them like that?

He went to ask Sylvia a delicate question about their finances, leaving the room to find her in the kitchen. As Eph turned the corner, Sylvia was replacing her wall phone. She stepped backward with a strange look on her face.

Eph was confused at first. "Who were you calling, Sylvia?"

The others came in behind him. Sylvia felt for the wall behind her, then sat down in a chair.

Eph said, "Sylvia—what's going on?"

She said, without moving, and with an eerie sense of calm behind her wide, damning eyes, "You're going to lose."

PS 69, Jackson Heights

KELLY USUALLY never turned her mobile phone on in the classroom, but now it sat to the left of her calendar blotter, set to silent. Matt had stayed out all night, not unusual for overnight inventories; he often took the crew out to breakfast afterward. But he always called to check in as well. The school was a no-cell-phone zone, but she had sneaked a few calls to him, getting his voice mail each time. Maybe he was out of range. She was trying not to worry, and losing the battle. Attendance was low at the school.

She regretted listening to Matt and giving in to his arrogance about not leaving the city. If he had somehow put Zack at risk . . .

Then her phone lit up and she saw the envelope icon. A text message from his mobile.

It read: COME HOME.

That was it. Two words, lower case, no punctuation. She tried to call him right back. The phone rang and then stopped ringing as though he had answered. But he didn't say anything.

"Matt? Matt?"

Her fourth-graders looked at her strangely. They had never seen Ms. Goodweather talking on a phone in class.

Kelly tried their home phone, and got a busy signal. Was the voice mail broken? When was the last time she'd heard a busy signal?

She decided to leave. She'd have Charlotte open the door to her classroom next door, keep an eye on her students. Kelly thought about packing it in for the day and even picking up Zack at the middle school, but no. She'd shoot home, find out what was wrong, then evaluate her options and go from there.

Bushwick, Brooklyn

THE MAN WHO MET THEM at the empty house filled most of the door frame. The shadow of a skipped shave blackened his jutting jaw like a dusting of soot. He carried a large white sack at his hip, one hand choking its neck, an oversize pillowcase with something heavy inside.

After the introductions, the big man went into his shirt pocket and unfolded a worn copy of a cover letter bearing the CDC seal. He showed the letter to Eph.

"You said you had something to show us?" said Eph.

"Two things. First, this."

Fet loosened the drawstring on his sack and overturned the contents onto the floor. Four furry rodents landed in a heap, all dead.

Eph jumped back and Nora gasped.

"I always say, you want to get people's attention, bring 'em a bag of rats." Fet picked one up by its long tail, its body twirling slowly back and forth under his hand. "They're coming up out of their burrows all across the city. Even in daytime. Something's driving them out. Meaning, something's not right. I know that during the black death, rats came out and dropped dead in the streets. These rats here aren't coming up to die. They're coming up plenty alive and plenty desperate and hungry. Take my word for it, when you see a big change in rat ecology, it means bad news is on the way. When the rats start to panic, it's time to sell GE. Time to get out. Know what I mean?"

Setrakian said, "I do indeed."

Eph said, "I'm missing something here. What do rats have to do with . . . ?"

"They are a sign," said Setrakian, "as Mr. Fet rightly states. An ecological symptom. Stoker popularized the myth that a vampire can change its form, transforming into a nocturnal creature such as a bat or a wolf. This false notion arises out of a truth. Before dwellings had basements or cellars, vampires nested in caves and dens on the edges of villages. Their corruptive presence displaced the other creatures, bats and wolves, driving them out so that they overran the villages—their appearance always coinciding with the spreading sickness and the corruption of souls."

Fet was paying close attention to the old man. "You know what?" he said. "Twice when you were just talking, I heard you say the word 'vampire.'"

Setrakian looked at him evenly. "That you did."

After a contemplative pause, and a long look at the others, Fet said, "Okay." As though he was starting to get it. "Now let me show you the other thing."

He led them down into the basement. The smell was one of foul incense, of something diseased that had been burned. He showed them the atomized flesh and bone, now cold cinder lying on the floor of the basement. The rectangle of window sunlight had elongated and moved, shining against the wall now. "But it was beaming down here, and they went into it, and it cooked them in an instant. But, before that, they came at me with this . . . *thing* shooting out from underneath their tongues."

Setrakian told him the short version. The rogue Master stowing away on Flight 753. The disappearing coffin. The morgue dead rising and returning to their Dear Ones. The household nests. The Stoneheart Group. Silver and sunlight. The stinger.

Fet said, "Their heads tipped back and their mouths opened up . . . and it was like that candy, that kids' candy—the one that used to come with *Star Wars* character heads."

Nora said, after a moment, "A Pez dispenser."

"That's it. You tip up the chin, candy pops out of the neck."

Eph nodded. "Except for the candy part, an apt description."

Fet looked at Eph. "So why are you public enemy number one?"

"Because silence is their weapon."

"Hell, then. Somebody has to make some noise."

"Exactly," said Eph.

Setrakian eyed the light clipped on the side of Fet's belt. "Let me ask you this. Your profession uses black light, if I am not mistaken."

"Sure. To pick up rodent urine traces."

Setrakian glanced over at Eph and Nora.

Fet took another look at the old man in the vest and suit. "You know about exterminating?"

Setrakian said, "I have had some experience." He stepped over to the turned property manager, who had crawled or dragged himself away from the sunlight, and was now curled up in the far corner. Setrakian examined him with a silver-backed mirror, and showed Fet the result. The exterminator looked back and forth between the property manager as he appeared to his eyes and the vibrating blur reflected in the glass. "But you strike me as an expert on things that burrow and hide. Creatures who nest. Who feed off the human population. Your job is to drive out these vermin?"

Fet looked at Setrakian and the others like a man standing on an express train, gathering speed out of the station, suddenly realizing he had boarded on the wrong track. "What are you getting me into here?"

"Tell us, then, please. If vampires are vermin—an infestation spreading quickly throughout the city—how would you stop them?"

"I can tell you that, from a pest control point of view, poisoning and trapping are short-term solutions that won't work in the long run. Picking these babies off one by one gets you nowhere. The only rats you ever see are the weakest ones. The hungry ones. Smart ones know how to survive. Control is what works. Managing their habitat, disrupting their ecosystem. Removing the food supply and starving them out. Then you get to the root of the infestation, and wipe it clean."

Setrakian nodded slowly, then looked back at Eph. "The Master. The root of this evil. Somewhere in Manhattan right now." The old man looked again at the unfortunate curled up on the floor, who would animate after nightfall, became a vampire, vermin. "You will step back please," he said, unsheathing his sword. With his pronouncement and a two-handed stroke, he decapitated the man where he lay. As pale pink blood eked out—the host was not yet fully turned—Setrakian wiped his blade on the man's shirt and returned it to the walking stick. "If only we had some indication of where the Master might be nesting. The site would have been preapproved and perhaps even selected by him. A lair worthy of his stature. A place of darkness, offering shelter from, yet access to, the human world on the surface." He turned back to Fet. "Do you have any notion where these rats might be rising from? The epicenter of their displacement?"

Fet nodded immediately, his eyes staring into the distance. "I think I know."

Church Street and Fulton

IN THE DECLINING light of day, the two epidemiologists, the pawn-broker, and the exterminator all stood on the viewing platform on the upper edge of the World Trade Center construction site, the excavation dug one block wide and seventy feet deep.

Fet's city credentials and one small lie—Setrakian was not a world-famous rodentologist in from Omaha—got them into the subway tunnel without an escort. Fet led them down to the same out-of-service track he had followed before, playing his flashlight upon the ratless tracks. The old man stepped carefully over the ties, picking his way along the bed stones with his oversize walking stick. Eph and Nora carried Luma lights.

"You are not from Russia," Setrakian said to Fet.

"Just my parents and my name."

"In Russia, they are called *vourdalak*. The prevailing myth is that one gains immunity from them by mixing the blood of a *vourdalak* with flour and making bread from the paste, which must then be eaten."

"Does that work?"

"As well as any folk remedy. Which is to say, not very well at all." Setrakian remained far to the right of the electrified third rail. "That steel rod looks handy."

Fet looked at his length of rebar. "It's crude. Like me, I suppose. But it gets the job done. Also like me."

Setrakian lowered his voice to cut down on the tunnel echo. "I have some other instruments you might find at least as effective."

Fet saw the sump hose the sandhogs had been working on. Farther ahead, the tunnel turned and widened, and Fet recognized the dingy junction at once. "In here," he said, shining a flashlight beam around, keeping it low.

They stopped and listened to the dripping of water. Fet scoured the ground with his light. "I put down tracking powder last time. See?"

There were human footprints in the powder. Shoes, sneakers, and bare feet.

Fet said, "Who goes barefoot in a subway tunnel?"

Setrakian held up a wool-gloved hand. The tubelike tunnel acoustics brought them distant groans.

Nora said, "Jesus Christ . . ."

Setrakian whispered, "Your lamps, please. Turn them on."

Eph and Nora did, their powerful UVC rays illuminating the dark underground, exposing a mad swirl of colors. Innumerable stains splashed wildly against the floor, the walls, the iron stanchions . . . everywhere.

Fet recoiled in disgust. "This is all . . . ?"

"It is excrement," said Setrakian. "The creatures will shit while they eat."

Fet looked around in amazement. "I guess a vampire doesn't have much need for good hygiene."

Setrakian was backing away. He had a different grip on his walking stick now, the top half pulled several inches out of the bottom half, baring the bright, sharp blade. "We must leave here. Right now."

Fet was listening to the noises in the tunnels. "No argument from me."

Eph's foot kicked something, and he jumped back, expecting rats. He shone his UVC lamp down and discovered a low mound of objects in the corner.

They were mobile phones. One hundred or more, piled up as though they had been thrown into the corner.

"Huh," said Fet. "Somebody dumped a load of mobile phones down here."

Eph reached for some on the top of the pile. The first two he tried were dead. The third had just one blinking bar of battery life. An X icon along the top of the screen indicated that there was no reception.

"That's why the police can't find all the missing people by their cell phones," said Nora. "They're all underground."

"Judging by the looks of this," said Eph, tossing the phones back onto the pile, "most of them are here."

Eph and Nora stared at the phones, quickening their steps.

"Quickly," said Setrakian, "before we are detected." He led the retreat out of the tunnel. "We must prepare."

Worth Street, Chinatown

It was early on the fourth night as Ephraim cruised past his building on the way to Setrakian's to properly arm themselves. He saw no police posted outside his place, so he pulled over. He was taking a chance, but it had been days since he'd changed his clothes, and all he needed was five minutes. He pointed out his third-floor window to them, and said he would lower the blinds once he was inside if there was no trouble.

He made it into the building lobby with no problem, then climbed the stairs. He found his apartment door open a crack, and paused to listen. An open door didn't seem very coplike.

He pushed inside, calling, "Kelly?" No answer. "Zack?" They were the only ones who had keys.

The smell alarmed him at first, until he realized it was the Chinese food left in the trash, from when Zack was over—which seemed like years ago. He entered the kitchen to see if the milk in the refrigerator was still good . . . and then stopped.

He stared. It took him a moment to understand what he was looking at.

Two uniformed cops lay on his kitchen floor, against the wall.

A droning started inside the apartment. Quickly rising to something like a scream, like a chorus of agony.

His apartment door slammed shut. Eph whipped around to the closed door.

Two men stood there. Two beings. Two vampires.

Eph saw this at once. Their posture, their pallor.

One of them he did not know. The other one he recognized as the survivor Bolivar. Looking very dead, and very dangerous, and very hungry.

Then Eph sensed an even greater danger in the room. For these two revenants were not the source of the drone. Turning his head back toward the main room took an eternity and it took only one second.

A huge being wearing a long, dark cloak. Its height taking up all of the apartment, to the ceiling and more, its neck bent so that it was looking down at Eph.

Its face . . .

Eph grew dizzy as the being's superhuman height made the room seem small, made him feel small. The sight weakened his legs, even as he turned to race toward the door to the hallway.

Now the being was in front of him, between him and the door, blocking the only exit. As though Eph hadn't actually turned but the floor itself had rotated. The other two normal, man-size vampires flanked him on either side.

The being was closer now. Looming over Eph. Looking down.

Eph dropped to his knees. Simply being in the presence of this giant creature was paralyzing, no different than if Eph had been physically struck down.

Hmmmmmmmmmmm.

Eph felt this. The way you feel live music in your chest. A hum rumbling in his brain. He averted his eyes, to the floor. He was crippled by fear. He did not want to see its face again.

Look at me.

At first Eph believed that this thing was strangling him with its mind. But his breathlessness was the result of pure terror, a panic of his very soul.

He raised his eyes just a bit. Trembling, he saw the hem of the Master's robe, up to the hands at the end of the sleeves. They were revoltingly colorless and nail-less, and inhumanly large. The fingers were of uniform length, all oversize except for the middle finger, which was even longer and thicker than the rest—and hooked at the end like a talon.

The Master. Here for him. To turn him.

Look at me, pig.

Eph did, raising his head as though a hand gripped his chin.

The Master looked down at him from where his head bent beneath the ceiling. It gripped the sides of its hood with its huge hands and pulled it back off its skull. The head was hairless and colorless. Its eyes, lips, and mouth were all without hue, worn and washed out, like threadbare linen. Its nose was worn back like that of a weathered statue, a mere bump made of two black holes. Its throat throbbed in a hungry pantomime of breathing. Its skin was so pale that it was translucent. Visible beneath the flesh, like a blurry map to an ancient, ruined land, were veins that no longer carried blood. Veins that pulsed with red. The circulating blood worms. Capillary parasites coursing beneath the Master's pellucid flesh.

This is a reckoning.

The voice rode into Eph's head on a roar of terror. He felt himself going slack. Everything muddled and dimming.

I have your pig wife. Soon your pig son.

Eph's head was swollen to bursting with disgust and anger. It felt like a balloon forcing itself to pop. He slid one foot flat beneath him. He staggered to his feet before this immense demon.

I will take everything from you and leave nothing. That is my way.

The Master reached forward in a fast, blurry motion. Eph felt, as an anesthetized patient feels the pressure of the dentist's drill, a gripping sensation on the top of his head, and then his feet were off the floor. He swung his arms and kicked out his legs. The Master palmed his head like a basketball, lifting him one-handedly toward the ceiling. To eye level, near enough to glimpse the blood worms wriggling like plague spermatozoa.

I am the occultation and the eclipse.

Lifting Eph to his mouth like a fat grape. The mouth was dark inside, his throat a barren cavern, a direct route to hell. Eph, his body swinging from his neck, was nearly out of his mind. He could feel the long middle talon against the back of his neck, its pressure at the top of his spine. The Master tipped Eph's head back as though cracking open the pop top of a beer can.

I am a drinker of men.

A wet, crunching sound, and then the Master's mouth began to open. His jaw retracted and his tongue curled up and back and his hideous stinger emerged.

Eph roared, defiantly blocking access to his neck with his arms, howling into the Master's savage face.

And then, something . . . not Eph's howl . . . something made the Master's great head turn ever so slightly.

The nostrils in his face pulsed, the sniffing of a demon without breath.

His onyx eyes turned back to Eph. Staring at him like two dead spheres. Glaring at Eph—as though Eph had somehow dared to deceive the Master.

Not alone.

A t that moment, coming up the stairs of Eph's apartment building two steps behind Fet, Setrakian gripped the handrail suddenly, his shoulder slumping against the wall. Pain burst in his head like a blinding aneurism, and a voice—vile and gloating and blasphemous—boomed like a bomb exploding inside a crowded symphony hall.

SETRAKIAN.

Fet stopped and looked back, but through wincing eyes Setrakian waved him ahead. A whisper was all he could muster: "He is here."

Nora's eyes darkened. Fet's boots pounded as he ran up to the landing. Nora helped Setrakian, pulling him after Fet, to the door, inside the apartment.

Fet hit the first body he encountered, an open field tackle, going in low and getting grabbed as he did, falling and rolling over. He popped up fast in a fighting stance and faced his opponent, seeing the vampire's face, not grinning, but with his mouth spread like a grin, ready to feed.

Then Fet saw the giant being across the room. The Master, with Eph in his grip. Monstrous. Mesmerizing.

The nearer vampire came at him and drove Fet back into the kitchen, against the refrigerator door.

Nora rushed inside, managing to switch on her Luma lamp just as the vampire Bolivar lunged for her. He hissed a breathless scream and reeled backward. Then Nora saw the Master, the back of his down-turned head against the ceiling. She saw Eph dangling by his head in the monster's grip. "Eph!"

Setrakian entered with his long sword bared. He froze for a moment when he saw the Master, the giant, the demon. Here in front of him now after so many years.

Setrakian brandished his silver sword. Nora, closing from a different angle, drove Bolivar back toward the front wall of the apartment. The Master was cornered. Attacking Eph in such a small space had been a cardinal mistake.

Setrakian's heart pounded in his chest as he turned the blade point out and ran it at the demon.

The droning inside the apartment expanded suddenly, an explosion of noise inside his head. And Nora's, and Fet's, and Eph's. An incapacitating shockwave of sound that made the old man shrink back for a moment—just long enough.

He saw a black grin snake across the Master's face. The giant vampire threw the flailing Eph across the room, his body slamming into the far wall and dropping hard to the floor. The Master hooked Bolivar by the shoulder with one of his long, taloned hands—and lunged at the picture window overlooking Worth Street.

A splintering crash shuddered the building as the Master escaped in a rain of glass.

Setrakian ran toward the sudden breeze, to the frame of the window edged with jagged shards. Three stories below, the glass spray was just hitting the sidewalk, glittering in the streetlight.

The Master, with his preternatural speed, was already across the street and mounting the facing building. With Bolivar hanging from his free arm, he went over the top railing and disappeared onto the higher roof, into the night.

Setrakian sagged a moment, unable to process the fact that the Master had just been inside that very room and was now escaped. His heart was throwing a fit in his chest, pounding as if it was going to burst.

"Hey—a little help!"

He turned, and Fet was on the floor holding off the other vampire, Nora assisting with her lamp. Setrakian felt a new burst of rage and went walking over, his silver sword straight out at his side.

Fet saw him coming, his eyes going wide. "No, wait—"

Setrakian struck, sweeping his blade through the vampire's neck, inches above Fet's hands, then kicking the decapitated body off of Fet's chest before the white blood could reach his skin.

Nora ran over to Eph, lying crumpled on the floor. His cheek was cut and his eyes were dilated and terrified—but he appeared unturned.

Setrakian whipped out a mirror to confirm this. He held it to Eph's face and found no distortion. Nora shone her lamp on Eph's neck. Nothing—no breach.

Nora helped him sit up, Eph wincing in pain when his right arm was touched. She touched his chin underneath his cut cheek, needing to embrace him but not wanting to hurt him any further. "What happened?" she said.

Eph said, "He has Kelly."

Kelton Street, Woodside, Queens

EPH TORE ACROSS the bridge into Queens. He used Jim's phone to try Kelly's mobile as he drove.

No ring. Immediate pickup by her voice mail.

Hi, this is Kelly. I'm not able to answer my phone right now . . .

Eph speed-dialed Zack again. Zack's phone kept ringing through to the mailbox.

He screamed around the corner onto Kelton and pulled up hard outside Kelly's front yard, vaulting the low fence and running up the stairs. He banged on the door and pushed the bell. His keys were hanging on a peg back inside his apartment.

Eph took a running start and put his sore shoulder into the door. He tried it again, hurting his arm even more. The third time he threw himself against the door, the frame splintered, and he fell, sprawling, inside.

He got to his feet and rushed through the house. Slamming into walls around corners, his feet kicking at the steps up to the second floor. He stopped at the door to Zack's bedroom. The boy's room was empty.

So empty.

Back downstairs three steps at a time. He recognized Kelly's emergency go bag next to the broken door. He saw suitcases packed but not zipped. She had never left the city.

Oh, Christ, he thought. *It's true.*

The others reached the door just as something struck Eph from behind. A body, tackling him. He fought back immediately, already primed with adrenaline. He rolled his attacker over, holding him off.

Matt Sayles. Eph saw his dead eyes and felt the heat of his over-amped metabolism.

The feral thing that was once Matt snarled at him. Eph braced his forearm against Matt's throat as the recently turned vampire started to open its mouth. Eph went up hard under his chin, trying to block whatever biological mechanism was about to unleash the stinger. Matt's eyes strained and his head shook all over as he tried to work his throat free.

Eph saw Setrakian drawing his sword behind Matt. Eph yelled, "*NO!*" and drew from a ready well of rage to kick Matt off him.

The vampire snarled, rolling to a stop, then popping up on all fours, watching Eph get to his feet.

Matt rose, standing hunched over. He was doing weird things with his mouth, a new vampire getting used to the different muscles, his tongue swirling around his open lips in lascivious confusion.

Eph looked around for a weapon, finding only a tennis racket lying on the floor outside the closet. He grabbed the taped grip two-handedly and spun the titanium frame on its side, going after Matt with it. All of his feelings for Matt—this man who had moved into his wife's house and bed . . . who wanted to be his boy's father . . . who sought to replace Eph—came surging up as he swung for Matt's jaw. He wanted to shatter it and the horror that lurked inside. The new ones weren't so coordinated yet, and Eph got in seven or eight good blows, chopping loose teeth and dropping Matt to his knees—before Matt lashed out, catching Eph's ankle and upending him. Some residual anti-Eph rage still boiled inside Matt too. He rose up gnashing his broken teeth, but Eph kicked Matt in the face, extending his knee and throwing Matt back. Eph retreated around the partition into the kitchen, and it was there he saw the carving knife stuck on a magnet strip.

Rage is never blind. Rage is uniquely focused. Eph felt as if he were looking through the wrong end of a telescope—seeing only the knife, and then only Matt.

Matt came at him and Eph strong-armed him back against the wall. He grabbed a handful of hair and yanked it back in order to expose the vampire's neck. Matt's mouth opened, his stinger swishing out, trying to feed on Eph. Matt's throat rippled and bucked, and Eph attacked it, stabbing, *knifeknifeknifeknifeknife*. Hard and quick, right through the throat and into the wall behind, the blade tip sticking and Eph pulling out again. Crunching cervical vertebra. White goo bubbling. Body sagging, arms flailing. Eph stabbing until the head remained in his hand but the body sagged to the floor.

Eph stopped cutting then. He saw, without truly processing it, the head in his hand with its stinger drooping *through the severed neck*, still twitching.

He then saw Nora and the others watching him from the open door. He saw the wall and the white mess dripping down it. He saw the decapitated body on the floor. He saw the head in his hand.

Blood worms wriggled up Matt's face. Past his cheeks and over his staring eyes. Into Matt's thin hair, approaching Eph's fingers.

Eph dropped the head, which struck the floor with a thud, not rolling anywhere. He dropped the knife too, which fell soundlessly into Matt's lap.

Eph said, "They took my son."

Setrakian pulled him away from the body and the infested vampire blood. Nora turned on her Luma light and irradiated Matt's body.

Fet said, "Holy, holy shit."

Eph said again, both as an explanation and as a nail to be banged more deeply into his soul: "They took my son."

The homicidal roar in his ears was fading, and he recognized the sound of a car pulling up outside. A door opened, soft music playing.

A voice calling out, "Thanks."

That voice.

Eph went to the broken front door. He looked down the walk and saw Zack getting out of a minivan, shrugging a backpack strap over one shoulder.

Zack made it only as far as the gate door before Eph wrapped him up in his arms. "Dad?"

Eph checked him over, grasping the boy's head in his hands, examining his eyes, his face.

Zack said, "What are you doing—?"

"Where were you?"

"At Fred's." Zack tried to wriggle out of his father's grip. "Mom never showed, so Fred's mom took me over to their place."

Eph let Zack pull back. *Kelly.*

Zack was looking past him, at the house. "What happened to our door?"

He took a few steps toward it, until Fet appeared in the doorway, Setrakian behind him. A big guy in a hanging flannel shirt and work boots, and an old man in tweed holding a wolf's-head walking stick.

Zack looked back at his father, the troubled vibe now fully setting in.

He said, "Where's Mom?"

Knickerbocker Loans and Curios, East 118th Street, Spanish Harlem

EPH STOOD IN the book-lined hallway of Setrakian's apartment. He was looking in on Zack eating a Devil Dog at the old man's small kitchen table, where Nora was asking him about school, keeping him occupied and distracted.

Eph could still feel the sensation of the Master's grip on his head. He had lived a life built on certain assumptions, in a world based on certain assumptions, and now that everything he thought he could rely on was gone, he realized he didn't know anything anymore.

Nora saw him watching from the hall, and Eph could tell by the look on her face that she was frightened by the look on his.

Eph knew that he would always be a little insane from now on.

He went downstairs two flights to Setrakian's basement armory. The UV alarm lights at the door were turned off, the old man showing Fet his wares. The exterminator was admiring the modified nail gun, looking like a longer, narrower UZI submachine gun, but orange and black, and with its loading nail magazine feeding the barrel on a slant.

Setrakian came straight over to Eph. "Did you eat?"

Eph shook his head.

"How is your boy?"

"Scared, but he won't let it show."

Setrakian nodded. "Like the rest of us."

"You've seen him before. This Thing. The Master."

"Yes."

"You tried to kill it."

"Yes."

"You failed."

Setrakian squinted, as though looking directly into the past. "I was not adequately prepared. I will not miss again."

Fet, holding a lantern-shaped object with a spike on the end of it, said, "Not likely. Not with this arsenal."

"Some parts I pieced together myself, from things that came into the store. But I am no bomb maker." He clenched his gloved claws as proof of this. "I have a silversmith in New Jersey who molds my points and needles."

"You mean you didn't pick this up at Radio Shack?"

Setrakian took the heavy, lantern-shaped object from the exterminator's hands. It was constructed of shaded plastic with a thick battery base, a six-inch spike of steel on the bottom. "This is essentially an ultraviolet light mine. It is a single-use weapon that will emit a cleansing spray of vampire-killing light in the pure UVC range. It is designed to clear a large room, and will burn very hot and fast once charged. You want to make certain you are out of the way when it does. The temperature and the radiation can get a bit . . . uncomfortable."

Fet said, "And what's with this nail gun?"

"This is powder actuated, operating on a shotgun load of gunpowder to drive the nail. Fifty nails per load, inch and a half brads. Silver of course."

"Of course," said Fet, admiring the piece, getting a feel for the rubber grip.

Setrakian looked around the room: the old armor up on the wall; the UVC lamps and battery chargers on the shelves; the silver blades and silver-backed mirrors; some prototype weapons; his notebooks and sketches. The enormity of the moment nearly overwhelmed him. He only hoped that fear would not turn him back into the powerless young man he had once been.

He said, "I have waited for this a very long time."

He started upstairs then. Leaving Eph alone with Fet. The big exterminator lifted the nail gun out of its charger. "Where did you find this old guy?"

Eph said, "He found me."

"I've been in a lot of basements in my line of work. I look around this little workshop here, and I think—here is the one crazy who's actually been vindicated."

Eph said, "He's not crazy."

"He show you this?" Fet asked. He crossed to the glass specimen jar, the afflicted heart suspended in fluid. "Guy keeps the heart of a vampire he killed as a pet in his basement armory. He's plenty crazy. But that's okay. I'm a little crazy too." He knelt down, putting his face close to the jar. "Here, kitty, kitty . . ." The sucker shot out at the glass, trying to get him. Fet straightened and turned to Eph with a look of *Can-you-believe-this?* "This is all a bit more than I bargained for when I woke up this morning." He sighted the nail gun on the jar, then pulled off his aim, liking the feel of it. "Mind if I claim this?"

Eph shook his head. "Be my guest."

Eph returned upstairs, slowing in the hallway, seeing Setrakian with Zack in the kitchen. Setrakian lifted a silver chain off his own neck—containing the key to the basement workshop—and with his crooked fingers he placed it over Zack's head, hanging it around the eleven-year-old's neck, then patted his shoulders.

"Why did you do that?" Eph asked Setrakian once they were alone.

"There are things downstairs—notebooks, writings—that should be preserved. That future generations may find helpful."

"You're not planning on coming back?"

"I am taking every conceivable precaution." Setrakian looked around, making certain they were alone. "Please understand. The Master has power and speed well beyond that of these clumsy new vampires we are seeing. He is more than even we know. He has dwelled upon this earth for centuries. And yet . . ."

"And yet he is a vampire."

"And vampires can indeed be destroyed. Our best hope is to flush him out. To hurt him and drive him into the killing sun. Why we must wait for the dawn."

"I want to go now."

"I know you do. That is exactly what he wants."

"He has my wife. Kelly is where she is for one reason only—because of me."

"You have a personal stake here, Doctor, and it is compelling. But you must know that, if he has her, she is already turned."

Eph shook his head. "She is not."

"I don't say this to anger you—"

"She is not!"

Setrakian nodded after a moment. He waited for Eph to compose himself.

Eph said, "Alcoholics Anonymous has done a great deal for me. But the one thing I never got out of it was the serenity to accept the things I cannot change."

Setrakian said, "I am the same. Perhaps it is this shared trait that has led us to this point together. Our goals are in perfect alignment."

"Almost perfect," said Eph. "Because only one of us can actually slay the bastard. And it's going to be me."

Nora had been waiting anxiously to speak with Eph, pouncing on him once he stepped away from Setrakian, pulling him into the old man's tiled bathroom.

"Don't," she said.

"Don't what?"

"Ask me what you're going to ask me." She implored him with her fierce brown eyes. "Don't."

Eph said, "But I need you to—"

"I am scared shitless—but I have earned a place at your side. You *need* me."

"I do. I need you here. To watch Zack. Besides—one of us has to stay behind. To carry on. In case . . ." He left that unsaid. "I know it's a lot to ask."

"Too much."

Eph could not stop looking in her eyes. He said, "I have to go after her."

"I know."

"I just want you to know . . ."

"There's nothing to explain," she said. "But—I'm glad you want to."

He pulled her close then, into a tight embrace. Nora's hand went up to the back of his head, caressing his hair. She pulled away to look at him, to say something more—and then kissed him instead. It was a good-bye kiss that insisted on his return.

They parted and he nodded to let her know he understood.

He saw Zack watching them from the hallway.

Eph didn't try to explain anything to him now. Leaving the beauty and goodness of this boy and departing from the perceived safety of the surface world to go down and face a demon was the most unnatural thing Eph could do. "You'll stay with Nora, okay? We'll talk when I come back."

Zack's preteen squint was self-protective, the emotions of the moment too raw and confusing for him. "Come back from where?"

He pulled his son close, wrapping him up in his arms as though otherwise the boy he loved would fracture into a million pieces. Eph resolved there and then to prevail because he had too much to lose.

They heard yelling and automobile horns outside, and everyone went to the west-facing window. A mass of brake lights clotted the road some four or more blocks away, people taking to the streets and fighting. A building was in flames and there were no fire trucks anywhere in sight.

Setrakian said, "This is the beginning of the breakdown."

Morningside Heights

GUS HAD BEEN ON the run since the night before. The handcuffs made it difficult for him to move freely on the streets: the old shirt he had found, and wound around his forearms, as if he was walking with his arms crossed, wouldn't have fooled many. He ducked into a movie theater through the back exit and slept in the darkness. He thought of a chop shop he knew over on the West Side, and spent a considerable amount of time making his way over there, only to find it empty. Not locked up, just empty. He dug through the tools he could find there, trying to cut the links joining his wrists. He even ran an electric jigsaw, held with a vise, and nearly sliced his wrists open in the process. He couldn't do anything one-handed, and eventually left in disgust.

He went by the haunts of a few of his *cholos* but couldn't click up with anyone he trusted. The streets were weird—there wasn't much going on. He knew what was happening. When the sun started going down, he knew that his time and his options would be running out.

It was risky going home, but he hadn't seen many cops all day, and anyway he was worried about his *madre*. He slipped inside the building, trying to keep his shirt-balled hands casual, making for the stairs. Sixteen flights up. Once there, he walked down the hallway and saw no one. He listened at the door. The TV was playing, as usual.

He knew the bell didn't work, so he knocked. He waited and knocked again. He kicked at the foot plate, rattling the door and the cheap walls.

"Crispin," he hissed at his dirtbag brother. "Crispin, you shit. Open the fucking door."

Gus heard the chain lock being undone and the bolt turning inside. He waited, but the door never opened. So Gus unwound the shirt covering his cuffed hands and turned the knob.

Crispin was standing back in the corner, to the left of the couch, which was his bed, when he came around. The shades were all drawn and the refrigerator door was open in the kitchen.

"Where's Mama?" said Gus.

Crispin said nothing.

"Fucking pipehead," said Gus. He closed the fridge. Some stuff had melted and there was water on the floor. "She asleep?"

Crispin said nothing. He stared at Gus.

Gus started to get it. He took a better look at Crispin, who barely rated a glance from him anymore, and saw his black eyes and drawn face.

Gus went to the window and whipped apart the shades. It was night. There was smoke in the air from a fire below.

Gus turned to face Crispin, across the apartment, and Crispin was already charging him, howling. Gus got his arms up and got the handcuff chain across his brother's neck, under his jaw. High enough so that he couldn't get his stinger out.

Gus grasped the back of his head with his hands and pushed Crispin down to the floor. His vampire brother's black eyes bugged and his jaw bucked as his mouth tried to open, which Gus's strangling grip would not allow. Gus was intent on suffocating him, but as time went by and Crispin kept kicking, and there was no blacking out—Gus remembered that vampires didn't need to breathe and could not be killed that way.

So he pulled him up by his neck, Crispin's hands clawing at Gus's arms and hands. For the past few years, Crispin had been nothing but a drag on their mother and a big pain in the ass for Gus. Now he was a vampire and the brother part of him was gone but the asshole part remained. And so it was retribution that moved Gus to wheel him head-first into the decorative mirror on the wall, an old oval of heavy glass that didn't crack until it slid down to the floor. Gus kneed Crispin, throwing him down onto the floor, and then grabbed the largest shard of glass. Crispin wasn't quite to his knees when Gus rammed the point through the back of his neck. It severed the spine and poked the skin out of the front of his neck without quite ripping it. Gus worked the glass piece sideways, slicing Crispin's head nearly off—but forgetting its sharpness against his own hands, cutting his palms. The pain stabbed at him, but he did not let go of the broken glass until his brother's head was removed from its body.

Gus staggered back, looking at the bloody slash across each of his palms. He wanted to make certain none of those worms wriggling out with Crispin's white blood got into him. They were on the carpet and hard to see, so Gus stayed away. He looked at his brother, in pieces on the floor, and felt sickened by the vampire part of him, but as to the loss, Gus was numb. Crispin had been dead to him for years.

Gus washed his hands at the sink. The cuts were long but not deep. He used a gummy dish towel to stop the bleeding and went to his mother's bedroom.

"Mama?"

His only hope was that she not be there. Her bed was made and empty. He turned to leave, then thought twice and got down on his hands and knees to look under the bed. Just her sweater boxes and the arm weights she'd bought ten years ago. He was on his way back to the kitchen when he heard a rustling in the closet. He stopped, listening again. He went to the door and opened it. All of his mother's clothes were pulled down off the hanging rack, lumped in a big pile on the floor.

The pile was moving. Gus tugged back an old yellow dress with shoulder pads and his *madre*'s face leered out at him, black eyed and sallow skinned.

Gus closed the door again. Didn't slam it and run off, he just closed it and stood there. He wanted to cry but tears wouldn't come, only a sigh, a soft, deep whimper, and then he turned and looked around his mother's bedroom for a weapon to cut her head off with . . .

. . . and then he realized what the world had come to. Instead, he turned back to the closed door, leaning his forehead against it.

"I'm sorry, Mama," he whispered. "*Lo siento.* I should have been here. I should have been here . . . "

He walked, dazed, into his own room. He couldn't even change his shirt, thanks to the handcuffs. He stuffed some clothes into a paper bag for when he could change, and crumpled it up under his arm.

Then he remembered the old man. The pawnshop on 118th Street. He would help him. And help him fight this thing.

He left his apartment, exiting into the hall. People stood down at the elevator end, and Gus lowered his head and started toward them. He didn't want to be recognized, didn't want to have to deal with any of his mother's neighbors.

He was about halfway to the elevators when he realized they weren't talking or moving. Gus looked up and saw that the three people there were standing and facing him. He stopped when he realized that their eyes, their dark eyes, were hollow too. Vampires, blocking his exit.

They started coming down the hall at him, and the next thing he knew, he was hammering away at them with his cuffed hands, throwing them against walls, smashing their faces into the floor. He kicked them when they were down, but they didn't stay down for long. He gave none of them the chance to get their stingers out, crushing a few skulls with the heel of his heavy boots as he ran to the elevator, the doors closing as they reached it.

Gus stood alone in the elevator car, catching his breath, counting down the floors. His bag was gone—it had ripped open, leaving his clothes strewn about the hallway.

The numbers got to L and the doors dinged open on Gus standing in a crouch, ready for a fight.

The lobby was empty. But outside the door, a faint orange glow flickered, and there were screams and howls. He went out into the street, seeing the blaze on the next block, the flames jumping to neighboring buildings. He saw people in the streets with wooden planks and other makeshift weapons, running toward the blaze.

From the other direction, he saw another loose gang of six people, no weapons, walking, not running. A lone man came running past Gus the other way, saying, "Fuckers everywhere, man!" and then he was pounced upon by the group of six. To an untrained eye, it would have looked like a good old-fashioned street mugging, but Gus saw a mouth stinger by the orange light of the flames. Vampires turning people in the street.

While he was watching, an all-black SUV with bright halogen lamps rolled up fast out of the smoke. Cops. Gus turned and chased his headlamp shadow down the street—running right into the gang of six. They came at him, their pale faces and black eyes lit up by the head-lights. Gus heard car doors open and boots hit the pavement, and he was caught between these two fates. He raced at the snarling vampires, swinging his bound fists and butting them in the chest with his head. He didn't want to give them a chance to open their mouths on him. But then one of them hooked its arm inside Gus's cuffs and twisted him around, dragging him to the ground. In a second, the herd was on top of him, fighting over who would be the one to drink from his neck.

There was a *thwok* sound, and a vampire squeal. Then a *splat*, and one of the vampires' heads was gone.

The one on top of him was hit from the side and suddenly knocked away. Gus rolled over and got to his knees in the middle of this street fight.

These weren't cops at all. They were men in black hoodies, their faces obscured, black combat pants and black jump boots. They were firing pistol crossbows and larger crossbows with wooden rifle stocks. Gus saw one guy sight a vampire and put a bolt in his neck. Before the vampire even had time to raise his hands to his throat, the bolt exploded with enough force to disintegrate his neck, removing the head.

Dead vampire.

The bolts were silver tipped and top loaded with an impact charge.

Vampire hunters. Gus stared in amazement at these guys. Other vampires were coming out of the doorways, and these shooters were throat accurate at twenty-five, even thirty yards.

One of them came up fast on Gus, as though mistaking him for a vamp, and before Gus could even speak, the hunter put a boot on his arms, pinning them against the road. He reloaded his crossbow and aimed it at the links joining Gus's cuffs. A silver bolt split the steel, embedding itself in the asphalt. Gus winced, but there was no explosive charge. His hands were apart, though still in cop bracelets, and the hunter hauled him up onto his feet with startling strength.

"Shit yeah!" said Gus, overjoyed by the sight of these guys. "Where do I sign up!"

But his savior had slowed, something catching his eye. Gus looked more closely into the shadowy recesses of his sweatshirt hood, and the face there was eggshell white. Its eyes were black and red, and its mouth was dry and nearly lipless.

The hunter was staring at the bloody lines across Gus's palms.

Gus knew that look. He had just seen it in his brother's and his mother's eyes.

He tried to pull back, but the grip on his arm was lock solid. The thing opened its mouth and the tip of its stinger appeared.

Then another hunter came up, holding its crossbow to this hunter's neck. The new hunter pulled back Gus's hunter's hood, and Gus saw the bald, earless head, the aged eyes of a mature vampire. The vampire snarled at his brethren's weapon, then surrendered Gus to the new hunter, whose pale vampire face Gus glimpsed as he was lifted aloft, carried to the black SUV, and thrown into the third-row seat.

The rest of the hooded vampires climbed back inside the vehicle and it took off, wheeling a hard U-turn in the middle of the avenue. Gus was the only human inside the SUV.

A smack to the temple knocked him out cold. The SUV raced back toward the burning building, bursting through the street smoke like an airplane punching through a cloud, then screaming past the rioting, rounding the next corner and heading farther uptown.

The Bathtub

THE SO-CALLED BATHTUB of the fallen World Trade Center, the seven-stories-deep foundation, was lit up as bright as day for overnight work even in the minutes before dawn. Yet the construction site was still, the great machines quiet. The work that had continued around the clock almost since the towers' collapse had, for the time being, all but ceased.

"Why this?" asked Eph. "Why here?"

"It drew him," said Setrakian. "A mole hollows out a home in the dead trunk of a felled tree. Gangrene forms in a wound. He is rooted in tragedy and pain."

Eph, Setrakian, and Fet sat in the back of Fet's van, parked at Church and Cortlandt. Setrakian sat by the rear-door windows with a nightscope. Very little traffic rolled past, only the occasional predawn taxi or delivery truck. No pedestrians or any other signs of life. They were looking for vampires and not finding any.

Setrakian, his eye still to the scope, said, "It's too bright here. They don't want to be seen."

Eph said, "We can't keep looping around the site again and again."

"If there are as many as we suspect," said Setrakian, "then they must be nearby. To return to the lair before sunrise." He looked at Fet. "Think like vermin."

Fet said, "I will tell you this. I've never seen a rat go in anywhere through the front door." He thought about it some more, then pushed past Eph toward the front seats. "I have an idea."

He rolled north on Church to City Hall, one block northeast of the WTC site. A large park surrounded it, and Fet pulled into a bus space on Park Row, killing the engine.

"This park is one of the biggest rat nests in the city. We tried pulling out the ivy, 'cause it was such good ground cover. Changed the garbage containers, but it was no use. They play here like squirrels, especially at noon when the lunch crowd comes. Food makes them happy, but they can get food just about anywhere. It's infrastructure that rats really crave." He pointed to the ground. "Underneath, in there, is an abandoned subway station. The old City Hall stop."

Setrakian said, "It still connects?"

"Everything connects underground, one way or another."

They watched, and did not wait for long.

"There," said Setrakian.

Eph saw a bedraggled-looking woman by a streetlight, some thirty yards away. "A homeless woman," he said.

"No," said Setrakian, handing his heat scope to Eph.

Eph saw, through the scope, the woman as a fierce blur of red against a cool, dim background.

"Their metabolism," said Setrakian. "There is another."

A heavy woman waddling, still getting her sea legs, staying in the shadows along the low iron fence ringing the park.

Then another: a man wearing a newspaper hawker's change apron, carrying a body on his shoulder. Dropping it over the fence, then clumsily scaling it himself. He fell going over, ripping one leg of his pants, standing back up without any reaction and picking up his victim and continuing into the tree cover.

"Yes," said Setrakian. "This is it."

Eph shivered. The presence of these walking pathogens, these humanoid diseases, repulsed him. He felt sick watching them stagger into the park, lower animals obeying some unconscious impulse, withdrawing from the light. He sensed their hurry, like commuters trying to catch that last train home.

They quietly stepped out of the van. Fet wore a protective Tyvek jumpsuit and rubber wading boots. He offered spare sets to the others, Eph and Setrakian choosing only the boots. Setrakian sprayed, without asking, each of them from a bottle of scent-eliminating spray with a picture of a deer in red crosshairs on the label. The spray of course could do nothing about the carbon dioxide emitted by their breath, nor the sound of their pumping hearts and coursing blood.

Fet carried the most. The nail gun was in a bag hung across his chest, complete with three extra loaders of silver brads. He carried various tools on his belt, including his night-vision monocular and his black-light wand, along with one of Setrakian's silver daggers in a leather sheath. He held a high-powered Luma light in his hand, and bore the UVC mine in a mesh bag over his shoulder.

Setrakian carried his walking stick and a Luma light, the heat scope in his coat pocket. He double-checked the pillbox in his vest, then left his hat behind in the van.

Eph also carried a Luma, as well as, in a sheath strapped across his chest, a silver sword, the twenty-five-inch blade and grip against his back.

Fet said, "I'm not sure this makes sense. Going down to fight a beast on its own turf."

Setrakian said, "We have no alternative. This is the only time we know where he is." He looked up at the sky, bluing with the first faint glimmer of day. "The night is ending. Let us go."

They made their way to the low fence gate, which was kept locked overnight. Eph and Fet scaled it, then reached back to help Setrakian.

The sound of more footsteps on the sidewalk—moving quickly, one heel dragging—made them hustle deep into the park.

The interior was unlit at night, and thick with trees. They heard the park fountain running and automobiles passing outside.

"Where are they?" whispered Eph.

Setrakian brought out his heat scope. He scanned the area, then handed the scope off to Eph. Eph saw bright red shapes moving stealthily through the otherwise cool landscape.

The answer to his question was: they were everywhere. And quickly converging on a point to their north.

Their destination became clear. A kiosk on the Broadway side of the park, a dark structure Eph couldn't make much more of from that distance. He watched and waited until the numbers of returning vampires declined, and Setrakian's scope picked up no other significant heat sources.

They ran to the structure. In the burgeoning light, they saw that it was an information kiosk, kept shuttered overnight. They pulled open the door, and found it empty.

They huddled inside the cramped space, the wooden counter taken up by wire racks full of tourist fliers and tour-bus schedules. Fet turned his little Maglite on twin metal doors in the floor. There were thick eyeholes at either end, the padlocks gone. The lettering across the twin doors read, MTA.

Fet pulled open both doors, Eph with his lamp at the ready. Stairs led down into darkness. Setrakian aimed his flashlight at a faded sign on the wall as Fet started down.

"Emergency exit," Fet reported. "They sealed off the old City Hall station after World War Two. The track turn was too sharp for newer trains, the platform too narrow—though I think the number six local still turns around here." He looked from side to side. "Must have demolished the old emergency exit, and put this kiosk up on top of it."

"Fine," Setrakian said. "Let us go."

Eph followed, bringing up the rear. He did not bother to close the doors behind him, wanting a straight shot to the surface if they needed it. Grime coated the sides of each step, the middles cleaned by regular foot traffic. Darker than night down there.

Fet said, "Next stop, 1945."

The flight of stairs ended at an open door leading to a second flight of wider stairs, leading down to what had to be the old mezzanine. A tiled dome with four arched sides, rising to an ornate skylight of modern glass, was just starting to blue. Some ladders and old scaffolding had been laid against the wooden ticket room along one rounded wall. The arched doorways were without turnstiles, the station predating tokens.

The far arch led to another flight of stairs no more than five persons wide, emptying into the narrow platform. They listened at the arched doorway, hearing only the distant screech of subway car brakes, then emerged fully onto the abandoned platform.

It was like a whispering gallery inside a cathedral. Original brass chandeliers containing bare, dark bulbs hung from the arched ceilings, the interlocking tile along the arches looking like giant zippers. Two vault skylights allowed light through amethyst glass, the rest having been leaded over due to air raid concerns after World War II. Farther away, light appeared through some surface grates, still very faint, but enough to give depth to their perception along the gracefully curved track. There was not one right angle in the entire place. The tile work was damaged throughout, including the glazed terra-cotta of the nearest wall sign, done in gold with green borders, around white plates containing blue letters spelling CITY HALL.

A film of steel dust along the curling platform showed the vampires' footprints, leading into the dark.

They followed the footprints to the end of the platform, jumping down onto the still-live tracks. Everything operated on a leftward curve along the train loop. They switched off their flashlights, Eph's Luma showing urine splashes everywhere, iridescent and multicolored, ending farther on. Setrakian was reaching for his thermal scope when they heard noises behind them. Latecomers moving off the mezzanine stairs into the platform. Eph switched off his wand and they crossed the three rails to the far wall, standing flat against the recessed stone.

The latecomers came off the platform, feet scratching the dusty stones along the rail beds. Setrakian spied them through his heat scope, two bright orange-red forms, nothing unusual about their shape or posture. The first one disappeared, and it took Setrakian a long moment to realize that it had slipped into a seam in the wall, an opening they had somehow missed. The second form stopped at that same spot, but turned there instead of disappearing, looking their way. Setrakian did not move, knowing the creature's night vision was advanced but not yet matured. His thermal reading registered the vampire's throat as its warmest region. A spill of orange down its leg cooled immediately to yellow as it pooled on the ground, the creature emptying its bladder. Its head lifted like an animal scenting prey, looking up the tracks away from their hiding space . . . then ducked its head and disappeared into the crack in the wall.

Setrakian moved back into the railway, the others following him. The foul smell of fresh, hot vampire piss filled the arched space, the burnt-ammonia scent holding dark associations for Setrakian. The others stepped around the stain on their way to the seam in the wall.

Eph slid his sword out of the sheath across his back, taking the lead. The passageway widened into a hot, rough-walled catacomb smelling of steam. He switched on his Luma light just in time to see the first vampire rising out of a crouch and driving at him. Eph could not get his silver blade up in time, and the vampire threw him back against the wall. His light lay on its side near the streamlet of sewage lying along the guttered floor, and he saw by its hot indigo light that she was, or had been at one time, a woman. She wore a businesslike blazer over a dirtied white blouse, her black mascara rubbed into menacing raccoon eyes. Her jaw dropped and her tongue curled back—and that was when Fet darted out of the passage.

He went at her with his dagger, stabbing her once, low in the side. She rolled off Eph and came back up in a crouch. With a yell, Fet jabbed at her again, this time right above where her heart would have been, into her chest, below her shoulder. The vampire staggered backward, only to rush forward again. With a howl he buried his blade in her lower belly, and she buckled and snarled—but again reacted with more confusion than pain. She was going to keep coming at him.

Eph had recovered enough by this time, and when the vampire went at Fet again, Eph stood and swung his sword at her with two hands, from behind. The impulse to murder was still foreign, and because of this he took a little something off his swing at the end, so that the blade did not find its way through. But it was enough. He had severed the spinal column, the vampire's head flopping forward. Her arms flailed and her body went into seizure as she pitched forward into the sewage in the center of the floor, like something sizzling in an overheated pan.

There was little time to be shocked. The *splash-splash-splash* sounds echoing in the catacomb were the footfalls of the second vampire running ahead—racing to alert the others.

Eph grabbed his Luma light off the floor and took off after him with his sword at his side. He imagined that he was chasing the one who had lured Kelly here, and that anger carried him along the steamy passageway, his boots splashing hard. The tunnel hooked right, where a wide pipe ran out of the stone and down the length of the narrowing hole. The steam heat fostered algae and fungal growth that glowed in his lamplight. He made out the dim form of the vampire ahead of him, running with its hands open, fingers clawing at the air.

Then another quick turn, and the vampire was gone. Eph slowed and looked all around, shining his lamp, panicking—until he spotted the thing's legs wriggling through a flat hole dug under the side wall. The being undulated with wormlike efficiency, slithering out of the passage, and Eph slashed at its filthy feet but they whisked through too fast, his sword stabbing dirt.

Eph got down on his knees, but could not see through to the other side of the shallow hole. He heard footsteps and knew Fet and Setrakian were still well behind him. He decided he could not wait. Eph got down on his back and started through.

He fed himself into the hole with his arms over his head, lamp and sword first. *Don't get stuck here,* he thought. If he did, there would be no way to wriggle back out. He wormed through, his arms and head emerging into the air of an open space, and kicked free of the burrow, getting to his knees.

Panting now, he waved the lamp around like a torch. He was inside another tunnel, but this one was finished off with track rails and stones, and had an eerie, unused stillness about it. To his left, not one hundred yards away, was light.

A platform. He hurried along the track and clambered up. This platform offered none of the splendor of the City Hall station; instead it was all bare steel beams and visible ceiling piping. Eph thought he had visited every station in the downtown area, but he had never stopped at this one.

A length of subway cars rested against the end of the platform, the door sign reading OUT OF SERVICE. The shell of an old control tower stood in the middle, plastered with old-school wild-style graffiti. He tried the door but it was sealed.

He heard scuffling back inside the tunnel. It was Fet and Setrakian coming through the burrow, catching up with him. Probably not smart, his running ahead alone. Eph resolved to wait for them there, in this oasis of light, until he heard a stone being kicked in the near track bed. He turned just in time to see the vampire breaking from the last subway car, running along the far wall, away from the lights of the abandoned station.

Eph raced after him, over the elevated platform to the end, then leaped down onto the tracks, following them back into darkness. The track bed veered right, the rails ending. The tunnel walls shuddered in his vision as he ran. He could hear the vampire's scuttling footsteps echoing, its bare feet upon the cutting rocks. The creature was stumbling, slowing. Eph drew closer, the heat of his lamp panicking the vampire. It turned back once, its indigo-lit face a mask of horror.

Eph swept his sword arm forward, decapitating the monster in midstep.

The headless body pitched forward, Eph stopping to shine the Luma light on its oozing neck, killing the escaping blood worms. He straightened again and his harsh breathing subsided . . . and then he held his breath altogether.

He heard things. Or, rather, sensed them. Things all around him. No footsteps or movement, just . . . stirrings.

He fumbled for his small flashlight and clicked it on. The bodies of New Yorkers were laid out all along the grungy floor of the tunnel. Their clothed bodies lined each side, like victims of a gas attack. Some eyes were still open, gazing with the narcotized stare of the ill.

These were the turned. The recently bitten, the newly infected. Attacked that very night. The stirring Eph had heard was the metamorphosis inside their bodies: no limbs moving, but rather the tumors colonizing their organs, and the mandibles growing into oral stingers.

The bodies numbered in the dozens, and there were many more ahead, vague forms beyond the reach of his beam. Men, women, children—victims from all walks of life. He rushed around, moving his beam from face to face, searching for Kelly—and praying he would not find her here.

He was still searching when Fet and Setrakian caught up. With something like relief, and at the same time despair, Eph told them, "She's not here."

Setrakian stood with his hand held against his chest, unable to catch his breath. "How much farther?"

Fet said, "That was another City Hall station, on the BMT line. A lower level that was never put into service, only used for layup and storage. That means we're underneath the Broadway line. This turn in the track takes us around the foundation of the Woolworth Building. Cortlandt Street is next. Meaning the World Trade Center is . . ." He looked up, as though able to see ten, fifteen stories through city rock to the surface. "We're close."

"Let's finish this," said Eph. "Now."

"Wait," said Setrakian, still trying to steady his heart rate. His flashlight beam played over the faces of the turned. He got down on one knee to check some of them with a silver-backed mirror from his coat pocket. "We have a responsibility here first."

Fet and Eph exterminated the nascent vampires by the light of Setrakian's flashlight. Each beheading was like a hack at Eph's sanity.

Eph too had been turned. Not from human to vampire, but from healer to slayer.

The groundwater deepened farther into the catacombs, with strange, sun-starved roots and vines and albino growths crawling down from the unfinished ceiling to feed off the water. The occasional yellow tunnel light showed a total lack of graffiti. White dust lay across the untouched sides of the floor, some of it very fine, coating the surface of pockets of stagnant water. It was residue from the World Trade Center. The three of them avoided stepping in it where they could, with the respect afforded a graveyard.

The ceiling got lower, gradually dipping below head level, approaching a dead end. Setrakian's search beam found an opening in the upper part of the shrinking wall, wide enough to admit them. A rumbling that had been vague and distant began to gather in force. Their flashlight beams showed the water at their boots beginning to tremble. It was the unmistakable roar of a subway train, and each of them actually turned around to look, though the tunnel they were standing in contained no rail beds.

It was in front of them, coming right at them—but on live tracks lifting over their heads, entering the active City Hall BMT platform above. The squealing, roaring, and shuddering became unbearable—reaching earthquakelike force and decibels—and at once they realized that this powerful disruption was their best opportunity.

They pressed through the crack, hurrying into another man-made, trackless passage, this one strung with unlit bulbs, construction lights dancing under the force of the passing subway train. Piles of dirt and debris had long ago been pushed back beyond steel beams rising some thirty feet to the ceiling. Around a long corner up ahead, jaundiced light shone faintly. They switched off their Luma lights and rushed along the dark tunnel, feeling it widen as they rounded the corner into a long, open chamber.

As the floor stopped trembling and the train noise faded like a passing storm, they slowed to keep their boot steps quiet. Eph sensed the others before he saw them, their outlines, sitting on or lying about the floor. The creatures were roused by their presence, sitting up, but not attacking. So he and Setrakian and Fet kept moving, wading forward into the Master's lair.

The demons had fed that night, and were bloated with blood, like ticks, lying about and digesting. Their languor was deathlike, they were creatures resigned to waiting for sundown and the opportunity to feed again.

They started to rise. They wore construction clothes and business suits and workout clothes and pajamas and evening wear and dirty aprons and nothing at all.

Eph gripped his sword, searching faces as he passed them. Dead faces with bloodred eyes.

"Stay together," whispered Setrakian, lifting the UVC mine thing carefully out of the mesh bag on Fet's back as they walked. With crooked fingers, he peeled back a strip of safety tape, then rotated the top of the globe to ready the battery. "I do hope this works."

"Hope?" said Fet.

One came at him then—an old man, maybe not as sated as the

others—and Fet showed him his silver dagger and the vampire hissed. Fet put a boot on the man's thigh and kicked him back, showing the others his silver.

"We're digging ourselves into a deep hole here."

Faces came out of the walls, flushed and leering. Older vampires, first or second generation, marked by their whitening hair. There were animal-like groans and glottal clicks from some, like attempts at speech blocked by the vile appendages grown beneath their tongues. Their swollen throats twitched perversely.

Setrakian said, walking between Fet and Eph, "When this spike makes contact with the ground, the battery should connect."

"*Should!*" said Fet.

"You must take cover before it ignites. Behind these supports." Rusted, rivet-studded beams stood at regular intervals. "You won't have more than a few seconds. When you do, shut your eyes. Do not look. The burst will blind you."

"Just do it!" said Fet, crowded by the vampires.

"Not yet . . ." The old man opened his walking stick just enough to bare the silver blade, and with the quick motion of flint striking stone he ran the tips of two crooked fingers against the sharp edge. Blood dripped to the stone floor. The scent went through the vampires with a visible ripple. They were coming from all over, crowding in from unseen corners, ever curious and ever hungry.

Fet swiped the dusty air with his dagger in order to maintain the few meters of open space around them as they moved. "What are you waiting for?" he said.

Eph searched faces, scanning the dead-eyed women for Kelly. One made a move toward him and he laid the tip of his sword against her breastbone and she shrank back as though burned.

More noise now, the front crowd being pressed closer from behind, hunger overriding hesitance, want trumping wait. Setrakian's blood dribbled to the floor, its scent—and the casual waste—driving them into a frenzy.

"Do it!" said Fet.

Setrakian said, "A few more seconds . . ."

The vampires pushed in, Eph prodding them back with the tip of his sword. He only then thought to turn his Luma light back on, but they leaned into its repulsing rays like zombies staring at the sun. The ones in front were at the mercy of those in the rear. The bubble was collapsing . . . Eph felt one hand grab at his sleeve . . .

"*Now!*" said Setrakian.

He tossed the spiked globe into the air, like a referee serving up a jump ball. The heavy thing righted itself at its apex, weighted spikes pointing straight down as it drove toward the floor.

The four-edged steel spike sank into the stone, and a whir started, like that of an old flashbulb rack recharging.

"Go, go!" said Setrakian.

Eph waved his light and swung his sword like a machete, making for one of the stanchions. He felt them grabbing at him, pulling, and felt the squishy thump of his sword cutting, and heard their groans and garbled howls. And still—he checked faces, looking for Kelly, and striking down all those who were not her.

The mine's whir became a growing whine, and Eph stabbed and kicked and swiped his way to the steel support beam, stepping into its shadow just as the underground chamber began to fill with a blazing blue light. He clamped his eyes shut and buried them in the crook of his elbow.

He heard the bestial agony of the shattered vampires. The melting, blistering, peeling sound of their bodies being desiccated at the chemical level, the collapsing of their innards like the charcoaling of their very souls. Their dumb cries strangled in scalded throats.

Mass immolation.

The high-pitched whine lasted no longer than ten seconds, the brilliant plane of cleansing blue light riding from floor to ceiling before the battery burned out. The chamber went mostly dark again—and when the only sound left was a residual sizzling, Eph lowered his arm, opening his eyes.

The nauseating stench of roasted disease rose in smoky steam from the charred creatures laid out over the floor. It was impossible to move without disturbing these rotted demons, their bodies crumbling like artificial logs hollowed out by fire. Only those vampires lucky enough to have been partially behind a beam remained animate, Eph and Fet moving quickly to release these crippled, half-destroyed creatures.

Fet then walked over to the mine, which had caught fire. He surveyed the damage.

"Well," he said, "that fucking worked."

"Look," said Setrakian.

At the far end of the steaming chamber, set on top of a yard-high mound of dirt and refuse, was a long, black box.

As Eph and the others approached it—with the dread of bomb-squad agents approaching a suspicious device without wearing blast suits—the situation felt terribly familiar, and it was only a moment before he placed it: he had felt exactly the same walking toward the darkened airplane on the taxiway, at the start of this whole thing.

This sense of approaching something dead and not dead. Some delivery from another world.

He got close enough to confirm that it was indeed the long, black cabinet from the cargo hold of Flight 753. Its top doors exquisitely carved with human figures swirling as though burning in flames, and elongated faces screaming in agony.

The Master's oversize coffin, set here on an altar of rubble and rubbish beneath the ruins of the World Trade Center.

"This is it," Eph said.

Setrakian reached out to the side of the box, almost touching the carvings, then pulling back his twisted fingers. "A long time I have searched for this," he said.

Eph shuddered, not wanting to meet this thing again, with its devouring size and ruthless strength. He remained on the near side, expecting the top doors to burst open at any moment. Fet went around to the facing side. There were no handles on the top doors. One had to slip one's fingers in beneath the lip of the middle seam and pull up. It would be awkward, and difficult to do quickly.

Setrakian stood at the presumed head of the cabinet, his long sword ready in his hand. But his expression was grim. Eph saw the reason for this in the old man's eyes, and it deflated him.

Too easy.

Eph and Fet wriggled their fingers in beneath the double doors, and on a nod of three, pulled them back. Setrakian leaned forward with his lamp and his sword . . . and discovered a box full of soil. He probed it with his blade, the silver tip scraping the bottom of the great box. Nothing.

Fet stepped back, wild-eyed, full of adrenaline he could not stifle. "He's gone?"

Setrakian withdrew his blade, tapping off the soil on the edge of the box.

Eph's disappointment was overwhelming. "He escaped." Eph stepped back from the coffin, turning to the wasteland of slain vampires inside the stultifying chamber. "He knew we were here. He fled into the subway system *fifteen minutes ago*. He can't surface because of the sun . . . so he'll stay underground until night."

Fet said, "Inside the longest transit system in the entire world. Eight hundred miles of tracks."

Eph's voice was raw with despair. "We never even had a chance."

Setrakian looked exhausted but undaunted. If anything, his old eyes showed a bit of fresh light. "Is this not how you exterminate vermin, Mr. Fet? By rousting them from their nest? Flushing them out?"

Fet said, "Only if you know where they're going to end up."

Setrakian said, "Don't all burrowing creatures, from rats to rabbits, construct a kind of back door . . . ?"

"A bolt-hole," said Fet. He was getting it now. "An emergency exit. Predator comes in one way, you run out the other."

Setrakian said, "I believe we have the Master on the run."

Vestry Street, Tribeca

THEY HADN'T TIME to properly destroy the coffin, and so settled for shoving it off its altar of rubble, overturning it and spilling the soil to the floor. They had resolved to return later to finish the job.

Getting back through the tunnels and out to Fet's van took some time, and more of Setrakian's energy.

Fet parked around the corner from the Bolivar town house. They ran the sunny half block to his front door with no effort to conceal their Luma lamps or silver swords. They saw no one outside the residence at that early hour, and Eph started up the crossbars of the scaffolding in front. Over the boarded door was a transom window decorated with the address number. Eph smashed it in with his sword, kicking free the larger shards and then clearing out the frame with his blade. He took a lamp and went inside, lowering himself into the foyer.

His purple light illuminated twin marble panthers on either side of the door. A winged angel statue at the bottom of the curling stairs looked down at him balefully.

He heard it, and felt it: the hum of the Master's presence. *Kelly*, he thought, misery aching in his chest. She had to be here.

Setrakian came down next, held from the outside by Fet, helped to the floor by Eph. Setrakian landed and drew his sword. He too felt the Master's presence, and with it, relief. They were not too late.

"He is here," said Eph.

Setrakian said, "Then he already knows we are."

Fet lowered two larger UVC lamps to Eph, then clambered over the transom himself, his boots striking the floor.

"Quickly," said Setrakian, leading them under the winding stairs, the bottom floor in the midst of renovation. They moved through a long kitchen of still-boxed appliances, looking for a closet. They found it, empty inside, and unfinished.

They pushed open the false door in the back wall, as it had been pictured in Nora's *People* magazine printouts.

Stairs led down. A sheet of plastic behind them flapped, and they turned around fast, but it was only riding the draft rising up the stairs. The wind carried the scent of the subway, and of dirt and spoilage.

This was the way to the tunnels. Eph and Fet began arranging two large UVC lamps so they could fill the closet passageway with hot, killing light, and thereby seal off the underground. And block any other vampires from rising up, and, more imperative, ensure that the only way out of the town house was into direct sunlight.

Eph looked back to see Setrakian leaning against one wall, his fingertips pressing against the vest, over his heart. Eph didn't like the looks of that, and had started toward him when Fet's voice turned him back around. "*Damnit!*" One of the hot lamps tumbled over, clunking to the floor. Eph checked to make sure that the bulbs still worked, then righted the lamp, wary of the radiative light.

Fet quieted him. He heard noises below. Footsteps. The odor in the air changed—became ranker, more rotten. Vampires were assembling.

Eph and Fet backed away from the blue-lit closet, their safety valve. When Eph turned back to the old man, he was gone.

Setrakian had moved back into the foyer. His heart felt tight in his chest, overtaxed by stress and anticipation. So long he had waited. So long . . .

His gnarled hands began to ache. He flexed them, gripping the sword handle beneath the silver wolf's head. Then he felt something, the faintest breeze in advance of movement . . .

Moving his drawn sword at the last possible moment saved him from a direct and fatal blow. The impact knocked him back, sending his crumpled body sliding headfirst over the marble floor to slam into the base of the wall. But he kept his grip on his sword. He got back to his feet quickly, swinging his blade back and forth, seeing nothing in the dim foyer.

So fast the Master moved.

He was right here. Somewhere.

Now you are an old man.

The voice crackled inside Setrakian's head like an electric shock. Setrakian swung his silver sword out wide in front of him. A black form blurred past the statue of the weeping angel at the foot of the curling marble stairs.

The Master would try to distract him. This was his way. Never to challenge directly, face-to-face, but to deceive. To surprise from behind.

Setrakian backed up against the wall beside the front door. Behind him, a narrow, door-framing window of Tiffany glass had been blacked over. Setrakian struck at the lead panes, smashing out the precious glass with his sword.

Daylight knifed into the foyer.

At that moment of breaking glass, Eph and Fet returned to find Setrakian standing with his sword raised, his body bathed in sunlight.

The old man saw the dark blur rising up the stairs. "There he is!" he yelled, starting after him. "Now!"

Eph and Fet charged up the steps after the old man. Two other vampires met them at the top of the stairs. Bolivar's former security detail, his Big-and-Tall-Store bodyguards now hungry-faced hulks in dirty suits. One swatted at Eph, who stumbled backward and almost lost his balance, grabbing the wall to keep himself from tumbling down the marble stairs. He stuck out his Luma light and the big dummy recoiled and Eph chopped at his thigh with the sword. The vampire let out a gasp and swung at him again. Eph gutted him, running his sword most of the way through his belly before pulling it back, the vampire sinking to the landing like a stuck balloon.

Fet held his at bay with his lamp light, sticking and cutting at the bodyguard's grabbing hands with his short-bladed dagger. He brought the light up, right into its face, and the vampire flailed and looked around wildly, temporarily blinded. Fet ducked him and got behind his back, stabbing the bodyguard in the back of its thick neck before shoving him hard down the stairs.

Eph's vampire tried to rise, but Fet dropped him again with a kick to the ribs. The bodyguard's head lay off the top step, and with a cry of anguish, Eph brought his sword down.

The head bumped down the stairs, gaining speed and rotation at the bottom, hopping the other vampire's body and rolling all the way to the wall.

White blood oozed out of its opened neck, onto the carmine runner. The blood worms emerged, Fet frying them with his lamp.

The bodyguard at the bottom of the steps was no more than a skin sack of broken bones, but he was still animate. The fall had not severed his neck, and so had not released him. His eyes were open and he stared dumbly up the long staircase, trying to move.

Eph and Fet found Setrakian near the closed elevator grate with his sword out, taking a swipe at a dark, fast-moving blur. "Watch out—!" called Setrakian, but before the words were out of his mouth, the Master struck Fet from behind. He went down hard, nearly smashing his lamp. Eph barely had time to react before the form flew past him— slowing down just long enough for Eph to see the Master's face again, his wormy flesh and sneering mouth—and he was thrown back against the wall.

Setrakian lunged forward, sweeping his sword two-handedly, driving the fast-moving form into a wide, high-ceilinged, floor-through room. Eph got himself up and followed, as did Fet, a lick of blood dribbling down his temple.

The Master stopped, appearing to them before the massive stone fireplace at the midpoint of the room. The town house had windows only at either long end—leaving no sunlight in the middle to assist them. The Master's cloak rippled and settled and his horrible eyes looked down on them all, but mainly Fet, no small man himself. The blood trickling down his face. With something like a howling grin, the long-armed Master grabbed up lumber and bales of electrical wire and any other debris within reach and hurled them at the three assassins.

Setrakian flattened against the wall, Eph taking cover around the corner, Fet using a chunk of wallboard as a shield.

When the assault ended and they looked up, the Master was gone again.

"*Christ!*" hissed Fet. He swiped the blood off his face with his hand, then tossed aside the wallboard. He threw his silver dagger into the cold fireplace with a clank and a thud—useless against this giant—and took Eph's lamp from him, giving Fet two, freeing Eph up to wield his longer blade with both hands.

"Stay after him," said Setrakian, pushing ahead. "Like smoke rising up a chimney, we must force him to the roof."

As they rounded the corner, four more hissing vampires came at them. They looked like former fans of Bolivar's with their razored hair and piercings.

Fet went after them with the twin lamps, pushing them back. One got through, and Eph played backup, showing her his silver sword. This one looked like a chubby Vampira in a denim skirt and torn fishnet stockings. She had that curious rapacity of the newly turned vampire that Eph had come to recognize. Eph aimed his sword at her from a crouch, the vampire feinting right, then left, hissing at him through white lips.

Eph heard Setrakian yell, "*Strigoi!*" in that commanding voice of his. The chopping sound of the old man cutting down vampires emboldened Eph. The chubby Vampira feinted too aggressively and Eph jabbed her, his sword tip slicing into the front shoulder of her torn black cotton top, burning the beast within. Her mouth opened and her tongue curled up, and Eph darted back barely in time, her stinger just missing his neck. She continued at him, mouth agape, and with a howl of anger, Eph ran his sword at her face. Straight at her stinger, the blade slicing right through the back of her head, the tip burying a few inches in the unfinished wall.

The vampire's eyes bugged. Her stinger was cut and leaking white blood, filling her mouth and spilling down her chin, which she could not move. She was pinned to the wall. She bucked and attempted to cough her wormy blood onto Eph. A virus will propagate itself any way it can.

Setrakian had slain the other three vampires, leaving the newly polished maple flooring at the end of the hall slathered in white. He returned to Eph, yelling, "Back!"

Eph released his sword, the grip quivering out of the wall. Setrakian swung at the vampire's neck, and gravity pulled the headless body to the floor.

The head remained speared to the wall, white blood spilling from its severed neck, the vampire's black eyes flaring wide at both men . . . then rolling upward and relaxing, holding still. Eph grasped the handle of his sword and plucked it from the wall behind her mouth, and her head dropped on top of her body.

There was no time to irradiate the white blood. "Up, up!" said Setrakian, walking along the wall to a different set of stairs, these circular with an ornate iron railing. The old man's spirit was strong, but his strength was flagging. Eph passed him at the top. He looked right and left. In the dim light, he saw finished hardwood floors and unfinished walls. But no vampires.

"We split up," said the old man.

"Are you *kidding*?" said Fet, grabbing hold of him and helping him to the top. "*Never* split up. That's the first rule."

One of his lamps fizzled. The bulb popped as the unit overheated, and suddenly burst into flames. Fet dropped it, crushing the flames underneath his boot. Now he was down to one lamp.

"How much more battery time?" Eph asked.

"Not enough," said the old man. "He will wear us down like this, having us chase him until nightfall."

"Gotta trap him," said Fet. "Like a rat in a bathroom."

The old man stopped then, turning his head to a sound.

Your heart is weak, you old wretch. I can hear it.

Setrakian stood still, his sword at the ready. He looked all around, but there was no sign of the Dark One.

He tapped the point of his sword on the floor. *Pick-pick-pick.* "Show yourself."

You have fashioned a handy tool.

"You don't recognize it?" said Setrakian aloud, with heavy breaths. "It was Sardu's. The boy whose form you took."

Eph pulled closer to the old man, realizing that he was in a conversation with the Master. "Where is she?" he yelled. "Where is my wife?"

The Master ignored Eph.

Your whole life has led to this point. You will fail a second time.

Setrakian said, "You will taste my silver, *strigoi*."

I will taste you, old man. And your clumsy apostles—

The Master attacked from behind, throwing Setrakian to the floor again. Eph reacted, swiping his sword at the breeze he felt, a couple of guessing swishes. When he pulled back the blade, he found the tip sticky with white.

He had hurt the Master. He had cut him.

But in the moment it took to process this fact, the Master returned and swatted Eph in the chest with his taloned hand. Eph felt his feet leave the floor, his back and shoulders ramming into the wall, his muscles exploding with pain as his body fell to the side.

Fet swept forward with his lamp, and Setrakian swung silver from one knee, pushing back the beast. Eph rolled over as fast as he could, bracing for more blows . . . but none came.

They were all alone again. They could feel it. No sound except the tinkling of construction lights strung along the ceiling, swaying near the foot of the stairs.

Eph said, "I cut him."

Setrakian used his sword to get to his feet, as one arm was hurt and hanging limp. He moved to the next flight of stairs going up.

There was white vampire blood on the unfinished planking of the stairs.

Sore but determined, they climbed the steps to the top. This was Bolivar's penthouse, the top floor of the taller of the two conjoined town houses. They entered the bedroom half, looking for vampire blood on the floor. Seeing none, Fet went around the unmade bed to the far windows, tearing down the room-darkening curtains, letting in light but no direct sun. Eph checked the bathroom and found it even larger than he had expected, with facing, gold-framed mirrors reflecting him into infinity. An army of Ephraim Goodweathers with swords in their hands.

"This way," gasped Setrakian.

Fresh streaks of white stood out against a black leather chair in the broader media room. Two arched and heavily draped doorways along the eastern wall showed soft light edging beneath the hem of the long curtains. The roof of the adjoining town house lay beyond.

There they found the Master standing in the center of the room, his worm-infested face angled down toward them, onyx eyes staring, the dangerous daylight behind him. Iridescent white blood dripped, slow and irregular, down his arm and off his elongated hand, falling from the tip of his unearthly talon to the floor.

Setrakian limped forward, his sword dragging behind him, scoring the wood floor. He stopped and raised the silver blade with his one good arm, facing the Master—his heart racing at too many beats per minute.

"*Strigoi*," he said.

The Master stared, impassive for the moment, demoniacally regal, his eyes two dead moons in clouds of blood. The sole indicator of his predicament was the excited wriggling of the blood parasites beneath his inhuman face.

For Setrakian, the moment was nearly at hand . . . and yet his heart was locking up, shutting him down.

Eph and Fet converged behind him, and the Master had no alternative but to fight his way out of this room. His face spread into a savage sneer. He kicked up a long, low table at Eph, which battered him backward, and with his good arm sent a club chair sliding at Setrakian. These moves had the effect of splitting them, the Master blazing through the middle, going straight at Fet.

Fet raised his lamp, but the Master dodged and came clawing at him from the side. Fet went down, falling, dazed, near the top of the stairs. The Master lunged past him, but Fet was fast, swinging the lamp on him—right into the Dark One's snarling face. The UVC rays staggered him, driving him back against the wall, the plaster cracking against his great weight. When the Master's claws came down from his face, his eyes were wider than before, and seemingly lost.

The Master was blinded, but only temporarily. They all sensed their advantage here, and Fet went right at him with the lamp. The Master flailed back wildly. Fet drove the towering beast back across the room toward the curtained doors, and Eph rushed after him, slashing at the Dark One's cloak, catching a bit of flesh. The Master's talon swung but struck no one.

Setrakian gripped the chair that had been slid at him, his sword clattering to the floor.

Eph cut down the heavy drapes over one of the arches, revealing bright sunlight. Decorative iron grating barred the glass doors, but with one chop of his blade, the latch cracked free in a spray of sparks.

Fet kept driving the Master backward. Then Eph spun around, looking to Setrakian to administer the finishing blow. That was when he saw the old professor laid out on the floor next to his sword, gripping his chest.

Eph froze, looking at the vulnerable Master, then at Setrakian, dying on the floor.

Fet, holding his lamp on the vampire like a lion trainer with a footstool, said, "What are you waiting for?"

Eph ran to the old man. He got down on his hands and knees and saw the distress in Setrakian's face, the distant stare. His fingers plucked at his vest, over his heart.

Eph set down his sword. He ripped open the vest and his shirt, baring Setrakian's sagging chest. He reached up under his jaw for a pulse, but couldn't find one.

Fet yelled back, "Hey, Doc!" He kept pressing forward, pinning the Master up against the edge of the sunlight.

Eph massaged the old man's chest over his heart. He didn't start CPR right away because he was worried about the man's bones, about crushing his rib cage. Then he noticed that Setrakian's old fingers were no longer poking at his heart, but were reaching for his vest.

Fet turned back in a panic to see what the hell was holding them up. He saw Setrakian laid out on the floor and Eph kneeling over him.

Fet looked for a moment too long. The Master clawed at Fet's shoulder and pulled him in.

Eph squeezed the pockets of Setrakian's tweed vest and felt something. He pulled out the little silver pillbox and quickly unscrewed the top. A dozen tiny white tablets tumbled to the floor.

Fet was a big man himself, but he was a child in the Master's grip. He still had the lamp in his hand, even though his arms were pinned. He turned it on the Master, burning his side—and the blinded beast roared in pain but did not relinquish his grip. The Master's other hand gripped the top of Fet's head and wrenched back his neck despite Fet's resistance. Then Fet found himself staring up into this unspeakable face.

Eph pinched up one of the nitroglycerin tablets and cupped the old man's head in his hand. He worked open his clenched jaw and slipped the pill in underneath the old man's cool tongue. He pulled out his fingers and shook Setrakian, yelling at him. And the old man's eyes opened.

The Master opened his mouth over Fet and extended his stinger, lashing about in the air above Fet's wide eyes and exposed throat. Fet fought mightily, but the compression of the back of his neck cut off the blood flow to his brain, so the room blackened and his muscles went limp.

Eph yelled, "No!" and ran at the Master with his sword, slashing the blade across the abomination's broad back. Fet fell to the floor in a heap. The Master's head whipped around, his stinger searching, his clouded eyes finding Eph.

"*My sword sings of silver!*" cried Eph, slicing at the Master's upper chest. The blade did indeed sing, though the Dark One flew backward and avoided it. Eph swung again—and missed again—the Master thrashing backward, out of control. He was in the sunlight now, framed before the twin glass doors, the full and broad daylight of a rooftop patio behind him.

Eph had him. The Master knew he had him. Eph brought his sword up with two hands, ready to stab it up through the Master's bulging neck. The king vampire stared down at Eph with something like outright disgust, summoned even more height, and raised the hood of his dark cloak over his head.

"*Die!*" said Eph, running at him.

The Master turned and crashed through the plate-glass doors and out onto the open patio. Glass exploded as the cloaked vampire fell rolling onto the hot clay tiles, in full view of the killing sun.

He came to a rest momentarily, hunched over on one knee.

Eph's momentum carried him through the shattered door, where he stopped, staring at the cloaked vampire, awaiting the end.

The Master trembled, steam rising from within its dark cloak. Then the king vampire stood to its full height, quivering as though in the grip of a violent seizure, his great claws curled into beastlike fists.

With a roar he threw off his cloak. The ancient garment fell away, smoking, to the tile. The Master's nude body writhed, his pearlescent flesh darkening, cooking, changing from fair, lily white to a dead black leather.

The slashing wound Eph had made across his back fused into a deep black scar, as though cauterized by the rays of the sun. He turned, still shaking, and faced Eph, and Fet standing in the doorway behind him, and Setrakian risen to one knee. He was ghoulishly lean, with a smooth and sexless crotch. His broiled black flesh writhed with pain-crazed blood worms.

With a most horrible smile—a sneer of intense pain and even triumph—the Master turned his face toward the sun and let loose an openmouthed howl of defiance. A true demonic curse. Then, with dizzying speed, he bolted to the edge of the patio, slid over the low wall at the edge of the roof, and raced down the side of the building to the third-story scaffolding . . . disappearing into the morning shadows of New York City.

THE
CLAN

Nazareth, Pennsylvania

In a long-abandoned and never-mapped asbestos mine, a netherworld a few hundred feet below the surface of the Pennsylvania woods, three Ancients of the New World conferred in a pitch-black chamber.

Their bodies, over time, had become worn smooth as river stones, their movements slowing nearly to imperceptibility. They had no use for exterior physicality. Their body systems had evolved to maximum efficiency, and their vampire mandibles functioned without flaw. Their night vision was extraordinary.

In the cages built into the deep western tunnels of their dominion, the Ancients had already begun storing food for the long winter. The occasional scream of a human captive ripped through the mine, reverberating like an animal call.

It is the seventh one.

Despite their human appearance, they had no use for animal speech. Their movements, down to the glances of their sated red eyes, were dreadfully slow.

What is this incursion?

It is a violation.

He thinks us old and weak.

Someone else is a party to this transgression. Someone had to assist him in his ocean crossing.

One of the others?

One of the New World Ancients reached out with his mind, across the sea to the Old World.

I do not feel that.

Then the seventh one has aligned with a human.

With a human, against all other humans.

And against us.

Is it not evident now that he alone was responsible for the Bulgarian massacre?

Yes. He has proven his willingness to kill his own kind if crossed.

He was indeed spoiled by the world war.

He supped too long in the trenches. Feasted in the camps.

And now he has broken the truce. He has set foot on our soil. He wants the entire world for himself.

What he wants is another war.

The tallest one's talon twitched—an extraordinary physical action for a being so steeped in deliberation, in elemental stillness. Their bodies were simple shells and could be replaced. Perhaps they had become complacent. Too comfortable.

Then we will oblige him. We must remain invisible no more.

The headhunter entered the chamber of the Ancients and waited to be acknowledged.

You have found him.

Yes. He tried to return home, as do all creatures.

He will suffice?

He will be our sun hunter. He has no other choice.

In a locked cage in the western tunnel, on a floor of cold dirt, Gus Elizalde lay unconscious, dreaming of his mother—unaware of the peril awaiting him.

EPILOGUE

Kelton Street, Woodside, Queens

They regrouped at Kelly's house, Nora bringing Zack home after Eph and Fet had cleaned up the mess that was Matt, burning his remains under leaves and brush in the backyard.

Setrakian lay on the fold-out sleeper in the sunroom. He had refused to go to a hospital, and Eph agreed that was out of the question anyway. His arm was badly bruised but not broken. His pulse rate was low, but steady and improving. Eph wanted Setrakian to sleep, but not with painkillers. So before going in to check on him after nightfall, Eph opened Kelly's kitchen liquor cabinet. He picked up a bottle of scotch, once his crutch, and set it aside, pouring the old man a more gentle brandy.

Setrakian said it wasn't the pain that bothered him. "Failure keeps one awake."

The mention of failure reminded Eph that he had not found Kelly. Part of him wanted to believe that this was still a reason to hope.

"You did not fail," said Eph. "The sun failed."

Setrakian said, "He is more powerful than I knew. I suspected it, maybe . . . dreaded, certainly . . . but never knew. He is not of this earth."

Eph agreed. "He is a vampire."

"No—not of this earth."

Eph was worried about the old man having taken a blow to the head. "We hurt him, bottom line. We marked him. And now he's on the run."

The old man would not be consoled. "He is still out there. It goes on." He accepted the glass from Eph, drank it, and sat back. "These vampires now . . . they are in their infancy. We are about to witness a new stage in their evolution. It takes about seven nights to become fully turned. For their new parasitic organ system to complete its formation. Once that occurs, once their bodies are no longer comprised of vital organs—heart, lungs—but only a series of chambers in the body, they will be less vulnerable to conventional weaponry. And they will continue to mature beyond that time—learning, becoming smarter, more used to their environment. They will band together and coordinate their attacks, and individually become much more nimble and deadly. Making it much harder to find and defeat them. Until eventually it will become impossible to stop them." The old man finished his brandy and then looked at Eph. "I believe what we saw up there on that rooftop this morning was the end of our kind."

Eph felt the weight of the future pressing down on them all. "How much is there that you haven't told me?"

Setrakian's eyes were rheumy as he stared off into the middle distance. "Too much to speak of now."

A short while later, he was asleep. Eph looked at his gnarled fingers twisting the hem of the bedsheet on his chest. The old man's dreams were feverish.

"Dad!"

Eph went out to the main room. Zack was sitting in the computer chair, and Eph gripped the boy from behind, wrapped him up in another hug, kissing the top of his head, breathing in the scent of his hair. "I love you, Z," he whispered.

"Love you too, Dad," Zack said back, and Eph ruffled his hair and let him go.

"Where are we with this?"

"Almost all set." The boy returned to the computer. "I had to create a dummy e-mail address. You pick a password."

Zack was helping Eph upload the video of Ansel Barbour in the dog shed—which Eph had not yet shown Zack—onto as many file-sharing and broadcast video web sites as possible. Eph wanted true vampire footage out there on the Internet for the world to see. It was the only way he could think of to reach people and make them comprehend. He wasn't worried about fostering chaos and panic: the riots continued, confined to poorer neighborhoods, though their spread was just a matter of time. The alternative of continued coordinated silence in the face of an extinction event was too absurd to consider.

This plague would be fought at a grassroots level now—or not at all.

Zack said, "Now I select the file, like this, and move it up as an attachment . . ."

Fet's voice came from the kitchen, where he was watching television, eating deli chicken salad out of a half-pound plastic tub. "Look at this."

Eph turned. Helicopter footage showed a row of flaming buildings now, and thick black smoke filling the air over Manhattan.

"It's getting bad," he said.

As Eph watched, he noticed all of Zack's school papers on the refrigerator door lift and flutter. A napkin wafted across the counter, drifting to the floor, at Fet's feet.

Eph turned to Zack, who had stopped typing. "What was that breeze?"

Zack said, "Back slider must be open."

Eph looked around for Nora. Then the toilet flushed, and she stepped out of the hall bathroom. "What's up?" she said, finding everyone staring at her.

Eph turned toward the other end of the house, looking at the corner that led around to the sliding glass door and the backyard.

A person turned the corner. Stopping there, her arms hanging limply at her sides.

Eph stared, paralyzed.

Kelly.

"Mom!"

Zack started toward her, and Eph reached out and grabbed him. His grip must have hurt Zack, because the boy pulled away in surprise, looking back at him.

Nora rushed over and wrapped Zack up from behind.

Kelly was just standing there. Looking at them. No expression, no blinking. She looked shell-shocked, as though deafened by some recent explosion.

Eph knew immediately. The pain in his heart was physical.

Kelly Goodweather was turned. A dead thing returned to its home.

Her gazing eyes found Zack. Her Dear One. She had come for him.

"Mom?" said Zack, seeing that something was wrong with her.

Eph felt quick movement from behind. Fet rushed into the hall and grabbed Eph's sword. He brandished it, showing Kelly the silver of the blade.

Kelly's face curdled. Her expression collapsed into evil and she bared her teeth.

Eph's heart dropped through his chest and into his gut.

She was a demon. A vampire.

One of them.

She was gone to him forever.

With a muffled groan, Zack recoiled at the sight of his demonized mother . . . and then blacked out.

Fet started after her with the sword, but Eph hooked his arm before he could follow through. Kelly recoiled from the silver blade, like a cat with its fur up. She hissed at them. She took one more baleful look at the unconscious boy, her intended . . . and then turned and fled out the back door.

Eph and Fet rounded the corner just in time to watch Kelly throw herself over the low chain-link fence separating their backyard from the neighbor's, and run off into the new night.

Fet closed the door and locked it. He drew the blinds over the glass, then turned to Eph.

Eph said nothing but returned to Nora, who was kneeling over Zack, on the floor, her eyes keen with despair.

He saw now how truly insidious this plague was. Pitting family member against family member. Pitting death against life.

The Master had sent her. He had turned her against Eph and Zack. To torment them. To take his revenge.

If the degree of devotion to a Dear One in life bore any correlation to their desire to reunite in death . . . then Eph knew that Kelly would never give up. She would go on haunting her son forever unless someone put a stop to it.

Their custody battle for Zack was not over.

Eph looked at their faces . . . and then at the fires raging on television . . . and then turned to the computer. He pressed the enter key, completing Zack's task. He dispatched video proof of the raging vampire into the world . . . and then went into the kitchen, where Kelly kept the scotch. For the first time in a long time, he poured himself a drink.

Turn the page for a peak at the next volume in Guillermo del Toro and Chuck Hogan's frightening and imaginative thriller series, *The Fall*, available from William Morrow and Harper, imprints of HarperCollins Publishers.

THE
FALL

Book II of The Strain Trilogy

Guillermo del Toro and Chuck Hogan

WILLIAM MORROW *An Imprint of* HarperCollins*Publishers*

Friday, November 26

It took the world just sixty days to end. And we were there to account for it—our omissions, our arrogance . . .

By the time the crisis went to Congress, and was analyzed, legislated, and ultimately vetoed, we had already lost. The night belonged to them.

Leaving us longing for daylight when it was ours no more . . .

All this mere days after our "uncontestable video evidence" reached the world—its truth drowned in thousands of smirking rebuttals and parodies that YouTube'd us beyond all hope.

It became a Late Night pun, smart-asses that we were, hardy-har-har—until dusk fell upon us and we turned to face an immense, uncaring void.

The first stage of public response to any epidemic is always Denial.

The second, Search For Blame.

All the usual scarecrows were trotted out as distractions: economic woes, social unrest, the racial scapegoating, terrorist threats.

But in the end, it was just us. All of us. We allowed it to happen because we never believed it could happen. We were too smart. Too advanced. Too strong.

And now the darkness is complete.

There are no longer any givens, any absolutes—no root to our existence. The basic tenets of human biology have been rewritten, not in DNA code but in blood and in virus.

Parasites and demons are everywhere. Our future is no longer the natural organic decay of death but a complex and diabolical transmutation. An infestation. A becoming.

They have taken from us our neighbors, our friends, our families. They wear their faces now, the faces of our familiars, our Dear Ones.

We have been turned out of our homes. Cast out of our own kingdom, we roam the outlands in search of a miracle. We survivors are bloodied, we are broken, we are defeated.

But we are not turned. We are not Them.

Not yet.

This is not intended as a record or a chronicle, but as a lamentation, the poetry of fossils, a reminiscence of the end of the era of civilization.

The dinosaurs left behind almost no trace of themselves. A few bones preserved in amber, the contents of their stomachs, their waste.

I only hope that we may leave behind something more than they did.

Knickerbocker Loans and Curios, East 118th Street, Spanish Harlem

THURSDAY, NOVEMBER 4

MIRRORS ARE THE BEARERS *of bad news,* thought Abraham Setrakian, standing under the greenish fluorescent wall lamp, staring into his bathroom mirror. An old man looking into older glass. The edges were blackened with age, a corruption creeping ever closer to the center. To his reflection. To him.

You will die soon.

The silver-backed looking glass showed him that much. Many times he had been close to death, *or worse;* but this was different. In his image he saw this inevitability. And still, somehow, Setrakian found comfort in the truth of the old mirrors. They were honest and pure. This one was a magnificent piece, turn-of-the-century, quite heavy, strung from the wall by corded wire, hanging off the old tile at a downward angle. There were, hung from walls and standing on the floors and leaning against bookshelves, some eighty silver-backed mirrors arranged throughout his living quarters. He collected them compulsively. As people who have walked through a desert know the value of water, so Setrakian found it impossible to pass up the acquisition of a silver looking-glass—especially a smaller, portable one.

But, more than that, he relied upon their most ancient quality.

Contrary to popular myth, vampires certainly do have reflections. In mass-produced, modern mirrors, they appear no different than they do to the eye. But in silver-backed glass, their reflections are distorted. Some physical property of the silver projects these virus-laden atrocities with visual interference—like a warning. Much like the looking glass in the Snow White story, a silver-backed mirror cannot tell a lie.

And so, Setrakian looked at his face in the mirror—between the thick porcelain sink and the counter that held his powders and salves, the rubs for his arthritis, the heated liniment to soothe the pain in his gnarled joints—and studied it.

Here he confronted his fading strength. The acknowledgment that his body was just that: a body. Aged and weakening. Decaying. To the point where he was unsure if he would survive the corporeal trauma of a turning. Not all victims do survive it.

His face. Its deep lines like a fingerprint—the thumb of time stamped firmly onto his visage. He had aged twenty additional years overnight. His eyes appeared small and dry, yellowed like ivory. His pallor was off, and his hair lay against his scalp like fine silver grass matted down by a recent storm.

Pic—pic—pic . . .

He heard death calling. He heard the cane. His heart.

He looked at his twisted hands, molded by sheer will to fit and hold the handle of that silver cane sword—but able to do little else with any dexterity.

The battle with the Master had weakened him greatly. The Master was stronger even than Setrakian had remembered or presumed. He had yet to process his theories spawned by the Master's survival in direct sunlight—sunlight that weakened and marked him, but did not obliterate him. The virus-smashing ultraviolet rays should have cut through him like the power of ten thousand silver swords—and yet the terrible creature had withstood it and escaped.

What is life, in the end, but a series of small victories and larger failures? But what else was there to do? Give up?

Setrakian never gave up.

Second-guessing was all he had at the moment. If only he had done *this* instead of *that*. If he could have somehow dynamited the building once he knew that the Master was inside. If Eph had allowed him to expire rather than saving him at that last critical moment . . .

His heart was racing again, just thinking of lost opportunities. Fluttering and skipping beats. Lurching. Like an impatient child inside him, wanting to run and run.

Pic—pic—pic . . .

A low hum purred above the heartbeat.

Setrakian knew it well: this was the prelude to oblivion, to waking up inside an emergency room, if there were any still operating . . .

With a stiff finger, he fished a white pill out of his box. Nitroglycerin prevented angina by relaxing the vessels carrying blood to his heart, allowing them to dilate, increasing flow and oxygen supply. A sublingual tablet, he placed it underneath his dry tongue, to dissolve.

There was immediately a sweet, tingling sensation. In a few minutes, the murmur in his heart would subside.

The fast-acting nitro pill reassured him. All this second-guessing, this recrimination and mourning: it was a waste of brain activity.

Here he was now. His adopted Manhattan called to him, crumbling from within.

One week now since the 777 had touched down at JFK. One week since the arrival of the Master and the start of the outbreak. Setrakian had foreseen it from the first news report, as surely as one intuits the death of a loved one when the phone rings at an odd hour. News of the dead plane gripped the city. Just minutes after landing safely, the plane had shut down completely, sitting dark on the taxiway. The Centers for Disease Control and Prevention boarded the plane in contact suits and found all passengers and crew dead, but for four "survivors." These survivors were not well at all, their disease syndrome only augmented by the Master. Hidden inside his coffin within the cargo hold of the airplane, the Master had been delivered across the ocean thanks to the wealth and influence of Eldritch Palmer: a dying man who had chosen not to die but instead to trade human control of the planet for a taste of eternity. After a day's incubation, the virus activated in the dead passengers and they arose from their morgue tables and carried the vampiric plague into the city streets.

The full extent of the plague was known to Setrakian, but the rest of the world resisted the horrible truth. Since then, another airplane had shut down soon after landing at London's Heathrow Airport, stopping dead on the taxiway to the gate. At Orly Airport, an Air France jet arrived stillborn. At Narita International Airport in Tokyo. At Franz Joseph Strauss in Munich. At the famously secure Ben Gurion International in Tel Aviv, where counterterrorist commandos stormed the darkened airliner on the tarmac to find all 126 passengers dead or unresponsive. And yet no alerts were issued to search the cargo areas, or to destroy the airplanes outright. It was happening too fast, and disinformation and disbelief ruled the day.

And on it went. In Madrid. Beijing. Warsaw. Moscow. Brasília. Auckland. Oslo. Sofia. Stockholm. Reykjavik. Jakarta. New Delhi. Certain more militant and paranoid territories had correctly initiated immediate airport quarantines, cordoning off the dead jets with military force, and yet . . . Setrakian couldn't help but suspect that these landings were as much a tactical distraction as an attempt at infection. Only time would tell if he was correct—though, in truth, there was precious little time.

By now, the original *strigoi*—the first generation of vampires, the Regis Air victims, and their Dear Ones—had begun their second wave of maturation. They were becoming more accustomed to their environment and new bodies. Learning to adapt, to survive—to thrive. They attacked at nightfall, the news reported "rioting" in large sectors of the city, and this was partially true—looting and vandalism ran rampant in broad daylight—but no one pointed out that activity spiked at night.

Because of these disruptions occurring nationwide, the country's infrastructure was beginning to crumble. Food delivery lines were broken, distribution delayed. As absences increased, available manpower suffered and electrical outages and brownouts went unserviced. Police and fire response times were down, and incidences of vigilantism and arson up.

Fires burned. Looters prevailed.

Setrakian stared into his face, wishing he could once again glimpse the younger man within. Perhaps even the boy. He thought of young Zachary Goodweather, just down the hall in the spare bedroom. And, somehow, the old man at the end of his life felt sorry for the boy—eleven years old but already at the end of childhood. Tumbling from grace, stalked by an undead thing occupying the body of his mother . . .

Setrakian stepped out to the dressing area of his bedroom, finding his way to a chair. He sat with one hand covering his face, waiting for the disorienting sensation to pass.

Great tragedy leads to feelings of isolation, which sought to envelop him now. He mourned his long-lost wife, Miriam. Memories of her face had been crowded out of his mind by the few photographs in his possession, which he referred to often and which had the effect of freezing her image in time without ever truly capturing her being. She had been the love of his life. He was a lucky man; it was a struggle sometimes to remember this. He had courted and married a beautiful woman. He had seen beauty and he had seen evil. He had witnessed the best and the worst of the previous century, and he had survived it all. Now he was witnessing the end.

He thought of Ephraim's ex-wife, Kelly, whom Setrakian had met once in life and once again in death. He understood the man's pain. He understood the pain of this world.

Outside, he heard another automobile crash. Gunshots in the distance, alarms ringing insistently—cars, buildings—all going unanswered. The screams that split the night were the last cries of humanity. Looters were taking not only goods and property—they were looting souls. Not taking possessions—but taking possession.

He let his hand fall, landing upon a catalog on the small side table. A Sotheby's catalog. The auction was to be held in just a few days. This was not a coincidence. None of it was coincidence: not the recent occultation, not the conflict overseas, not the economic recession. Like orderly dominoes we fall.

He lifted the auction catalog and searched for a particular page. In it, without any accompanying illustration, was listed an ancient volume:

> Occido Lumen (1667) — A compleat account of the first rise
> of the Strigoi and full confutation of all arguments produced
> against their existence, translated by the late Rabbi Avigdor
> Levy. Private collection. Illuminated manuscript, original
> binding. In view upon appointment. Estimated $15–$25M

This very book—not a facsimile, not a photograph—was crucial to understanding the enemy, the *strigoi*. And vanquishing it.

The book was based on a collection of ancient Mesopotamian clay tablets first discovered in jars inside a cave in the Zagros Mountains in 1508. Written in Sumerian and extremely fragile, the tablets were traded to a wealthy silk merchant, who traveled with them throughout Europe. The merchant was found strangled in his quarters in Florence and his warehouses set on fire. The tablets, however, survived in the possession of two necromancers, the famous John Dee and a more obscure acolyte known to history as John Silence. Dee was Queen Elizabeth I's consultant, and, unable to decipher them, kept the tablets as a magical artifact until 1608 when, forced by poverty, he sold them—through his daughter Katherine—to the learned Rabbi Avigdor Levy in the old ghetto of Metz, in Lorraine, France. For decades, the rabbi meticulously deciphered the tablets, utilizing his unique abilities—it would be almost three centuries before others could finally be able to decipher similar tablets—and eventually presented his findings in manuscript form as a gift for King Louis XIV.

Upon receipt of the text, the king ordered the elderly rabbi's imprisonment and the destruction of the tablets, as well as of the rabbi's entire library of texts and devotional artifacts. The tablets were pulverized, and the manuscript languished in a vault alongside many forbidden treasures. Secretly, Mme de Montespan, the king's mistress and an avid dabbler in the occult, orchestrated the retrieval of the manuscript in 1671. It remained in the hands of La Voisin, a midwife who was de Montespan's sorceress and confidante, until her exile following her implication in the hysteria surrounding the Affaire des Poisons.

The book subsequently resurfaced briefly in 1823, appearing in the possession of the notorious London reprobate and scholar William Beckford. It appeared listed as part of the library in Fonthill Abbey, Beckford's palace of excess, where he accumulated natural and unnatural curiosities, forbidden books, and shocking objets d'art. The Gothic Revival construction and its contents were sold to an arms dealer in order to satisfy a debt, and the book remained lost for nearly a century. It was listed erroneously, or perhaps surreptitiously, under the title *Casus Lumen* as part of a 1911 auction in Marseille, but the text was never produced for display and the auction summarily canceled after a mysterious outbreak gripped the city. In the ensuing years, the manuscript was widely believed to have been destroyed. Now it was at hand, right here, in New York.

But $15 million? $25 million? Impossible to get. There had to be some other way . . .

His greatest fear, which he dared share with no one, was that the battle, begun so long ago, was already lost. That this was all an endgame, that humanity's king was already in check, yet stubbornly playing out its few remaining moves upon the global chessboard.

Setrakian closed his eyes against a humming in his ears. But the humming persisted—in fact, grew stronger.

The pill had never had this effect on him before.

Once he realized this, Setrakian stiffened and rose to his feet.

It was not the pill at all. The hum was all around him. Low-grade, but there.

They were not alone.

The boy, thought Setrakian. With great effort, he pushed himself up and out of the chair, starting for Zack's room.

Pic—pic—pic . . .

The mother was coming for her boy.

Zack Goodweather sat cross-legged in the corner of the roof of the pawnshop building. His dad's computer was open in his lap. This was the only spot in the entire building where he could get connected to the Internet, trespassing on the unsecured home network of a neighbor somewhere on the block. The wireless signal was weak, varying between one and two bars, slowing his Internet search to a crawl.

Zack had been forbidden to use his dad's computer. In fact, he was supposed to be asleep right now. The eleven-year-old had enough difficulty sleeping on normal nights, a decent case of insomnia he'd been hiding from his parents for some time.

Insomni-Zack! The first superhero he ever created. An eight-page color comic written, illustrated, lettered, and inked by Zachary Goodweather. About a teen who patrolled the streets of New York by night, foiling terrorists and polluters. And terrorist polluters. He never could get the blanket cape folds to come out right, but he was passable with faces, and okay with musculature.

This city needed an *Insomni-Zack* now. Sleep was a luxury. A luxury no one could afford—if everyone knew what he knew.

If everyone had seen what he had seen.

Zack was supposed to be sacked out in a goose-down sleeping bag inside a spare bedroom on the third floor. The room smelled like a closet, like an old cedar room in his grandparents' house—one that no one opened anymore except for kids who liked to snoop. The small, oddly angled room had been used by Mr. Setrakian (or Professor Setrakian—Zack still wasn't clear on that part, seeing how the old man ran the first-floor pawnshop) for storage. Tilting stacks of books, many old mirrors, a wardrobe of old clothes, and some locked trunks—really locked, not the fake kind of lock that can be picked with a paper clip and a ballpoint pen (Zack had already tried).

The exterminator, Fet—or V, as he had told Zack to call him—had hooked up an ancient, cartridge-fed, 8-bit Nintendo system to a pawned Sanyo television set with big knobs and dials on the front instead of buttons, all brought up from the showroom downstairs. They expected him to stay put and play *The Legend of Zelda*. But the bedroom door had no lock. His dad and Fet had mounted iron bars onto the wall over the window—mounted them on the inside, rather than the outside, bolted to the wall beams—a cage that Mr. Setrakian said was left over from the 1970s.

They weren't trying to lock him in, Zack knew. They were trying to lock *her* out.

He searched for his dad's professional page at the Centers for Disease Control and Prevention, and got a "Page Not Found." So they had already scrubbed him from the government Web site. News hits for "Dr. Ephraim Goodweather" claimed he was a discredited CDC official who fabricated a video purporting to show a human-turned-vampire being destroyed. It said that he had uploaded it (actually, Zack uploaded the video for him, one that his dad wouldn't let him view) onto the Internet in an attempt to exploit the eclipse hysteria for his own purposes. Obviously, that last part was BS. What "purposes" did his dad have other than trying to save lives? One news site described Goodweather as "an admitted alcoholic involved in a contentious custody battle, who is now believed to be on the run with his kidnapped son." That left Zack with a lump of ice in his chest. The same article went on to say that both Goodweather's ex-wife and her boyfriend were currently missing and presumed dead.

Everything made Zack feel nauseous these days, but the dishonesty of this article was especially toxic to him. All wrong, every last word. Did they really not know the truth? Or . . . did they not care? Maybe they were trying to exploit his parents' trouble *for their own purposes?*

And the talkback? The comments were even worse. He could not deal with the things they were saying about his dad, the righteous arrogance of all these anonymous posters. He had to deal right now with the awful truth about his mom—and the banality of the venom spewed in blogs and forums missed the point completely.

How do you mourn someone who isn't really gone? How do you fear someone whose desire for you is eternal?

If the world knew the truth the way Zack knew the truth, then his dad's reputation would be restored, and his voice heard—but still nothing else would change. His mom, his life, would never be the same.

So, mostly, Zack wanted it all to pass. He wanted something fantastic to happen to make everything right and normal again. As when he was a child—like five or something, he broke a mirror and just covered it with a sheet, then prayed with all his might for its restoration before his parents found out. Or the way he used to wish his parents would fall back in love again. That they would wake up one day and realize what a mistake they had made.

Now he secretly hoped that his dad could do something incredible. Despite everything, Zack still assumed that there was some happy ending awaiting them. Awaiting all of them. Maybe even something to bring Mom back to the way she was.

He felt tears coming, and this time he didn't fight them. He was up on the roof; he was alone. He wanted so badly to see his mother again. The thought terrified him—and yet he yearned for her to come. To look into her eyes. To hear her voice. He wished for her to explain this to him the way she did every troubling thing. *Everything is going to be just fine . . .*

A scream somewhere deep in the night brought him back to the present. He peered uptown, seeing flames on the west side, a column of dark smoke. He looked up. No stars tonight. And only a few airplanes. He had heard fighter jets zooming overhead that afternoon.

Zack rubbed his face in the crook of his elbow sleeve and turned back to the computer. With some quick desktop searching, Zack discovered the folder containing the video file he was not supposed to view. He opened it and heard Dad's voice, and realized Dad was operating the camera. Zack's camera, the one his dad had borrowed.

The subject was hard to see at first, something in the dark inside a shed. A thing leaning forward on its haunches. A guttural growl and a back-of-the-throat hiss. The slinking noise of a chain. The camera zoomed in closer, the dark pixilation improving, and Zack saw its open mouth. A mouth that opened wider than it should, with something resembling a thin silver fish flopping inside.

The shed-thing's eyes were wide and glaring. He mistook their expression for one of sadness at first, and hurt. A collar—apparently, a dog collar—restrained it at the neck, chained to the dirt floor behind it. The creature looked pale inside the dark shed, so bloodless it was nearly glowing. Then came a strange pumping sound—*snap-chunk, snap-chunk, snap-chunk*—and three silver nails, propelled from behind the camera (from Dad?) struck the shed-thing like needle-bullets. The camera view jerked up as the thing roared hoarsely, a sick animal consumed with pain.

"*Enough,*" said a voice on the clip. The voice belonged to Mr. Setrakian, but it was not a tone like anything Zack had ever heard out of the kindly, old pawnbroker's mouth. "*Let us remain merciful.*"

Then the old man stepped into view, intoning some words in a foreign, ancient-sounding language—almost like summoning a power or declaring a curse. He raised a silver sword—long and bright with moonlight—and the shed-thing howled as Mr. Setrakian swung the sword with great force . . .

Voices pulled Zack out of the video. Voices from the street below. He shut the laptop and stood, staying back, peering over the raised edge of the roof down to 118th Street.

A group of five men walked up the block toward the pawnshop, trailed by a slow-moving SUV. They carried weapons— guns—and were pounding on every door. The SUV stopped before the intersection, right outside the front of the pawnshop. The men on foot approached the building, rattling the security gates. Calling, "Open up!"

Zack backed away. He turned to go to the roof door, figuring he'd better get back to his room in case anyone came looking.

Then he saw her. A girl, a teenager, high school probably. Standing on the next roof over, across an empty lot around the corner from the shop entrance. The breeze lifted her long nightshirt, ruffling it around her knees, but did not move her hair, which hung straight and heavy.

She stood on the raised edge of the roof. The very edge, balanced perfectly, no wavering in her posture. Poised at the brink, as though wanting to try to make the jump. The impossible leap. Wanting to and knowing she would fail.

Zack stared. He didn't know. He wasn't sure. But he suspected.

He raised a hand anyway. He waved to her.

She stared back at him.